The REBELS OF GOLD

keymaster press

The REBELS OF GOLD

ELISE KOVA

Published by Keymaster Press
3971 Hoover Rd. Suite 77
Columbus, OH 43123-2839

Edited by: Rebecca Faith Heyman
Cover Design by: Nick D. Grey
Proofreading by: Loan Le
Layout Design by: Gatekeeper Press

ISBN: 9781619846531
eISBN: 9781619846548

Library of Congress Control Number: 2017954348

Printed in the United States of America

Also by Elise Kova

LOOM SAGA
The Alchemists of Loom
The Dragons of Nova
The Rebels of Gold

AIR AWAKENS SERIES
Air Awakens
Fire Falling
Earth's End
Water's Wrath
Crystal Crowned

GOLDEN GUARD TRILOGY
The Crown's Dog
The Prince's Rogue
The Farmer's War

for Rebecca
the woman who can turn black text gold

Contents

Lysip

the
Islands
of Nova

ieuri

TEMPLE
OF LORD
XIN

EASTWIN

NAPOLE

VENYS

ABILLA

XIN
MANOR

Ruana

PART
ONE

ARIANNA

rip.

Some kind of coupling or welding had come loose.

Drip.

Arianna groaned softly. The sound brought her body back to life from what felt like death itself.

Drip. Drip.

There was not a section of muscle tissue that didn't protest in fiery agony at her insistence on movement. She was in tatters from head to toe, her mental state no better. Her fingers twitched and the joints popped softly.

Drip. Drip. Drip.

"If a Rivet doesn't fix that soon, the wrench will touch their temple before it touches the pipe." Using her voice—what there was of it—was enough to make her head feel as though it was splitting open.

A loud *clang* shot between her ears as metal met cement. The aforementioned tool slid across the ground with all the cacophony of an industrial machine gone awry, and came to a stop at her toes.

Arianna's eyes cracked open.

The room came into focus slowly, very, *very* slowly. Hazy orbs formed into the cold glow of electric lighting, two sconces

illuminating the weeping condensation that poured down the wall
she faced. A skeleton of piping ran across the ceiling. Arianna's
eyes followed the lead lines to the corner where one usually found
such imperfections and sure enough . . .

Drip.

"Convenient for me. It seems I have a Rivet right here who
could perform the fix."

Her lolling eyes stilled. Arianna could only muster the
strength to move so much of her body at one time. Refocusing,
she tilted her head forward off the cold metal. She drew her
shoulders in, only to be arrested by the restraints strapped
across her entire body.

A crimson face loomed before her.

Yveun'Dono, the Dragon King.

Arianna snapped her eyes shut and used the darkness
to drop a curtain on the memory of the last time she was so
confined. The last time someone had held her captive.

"I'll need more than a wrench for that . . ." she mumbled.
No matter how broken her body was, the machinations of
her mind ground to life around numbers. She had to keep
herself moving, couldn't allow herself to freeze. The pipes were
lead construction, likely fifty years old based on the jointing
techniques. "I'd need a welding tool."

She shifted her vision from the ceiling to look at the
speaker. A corpse lounged in a chair pressed flush against the
door and stared back at her. He was lanky, all knobby bones
and translucent skin. His black hair was pulled back tightly,
stretching the skin of his face and turning his beady eyes to
near slits.

She had traded being the captive of one king for another.

"King Louie."

"Not so much a king anymore." The man grinned wide enough to show teeth yellowed with age. "Kings need kingdoms."

She put a pin in that statement. It was too early to ask questions. So Arianna said nothing, and let Louie continue in the face of her silence.

"It's well past time we met face-to-face, my dear White Wraith."

A single sentence had never said more. He knew who she was. She knew who he was. "Glad there's no need for pretense." Arianna continued to take stock of her situation. "And I am not 'your dear.'"

"You're not? And here I was hopeful that the White Wraith would be fond of me."

"Not in this lifetime," she muttered, wishing her voice sounded stronger. Her head ached, but Arianna didn't allow the pain to betray as anything more than a narrowing of her eyes. *How did she get here?*

Arianna quickly assessed herself. She was likely underground, judging from the condensation on the walls and the heavy stillness that often came from such locations. Louie was here, a man she'd never interacted with before and certainly wouldn't have gone to for help. And she'd been right to avoid him, evidenced by the restraints holding her against an organ harvesting table—a tilted contraption that propped her at an angle, bound her down so she couldn't escape or struggle as someone, theoretically, cut her flesh from her body.

Yes, she knew where she was as it pertained to this singular room. But none of it indicated how she had arrived here. For that, she needed to go back further.

She'd escaped the Dragon King's prison with Cvareh's help. *Cvareh.* The name brought on a deluge of emotions, none of which she was equipped to handle under the circumstances. Arianna pushed the onslaught from her mind. Just another item to put a pin in, for now. Tackle one problem at a time.

She'd stolen a glider. Yveun's voice rattled through her mind again. *"Let go."* Her memories after that numbered three snapshots: Nova shrinking above her. The glider's metal handles just under her fingertips. Her body slamming against the contraption as she hit the clouds that separated the two worlds.

Then, nothing.

She must have fallen down to somewhere in Dortam, close enough to Mercury Town for Louie to get his grubby little hands on her.

"How did you know who I am?" Arianna willed her voice to sound the slightest bit more stable. Maybe it would, if she weren't diverting so much focus to merely keeping screams of pain and frustration dormant. Her mind was moving too slowly for her to tolerate. "I always sent someone else to meet with you."

"Your coat—among other factors—was a giveaway." Arianna desperately wanted to know what these "other factors" were. "And 'someone else'? Let's call her by name, shall we? *Florence.*"

If she were more in her right mind, she never would have given him the chance to say the name. Nor would she have risked giving away how much that single utterance meant to her with her traitorous face. Horror and heartache swept across her like a burst steam pipe, no doubt altering the landscape before she could patch the rupture. In a matter of moments she mastered herself once more—but Louie watched her closely, and the scalding emotion had left its mark.

"Quite a little upstart, that one." Louie made a display of picking lint off his knee to hide his satisfied grin. "Are you certain she's not a Rivet? Because she seems to be redesigning the world according to her own secret schematics." His eyes returned to her slowly in the wake of her silence.

Arianna struggled to keep her face impassive, to betray nothing, to give up no more weaknesses—for Florence's sake, if no one else's. But her heart screamed for any word of the young woman who had been her ward for years. The less she said before she had full control of her mind, the better.

"You don't know . . . do you?" Louie whispered like a child just discovering where their parents hid the sweets.

"I know enough."

"Where are we?" He called her bluff without so much as blinking.

"Mercury Town," Arianna surmised. The slowly widening grin—almost a snarl—on his face convinced her she had guessed wrong. "Oh? Did you find some new hole to terrorize?"

"Mercury Town is the hole." Louie shifted, bringing his left foot off his right knee and settling it to the floor. Leaning forward, he placed his elbows on his narrow thighs. "I suppose it's going to be hard to strike a deal with you if you don't understand the situation you're in."

"What makes you think I'd strike a deal with you?" She hated the feeling of ignorance. It was like drowning in a sea of ink, the world obscured, clarity lost. Her mind didn't know how to proceed in such a void.

"I have no doubt you'll prefer it to the alternatives."

"And what are those?" *Give me information,* her hungry mind pleaded. *Something, anything.* She needed just enough for a direction. For a strike to her flywheel to get things moving again. Her magic was slow, body aching, mind stunted. Something had to improve, or everything would break.

"Alternative one." Louie held up a skeletal finger. "I keep you here forever, and harvest you as I would any of my other pets."

"Resorting to harvesting and trying to pass off black organs? That's a new low, even for you."

"Black organs? No, no." He let out a wheezing chuckle and lifted another finger. "However, that does bring me to alternative two—I sell you back to your Florence and her rebellion for the heftiest sum I can imagine."

"Florence wouldn't pay for me." Arianna hoped. She didn't want the girl to waste any resources on her. She didn't want Florence to risk anything further by being near Louie and the dangers that seemed to lurk perpetually around him.

"Oh, I think she would. How else will she live up to her promise of producing a Philosopher's Box?"

Arianna barely missed the final point over the ringing in her ears.

"Or three . . . You cut me in on the deal to produce the infamous box. You show me what's been making you so deadly all these years. You show me the schematics that let you bleed gold."

All at once, the pain vanished. The buzzing between her ears stopped. And everything went numb.

FLORENCE

Wind blew dust over the ramparts of Ter.0, curling around the ghosts that were the only other occupants of the crumbling glory of a world long lost.

It was a wasteland of sand and rock, littered with hollowed skeletons of gnarled iron and cement that rose insistently from their shadowed graves. Florence tilted her head back to gaze at the shifting skies and semi-translucent clouds that swirled between worlds. Her pale companions played a game of hide-and-seek—mostly hide—with the moon.

She was the only creature alive here. She was the beating heart and shallow breaths of a land forgotten. She was the only remnant of life to return to this broken corner of their world.

No, she wasn't the only one. She was merely the *first*. All of Loom would come to converge in this once-hallowed place of knowledge. They would return, and the Vicar Tribunal would be born anew.

It was a beautiful idea—one she'd believed in enough to shoot a dangerously stubborn vicar between the eyes for. But now Florence was forced to admit her hasty plan that led her to this point hadn't been thought through as much as she would've liked.

Somehow, everything would work itself out, as it had her entire life.

The next morning, Florence moved again. She traversed the cracked earth and rubble toward a structure that was once a distant point on her horizon. Like a mighty hand's fingers stretching up from the horizon, five points reached toward the sky as if to grasp the universe.

Florence trudged along. She didn't have much—just the basic necessities she'd collected in Ter.2.3 before chartering a boat. Her pack grew lighter with each fading night.

On her seventh day in Ter.0, she crossed through the gate. The wall housing it had been blown apart on either side, but the gate still stood, a symbolic entrance standing in defiance of time—and Dragons.

Florence stopped to adjust her tattered frock. She combed her fingers through her hair, though she imagined this did little to tame it. Her knuckles brushed the tattoo that marred her cheek. But Florence gave it no thought, choosing instead to adjust the tilt of her top hat.

The hatter in Ter.2.3 had only a few options for her. The current top hat she was sporting offered only one buckle around the base and a *single* feather. It was a style from two years ago, and nothing like the fashions she'd seen in the windows of Dortam practically a lifetime ago.

But it was something.

It was the regalia of the woman she had once been. She'd carry the remnants of her past life into this old world so that both could be rebuilt together. Florence dropped her hands and continued through the gate.

Ter.0 was once the breeding center for all of Loom. Every year, the five vicars converged upon this place to share knowledge, and initiate their reproductive cycles together. A selection of initiates, journeymen, and masters from each guild remained after the tribunal, to teach the children the fundamentals of thought and the basis for the world in which they all lived.

Florence was born here, but she had no recollection of this place. She was one of the thousands of children split among the guilds when the Dragons assumed control of Loom. She was selected for the Ravens and left to die.

And she would have, if she hadn't fought her way out.

The main entry to the Hall of Ter.0, the most important building in the world, was blocked. Its massive doors had splintered off their hinges and tilted against each other drunkenly, leaving Florence to seek another entrance. Windows cut beams of light from the hollow center of the hall through to the shaded ground below. Florence strolled across their beacons until she came upon a rubble-strewn entry she could crawl through.

Inside, an anterior passageway snaked around the perimeter of the hall. Florence pressed forward until she reached the grand atrium—the center for all learning and knowledge. The grandiose glass dome that had once arched above it all was shattered into hundreds of shards that painted rainbows across the marble floor.

With glass grinding beneath her heels, Florence stepped into the sunlight, and onto the stage of destiny.

She strode to the center of the atrium, surrounded by still-standing statues of the five guild symbols. The revolver chambers, the raven, the sickle, inverted triangles, and crossed tools for the Rivets—they were all there, but none seemed to fit her. None defined her. She did a half-turn, taking in the remnants of what was once the foundation of Loom.

"It'll do," she mumbled. It wasn't much by way of fortification or construction. But, for now, it could house the pieces of their ailing world. It could hold the Vicar Tribunal on ceremony alone, if nothing else.

Glass cracked and snapped under footsteps.

Florence turned. Her pistol was drawn and pointed at the source of the sound before she could blink.

A woman emerged from the shadows. Her hair was loose, flowing like moonbeams down her back and around her face. The pristine shade reminded Florence of Ari, but this woman's skin was a deeper hue, a more shadowed slate, not unlike Florence's own flesh. She wore a smart bronze-colored coat with gigot sleeves, offset by a stripe of steel blue tied in a bow around her bicep. The composition brought out the powder blue stitching of her dress.

"I am not your enemy."

Florence uncurled her fingers from the pistol grip, easing off the trigger, and returned it to its holster. "So it would seem. You're not Dragon." Florence looked over the stranger, and the contrast of soft curves and delicate fabrics that seemed to protest against the gritty world in which they existed. "Who are you?"

The woman brought a finger up to the filled tattoo on her cheek. "Shannra, the Revo."

"Florence, the Revo."

"I know who you are." Shannra crossed the distance between them with deliberate steps. "All of Loom knows who you are."

"Do they?" Florence couldn't stop her fingers from twitching toward the gun. The last time she'd been out of hiding as a named entity in the world was the night she killed the Vicar Alchemist. It would make sense if they were hunting her. Though she had heard no word of a manhunt while she was in Ter.2.3, and vicarcide would have prompted both—rumor and hunt.

"Of course. The woman who inspired the first Vicar Tribunal in years, who sparks rebellion like wildfire, would be known across the world."

"The Dragons did the work for me in sparking a rebellion," Florence said warily. It was true. Uprising was an easy sell when the world was kindling to burn at the hands of their oppressors.

"Perhaps, but you directed it." Shannra played with a particularly large shard of glass, sliding it with the toe of her boot. "You organized us."

"I've done nothing yet." There were many more steps for Florence to take, and even if she took them, she could well be marching the world she loved to its death.

Shannra just hummed, giving a wide sweep of her arms and motioning to the room around them. There was a delicate deadliness to her, Florence decided quickly, and secrets sewn between the powder blue stitching of her skirts.

"Why are you here, Shannra?" The girl had a filled Revo tattoo on her cheek. No doubt she was younger than Florence, and already achieved Journeymen.

"I'm here to see the world die, and begin anew."

"Cryptic." Florence put her hands in her pockets in an effort to seem less intimidating. It was a meaningless gesture; even with palms stuffed against her thighs, she could still outdraw almost anyone. Of that she was confident. She had to be, or she would hesitate when the moment mattered most.

Shannra laughed, a sound like the crescendo of a chorus. "Fair, fair . . . Then I'm here to help give you what you need."

"And what is that?"

"The Philosopher's Box."

Her heart stilled. The magic in her blood pushed inward, as if to guard her immediate, instinctive response of hope. Hope was dangerous. And yet, Florence had positioned herself as the harbinger of it, because it made the people around her so much more effective. Hope was indeed a danger—but it was also excellent leverage.

"What do you know of Arianna?" Florence asked finally. Her hands were still conveniently close to her guns and, depending on what this beautiful Revolver said to her, she could easily reach for them.

Shannra twirled a strand of hair around her fingers with a coy smile, knowing exactly where Florence's mind had gone. One look told Florence that she knew too much. More than anyone should.

"King Louie sends his regards."

Florence reached for her pistol without a second thought.

ARIANNA

D amn the man for having the foresight to tie her down, because if he hadn't, she would've spent her dying breath savoring the feeling of his skull disintegrating against her fingers as she clawed out his eyes.

"I don't know what you're talking about," she said, wishing she hadn't taken so long to voice her denial. Arianna curled and uncurled her fingers, moving something, anything, trying to get blood pumping to her brain at any cost. Louie made almost the same motion before he spoke.

"Oh, White Wraith, don't you think we have a better rapport than that? Since when have you known me to seek something I cannot easily attain?"

"I don't think *you* ever actually attain anything. As I recall, I did most—all—of the work on every heist." Arianna added a scoff in an attempt to get a rise out of the man. If she could throw him off his emotional center, she could regain some vantage.

"All the more poetic, then. As it seems this time will be no different." Louie shifted stiffly, folding his skeletal hands together, seeming utterly unbothered.

"I can't give you something I don't know how to create." If changing the topic didn't work, she'd try denial next. She'd try everything until something stuck, until her mind was solid enough again to think clearly.

"There was a time when I might have believed you." Louie stood slowly. Arianna narrowed her eyes at his deliberate, yet unsteady, motions. She expected the King of Mercury Town to have a little more . . . grace?

He reached for a holster on his hip and drew a tiny one-shot pistol barely larger than his hand. It was the sort of gun Arianna imagined Florence laughing at, if she ever saw it. The man pointed the weapon at her shoulder.

Arianna narrowed her eyes down at him. "You sure you can handle that? Seems like you're having trouble."

"Point blank shot at a tied-down target? I'll take my chances." Louie tightened his grip on his gun. "Question is, do you want to? I don't have any interest in shooting you, really. We had such a good stretch as business partners, and I'd much rather not poison the waters with a gunshot to prove a point."

Her scowl was so deep it hurt. She knew exactly what he was doing. Proof of her being the Perfect Chimera pumped through her veins. One shot wouldn't kill her. Bloody cogs, against all the other pain, it likely wouldn't even register. But there would be no denying after that.

"How did you find out?" Arianna asked. She instantly loathed the smug look on his face.

"You have your Florence to thank for that." Louie made a show of re-holstering his gun, as if he was doing her some grand favor. "After all, she was the one who let the world know that you, Arianna, the Master Rivet, pupil to the renowned Oliver, and the woman who supposedly perished alongside the Council of Five in the last rebellion, can make the Philosopher's Box."

"You know your history." Her voice had gone soft. But unlike the delicacy forced on her when she first awoke, this was a deadly sort of quiet that she found suited her much better.

"When I found you, bleeding gold, dressed in white . . . it was all too much of a coincidence to write away."

"And I confirmed my identity when I woke."

"Now, don't be too hard on yourself."

"Placate me again, old man, and—"

"No need for name-calling." Louie's chuckle devolved into a wheeze. "It makes things much more efficient like this. You know the situation; no need for us to play coy. So, which option—"

"You said Mercury Town was a hole." Her brain was beginning to work again, and she wasn't going to let him get away with spewing nonsense. The twitch of Louie's lips was the only thing that betrayed his annoyance at her interruption, but it was more than enough to satisfy her.

"The Revolvers saw to that." He settled back into his chair. "How much does Nova really know?"

"Assume I know nothing."

"Seems an easy assumption." It was now her turn to prevent her lips from twitching in annoyance. "The Dragon King ordered the guilds destroyed."

"Destroyed," she repeated involuntarily, as though it would make more sense if she said it again herself, slowly. It didn't.

"Destroyed." He echoed her horror in what was notably the first time they'd agreed on something. "For our insolence. The Harvesters were the first and they were hit the hardest. From what I hear, most of the masters were at the guild for a vote when the King's Riders dropped the bombs. The Alchemists were next. They lost their hall and at least a third of their members.

"The Revolvers . . ." Louie paused, as if offering a moment of silence to the noble fools of the weaponry guild. "They'd fought it from the start."

"They sought to protect Loom from their own mechanizations," she murmured.

"They quickly realized there weren't many options, and less time," Louie continued.

"They killed themselves."

"In a blaze of glory. It was an explosion befitting a funeral for the Vicar Revolver himself."

"The Ravens? Rivets?" It was terrible news atop terrible news. Still, she wanted to know the fate of her guild.

"Ravens were spared, thanks to the Revolver's efforts. The Rivets were hit, but the Riders didn't have the same firepower to raze them. Bent but not broken, from what I hear."

Ari took a moment just to breathe. The Rivets guild, in all its gorgeous mechanical glory, still ticked along. "And Florence?"

"Ah, yes, Loom's champion."

Arianna tried to keep her face passive—*just the facts*. But judging by Louie's reaction as he spoke, she failed. At last, she acquiesced; her hand had been shown for what it was. "She's alive then?"

"She thrives." He paused, clearly for dramatic effect. "So says my confidant."

"Confidant?" Arianna asked cautiously, though she didn't know why. She already knew what game Louie was playing at. He wanted the box and proximity to power; he wanted her to play along. Putting a loaded gun right next to Florence was the frustratingly perfect move.

"I sent a good friend of mine to her, just to help see things set up properly on Ter.0. After all, Florence is the one who got the Vicar Harvester to call the Tribunal."

"There's to be another Vicar Tribunal?"

"It's been a while, hasn't it?" Louie massaged his knees and Arianna wondered if they ailed the man. She could only speculate about his age . . . but he must be well into his forties, practically ancient for a Fenthri. "Children who have never even stepped foot on Ter.0 will be caucusing there for the first time to determine the fate of the world. Reminds you of the old days, doesn't it?"

"Take me to her, to Florence."

"I don't think you're in much of a position to make demands, Arianna."

"You were willing to make a deal before." She had to speak his language, stick to safe territory, stick to business.

"Give me access to the schematics for the Philosopher's Box and I will take you anywhere in this wide world you want to go. Even back up to Nova."

"Florence," she repeated firmly.

"The box?"

He was relentless. And even though Arianna knew the answer, she asked the question anyway. "Why do you want it?"

"Reasons that I think should be obvious."

And they were.

There was a time when he who owned the gold owned the power. But such a time was ending. Now, Loom and Nova stood on a new precipice, an age where power came from those who could manufacture weapons in the shape of people that bled gold. There was abject disgust at the notion that she would help usher in such an age.

But it was an age Loom had been headed toward since the first Chimera. If it hadn't been her, it would've been someone else.

"If I agree, you'll take me to her?"

"You have my word." Louie put his hand over his vested heart. "It's bad for business if I go back on my deals. Plus, we both have far, far more to gain by being friends."

"If I agree, you'll do as I say?"

"Within reason."

She settled back against the harvesting table, looking at him with narrowed eyes. She had to get something out of this, for the time being. There was no possible way she'd give Louie unrestricted access to the Philosopher's Box. For as long as she could manage, she'd regulate who knew what.

"On Nova, there is a flower for the Lord of Luck. This flower has four petals . . ." Her voice trailed off for a moment and Arianna thought back to her night with Cvareh on the island. She wanted to feel the same anger she felt toward him previously, but it was already weakening into an uncomfortable question: *What are we?* "Be my Lord of Luck here on Loom and grant me four wishes. Four things, whatever I design to help the rebellion, to help Loom, in the coming months. And when we are finished, you will have your schematics."

"I'm not a Dragon." Louie chuckled. "I think what you seek is a boon."

"I actually already have one of those. So I suppose you could call me a collector of sorts . . ." Arianna spread her lips and barred her teeth like a ravenous Dragon. "Plus, a boon is only *one* wish. I want four of you."

"You ask too much." He ran his fingers over his lips. Arianna could practically hear him thinking through the admission of her holding a boon.

"You ask for the power to change the world—to make you richer than ever before, and ten times as formidable. I ask you to honor four favors." She managed to shrug against the tight restraints. "Seems more than fair."

Louie stood, pulling his chair away from the door. "Very well, Arianna, you have your deal." He reached for the door latch, clicking it open. "We shall leave at dawn for Ter.0, and your Florence."

CVAREH

The skies above the floating islands of Nova were always peaceful. Even when his heart was heaviest and his mind in turmoil, the unhindered wind and free cries of the wild boco traversing its currents evoked a sort of calm. There wasn't another flyer anywhere around him, leaving the Xin'Ryu mostly to his thoughts.

Dawn began to seep between the stars—a melancholy hue that marked the end of Lord Xin's hour and the start of Lord Rok's.

Rok.

The mere thought had Cvareh looking over his shoulder. Far in the distance, hazy with the wisps of the God's Line, was the ghostly silhouette of the Rok Estate. He squinted against the darkness, pushing magic into his eyes and piercing the shadows, but another boco was nowhere to be seen.

He had split from his sister, Petra, to allow her to make a distraction while he went in search of Arianna. What sort of distraction Petra had in mind, he couldn't fathom, and now he wished he'd had an idea. Cvareh looked forward again.

His sister would be waiting for him back at the Xin Manor.

The isle of Lysip grew before him. It was a familiar shape. Cvareh knew every cut of the mountains and every switchback that wandered through its rolling jade hills, down into the great city of Napole at the far end.

But there were no festivities in Napole, no flame dancers on rooftops or revelers pouring wine until the bottles ran dry. As Cvareh rode his boco, Saran, as their shadows cut across the city below him, he was staggered by the quiet. *This* was a city in mourning, a place where men and women had lost family, loved ones, to the tyrant known upon their wide world as Yveun'Dono.

Cvareh tightened his grip on his boco's reigns. There was no bottom to the depths of Rok depravity, and in that endless pit was where they had found the will to poison the wine and bring an abrupt, dishonorable end to the Xin and the Crimson Court. While none could pin the act on House Rok, it was known. Cvareh could almost feel the truth being whispered behind tightened shutters and on the shuddering rasps of mourning lovers.

Roks may have weakened them, but in the same act, had provided House Xin with all the rationale and motivation ever required to stage a rebellion.

And that rebellion hinged on one person—a Chimera who smelled of honeysuckle and tasted of dreams. There were competing motivations in him. The first was admonishment that he had ever let Arianna return to Loom. He had let go the singular person who could provide Xin an army that could stand against the might of Rok.

But had he not released her, she would've never fought for—alongside—them. The other voice in his mind reassured him of the fact, just as it reassured him that for all her pain and anger, and for all that she put a world between them, her heart still spared a beat for him.

Cvareh swallowed the debate and ignored the aftertaste, focusing on his flight path. The Xin Manor was beginning to peek around the mountains ahead. Before he could even contemplate Arianna's mind and motives and if she would ultimately support House Xin, he had to think first about how to stave off Petra's ire for letting their inventor return to Loom unhindered.

At least, Cvareh hoped she had returned to Loom unhindered. He'd seen a glider rise from the Rok Manor on his way back to his boco. Then a second, not long after. But anything else . . . that was in the hands of the Lord of Luck Cvareh had been born under.

The shroud of silence hung heavy even at the Xin Manor. It was early yet, and no servants arrived at his usual landing balcony to attend to Saran.

"You know your way to the stables, right?" Cvareh patted the beast's feathery neck before dismounting.

It cooed softly, tilting its head in reply.

"If you want to stay here, you're welcome to," Cvareh added. Cvareh had always known that Raku, Petra's trusty mount, was the smartest of their birds.

His chambers had been tidied. He'd left them a sopping mess, only returning to ransack his clothes to find acceptable garb for his excursion. Those articles now smelled of Rok, and Cvareh was prompt to strip them off and cast them over the balcony rail. He paused, watching the trousers and arm adornments be swallowed up by the God's Line, and hoped they didn't fall on some poor unsuspecting Fenthri's head. Knowing his luck, they would, and that Fenthri would be Arianna.

With a sigh, Cvareh went inside. He had only begun to receive his latest tailor orders. No clothing seemed quite appropriate for the situation. So he donned a loose fitting robe, a sort of belled sleeve and wide-sashed ensemble that put the masculine lines of his chest and abdomen on display in a way he was rather fond of. It was most certainly a color from last season, but it brought out the dark umber notes of his blood-orange hair in a way he'd always liked.

He only had to look presentable enough for Petra.

His door clicked closed quietly behind him, and Cvareh descended the window-lined hall that would lead across the manor to Petra's chambers. Footsteps drew his attention; Cvareh's eyes locked with another set of golden irises.

Cain—his childhood friend, his confidant, aspiring mate to his sister—looked at Cvareh with an unfamiliar expression. Cain opened his mouth to speak, then promptly closed it before opening it again.

"What will we do?"

Cvareh couldn't help but grimace. No doubt, Petra had correctly anticipated or deciphered his actions of letting Ari go. "Arianna will continue to support us," he assured. "Even on Loom, she's returning to reunite with the rebellion and—"

Cvareh lost the final word. Cain crossed to him in a tempest. He grabbed Cvareh's robe by the lining of the collar, the man's claws punching holes through the silken fabric.

"Cain—"

"You think I care about your Fen pet right now?" he growled. Cvareh was instantly reminded of one of their last fateful encounters in the stables at the Crimson Court. He'd hoped the tension of that meeting had been washed away by the events of the past day.

"You'd do well not to refer to her in that way."

"Petra is dead and all you can think about is Loom?"

Cvareh froze. He didn't care for the ribbons that Cain was slowly cutting into his fine clothing. He didn't even pay attention to the full depth of rage and pain in the other man's eyes.

Petra is dead. These three words echoed so loudly in Cvareh's mind that he went deaf. He saw Cain's mouth moving but no sound accompanied it.

Petra is dead. Petra is dead. *Petra is dead.*

"What?" Cvareh blundered his way back into Cain's speech. "What about Petra?"

"You . . . you don't know." Cain's grip relaxed. His golden eyes changed from a fiery hue, alight with magic, to a smoldering ache. They glistened in a way Cvareh had never seen before. "She was with you, Cvareh. Your Oji was with you. How do you not know?"

Before Cvareh had a chance to explain his and Petra's plan—how they had split up for effectiveness—and before he had time to ask again what Cain meant, he was interrupted again.

"Cain'Da, Cvareh'Ryu." There was a note of genuine surprise on the quiet words of a servant who had appeared in the hall below them. "Your presence is requested back in the main hall."

Throne room. It had been the throne room before. Cvareh wanted to correct the boy. He wanted to be like Petra and inspire fear over something as simple as the use of a proper name. But he couldn't speak.

If he opened his mouth, he would scream. Or vomit. Or beg for answers. Or some combination thereof.

There must be some mistake, his mind protested as they descended through the fresh opulence of the Xin Manor. It stood in contrast to the Rok Estate's antiquity, a fact underscored even more by having just sneaked through the latter's halls. But Cvareh saw none of it. His mind barely registered that his robe was reduced to tatters. He moved on instinct and somehow found himself at his sister's most beloved room.

The stained-glass floor was illuminated with the first light of dawn. It splashed colors on the ceiling and walls of the long hall in happy contrast to the heavy melancholy that dominated the air. Most of the staff and servants were lined in rows, looking toward the raised platform where Petra's meticulously fashioned throne stood.

In front of that throne was a ruby-skinned man. Cvareh didn't know him but he recognized the beads of a King's Rider when he saw them.

"Good of you to join us, both of you," the Rider praised brightly. "We heard you had returned, Cvareh'Ryu, from your late-night *adventures*."

Cvareh didn't believe for a moment that the Rider didn't know exactly where he'd been. Cvareh barred his fangs in a wide grin. He was not to be tested right now. The past day was beginning to tug on his shoulders to the point of pain, contorting his muscles under the weight of something he couldn't yet fathom.

"Don't you mean Cvareh'Oji?" Cain corrected darkly from his side. For all their differences, and even when he dripped with anger, Cain still stood for Xin. If that fact ever changed, Cvareh's world would truly have ended.

"Not quite." The Rider turned back to Cvareh, smiling, fangs gleaming. "Cain Bek was gone for a while. I trust he informed you of the death of your sister."

Petra is dead.

"I require some clarity." It was all Cvareh could muster. Something had to begin making sense. The sad eyes of his House surrounded him, wary gazes begging for an answer he didn't have. He didn't even know the questions to ask.

"Ah, well, then allow me to inform you that your sister, Petra Xin'Oji To, has perished on this day."

Cvareh could see the ghost of his sister behind the man, sitting proudly on her throne. Her golden curls cascaded over her shoulders and down to the curve of her hip. A woman among women, and warrior who could best them all.

"She was challenged to a duel in the Rok Estate," the Rider continued.

There were whispers now, but all Cvareh could focus on was the ghost of his sister. It was a figure that already threatened to haunt him until the end of his days.

"A duel between whom?" Cain asked. "A Rok, no doubt. For if she was slain by a Rok, the title of Oji falls to Cvareh."

"I know well how titles work," the Rider chided with a condescending smile. "We use the same ones in House Rok. And you would do well, Cain Bek, to remember where House Rok sits." *At the top*, the Rider allowed everyone to mentally fill in the words. "No, she was challenged by a Xin."

They all knew who it was. There was only one man it could've been. For the only other Xin present at the time of Petra's death was Cvareh, and every last man and women assembled knew that Cvareh would have never challenged his sister.

"On the fifteenth day of the month of Soh, eleven years after the annexation of Loom, Petra'Oji was slain by Finnyr'Kin in a duel of her challenging."

Cvareh stared through the Rider. He looked back to the ghost of his sister in all her power and glory. She had a might that should only be thwarted by the Gods themselves, and Finnyr was no God. There was foul play here. Deceit and lies abounded everywhere Rok stood.

"Coletta Rok'Ryu and Yeaan Rok'Soh bore witness to this honorable challenge and kill. It determines before the Divine Twenty and the mortals below that Finnyr Xin'Kin To will henceforth be known as Finnyr Xin'Oji To."

In this moment, the Rider's words were muffled, garbled. The visage of his sister moved her lips, and all he heard was Cain's voice again, ripe with pain and colored in grief—*Petra is dead*—before the ghostly presence vanished, and left the halls of the Xin Manor forever.

ARIANNA

She was relieved to be free of her bonds. The feeling of entrapment in that dank little room was too similar to what she had endured on Nova at Yveun's hand. Even though the man before her was the antithesis to the hulking Dragon King, and her surroundings looked nothing like the architecture found in the sky world, there was something disturbingly similar to both situations.

"So, where are we?" Movement helped, but thinking helped more.

"Suburb of Ter.5.2." Louie moved at a snail's pace, and Arianna was reduced to a shuffle to avoid striding past him. "It was a warehouse I was using to transfer goods from Dortam to the port of Ter.5.2, and vice versa."

"How far does your reach actually extend?" Arianna didn't know why he was suddenly sharing all this information with her, but if his tongue was well oiled, she'd encourage the words to flow.

"Far enough." Louie paused at one of the switchbacks, giving her a smug smile.

"I suppose you weren't known for your transparency."

"The opposite, actually."

He pushed open a door that was quite light when Arianna caught it, despite the heavy-looking wood-and-bronze framing. They arrived in a homely upstairs room far more domestic than Arianna expected. A long wooden table was lined with pewter stools, one of which was occupied by a red-eared Chimera.

"Adam, go fetch our little crows from their tinkering."

The man named Adam stood and Arianna regarded him warily. She knew Chimeras got the luck of the draw when it came to organs, but seeing red Dragon flesh evoked a completely new response in her. He was oblivious to her apprehension, however, and left the notes he'd been looking over to disappear through a galley door.

"I'm going to need your help." Louie drew her attention from the table as he rounded it in his deliberate manner.

"With what?" Arianna was surprised when he slid the papers toward her. It seemed her needlessly complex planning for how to sneak looks at them was no longer necessary.

He fanned out the papers, an assortment of technological specifications, schematics, unit numbers, and more. "We need to outfit this airship for magic, using this much gold." His finger settled on a quantity.

Arianna scoffed. "Impossible."

"You seem to be someone who makes the impossible, possible."

"I'm an engineer, not a wizard."

"Well—" Louie was cut short by the galley door opening again. Two children strode through. "*Ah*, thank you for joining us."

"A delight to be here, m'Lord!" Helen gave a dramatic bow in Louie's direction.

Arianna tapped her fingers against the table. Magic rippled through the muscle and bone of her forearm, pooling in her fingertips. It was a conscious effort not to unsheathe her claws and throttle the two Ravens.

"If it isn't Helen and Will . . ." Why was she surprised? She really shouldn't be. Arianna had last seen the girl barreling through the underground at breakneck speeds. Anyone who possessed such equal parts stupidity and suicidal tendency would certainly find her way into Louie's employ.

"Been a while, huh?" Helen raised her hand in greeting, nonchalantly strolling over to the table. "What a small world. You work for Louie, I work for Louie…"

"I do not work for Louie," Arianna corrected. "He works for me."

Helen seemed taken aback by this, and her eyes swept to Louie.

"We have an arrangement." It wasn't much in the way of concession on Louie's part. But Arianna was operating under the idea of choosing her battles at present, and this one wasn't worth fighting.

"I knew you stooped low, but working with children, Louie?" Arianna keenly remembered Louie's statement regarding Florence being "observed" by one of his lackeys. Was he keeping Helen and Will here by force, to get back at the girl? "What threats did you have to make?"

"Flor introduced us," Helen announced, as if it was something to be proud of. Well, Ravens were notorious for rushing in headfirst with reckless abandon. "She's been busy while you've been having a vacation on Nova."

"I was *not* on vacation," Arianna snapped.

"Whatever you'll call it then."

"Enough of that, both of you." Louie leaned against the wall, looking as though he could hardly stand for another moment. "We're all on the same side. No need to be at each other's throats."

Arianna could think of quite a few reasons to be at the throats of everyone in the room. But, begrudging as she was to admit it, for now it did suit them all to get along.

"I've already begun to fill in the Wraith on our airship," Louie said to Helen and Will.

"I had some ideas for that." Will approached with caution, and Arianna regarded him in kind. At her side, he leaned over and pointed at a hollow point in the wing of the glider. "I think, right here, we can use it as a main sort of magic artery for lift in both wings."

"Save on gold by piping in the wings instead of on the outside . . ." Arianna's mind folded and unfolded the idea onto the blueprints before her, seeing how they laid atop the glider. "It could be possible." She pointed to the back of the wing. "Discharge through here?"

"Not unless you don't want us to be able to turn." Will shook his head. "Need movements in the flaps."

"How about the end of the wing then?" It was like her mind betrayed her; helping them along was the last thing she wanted to be doing. But it would get her to Florence. And perhaps even more important, it stretched her brain in ways it hadn't been for months on Nova.

It was good to be home.

"That might work. I'll need to check."

Arianna nodded, glancing over the quantity of gold. "I'll need a proper drafting table." She looked up to Louie. "Somewhere I can work."

"Does this count as a wish?" The coy bastard grinned his thin, little smile.

"Hardly." Arianna kept her voice level, scooping the papers and tapping them on the table. "It's a demand, and it's necessary to give you what you asked for."

"Yes, yes, there's somewhere by the hangar that should suffice."

Arianna wondered what constituted a "hangar" in Louie's makeshift world. She wondered what counted as "suitable" too, and was more afraid of the latter than the former.

"Then let's get to work, children."

"I am not a child!" Helen said.

"Let's go." Will grabbed his friend by the elbow, tugging her from the room. Ari was short behind.

"One more thing, Arianna."

"Yes?" She stood with the door half-open, but let it close when he gave it a pointed look. "We will stop in Holx for refueling."

It made sense; Holx was the capital of Ter.4, and even when the world was in disarray it'd still be well stocked. "Helen and Will know you're taking them back to the guild they escaped from?"

"They have faith I'll look after them." Louie waved away the concern. Arianna's only faith in Louie was that he'd look after no one but himself. "While we're there, I need you to acquire something for me."

"Acquire? You mean steal."

Louie hummed his affirmation. "You must think so poorly of me."

"Louie, I have to care about you to think poorly of you. Die in a ditch for all it concerns me."

"You should be more concerned, as I give you great power in this world." Sure, he was well connected, but Arianna had every faith she could be self-sufficient without him if she needed to be. It merely suited her to go along with him, for now, as the path of least resistance.

"So, what is it that you need the White Wraith for?"

"I'll give you the details when we arrive. In the meantime, focus on the airship and fixing your tools. They were badly damaged in your little fall."

Arianna snorted at the word "little." There was a time where not having her daggers would have been cause enough for panic. But now that she could produce claws from her fingertips, they seemed slightly less critical.

Arianna moved for the door but stopped. "One more thing." She looked at the little man. "If you go back on our deal, if you give me one reason to suspect you're out of line—"

"I'm always out of line."

Arianna resisted the urge to roll her eyes, and chose, instead, to hold her gaze level. "I will kill you and everyone you ever loved, horribly."

"Of course." His mouth cracked into a smile, a wild, little grin of pure mirth. Arianna knew where his mind was before he opened his mouth to speak. "That will be easy for you, as I've never loved anyone but myself."

Arianna let him have the last word. She needed time to think over how to threaten someone who fought for nothing but himself.

COLETTA

The first sip was always the hardest.

Coletta poured liquid fire into her mouth. She swallowed it down, a blessing that tasted of damnation. Her fingers cupped the stone mortar, one hooking the pestle to keep it from her face. Her elbows trembled from the weight of the vessel, and the pain.

The poison reached her stomach like a throbbing punch that made her abdomen clench so tightly it pushed the air from her chest and collapsed her lungs. It unfurled agony like the wings of death and took flight through her veins, ravaging her insides. Her magic pushed against the poison on instinct, fighting to keep her knees locked, striving for consciousness.

Still, she drank from the mortar like a babe to a tit. There was delight in the hurt that came from allowing her body to be brutalized by a concoction of her own creation. She charged toward the threshold where pain became pleasure, and nimbly leapt over the edge. Death transformed to triumph.

She killed herself time and again to feel her body reborn, to emerge stronger with each draught.

Coletta lowered the bowl, the sticky residue of the poison weeping down its sides in faintly umber-colored rivulets.

Another day, another draught, and death yet avoided. There would soon be no poison, no concoction or illness that could fell her.

She pulled a sheer, silken shawl back over her shoulders from where it had slipped down her back. The last of the poison was finishing coursing through her system, and Coletta decided a walk would keep her joints moving through the final shivering aftershocks. She stepped away from her sheltered outdoor laboratory, and into the gardens proper.

Flora and fauna encroached on the narrow, ruby-tiled walking path. Flowers uncurled their petals in a vibrant rainbow of color. There were thorny vines that had the most delicate of buds, long stalks that drooped with too-heavy blossoms, and spindly wide-leafed trees that clung to each other like happy drunks.

Two large, mostly harmless, trees sheltered the garden from prying eyes that might glide past on the back of a boco. Yveun's cautiousness had led her to plant the giants of her little kingdom, his concern that her "hobby" be discovered by someone undesirable was both charming and unnecessary. Dragons never saw plants as anything more than ornamentation.

It was a battle easier conceded to her mate than fought. She would kill any who learned the truth of her garden before they could utter it to another soul. And if she was honest, she liked the shade the trees gave, even if it made the garden a touch cooler in the ever-encroaching winter.

"Coletta'Ryu." A woman emerged from around the bend of the path. Ulia. She kneeled, head bowed.

"He has returned?"

"He has, my queen."

Around the woman's neck was a pendant—a small white flower, lacquered. Her mate had his collars of gold, tempered only to his magic, nooses at his command. Coletta's markers were far subtler, yet known well enough, and just as effective.

"This flower . . ." Coletta shifted her fingers, reaching up to touch the delicate petals of a flower identical to the one Ulia wore. "Do you know what it is?"

"A snow bud."

"Indeed. An unassuming name, isn't it?"

"It is." There were times, brief times, when Coletta wondered if the little buds that did her bidding actually agreed with her *unique* approach to conflict. But the second she exhausted mental capacity on such musings, she remembered that she didn't care. Obedience earned in fear was no different than that engendered through love, honesty, or deceit.

"Do you remember what it does?"

Ulia's eyes fell on the living version of her pendant, still cradled in Coletta's long fingers. She was young for a flower—just thirty-nine—but Ulia had proved her loyalty in a very short time.

"Paralysis," Ulia said finally.

"Yes, but only the stigma." Coletta touched her fingertip to the red knob that extended out from the center of the flower. "The petals actually provide the antidote to this natural immobilizer. Most don't even realize these properties exist, since consuming or brewing the flower neutralizes the negative effect." She dropped her hand and stepped over to the kneeling girl. Coletta reached out the same hand, guiding Ulia's face upward to meet her eyes. "Remember that, Ulia. One thing can both give and take away."

"Should I fall from your favor, it would be an honor too great for a wretch like me to die by a potion crafted by your hand, Coletta'Ryu."

The corners of her mouth twitched upward in the nearest imitation of a smile Coletta would ever give. "Yes, sweet Ulia, you will never betray me."

"Never." Ulia slowly, reverently, and with the slightest scent of fear in her magic, brought Coletta's hand to her mouth, kissing her knuckles once.

"Now." Coletta pulled her hand away, her dominance reaffirmed. "Take me to dress for dinner."

"My queen, Yveun'Dono is . . . occupied."

"I realize." The girl was young enough to underestimate her. It was endearing, to a point. "I would care to look on him before he is finished."

"As you wish." Ulia stood and bowed her head as Coletta strode past. She waited three breaths before falling into step behind.

There were two entrances to Coletta's garden—one to her private quarters and one to Yveun's. She rarely had reason to cross through the latter. Barring dinner, her mate usually came to her.

Her own portion of the Rok Estate was smaller but no less opulent than the rest. Red lacquered beams cut across a pitch-black ceiling, every fourth beam framed by two posts on the whitewashed walls. It was simple, striking, and reminiscent of all her favorite poisonous flora.

At the end of the hallway stood her primary sitting room. Hexagonal in shape, every wall had a door, perfectly centered and mosaicked in ruby. The door directly across from the hall was her bedroom; spiraling right around the room were the portals to her bathing room, second laboratory, library, and dressing room. Of these, the little buds that served as her personal handmaidens were only given permission to enter the last.

"Do you have a preference this evening, Ryu?" Ulia asked as Coletta seated herself on the oxblood leather ottoman at the room's center.

"I do not." All her life, the world had whispered of her shortcomings, *What a terrible Dragon she made.* Coletta cared nothing for fashion and in many cases preferred function over form. She appreciated fineries, but only insofar as they had purpose. But ignoring trivialities uncluttered her mind, allowing her to dedicate all her energy to a singular focus: domination. In this way, she was one of the greatest paragons of her species. If only the rest of Nova knew.

"How about the lavender?" Ulia asked from behind her. "It brings out the shades of wine in your skin."

Coletta smiled, wide and wicked, at the word. Rarely did she reveal her nubby teeth and rotten gums, ravaged by years of poisoning herself for the sake of immunity, for strength. But thoughts of her grand display on the Isle of Ruana—and of Petra shuddering on the floor of the Rok Manor—made it near impossible to contain her pleasure.

By the time Ulia's footsteps neared, Coletta's face was as blank and composed as daylight: emotions drawn inward, face passive, eyes hard—this was the way to greet the world.

Ulia presented a simple, armless sheath that slipped over Coletta's shoulders and split into strips at her hips. They danced and swirled around her legs as she walked. The silken material stitched with gemstones betrayed its finery, but it was otherwise simple. It showed off her thin frame and the soft, squishy skin clinging to her bones.

Demure. Frail. Delicate.

Three things no Dragon wished to be. The world whispered it of her, even as she slipped death into their drinks and food, and between their ribs.

"I do not need you to escort me to the dining room this evening, Ulia," Coletta said as they traversed back through her garden.

"As you wish." The girl gave a small bow. Coletta appreciated her unquestioning obedience, even when she broke form. Actions like that kept Ulia close. If the girl knew it or not, they kept her alive.

"I would, however, ask you to see that wine is set out." She felt the corners of her mouth twitch again in a near-smile. But letting the same person see her smile more than once in a single week—in a single day no less—was far too much. "Go to the cellars. There should be a newer vintage from a winery here on Lysip."

"Yes, my lady."

Coletta gave the girl a nod of dismissal and started in the opposite direction.

Yveun's halls were cluttered compared to hers. Ironwork, reminiscent of the fanned wings of a Rider's glider, arched over her with curling tendrils of metal lacework reaching down in wide, concentric circles. Beyond was what Coletta had termed the sailcloth room, a billowing half-glass roof that looked like the puffed sail of a lake boat. On and on, the walls were adorned and the floor gleamed with a proud, polished finish.

On and on, Coletta ignored it all.

She listened, but there was not another soul to be heard. Even magic hearing would not have revealed a single sound. Yveun had likely sent away every Dragon, high and low.

Nearing his chambers, Coletta pressed on a wall. It looked no different from anything else, the wood paneling near flawless. *Near flawless.* A small groove betrayed the narrow door that swiveled open at her insistent force.

Clicking the door back into place, Coletta found herself in an unlit, narrow hall that ran parallel to the first. There were many secrets in the manor, and she made it a point to know them all.

Coletta walked without light, running her fingertips along the wall as she proceeded with measured steps. She avoided pushing magic into her eyes, for that could be sensed—or worse, smelled. The darkness slowed her steps, prevented the carelessness of haste that might give her away.

It seemed, however, there were some allowances that could be made for noise.

Yveun, for all his strengths, was still a man and a Dragon. A man with desires, and a Dragon bent on domination. When the two forces combined, the results were hardly silent.

Coletta heard them—heavy breathing, gasping, grunting, growling. Ahead, a few beams of gray light broke through the darkness. Coletta walked toward them like a beacon.

Where the main hall sloped downward, her private corridor remained level. She now found herself peering down at a familiar room—Yveun's private sleeping chamber.

Blood dripped from his back where long gashes, already healing, had been dragged across his skin. Beneath him, a woman as green as Coletta's fauna writhed and arched her back as they rutted like dogs and sounded much the same. Yveun's face twisted, his head thrown back in a snarl of pleasure that was nearly drowned out by the smacking of his hips against the woman's backside.

It was the first time she'd laid eyes on the creature her little buds had selected for their Dono. Fae, they had said her name was. Little and less was known about her, but Coletta knew the one thing that mattered more than all others: Yveun had taken a liking to her.

Unlike Leona, he had charged forward with this one. He had mounted the creature like an animal, and like an unbroken boco, she was fighting back. The lovers rolled over, and Fae swiped at Yveun's face, drawing yet more blood. He snarled in kind, digging his own claws down her arm.

Their mouths met before smearing golden blood over each other's skin.

They were drunk on each other. Coletta watched as her life mate, her king, sexed another woman in a way he had never done to her. His face contorted in bliss; Coletta looked away, having both seen and affirmed enough.

Fae might own the Dono, but Coletta owned Fae. Everything was moving according to plan on Nova. Now, before she'd give in to the demands of her quietly grumbling stomach, she would check in with her odd little Fenthri to see how things were progressing down on Loom.

ARIANNA

When dusk settled upon the world, Arianna was nothing more than a white smudge against a gray sky. She peered down at Holx through her modified goggles from the rooftop of one of the airship yards. She'd been scouting since the afternoon, observing people's comings and goings, studying the flow of machine and man alike.

The home of the Ravens' Guild was unnaturally quiet. Or perhaps the quiet was *too* natural. Arianna heard howling winds and cawing birds, benign sounds at odds with the screeching trikes and revving engines Holx was famous for.

The one guild the Dragons supposedly hadn't touched had, nevertheless, ground to a slow crawl in the wake of the fall of their world. It was unnervingly somber, a quiet testament to the devastation the Dragon King had reaped from his sky city.

Malice sparked within her and was promptly quieted by the thought of Yveun. *Looking down on her, his claws on her flesh . . .*

Arianna rubbed her neck, urging tension and the memory away.

She had a job to do, and there wasn't nearly enough time to properly prepare for it. All she had was some basic information from Louie—oddly specific in some areas, completely blank in others—and whatever she could observe before nightfall.

It wasn't nearly enough time to break into the guild's hall.

As the sun fell behind the clouds that perpetually blanketed Loom's sky, Arianna rose. She held out her hand. Magic pulled against her palm, drawing out a line from her winch box like a serpent from its den. The cord was cast in gold and tempered to her magic alone, the closest thing to a loyal friend she had at the moment. It was time to shake off the dust that had settled on her shoulders in Nova.

Arianna looped the cord around a heavy pipe that ran around the rooftop, clipping the line to itself. She walked to the edge of the building and put everything else behind her. Up here, she didn't need to be Arianna the Master Rivet. She could cast aside the loose ties to Nova as Ari Xin'Anh Bek. She would ignore that her shroud of anonymity as the inventor of the Philosopher's Box, the Perfect Chimera, had been lifted. She certainly wouldn't spare a thought for Arianna, the rebel who had twice failed to slay the Dragon King.

She was merely the White Wraith—nothing more, nothing less. She was a vessel for her benefactors. All the rest, she would leave on the rooftop.

With a wide step and a whir of gears, Arianna tipped herself over the edge.

Golden cabling spun from the spools attached to her belt by the winch box. She ticked off seconds in her mind, calculating how much line she'd used based on the speed of her free fall and the distance covered. She'd know when to stop and swing onto a ledge, to magically unclip her line and cast it toward the next building, swinging from ledge to ledge until she reached her target.

Holx was a city of layers, each stacked on the next to create a labyrinth of tracks and walkways. She followed one track now; it had virtually no lights along its sides and would be almost impossible for Fenthri eyes to pick out in the growing dark. But with her Dragon eyes and refined goggles, she had little issue.

"Follow the red-lined trike path to the guild," Louie had instructed. It was one of his more oddly specific notes, and was followed immediately by one of his decidedly less specific: "Once you get to the end, you'll figure out a way in."

Thanks, Louie, Arianna thought grimly as she reached the end of the red-lined path. Arianna waited for headlights and the roar of engines to vanish before easing herself down from the mostly abandoned upper paths she'd been traversing. But where there should have been an egress awaiting her, she found instead the fresh cement of a portal recently sealed.

She looked back up. There hadn't been another ledge on her descent, no other obvious doorway. "Up" wasn't an option, and before her was blocked, which only left . . . down.

The depths of Holx held a darkness that even her goggles and eyes couldn't penetrate. She presumed she was somewhere close to the ground, or already below it. She might even be closer to the land known as the Raven's Folly—the Underground—than she was the airship. She dared progress no farther without some kind of light; begrudgingly, she drew the duller of her two daggers.

She pushed her magic into the hilt and up through the blade—just enough to heat the metal to a faint, reddish glow. She'd fix the dulled point later. For now, the ambient light of semi-molten gold was enough to reflect off her surroundings and give her a rusty picture of where she was.

To her right was another track that dead-ended in a walled-up portion of the guild. Below and to her left was a perpendicular road that intersected with a narrow bridge. Arianna squinted. She moved her blade left and right, watching the shadows dance away in opposite directions.

One shadow didn't budge.

Letting loose more slack in her line, Arianna's winch box clicked her further down the narrow gap between guild and street, leaving no doubt she had crossed the threshold into the Underground. Just above the narrow bridge, she cycled her legs in a running motion along the wall—back and forth, building speed.

One hand on the dagger, the other on her winch box, she prepared for her one chance to successfully make this jump. There wasn't even a ripple of apprehension across her nerves. At the apex of her parabola, she pulled the linchpin on her cable.

Arianna's stomach shot into her chest as she went into a free fall. She clutched the dagger with all her might.

The wooden bridge groaned under her, sagging with her weight. Arianna tumbled and dug her free hand into the grooves, using claws and splinters to gain purchase on the decaying walkway.

Now her nerves raced. Her chest heaved. Her eyes dilated, adrenaline providing a clarity no magic could ever match. Arianna grinned into the blackness, holding her cooling dagger away from both herself and the wood.

It felt good to be back at work.

She rolled onto her stomach and hopped up. Letting the fading heat of the dagger continue to give her just enough light, Ari summoned her gold line back to her spool. When it was wound up tightly, she focused on her next challenge.

The door was old and rusted, and the lock looked equally frail. Arianna sighed. She had so wanted an actual challenge when it came to breaking into the guild—the opportunity to exercise a bit of finesse.

With a smash of her boot, the door nearly fell off its hinges and alerted the ghosts of the Ravens' Guild to her forced entry. This doorway had been long forgotten; not a soul stirred in the dark tunnel it revealed. She moved forward fearlessly, guided by the light of her dagger.

Eventually, she came to a circular room with six connecting archways. Arianna paused in the room's center. Bruising had started to blossom on the fingers that clutched the dagger, working up her wrist with slow purpose. As her magic exhausted, her body began to break down, one burst blood vessel at a time.

She had to find her way up before her light faded.

In the thin layer of dust that coated the floor, a single track led from one hall to the other. *Someone must be using this old intersection.*

The two halls breathed from one to the other as if they were old friends, whispering little secrets. Wind pushed the flaps of her coat against the backs of her calves ever so slightly. Arianna chose her path based on the knowledge that cool air sought out warmer temperatures.

Her suspicion was affirmed as the hallway began to rise. The faint roar of engines guided her upward past two forks.

She was nearly breathless from magical exertion by the time she saw light, and Ari took a moment to compose herself. The faint glow of a doorway three pecas away told her she'd finally found a way out. She didn't know if it would lead her into the guild proper; she wouldn't have been surprised if she'd somehow overshot the hall entirely.

Arianna tilted her head back and closed her eyes, letting her breathing slow and her skin mend. In so many ways, she was her best in moments like this: alone, working for what she needed, taking odd jobs with a clear beginning and end.

But that would mean leaving Florence adrift in a rising sea of chaos. It would mean never seeing Cvareh again. Arianna didn't want to admit why that fact put such a profound ache in her chest. A life of crime and obscurity would have to wait, at least for now.

Arianna opened her eyes and kept moving.

The doorway opened onto a walkway above a large track. As she crossed the threshold, a trike came whizzing around a far corner, speeding underneath her in a blink. She couldn't even make out that a person was driving the machine, and for that reason alone she was confident there was no way the Raven would've seen her as anything more than a rogue guild member wandering the halls.

The Ravens' Guild had a helix of two tracks spiraling around a central core. The only way to get up, according to Louie, was by driving one of those chaotic machines to the desired level. Down the curving track, a large yellow "2/1" was painted on the far wall.

Well, that's convenient. She didn't have far to go. The item Louie had asked her to procure could supposedly be found on level two—the main train terminal for the guild.

In the distance, another catwalk loomed above the track. She waited for two more trikes to pass before casing her line and perching on the railing. The drivers may not notice a random person on the catwalk, or a relatively thin golden line, as they no doubt focused more on not dying in a splatter on one of the curving walls . . . but they would likely not be able to miss a woman swinging from walk to walk.

The sound of an engine in the distance announced the impending arrival of another rogue trike. Four more sped by, then there was a brief stint of quiet. Arianna took her chance, jumping off and using her magic winch box to pull her to the far walk.

It only took three more leaps to arrive at the landing for level two. Steam billowed out from a large archway, half-blocked by a heavy steel door that hung partially closed. The tinny screech of train brakes echoed through the halls.

Arianna watched as men and women flowed in and out of the entryway. Louie hadn't warned her of this.

The Ravens' Guild managed the shipping and transport for the world, often using their guild hall itself as a key hub. It made sense there would be only one entrance—an entrance that could be locked down in the case of a nefarious force trying to gain entry.

Arianna did the only thing she could think of: wait and watch. Ravens pulled up in their various vehicles, parked them, and went about their business. There was seemingly no order to their comings and goings.

If only I'd brought my grease pencil. Etching the guild's mark on her cheek would have made things easier, but she was hardly dissuaded. It was almost mechanical now, seeing different ways to gain access wherever she wanted to go.

Arianna fastened the toggles on her white coat as high as they went, obscuring most of her face to the nose. She reached under the catwalk and ran her hand along the thick layer of exhaust grime that coated the wood and iron from years of use by all manner of vehicles. As suspected, her gray skin was turned black; Arianna rubbed it on both hands and applied it to her cheeks, then to her coat.

She had three more requests of Louie. If she had one to spare, she'd spend it on demanding the man wash her coat himself, just for the sake of seeing the king get his hands dirty once.

Goggles down, hood up, covered in soot and grease, she might be able to pass as a Raven. Between racing trikes, Arianna descended quickly using her golden cable. She scampered up to the parking area, crouching as one odd-looking four-wheeled vehicle pulled away.

By the time another Raven approached, all they would see was a grime-covered woman hunched with her eyes on the floor, striding with purpose into the most important terminal in the world.

She may not agree with the Raven mindset or methods, but Arianna couldn't deny a cathedral of innovation when she saw one.

Fifteen tracks, neatly lined and almost all occupied, sat underneath a vaulted ceiling high enough to stack half the trains on top of each other with room to spare. There were passenger vessels and cargo transports alike. One engine made Arianna do a double-take.

It was no doubt experimental. Arianna had never considered that placement of gold before to help drive thrust. Half of it made sense, but the other half would likely result in inefficiency. Unless . . .

She pried her eyes away. That was *not* what she was here for. She refocused on the windows that lined the wall opposite the end of all the tracks—the terminal offices.

It reminded her of the last time she'd broken into an office for shipping information. Back then, she'd been ferrying a particular Dragon.

"Watch where you're going!" A Raven threw her a rude gesture as they narrowly avoided a collision.

Arianna put her head down and kept moving forward. She had to get what she came for, and get out. She was allowing Arianna the Rivet and Ari Xin to exist where there should only be the White Wraith.

It was amazing how little mind the guild members paid her. They continued along with their duties, oblivious to the intruder in their midst. There seemed to be fewer than she would've suspected, however. Perhaps they were thinned as a result of the shifting efforts due to the budding rebellion?

Up two flights of stairs, Arianna found herself in another empty hall. This one was lit—a far significant improvement over her earlier wandering.

Every office, save the first she passed, was quiet. Almost unnervingly so. Low numbers of initiates and journeymen, desks without people to man them . . . This was supposedly one of the busiest stations in the world. Why was it so quiet?

Arianna made quick work of the door lock, easing herself into the dimly lit office. A single light for which there was no switch glowed overhead. A beacon perpetually shining, waiting for the trains that never stopped, even long after people stopped tending them.

There was nothing particularly special about the room. But every detail was exactly as Louie had described. The desk— suspiciously wounded with a deep notch in its right corner—faced the doorway. Two bookshelves stood on her right-hand side, three on her left. Arianna went to the shelf in the farthest corner.

19.32

The innocuous number was imprinted on the second-highest shelf. Binders of identical size, shape, and color were slotted side by side along its entire length. Each bore a number on its spine in ascending order, the last marked 1081.

This year.

This was where Louie's dictation had ended. All his careful instruction had taken her to this shelf, to the records all the way to the right. This was what he wanted her to steal.

She opened the unmarked folio. A sort of Raven's code was scribbled across from dates. Numbers and symbols, nothing more.

Louie had no doubt assumed she couldn't decipher the meaning. And, without more time, she couldn't. But he was underestimating her, a mistake that many found harmful to their health.

Arianna might not know the Raven's code offhand, but she knew she was in the main terminal for the transport of all goods and peoples across Loom. She knew that 19.32 was a very specific number, identical to a certain density. And she knew one alchemical symbol that continued to appear across the pages: a circle with a ring around it.

The symbol for gold.

"All right, Louie," she whispered. "I got your book." The only linger question was what exactly Louie planned to do with it.

CVAREH

"Say it again." Cain's voice was the first to break the silence. "Say it again!" Never before had a Dragon growled with such rage. It would be enough to startle the Goddess of Warriors herself.

"In light of these events," the Rider continued, ignoring Cain, "Yveun'Dono, in all his generosity, has been gracious enough to allow Finnyr'Oji to return to these halls as your House's leader."

"Gracious enough?" Cain snarled. "*Gracious enough?* He likely killed her himself!"

"Cain Bek, I will let this slide without a challenge, seeing as House Xin is currently in a time of transition—" The Rider would not even say *grief.* He wouldn't give them that decency. "—But your Ryu is still present and, in such a case, can authorize a duel."

The mention of Ryu brought Cain's eyes swinging back to Cvareh.

Cvareh wasn't ready for all the emotions and demands wrapped up in his friend's gaze. He could barely handle his own emotions; how would he handle another's? What did Cain think he could do?

Petra had trained him to be her right hand, to function as she needed. He was a vessel for his sister and without her . . .

"Are you really going to let them get away with this?" Cain demanded. It was a verbal slap across the face, a violent tug out of the ocean of his grief and onto the beach of reality. It was what he *needed*. But what he *wanted* was to sink into those forever depths that had the same chilling embrace of Lord Xin. "If Petra is dead, then—"

"Enough, Cain." Cvareh grabbed for the other man's wrist the moment he saw the tension ripple down Cain's bicep. If the man unsheathed his claws now, a duel would be inevitable. Even if Cain won, it would just throw the situation with Rok into further chaos.

All eyes had turned to the altercation between the two men. The brother, and the would-be lover of the woman who had led them fearlessly toward a vision so many generations had never even dared to whisper, let alone desire. Cvareh didn't know what to do with their attention.

Petra would have known what to do.

He cleared his throat and spoke words he never thought he'd say. "When will Finnyr'Oji—" his brother's name tasted of bile "—be arriving?"

The Rider's mouth curled back in a triumphant smile. House Xin had always been the lowest in Dragon society, but this was a new feeling.

"He will be sent within the day." The Rider stepped leisurely down from the pedestal. "I hear the duel was fearsome. He's taking time to recover."

Cvareh remembered Finnyr's last altercation with Petra. *That* had been fearsome. He had seen it with his own eyes:

his sister atop his brother, knees digging into chest, blood from his shredded face up to her elbows.

"Recover under a Rok roof," Cain mumbled, not quietly enough.

"Well, he does feel quite at home there," the Rider goaded easily. "After all, he's lived under the generous care of the Dono himself for years. I couldn't imagine actually wanting to return to these bleak halls."

"I chall—"

"Cain'Da, silence!" The echoes of Cvareh's voice seemed to resonate from half the open mouths in the room. Even his friend was stunned to silence. "The Rider had quite the trip here, and will have another long journey home. I suggest we let him leave with haste."

It was phrased to Cain as a suggestion, but it was a poorly veiled demand.

The Rider flashed his canines to Cvareh first, then Cain, and then every Xin assembled at the manor on his way out.

"You shouldn't have let him walk out alive." Cain's bloodlust was insatiable. Cvareh expected it would be for some time.

"Dueling him would serve little purpose."

"Petra would not have let him leave after such disrespect." Cain found the spot and pushed hard.

"Petra is not here!"

Silence, again.

The two men squared off, huffing short breaths that could just as easily become tears as they could become screams of anger. Cain's magic ballooned to three times his size. Cvareh's claws itched for extension.

But Cvareh took a breath and stepped away.

"Petra is not here," he repeated, softer. "Fighting that Rider will not bring her back and neither will fighting me."

"So we are to tolerate disrespect now?" Cain motioned as though he was somehow speaking for the whole of House Xin. "We are to let them walk on us?"

"We are to survive." *It's what she would've wanted.* Cvareh didn't have to speak the thought to know the entire room was in agreement.

All eyes were on him. They looked to him for answers he didn't have, for plans he had yet to formulate. He didn't even know what Petra had intended, all the moving parts that only she had kept track of.

"This is what Yveun wants." Cvareh didn't know if it was pain or loathing that made him drop the Dono's title in that moment. But he prayed it wouldn't become a habit, and that the Rider was far enough away not to hear. "He wants us weakened, divided. He is doing to us what he did to Loom."

"Loom?" Cain was at him again. "You bring up Loom *now*? Are you Cvareh Xin, or have you given up your name like a Fen? What next? Will you paint your skin gray?"

"I said silence, Cain." Cvareh's voice had gone quiet. He didn't want to fight Cain, but the majority of the House didn't know where he had spent the past months. They didn't know who Ari Xin really was. "And yes, I bring up Loom . . . because they are the one chance we have to fight our way out from under Yveun's thumb."

Cain eased away.

Without the immediate threat, Cvareh could properly appreciate the confused looks on the faces of the other members of the House. Was now the right time to tell them? When would Petra have said it?

"I will explain, in time." The fewer people who knew right now, the better. Powers were shifting, and the world was changing around him. "For now, I need your faith."

"You have it." A man Cvareh did not recognize spoke up from the crowd. Agreement was slowly voiced from all around him.

Cain continued to glare.

"Then we shall prepare for the arrival of my brother." He couldn't bring himself to say "Finnyr'Oji," not just yet. "See that his quarters are cleaned and properly appointed."

Cvareh waited for someone to move, to execute his order, but all bodies in the room remained eerily still, all eyes trained on him, expectant. Finally, a woman spoke.

"Prepare his chambers?"

"Yes." He didn't see how he'd been unclear on the matter.

"But Cvareh'Ryu . . . Will you not challenge him? Will you not fight to be our Oji?"

Cvareh would have given anything to not have to answer that question.

COLETTA

The Rok Estate housed the most wonderful dining room in the entire world. It had a table made entirely of iron that stretched long enough for forty people to sit underneath a ceiling of frescos, lit by a thousand candles. It was a room of pure magic and power that would make even the finest Dragon blush at its decadence.

That was not the room where she and Yveun dined.

Instead, they sat at a basic wooden table, barely large enough to seat four comfortably. The windows were simple rectangles, the mullions made of pine. There were no adornments here, no paintings or carefully sculpted statues. Carved into the only entrance and exit was the symbol of House Rok. It took up the top half of the doorway: three triangles supporting a crown.

Coletta looked down as the servants delivered their food from the kitchens. Her flowers would take over during the second half of dinner, when discussion actually began. For now, she'd let the average man and woman see her as the weak Ryu they all expected her to be.

When the servants retreated, Yveun raised his glass first to his lips, then toward her. "You picked as stunning a vintage as ever, my Ryu."

"This is a new one I wanted to try." Coletta watched how the crimson liquid coated the inside of the glass, trickling down in tiny lines. "It's grown here on Lysip."

"On Lysip? Where?"

"To the north. The rocky earth and claylike soil give it that mineral taste." Coletta set down her glass. Putting her fingers on either side of its stem, she swirled it around thoughtfully. "It's about time viticulture came to Lysip. While I appreciated the irony of House Xin making a crimson beverage I think it's far more fitting for this to be an area of Rok expertise."

"I never thought of the color." Yveun copied Coletta's motion before setting the glass aside.

Coletta did the same, and the atmosphere shifted.

"Fae is to your liking?" She phrased it as a question, but they both knew better.

"More so than Leona, even."

That was the answer Coletta wanted to hear. "I believe she will be good for us."

"I couldn't agree more." Yveun chewed his food for a long moment. "She will be the ideal asset to finally hunt down the Perfect Chimera. Truly fitting."

Coletta hummed thoughtfully.

"You disagree."

"Let the Chimera be." Like always, the Dono was narrow-minded when it came to things that eluded him, things he felt entitled to. Ah, to have the mind of a man, and have the world rendered as such a simple, linear place. "She has already made a fool of you too many times."

"Which is precisely why—"

"Why we will not allow it to happen again." Coletta did not appreciate being interrupted. She inhaled. Yveun made no motion to speak, so she continued. "The next time you see the Chimera will be when her death is assured. For now, we must keep Fae here to secure order on Nova."

"On Nova?" His pores practically oozed sex at the idea.

"She will go with Finnyr."

Yveun paused mid-drink, then slowly lowered his glass to the table. He ran the pads of his fingers over the rim of the glass. She could almost see him working out how quickly a boco could get to Ruana and back.

"Would it not be better to keep her here? It will be hard for her to earn the respect of the other Riders if she is off in the Xin Manor. How will she win beads?"

"She has enough beads for three strands of hair." Coletta took a small bite of the meal. The flavors were well balanced.

"Underground fighting pits and back alley brawls do not a Rider make. We can't recognize those kills for beads."

"Do you think she cares?" Coletta reached for her wine again.

There was a good reason she always saw wine set out. If Yveun was well mannered, they enjoyed it together. If he was stubborn but tolerable, she enjoyed having something to take the edge off. The few times he was outright unpleasant toward her, Coletta fantasized about how easy it would be to place a lethal dose of poison in his glass.

"So she goes with Finnyr, then." Yveun finally resigned. "For what purpose? House Xin will not appreciate us sending a bodyguard for a man they no doubt want to kill."

"Since when have we cared what House Xin thinks?"

Yveun laughed. It was a delightful sound, so genuine that even Coletta could admit it made him particularly attractive.

"Petra is dead. They are clawless. Now is the time to press harder, not pull back. No half-measures."

He repeated their House motto, toasting her as he did. "'Break them again when they are already broken, and see they rebuild in a way we find fitting.'"

She raised her glass to her lips with a smile. Yveun had the look of a king, but his mind was always a step behind hers. They made for a formidable pair in that respect. He was every inch what Nova wanted and Loom needed in a Dragon King; she was every scheming thought required to maintain the façade of his qualifications.

"I believe Fae has magic in her ears. Set up a whisper link with her so that we may know what's going on," Coletta suggested.

"But—"

"I will not be going anywhere." She waved the notion away. It was kind, but unnecessary for him to reserve that channel of communication for her alone. Allowing him to establish a link with Fae would not only give them a direct line to the Xin Manor, but would also please her mate, deepen his bond with Fae. "Set up a link with her."

"If you insist." Yveun couldn't conceal his excitement at the notion, though he mastered his face into seriousness. "There's another matter I wish to discuss about the woman."

"You have my attention." And what a rare commodity that was.

"I assume you know of her . . . *tastes*."

"You mean her proclivity for imbibing?" The delicate manner in which Yveun brought it up made it clear they were speaking about more than feasting on the heart of a fallen foe. This was imbibing from the living. "Yes, I am aware."

"An idea has crossed my mind."

"Oh?" Coletta always enjoyed Yveun's ideas. They were either fantastic—an equal match for her own—or they reminded her why she was usually the strategist between them.

"All this nonsense over a 'Perfect Chimera'—a Fenthri that can possess all Dragon organs containing magic without falling. Why not a perfect Dragon?"

Coletta paused, considering the idea. The difficulty of a perfect chimera for the Fenthri came from the fact that their bodies weren't meant for magic; they struggled to combat the rot that resulted from forcing magic on a body not intended to contain it. Dragons did not share this same barrier.

"You want to give Fae organs as a Fen Chimera would receive."

"I want to make her strong."

"The woman is plenty strong as the gods made her." Coletta ran her fingertip across the lip of her wineglass until it hummed softly, stopping the moment the vibrations made sound. "But I agree with you, Yveun. And I do not think she would be opposed to the idea."

"Excellent. Then we shall keep her here until such time as—"

"No, she will leave with Finnyr as planned." It was one of Yveun's better ideas, and Coletta would reward him for it—in time, in her own way. But keeping Fae on Ruana while sending Finnyr to the snake pit unprotected would not be that reward. "That is most important. I will seek out Fen slaves who bear the Alchemist triangles, and we shall experiment first. After all, if Fae is to be sculpted as the perfect Dragon, we must perfect our process foremost."

"Very well." He hummed. "Speaking of that which we will sculpt to perfection . . ."

"Loom?"

"Loom." Yveun rested his elbows on the table, lacing his fingers in front of him. "What word have you from your little flowers on the gray rock?"

"The Fen are, indeed, demoralized. But it seems that one is spurring another rebellion."

"Stubborn, suicidal creatures." Yveun shook his head as a father might, faced with a petulant child.

"They are convening on Ter.0 for a Vicar Tribunal," Coletta continued, reciting her information, not bothering to correct Yveun's incorrect assumption that it came from a Dragon on Loom. Even Fenthri would sell out each other for the right price.

"Vicar Tribunal. How long has it been since I've heard such a notion?"

"Not long enough."

"Indeed." Yveun laced and unlaced his fingers in thought. "I suppose I should be impressed that enough vicars survived to have such a gathering."

"Fenthri lives are fleeting." Coletta sat back in her chair, thinking of the brief periods of time the Fenthri walked the earth. A Dragon could easily live upwards of one hundred twenty years; Fenthri were lucky if they saw forty-five. How did one approach life knowing existence would be nothing more than a wink in time's great eye? "I'm sure they rotated new ones in hastily."

"Too true." Yveun placed his wine glass down. "I shall go to this Tribunal."

Coletta's eyes fluttered closed as she inhaled slowly. "Why would you deliver yourself to them?"

"Did we not raze them as vengeful gods do? Now, I shall descend as a god appeased, merciful and calm. I will show them the beauty of their submission."

"You mistake poetry for practicality." Coletta shifted uncomfortably in her seat. She knew from the look in her mate's eye that the battle was lost.

"I will bring order and offer peace. Even House Xin was offered that."

"And what great dividends that paid."

"The Fenthri know they have been beaten."

"They have not known it ever. How many times must we destroy them before you see that they will never bow willingly?"

"We have never destroyed them so completely before," Yveun countered.

Coletta was ready to strike back by pointing out the fact that they were far from destroyed if they were already organizing a Tribunal. But she knew when his mind was made up. There was little point in fighting the matter now.

"Very well." Coletta gripped and released the arms of her chair. "Go to them when you please. But meet with the leaders only, and do so under the banner of peace. Outnumber them in manpower, but avoid striking."

"It is hard to parlay for peace when claws are drawn."

"If they accept the natural order of things—" Dragons on top, Fenthri groveling far below "—then we shall all rejoice for the peace and prosperity our world will share. However, should they refuse—" and Coletta already knew they would "—then you shall heed me on such matters henceforth until Loom has returned to sense and order."

Yveun was silent for a long moment. Long enough that Coletta was afraid he truly had lost all sense and was going to deny her. "Very well. Your guidance has yet to lead me astray. And in any case, should Loom deny me yet again, I fear my patience will have been exhausted for good."

Coletta was counting on exactly that.

ARIANNA

L ike a swarm of angry hornets, airships of all shapes and
sizes buzzed in the skies above Ter.0. The roar of engines
below mirrored the sound, magnifying it, harmonizing
with it. It was more life than the barren earth had seen
in years.

Arianna stood on the deck of Louie's airship, goggles on,
wind whipping her hair across her face. She could barely see
land from around the back fin of the vessel and the stretch of
the wings, but what was visible filled her with curiosity and
dread. Ter.0 had been the foundation on which the order of
Loom once stood. What would this new world order look like,
built on the ruins of the old?

The airship touched down on a rocky stretch of mostly flat
earth. Arianna worked her way through the narrow interior to
the hatch that was currently being opened by one of Louie's
other lackeys—a man whose name Arianna had never thought
learn.

A sliver of light peeked from behind the door as the latches
disengaged. Arianna's eyes adjusted quickly as the door swung
open wide. Nothing would ever be as bright as the sunlight on
Nova.

Raven-tattooed men and women rushed around the makeshift airfield, waving flags and directing passengers off landing strips. Runners sprinted between high points of rock, delivering messages after every new ship landed.

There were massive ballooned ships and tiny glider-like vessels parked side by side. Most were Raven-marked; the next most common guild symbol was for Rivets. After that, Alchemists . . .

Arianna didn't see a single Revolver or Harvester.

"You may find it easier if you disembark." Louie's voice cut through her thoughts.

She offered no explanation or apology for her hesitation and ignored the man trying to work around her to get the departure stairs set up. Impatient, Arianna jumped the short distance from the airship to the ground. She landed in a crouch, then recovered, taking in the sights and smells of the world she was no longer observing from the shadows.

This was the land where the Vicar Tribunal was founded. This was where Loom had thrived, where she had been born. This was where the Council of Five banded together against the Dragons, where her lover died, where her life was forever changed. It seemed a piece of cosmic poetry that this could well be where she would die.

As promptly as the thoughts came, Arianna moved on from the notion of her own mortality. That was something she'd written off as unimportant years ago.

"Where are you going?" Helen called after her.

"To find Florence," Arianna shouted back, half-turning. They had now exchanged a total of seven words in one week.

"Perhaps you may find it faster to come with us." Louie motioned toward the trike lurching to a stop beside them.

A woman with long white hair, hanging loose and becoming a knotted mess, pushed a pair of streamlined, single-lens goggles up onto her forehead. "Sorry I'm late," she said, speaking directly to Louie.

"Hardly so." Louie walked around to the cart attached to the back of the trike, accepting one of his bigger lackey's help in getting into it. "How is our favorite rebel?"

"Fine, fine. It's a bit of a mess here, with everyone."

"A Raven's nightmare." Arianna was close enough to hear Helen mumble.

"Logistically, yes, but it's kind of like the Underground, I've heard some say. They never get to have this much fun driving or piloting in the sunlight. Not a single rule or regulation on vehicles in sight. Speaking of, looks like your ship had some interesting modifications . . . Heard you'd have a rainbow tail, didn't expect it to be so clean."

Arianna couldn't stop herself from rolling her eyes as she began to make her way to the benched cart with everyone else.

"We had a Master Rivet to conceive and implement the modifications." Louie motioned to her, bringing their driver's attention with it.

"You must be Arianna." The slate-skinned woman didn't miss a beat.

"And you are?"

"Shannra," the woman replied. "Florence told me all about you."

Arianna's blood seemed to boil and freeze at once. She wanted to know everything about Florence and didn't want to think of some random stranger knowing more than her. Fear at this idea rose like bile.

So much had happened. Would Florence still look to her for guidance as she once had? Would the girl value her as she once did?

"I look forward to her telling me all about you."

"Typical Arianna." Shannra laughed but had the decency to heed the conversation's conclusion. She turned forward, revving the engine to life.

The lurch of the trike jolted some tension from Arianna's muscles. The airfield passed in a haze of Ter.0 dust, airships, and homeless Fenthri. She was close to Florence now and the only thing that mattered was seeing her again. Everything else in the world could wait.

Off in the distance, the spires of Ter.0 grew in size. Arianna squinted at the diffuse light of Loom, trying to better make out their shape.

"They're stabilizing them," Louie explained without invitation. "Won't look like they did before the Dragons descended—that'd take years."

Arianna didn't miss how Louie did not imply if they did or didn't have years to take. "Assuming the Dragon King doesn't kill us all first."

"I doubt he'll do that."

"Let me guess: you're also now some expert on Nova's politics?" Arianna refrained from commenting that, of the two of them, *she* was the one who had just spent extended time on the floating islands. She was the one who had an all-too-personal encounter with the Dragon King.

"I am the best organ dealer in all of Loom." Louie's chest swelled against his vest—so much that Arianna was afraid he might crack a rib. "It is important I pay attention to inter-world politics."

"'The best' may be a bit of a stretch." Arianna leaned back against the railing behind the bench.

Louie cracked a smile. It wasn't one of his usual thin-lipped, tight expressions. It showed his teeth, yellowed with age, and his black gums that recessed away from them.

Black gums. The man was a Chimera. Arianna made careful note of the information, filing and storing it safely away. He had no visible Dragon parts, which meant he only had blood. Or he had something unseen to the naked eye, like a stomach . . . or lungs.

The gears of her mind ground to a halt.

There was an odd disconnect between her body as it moved closer to Florence, and her mind as it thought back to the only Dragon she'd known personally with magic in the lungs—Cvareh. She wanted to be in both places at once. It was a divided soul that Arianna had never known before.

Arianna played off her silence by twisting to get a better look at the once-great towers of Ter.0.

"What did they look like before?" Helen asked.

Louie and Arianna both opened their mouths at the same time.

"After you." He motioned with his bird-boned hand.

"No, I'm curious what you'll say," Arianna admitted. "The last time I was here . . ."

"You couldn't have been older than twelve."

Ten, actually. Arianna kept the thought to herself, owing Louie no information on her past. She turned it back on him instead. "How old were you, Louie?"

"Well, I was here a few years before the One Year War ended." He paused. "I would guess around . . . twenty."

Arianna didn't know what surprised her more: the fact that Louie was easily over forty years of age, or that he outright admitted to the fact. She inspected him as he continued speaking to Helen.

His black hair was carefully pulled back, so taut it stretched wrinkles in his forehead and around his eyes. The parchment-whiteness of his mouth was lined with folded shadow around his lips. And his eyes, as sharp and piercing as a hawk's, had a cloudiness to them that one commonly found in advanced age.

Even with his Dragon blood, Louie was a man well into his twilight years. What did someone with such little time left fight for? Arianna looked over to Helen and Will, who were both listening intently to Louie's descriptions. What were any of them fighting for?

Dusk promised dawn to no man.

"All around here—" Louie gave a small wave of his hand "—were schools and dormitories."

"Where breeding happened?" Helen clarified.

"Indeed."

"Where you were born." It was impossible to tell from the upturned slabs and forlorn remnants littering the road that this place had once been anything more than a rubble field. But Arianna still remembered what it used to look like with precision.

"Not quite." Helen gave a sly grin. "I was born in Holx, just after the Dragons instated family law."

Arianna couldn't stop her jaw from dropping. Helen was eleven. Oh, the girl's insufferably childish nature made sense now. She was a Raven, an explorer, a curious soul, one who had seen beyond her years. But she was five years younger than Florence and had yet to reach adulthood.

"I know, I'm clever for my age." Helen beamed proudly.

"Makes sense why the Dragons didn't kill you." Helen's time in the floating prison of Ter.4.2 finally had an explanation. The guild had locked up a child rather than executing her for running, to preserve what would no doubt be one of the greatest Raven minds of their generation—as loathe as Arianna was to admit it.

"I suppose I should be grateful." Helen's face fell as she looked out at the wasteland. Arianna wondered if she saw the iron bars of her cell in the curved rods of steel that protruded from the ground like industrial saplings, growing from the remnants of the old world. "So all this was beautiful?"

"It was . . ." Arianna answered this time. She, too, had finished her schooling early, choosing the Rivets' Guild and meeting Master Oliver when she was younger than even Helen. She remembered the land as it was then. It was a different sort of beauty than she'd seen on Nova. But her memories of Ter.0 glittered more brightly than the floating sky world and all its colors. "It all moved like clockwork. Teachers from every guild took up residence. We learned from the best in all disciplines."

"Sounds boring." Helen yawned. "All I want is maps and speed."

Arianna huffed in amusement. The girl was such a little crow. "Why did you run away from the guild, if you are so akin to it?"

Helen shrugged. "Freedom. Isn't that what all Ravens want? Freedom to explore, go where you want, when and how. Take your life back from the world and hold it in your hands?"

"Who knew it was possible?"

"What?" Helen asked.

"We can agree on something."

Helen looked just as surprised as Ari felt.

At the center of Ter.0 was the old meeting hall of the Vicar Tribunal. Where the dormitories and labs occupied the surrounding area, the five-towered hall stretched up and casted its long shadows like hands on a clock. Louie had been correct: work had begun to stabilize the Towers and reinforce them as residences.

Shannra drove the trike around the main entrance to a flat area on the side that had been allocated for parking.

"This is it!" she announced, quieting the engine and hopping down onto the dusty ground.

"This isn't going to fall on us . . . is it?" Will asked skeptically, stepping out of the cart.

Arianna couldn't fault the boy for his skepticism. The towers above them tilted uneasily and the winds that blew plumes of dust around them created an illusion of a drunken sway. Arianna adjusted her goggles over her eyes, squinting upward against the filtered sunlight from the clouds above Loom.

"They took a beating at the end of the One Year War. But structurally, they're still intact." She saw the straight lines of load-bearing pillars and walls running up like arteries underneath the crumbling cosmetics. "Foundation's holding. Just the aesthetics—" what little aesthetics Loom ever indulged in "—that seem to be falling off."

"Wonderful. So I won't die from the whole thing collapsing, but from a bit of debris dropping on my head." Helen rolled her eyes and folded her hands on top of her head.

"And if you don't die from either of those, I'm certain the Dragons will see to it," Louie noted as he disembarked.

Arianna grimaced at the notion. Ter.0 hadn't survived the last Dragons' attack. What did they hope to accomplish by holing up here for the next one?

What was Florence thinking?

"This way to Florence." Shannra started for an archway, as if reading Arianna's mind. "It's a bit mad if we go through the main hall."

They ascended a steep flight of stairs. Old piping clung to the smooth, industrially plain wall, cracking the stone where it protruded. On the first landing, Arianna heard voices, but it wasn't until the second landing area that she managed to see their source.

Below them, in the center of the five-towered hall, was the central meeting area. She remembered it from her classes as a child. But her most vivid memory was standing with Oliver, masters from each of the four other guilds, and a handful of others who were ready to die for Loom.

Now, where they had stood, where the Council of Five had made their pact to stand against the Dragons, to stand for Loom, wayward and homeless Fenthri roamed in a sort of controlled chaos.

Men and women poured in through the main entrance, funneled from the airfield and no doubt the few water ports still viable for docking. Some carried luggage, some had their hands laden with books. Others had empty palms and tattered clothing.

Barefoot and booted, the masses of Loom were ushered into the one place that had always stood against the Dragons: Ter.0. It was the home of the Vicar Tribunal and testament to the old ways. It had been the Territory people didn't dare speak of, for fear of being accused of inciting rebellion. And now it was where Loom would begin anew.

Arianna no longer had trouble understanding Florence's logic.

When Loom was all but destroyed, one place would always be home to every Fenthri, regardless of one's guild. The wayward Raven Arianna had taken in years ago had the wisdom to bring them back there.

A smile snuck up on her as Arianna looked through the arcade of windows, at the flow of people below. It was a smile that quickly faded at the sound of a lone voice.

"Arianna?"

Arianna turned to meet two dark eyes, black as the outlined Raven on the girl's cheek. The filtered light seemed to shine brighter, and the crumbling world built itself anew, simply because *she* was in one beautiful piece.

"Florence," Arianna whispered.

FLORENCE

"A rianna . . ." The name flowed from her like a familiar creed. It echoed old sentiments and resonated off the new corners of her personality that had been built in the white-haired woman's absence.

There she was, Florence's teacher and guardian, just as she remembered her. They'd been separated for months, and Florence had traveled half the world, across three territories, since they'd parted. She had seen guilds fall and good men die. She had the scars to speak of the battles she'd won, and lost.

In contrast, Arianna was the same as ever. Her white coat was far more tattered and soiled than Florence had ever allowed it to get previously, and she had to combat the urge to demand Arianna remove the article of clothing so that it could have a proper wash. But Florence had plenty of her own dirty laundry to attend to; she didn't have time for Arianna's any more.

"Florence," Arianna echoed.

What did they do now? How could Florence hope to bridge the gap between them?

"I require a word with Arianna," she announced decisively. It was then that Florence took in the rest of the room, those who had accompanied Ari to Ter.0. Louie opened his mouth to speak but Florence snuck in the first, and second, word. "Louie, I appreciate your *assistance* in helping Arianna get here." The tone of "assistance" had the requisite bite. "I will discuss matters with you later."

"I think—"

"I think if you would like whatever end game you're playing toward, you will vacate this room immediately." Her tone left no room for misinterpretation. There were many whom Florence would defer to. Louie was no longer one of them.

The man merely smirked. "You have grown, haven't you, wayward little crow?"

"One part of that was correct, the other incorrect." Florence pushed aside her smartly tailored jacket, resting her hand on the hilt of one of the revolvers that tugged on a thick belt around her hips.

"Of course. An easy mistake to make." Louie tapped his cheek, referencing the Raven outline on Florence's own.

"I wouldn't test me."

"Nor I, me." The skeletal man gave her a long and piercing stare, but it didn't even scratch the surface of her resolve, much less crack it. She had shot more frightening, powerful people than Louie point-blank. And all she had to do was remind herself of that fact whenever someone—anyone—tried to intimidate her. "We have far more to gain by working together, Florence."

"As does all of Loom." On that point, she could agree with the former king of Mercury Town.

Florence watched Louie and his crew depart down the stairs. They were like specters from a former life, creeping up from the shadows of her past. Eventually, she'd have to catch up with Will and Helen, but there was a sort of understanding there that came with old friends who had endured trials together.

Florence had history with everyone in the group, save Shannra. The moonlight-haired woman glanced back at her and gave Florence a hefty wink. They were still taking their time together, still evolving, and Florence couldn't stop a grin at her newest companion's antics.

Louie was ever unexpected. As loathe as Florence was to admit it, Shannra had been welcome company on Ter.0 while Florence had been organizing the initial structure of the resistance. Plus, the strange little man had brought Arianna back to her.

Her eyes swept back. Arianna had rested her goggles atop her forehead, at last revealing her striking, vermillion eyes—a bold splash of color in their gray world.

She didn't know what to say, and it seemed Ari was equally at a loss.

"Walk with me." The words strummed the tension delicately, rather than snapping it. She didn't know where she'd take Ari just yet, but movement would help. If she could move her feet, her mind might follow.

Arianna continued beside her in silence, peering periodically through the inner windows at the hollow-structured, densely populated core of the five-towered hall.

"You orchestrated all this?" Arianna's tone was thoughtful, almost gentle.

"I—" Florence worked to let go of modesty. "I did." She stopped, resting her hand on the gritty cement of a window sill, looking over Ter.0. Airships never stopped their assault on the skies and the trikes tore up the dust that had settled across the whole of the wasteland. For all the Dragons had killed, there were still more Fenthri left than Florence could've ever imagined. Loom itself was more than Florence could've ever imagined.

"Flor, what do you hope to achieve with this?"

Florence turned, searching Ari's face for some explanation. She had gone from pure admiration to admonishment in a breath.

"Drawing together Loom, the Dragon King only has only to attack one place," Arianna continued.

It was an argument Florence had heard before, and she could diffuse it like a simple bomb. "He has no more large-scale weapons to do it with. The Revolvers saw to that." She had never studied in the guild hall proper, but the Revolvers were her own people. The mere idea of their noble sacrifice put a lead slug in her gut. "Separate, we're disorganized, confused. He can pick us off bit by bit, convert those that remain. We're under his thumb. Together, there's strength in numbers. We need all of Loom to see that we are still strong, that we can be one and stand on our own again. We need the king to see that we are not to be underestimated."

She wished she knew what went on in Arianna's head. But, unlike all other times when Florence had awaited her mentor's judgment, she wasn't jittering with nerves, waiting for a verdict. She wanted Arianna's approval as a peer, an equal—not as a pupil or child.

"He's ruthless, Florence. The Dragon King will—"

"You do not need to tell me of his ruthlessness," Florence interrupted. "I was there, Arianna, when the Harvesters' Guild fell. If it weren't for the Vicar Harvester, I would not have made it out alive."

Arianna moved, crossing that seemingly unbreachable gap between them, present the first moment they'd laid eyes on each other. Her arms closed around Florence's shoulders and pulled her close. Frozen shock quickly thawed, warmed by the heat that swelled in Florence's chest at Arianna's closeness.

The woman smelled of cedar . . . and another floral scent that Florence couldn't quite place. Had she always smelled like this? There was a sort of newness to Arianna's embrace that Florence couldn't quite explain.

"I was so worried about you," Arianna whispered. "I thought of you every day on Nova."

Florence's fingers curled fistfuls of Arianna's tired white coat. "I was worried for you too," she confessed easily. "You do have a way of finding trouble."

Arianna snorted and pulled away, resting her palms on Florence's shoulders. "A habit you seem to have inherited."

"There will be a lot more trouble before all this is over." Florence stepped out of the woman's reach. She wasn't a child for Arianna to protect any longer. "Can I count on you, Arianna?"

"Without question."

The lack of hesitation reassured Florence immeasurably. "The first Vicar Tribunal will assemble in two days' time. At that point, I'll need you to discuss the Philosopher's Box."

Florence watched Arianna's face at the mention of the infamous box. Surely, Arianna had learned by now—from Louie, no doubt—that Florence had outed her ability to make the box. She searched for anger or pain. But whatever emotion Arianna was feeling, she kept it guarded. It was a barrier Florence wanted to break down. She wanted to be as close as they had been in Dortam, but as the women they were now.

"About that . . . Louie has requested unbridled access to the schematics for the box."

Florence's hand found its way back to the hilt of her gun at the mere mention of the conniving little man. "I assume you refused."

"No."

"What?" Florence hissed. She'd taken Arianna to be much smarter than that. "Ari, you know him, and you know what he intends to use the box for. Furthermore, we must keep the mechanics of the box as secret as possible, at least until—"

"If you wanted it to be secret, Flor, sharing its existence with the world was a strange choice."

"Loom has no other way to stand against the Dragons." She was not going to allow Arianna to make her feel guilty. "As we are, we will die. As Perfect Chimera, we have a chance. Plus, I saw no other way to unite the vicars after the destruction of the guilds." Florence sighed, allowing the tension to defuse. She quickly took her hand off her gun, not wanting Arianna to misinterpret the motion. "But we need to make sure that we don't have splintering factions. That those who are made into Perfect Chimera are loyal to Loom and know what they must do."

Arianna sighed heavily, her eyes glazed with a familiar, faraway look.

"Don't let your vision be clouded by the past." Florence took a step closer to her teacher. Arianna was head and shoulders taller than her, so she had to stand on her tiptoes to be in her field of vision. "I need you here, Arianna."

"And I will be." Arianna's focus was solely on Florence. "You lead, Flor, and I will follow."

"Good." That was how she wanted Arianna to look at her, as an equal. Florence believed her, wholly and completely. "Now, what are we going to do about Louie?"

"He served a purpose." Arianna shrugged. "And as long as he thinks he's getting access to the schematics, he owes me three more requests. Getting me to you was the first. The means justified the ends on this."

Florence shouldn't have doubted her former mentor and couldn't stop herself from noting the fact that she had been Arianna's first request. "And if he actually gets around to requesting those schematics?"

Arianna hummed noncommittally. "We can decide then."

"It's not like you to not have a plan calculated, with every contingency accounted for." Florence half-squinted, quizzical. It had been a short period of time on Nova, but could a few months really change a person so much?

She wondered if Arianna could possibly be feeling the same about her. The world had forced its change on Florence as well.

"There are a lot of moving parts to consider. He's in our pocket for now, and if he comes to demand the schematics . . . Later? Well, war is coming, Flor. There will be casualties."

"Indeed." Florence's mind instantly went to Sophie. "In a world like this, accidents can be quite common." Deeming the matter of Louie settled—for now—Florence's mind shifted. "Did you find what you were looking for on Nova?"

"I did." Arianna nodded. "The Dragon King has two rebellions he'll need to face. One here, and one up there."

"House Xin?"

"They're going to help us," Arianna affirmed. "As long as we help them."

Florence would come back to what that meant in a moment. But first, there was a man she wanted to inquire after. A man whose blood flowed through her veins. The only Dragon Florence could stomach thinking of with any sort of fondness. "And Cvareh?"

Ari stilled, so much that Florence couldn't have been certain even from a hand's width away that she breathed.

"His sister, Petra, leads House Xin . . ." Arianna began.

Florence leaned against the wall, settling in to absorb all the information Arianna saw fit to impart on her. She listened to tales of the sky cities she could hardly imagine, supported on magic and blood sport. But despite her every effort to pay careful attention to each detail that might someday prove important in her fight against the Dragon King, one question continued to creep up in her mind: What, exactly, had happened between Cvareh and Arianna on Nova?

COLETTA

Usually, after supper, Coletta preferred to retire to the company of her plants. On rare occasions, she treated herself to chilled mead out of a crystal snifter to sweeten the sunset over Lysip. Tonight, in a rare occasion, Coletta treated herself to blood.

It had been a busy day, but one full of triumphs. Nevertheless, there was no reprieve for the righteous, and Coletta had a few more items of key importance on her agenda to complete before the candle wax burned out for the day. It was a list mostly comprised of what her and Yveun had discussed, and the ideas he'd seeded in the back of her mind.

That, more than anything else, was what she valued him for. Certainly, his other uses were vast and important. But he was the one to inspire great thoughts in her. He was the muse, not the painter. Fortunately for them both, she had skill enough with the brush.

"Ryu, your nightly libation has been set out in the garden." Ulia emerged, hands folded and head bowed, from a side hall.

"Return it to the chill box for tomorrow." The girl had to scamper to keep up when Coletta took an unexpected turn from her usual pathways back to her quarters. "Fetch me Topann. I shall be waiting in the gray receiving room."

"Gray receiving room?" Ulia repeated, clearly confused.

"Topann will know where it is."

The orders given, Coletta continued alone.

Toward the top of the Rok Estate was space to store gliders for Riders, as well as the necessary landing and departure areas that accompanied them. But down the slope of the hill, on the side of the estate that faced the edge of the island, was a series of chambers burrowed into the ground below. There, amid the desolate stone walls and dimly lit halls, was another landing area for gliders. One room was connected to the barren track of stone, aptly named for its decor and function.

The gray receiving room was vacant and dark, the air stale. Coletta left the door to the hall open as she walked over to a thin countertop along one wall. It was barren, save a striker.

She picked up the tool that resembled a pair of shears, steel on one side, flint on the other, and lit the two iron oil lamps bolted into walls on either end of the room. It was barely enough light to scare darkness away from the corners and, if anything, seemed only to accentuate the inky blackness that clung to the edges of the room.

This will do nicely.

She leaned against the table and passed the time by inspecting her claws until Topann arrived.

"I apologize for my delay." Topann gave a small bow as she entered the room, shutting the door firmly behind her.

"You were not delayed," Coletta pointed out. She knew how long it took to arrive at the Gray Room from Topann's quarters among the flower fields on the opposite end of the estate. "If anything, you hurried."

"I do not like to keep my lady in wait." Topann crossed the floor, taking Coletta's hand in hers. The woman's red fingers curled around her wrist and she brought Coletta's knuckles to her lips.

"A trait of yours I appreciate." Coletta freed her hand from the prostrating woman. "Tell me, have we heard anything from our Fen traitor?"

"He has acquired information on the stores of gold on Loom."

"Excellent."

"However, he seeks to negotiate before he shares this information."

"Negotiate for what?" she inquired.

"I do not yet know."

Coletta thrummed her fingers against the table, annoyed. Her day had been going so well, so smoothly. She was not about to let a Fen be the blemish upon it.

"Very well . . ." Coletta hummed. "You shall go see what he wants."

"Ryu?"

No, she wouldn't understand. "Yveun will go to Loom himself to bring the Fen to their senses."

"I see." Her tone proved she agreed with Coletta that such a course was inherently foolish.

"Yes, well, I would like you to go with him. Take the opportunity to squeeze this Fen for all the information he's worth, and be my eyes and ears."

"Such a mission would be my honor."

"Before that," Coletta continued, "I require your assistance with something."

"Anything."

Coletta knew it to be true. Topann was the oldest of her little buds and had bloomed into a loyal zealot. Though, zealots were easy enough to create. All it took was saving someone whose desperation to be free of something had reached a critical mass. Whether the shackles took the form of a person or a place, Coletta broke her flowers' chains. Thereafter, they were hers.

In that way, all her little flowers were the same. Buds that had grown on the underside of Lysip. Girls that would have sprouted from nothing, into nothing, and died nothing . . . and yet, they had been saved from their fate, given a taste for greatness.

"I need you to find me an Alchemist from among the Fen."

"Ryu, with every respect, I did not think we kept Alchemists here—only Rivets to maintain the gliders."

Coletta ran her fingertips across her lips in thought. "I once brought an Alchemist from Loom to give me their knowledge on the plants and herbs of their world . . ."

Extracting that knowledge had been bloody, at first. But there was an unsurprisingly direct inverse correlation between the willingness of a person to impart their knowledge and the number of toes they still possessed. So unfortunate for the Fenthri that they could not regrow body parts as a Dragon could. It truly was a wonder the gray race had survived at all.

"But," Coletta continued, "that may have been twenty years ago. He could be dead by now." She sighed heavily. "Oh, the Fenthri and their life spans."

"I shall go to the Fen pens and search." Topann was unswayed. "Should I not find one, I will bring one back for my lady from Loom." She said it as though she were bringing back a souvenir from a leisure trip, not a creature, live and resistant.

"Good. The other thing I require shall be easier to procure." Coletta looked about the room again. Sturdy walls, thick, built to dampen sound. "Go below Lysip, and find me an organ donor."

"Any preferences?" It was not the first time Topann had received such a request. Coletta had been using organs to bargain with powers on Loom, and Nova, for years.

"Yes. Where is your magic, Topann?"

"Mine?"

Coletta nodded.

"Hands. Eyes. Ears."

It was a standard set of magic for a Dragon. Coletta was pleased. It would be simple to measure the effects on one such as Topann, who possessed so little magic to begin with. "Find a stomach."

"Of course." There was the beginning of understanding hovering beneath Topann's words. But the woman was undeterred. Coletta had long-held Topann's life in her claws.

"Good." Coletta walked over to her loyal subject. She stretched out a hand and cupped the woman's cheek in a sign of affection that was almost never seen. Topann stilled, taking a shallow breath. "You have been with me throughout the years, my flower, and I will reward your loyalty."

"You have given me more than enough," Topann whispered. "You showed me the sun, Coletta'Ryu."

Coletta smiled fondly on her first test subject. "Yes. And now I shall show you what it means to be made perfect."

CVAREH

Cvareh lay in bed, debating with the dawn. Was it too early, or not early enough? Was the sun duller than normal, or did it shine with its usual strength? He wondered if he could somehow delay time by whittling away the seconds, question by question.

Today, Finnyr would arrive.

Lord Xin's presence was palpable in the manor. Cvareh could feel it in the stillness of his room, in the quiet that seemed to seep into the stones.

He stared at the ceiling above his bed, wanting to scream. But his mouth could no longer make sound. He breathed slow, shallow breaths, until tears fell like tiny waterfalls off his cheeks and onto the pillow.

He realized Petra would never see the Xin Manor completed. She would never see House Xin ascend the ranks of Dragon society. Though the likelihood of either coming to pass now seemed slim.

One bright spot: She wouldn't see their family crumble away to nothingness, either.

Daylight inched its way across his ceiling, creeping in through his windows like an unwelcome guest. His attendants were not long to arrive. Cvareh wiped his face with his palms and sat upright.

He could allow himself this weakness only in private. Among Xin, he was the face of his house. Every man and woman had made that abundantly clear with their silent expectation that he would duel Finnyr.

Cvareh stood and went to his dresser. He pulled open his favorite drawer, running his hand over the silks and satins. All the beautiful colors clashed and complemented each other, a rainbow contained in a wooden box.

"Cvareh'O—Ryu." The attendant in the doorway quickly corrected himself.

Cvareh didn't spare the man a disapproving look. They could *not* call him Cvareh'Oji. "What did you have in mind for today?" the man asked, quickly moving between Cvareh and the dresser of fineries.

What did one wear to meet his sister's murderer . . . who also happened to be his brother?

He rubbed his temples. Cain was right; he had learned a deep and profound sympathy and appreciation for Loom. For as backwards as the idea of not having a family was, at least on Loom they weren't killing their own flesh and blood for power.

Which world, again, was the uncivilized one?

"White," he finally decided on.

"White?"

"Yes."

"I—Well, I'm sure there's something in here . . ."

Cvareh honestly didn't know if there would be. He couldn't recall a time he'd ever worn white. But today, he needed strength. He had lost one woman who he thought was invincible, and wanted to feel closer to the other woman he knew who had the same power of conquest, the same bravery, the same drive.

In the end, it was as he suspected. Nothing in the drawer was white, or black, or grey. He wore a light seafoam color that had a rough-cut lace overlay in white.

While it was a far cry from Arianna's coat, the tight-fitting trousers that hugged his thighs and matching shoulder embellishments accentuated his physique, and seemed to give a deeper, richer hue to his skin—which he hoped also reminded Finnyr of their midnight-skinned sister. It wasn't precisely what he'd had in mind, but as Arianna's coat fit her for conquest, this was his own battle-ready armor.

A woman appeared in the doorway, breathless. "Cvareh'Ryu, bocos have been spotted in the western skies."

Eyes were on him, expectant, waiting for his reaction. Cvareh waited as well, to see what rose within him. But the waters of his soul were dark and calm, concealing much in their depths, concealing his true feelings—concealing *him*.

"Then we should go to the arrival platform," Cvareh said, and strode past the woman to lead the way.

The morning's light had lost its luster. It shone through the windows as gray, bland, like the light filtered down to Loom. Cvareh adjusted his shoulder adornments, the beaded silver that dangled from them clinking softly, then dropped his arms limp at his sides. There was a danger to this dark ocean that House Rok had poured into the pit of his soul; it drowned his heart and overflowed into his mind. He didn't hold anger in balled fists. He kept it coiled in the tense muscles of his wrists, ready to unsheathe his claws in a breath.

More people followed as he ascended the stairs and halls of the Xin Manor toward the wide platform that was used to receive people of importance. Sculptures laden with rare gemstones and lined with gold rimmed the platform where the other half of the manor waited with Cain.

They formed a wide arc, leaving the open end of the platform barren to the air and bocos off in the distance. Was this a receiving party, or a dueling ring?

Cvareh, himself, did not know.

"What will you do?" Cain asked. The man always seemed to know just where and how to push. There was never a question of Cvareh's insecurities, uncertainties, or weaknesses when Cain was around. That made the man a strong ally. Invaluable.

"Do you trust me, Cain?" Cvareh asked, loud enough for the house to hear. Cain had been a favorite of his sister, and it was not by chance that half the family had chosen to stand behind him.

Cain studied him a long moment. Cvareh knew the man understood what he was asking, what he was saying. If they fractured and broke now, Rok could stab a fatal wedge into the foundation of House Xin.

"I trust you, Cvareh'Ryu," Cain affirmed. He didn't hesitate, but the words betrayed his uncertainty. The truth was clear: Cain trusted him, but questioned his methods.

"Good." The bocos were close enough for him to make out their colors. His claws itched for release. "I will only do what I feel is best for House Xin. It is all Petra ever demanded of me."

Cain said nothing more on the matter, settling instead for a small nod. He looked forward again and couldn't contain a growl. "He means to make war with his mere arrival."

The other man had no doubt seen the detail of Finnyr's boco as well. "He seems to be having trouble doing it." Raku,

Petra's trusted mount, was very clearly begrudging the notion of having Finnyr ride him. The bird squawked in protest, ruffling its feathers with every few flaps of its mighty wings.

Cvareh was more focused on Finnyr's companions. Two Riders, with only a handful of beads each, flew both sides, and the hulking form of a Tam woman flew closest to Finnyr. Cvareh recognized one of the Riders as the man who had delivered the news yesterday, and the other he'd seen in the king's entourage . . . but the woman was new.

She had but one bead. It should mean she was as green to combat as the color of her skin.

But Cvareh didn't believe the symbolism for a moment, and every look he took at her as she approached reaffirmed the fact. Yveun was playing one of his games with this one. He wanted them to assume the woman was no one of importance.

Cvareh instinctively knew better.

The party of four landed. Raku immediately bucked, trying to take to the skies again. Finnyr pulled hard on the reigns, only managing to upset the bird more.

The rest of House Xin watched, saying nothing. Not one servant moved to help the Oji as he dismounted.

Raku promptly flew away the first second he was able. Cvareh sympathized with the creature. He too wished to ruffle his feathers, cry indignantly, and take off for the horizon. Eventually, the bird would return; Raku was too loyal not to, and those hard-formed habits had long since turned into instinct.

"Is this all the welcome the *mighty* House Xin can muster for their Oji's arrival?" It was fitting the large Tam—no, she bore a Rok symbol on her cheek—was the first to speak. Finnyr couldn't even muster the strength to look any of them in the eye for longer than a moment.

"Welcome back to Ruana, Finnyr'Oji." Cvareh wouldn't allow himself to be a coward. He was better than his brother. But that didn't mean that he could bring himself to say "home" to the man who had seen their sister, the best among them, die at the hand of Rok.

The moment Finnyr's eyes met his was the moment Cvareh knew that he was, indeed, capable of killing his brother.

"It—" Finnyr coughed, trying to clear his throat. He continued, stronger, "It is good to return home to the land of my forefathers as your Oji."

At the word "Oji," an unspoken tension coursed through House Xin. Every man and woman felt it. Even Cvareh's chest tightened around the sound.

It was a pull to the title, a desire to recognize the rank and file that every element of Dragon society had told them from birth was the only thing separating them from destruction and discord. But it didn't feel right when directed at Finnyr, of all people.

From the corner of his eye, Cvareh saw Cain looking to him.

Cvareh's legs itched to move, but his feet stayed. Something about this still wasn't right.

"I have seen your chambers prepared in advance of your arrival."

"At least someone on this dreary rock has sense." The woman at Finnyr's side sneered at the statues that surrounded them, at the men and woman assembled.

"Thank you, Cvareh."

It was a testament to House Xin's steadfastness that an audible, collective gasp didn't rise like a wind at Finnyr's disrespect. To speak Cvareh's name without a suffix . . . to rob him of the title that had been there for so long . . . Cvareh hardly knew what his name sounded like without it.

Cvareh's hate for his brother worsened by the moment.

Cvareh gave a small bow of his head, forcing the interaction to continue. There was nothing he could do, for now, and he wanted it over with.

The people began to shift. There was a whisper, too quiet to discern clearly. Cvareh felt the weight of his family's eyes on him again. Cain wordlessly heaped expectations on him like shrouds of lead.

Cvareh knew what they wanted, especially now that a whiff of a potential slight was in the air.

Finnyr began to walk forward; Cvareh and Cain both parted to allow him to pass. The woman remained glued at his side, always within half a step of Finnyr. Up close, Cvareh could feel her magic. And he could see her eyes—a beautiful, and unnervingly familiar, shade of lilac.

"Are you going to let him go?" Cain finally snapped. His words were hushed and hurried, but anger distorted volume.

"What's this?" The woman turned. "Is this a challenge I hear?"

Cain balled and uncurled his fingers. Cvareh knew the motion his friend made when trying to fight against unsheathing his claws.

"Not a challenge." Cvareh stepped between Cain and the woman. "Cain'Da is merely curious when Finnyr and I will find time to regroup on the current status of the house and affairs of Xin."

"I see . . ." The woman smiled, wide enough for her fangs to be a challenge in their own right. Her eyes were indeed familiar. Not just in color, shape, and shade . . . but in the level of bloodthirsty ruthlessness he had also seen in Arianna's gaze. It was a lust for revenge he was starting to understand too well. "So good to have one so loyal to your house."

"We are lucky." Cvareh held his position. He didn't want to get into a brawl here—not with two Riders on the ground, with this mysterious woman, with Finnyr being a worthless coward the house could tear limb from limb, and especially not with a Dragon King only a half-day's ride away, who was no doubt itching to unleash his full power and lay waste to House Xin.

"Speaking of great loyalty . . ." The woman looked around at those assembled. "The Dragon King has sent me to stay with Finnyr during his transition as Oji. I am Master Rider Fae Rok'Da To, and I will ensure that there is no conduct unbecoming toward those who are, no doubt, loyal to his supreme rule throughout this trying time."

"We are to be babysat by—"

"Cain, enough." Cvareh hated himself. He hated that the moment his claws were unsheathed, it was to direct them at his friend, the most loyal among them to their name.

But his hand drawn back, claws shining faintly in the sunlight, had the right effect. Cain was stunned into silence. He turned to Cvareh in a rage that was quickly quelled.

Cvareh poured it all into his face now that he was turned away from Finnyr and the woman, and the other two Riders were on the far end of the platform, already mid-departure.

They were all angry. Every member of House Xin was angry and bearing the uncomfortable badge of mourning. But he would not have them act in foolishness that would get them killed.

"Forgive me, Cvareh'Ryu." Cain lowered his eyes.

"Shouldn't you be seeking my forgiveness?" Fae's voice sent shivers up Cvareh's spine. "After all, I stand for Yveun'Dono here."

Cain was silent. Cvareh implored him without words. He didn't want blood on these stones, not Cain's.

"I look forward to the honor of having one whom our Dono holds in such high esteem among us," Cain bit out.

The woman knew he was insincere just by her smile. That much was apparent. But she accepted the platitude and returned to Finnyr's side.

With the tension slightly allayed, for now at least, the other Riders took to the skies, no doubt to report back to Yveun at the first possible moment.

None of the other members of House Xin moved. Once again, they all looked to Cvareh for answers he didn't yet have. The home he so loved was quickly devolving into a battleground.

Cvareh started in first.

A familiar set of footsteps fell in close behind.

Cain followed him all the way back to his room, stalking like some predator. Cvareh kept his hands in plain sight, relaxed, claws sheathed. He hadn't spent so much effort on the receiving platform just to flay Cain in private.

Cvareh started for his dresser first thing. He needed new clothes. These were now soiled with the memory of calling Finnyr "Oji." He looked at the heap of fabric on the floor. He would need to get a new tailor on retainer if he was forced to discard clothing just because he used "Oji" in relation to his brother.

"What was that?" Cain finally spoke from where he leaned against the door.

"I don't know yet," Cvareh admitted quietly. He was still trying to figure out all the moving parts at play, and felt blind with no ears or eyes on Rok.

"You just let him come in here—"

"Cain—"

"—don *her* title and—"

"It was not her title!" Cvareh roared in frustration. "We are Dragons, Cain. We live. We fight. We die. All by each other's hands. Petra knew that, and she loved it. Eventually, someone was going to kill her. She knew that." It was why she prayed every day to Lord Xin, Cvareh realized in that instant. "And her death will mean nothing if we throw away our lives and House Xin by challenging my brother."

"Throw away our lives? You don't think you can beat Finnryr?"

"*Think* about this, Cain." His friend was blinded by his sorrow. But Cvareh could permit it no longer. He had shed his tears and moved on; Cain needed to do the same. "If you or I had challenged, the Riders would have stood for him. Finnyr would approve the duel as Oji."

His friend cursed, turning away with a quick spin.

"That woman, the new Master Rider, Fae . . . She seems . . . different. Surely you felt it, too?"

"She seemed as much trash as everything else Yveun dredges up," Cain growled.

"Trash with fearsome power."

Cain didn't argue the fact.

"Yveun wouldn't have sent her unless he believed she could guard Finnyr. Don't let the lack of beads fool you."

"She can't stop all of us."

"Together? No," Cvareh agreed. "But that would be an act of all-out war, a disregard for duels. It would be a complete affront that would sway Tam to stand behind Yveun in a way they never had, for a crusade across our land. Future generations may not even remember Xin's name. If we are to throw all Dragon law aside and bet everything, we better do it when we think there's a good chance we can win."

Cain cursed again and slammed his fist against the door. "So we are to sit here and tolerate all this? We are to accept it, bow to it, smile in the face of this affront?"

Cvareh wished he had a different answer for his friend, for himself, for their house. But he didn't. The truth changed with work, not wishes.

"Smiling or not is up to you. But you will tolerate it, for now."

"If you insist, Cvareh'Ryu." Cain reached for the door handle.

"Cain."

He stopped, but didn't turn.

"I need you with me. I need you to trust me. I can't do this without your help."

Cain sighed softly. When he turned, Cvareh could've guessed what he was about to say from his expression alone. "I already told you once today, you have it. Nothing has changed since Finnyr's arrival. Hopefully, not even your title."

"Thank you." Cvareh looked to the window. "I will figure out a way for our family to not just survive, but thrive."

"For her?"

Cvareh nodded. "For all of us."

The answer was enough. Cain's anger dissipated, and he gave a small bow before departing. Cvareh stared at the door long after Cain disappeared through it. There was work to be done, much work. But underneath it all, his friend persisted. It was a relationship Cvareh already knew he would need in the coming days.

Cvareh leaned against his dresser. The weight of it all had become too heavy. He needed the support, if just for a moment, when no eyes were on him and no expectations accompanied them.

Petra would know what to do. But Petra wasn't there. It was just him, a vicious king, and a gray world far below that was House Xin's only ally against the rising tide. Cvareh tried to organize his mind and, for the first time, plan his next steps.

A sound summoned him back to reality, and Cvareh walked over to the window. He cracked it, slightly, to better hear the low, sad song that echoed off every rock and crag surrounding the Xin Manor. Cvareh leaned against the window frame, and wondered who else paused to listen to Raku's dirge as the masterless boco cried it into the wind.

ARIANNA

Her quarters were more accommodating than she'd expected. Physically, at least.

There was an actual bed. The mattress was a lumpy mess of collected and questionable fabric, but it somewhat held its shape. It was, dare she even think it, almost comfortable when she nested into it far enough.

The world was cooling for winter, but the day's heat soaked into the stones of the five-towered hall and radiated warmth through the night's chill. It was practical. Nothing unnecessary, nothing out of place. It was a world Arianna was familiar with and was glad she could still find comfort in.

She'd needed a good night's rest before this morning.

A sharp rap on her door revealed Florence, promptly at the time she'd informed Arianna she'd be by the night before.

"Good morning, Flor." Arianna couldn't stop herself from smiling. It was good to see the girl, to know she was near, even under present circumstances.

"I hope it's a good morning." Florence took off her top hat, dusting off some imaginary specks before putting it back on and adjusting it several times over as they started to walk down the stairs. Arianna recognized her nervous tell instantly. "At the very least, we'll be able to stop agonizing over what state the tribunal will be in."

Arianna still couldn't believe the notion. Despite the reasoning behind it, despite the ramshackle location, there was to be a Vicar Tribunal. It was an event she had written off ever seeing in her lifetime.

"What are you expecting?" She put aside the odd excitement at the prospect of the day's events. There was work to be done, and Florence needed her focused.

"I know Vicar Harvester will be here. The Vicar Raven may be a question, with all the help the guild is giving to collect up Loom and bring them here . . . I heard Vicar Rivet and Vicar Alchemist arrived last night."

Arianna grimaced at the very idea of seeing Sophie again.

"What?" Florence didn't miss the distasteful expression. Then again, Arianna had done almost nothing to hide it.

"I went quite a few years without seeing Sophie. I could go quite a few more," she admitted. This was Florence, after all. The one person Arianna would make the Philosopher's Box for. If Arianna couldn't trust Flor with the truth, who could she trust?

"That won't be an issue." Florence adjusted the holster that held her guns on both sides of her ribs.

"It won't? She didn't make it through the Dragon's attack?" Arianna didn't feel bad in the slightest. Sophie was intolerable and, had the roles been reversed, Arianna had no doubt Sophie would be thinking the same thing about her.

"She survived. An accident after did her in, I believe."

"An accident?" The notion was almost delicious. Sophie, with her ability to stubbornly survive anything, done in by some innocuous happenstance. "Of what kind?"

Florence shrugged. "Not sure. You know how the Alchemists are . . . ever the secretive bunch."

Ari knew all too well. It had taken her years to penetrate Eva's shell and get the woman to trust her enough to share her research. So, she let the matter with Flor drop entirely, and put it from her mind as one small, golden lining to the whole madness that had become her world.

They rounded into the entrance hall. Even at this hour, people continued in a steady stream, led by Ravens and ushered into the various towers the Rivets had reinforced enough to be usable.

"What a mess we are," Arianna murmured.

"Maybe so . . . But to be a mess, we have to exist. Which is more than a lot of Loom can say."

Arianna kept quiet from then on, watching Florence interact with the people who seemed to know her already. They greeted her respectfully and bowed their heads and tipped their hats as she passed by.

And the day had only just begun.

"We'll be in here." Florence motioned to an open set of doors. "There are similar halls in the other towers, but this one was in the best condition and still happened to have working doors."

"I remember studying in here, once." Arianna paused to run her hand over the wood of the door. It was dusty and dented, but managed somehow to hold all the memories of her time on Ter.0 as a child and a young adult.

"Did you?" Florence paused as well.

"I was just a girl . . . and it was only for one lecture. This had been the Alchemists' tower, so the talk took place in here." Arianna could barely remember what was said and hated herself for the fact.

"Perhaps, someday, we will see lectures in here again."

"Perhaps." Such a day seemed so far away given their present circumstances that it was pointless to even think of.

At tight capacity, the room could hold maybe one hundred people. Large, but not the sort of room that would dwarf the speaker on the floor. Arianna and Florence walked down a sloping aisle that stretched along one of the five points of the pentagon-shaped space.

The floor was tiered in traditional lecture hall-style seating, with the occupants intended to sit directly on the edge of the tier, their feet over the edge. At the lowest point, where the lecturer would stand to address the room, the five guild symbols had been painted, one in front of each side of the pentagon.

"Florence?" A man's voice drew the girl's attention.

"Vicar Powell, it's so good to see you again."

Her apprentice, the girl she had pulled from the Underground, shaking and scared, now stood a woman who was bold and brave and capable. Florence was speaking with a vicar as though they were casual friends; Arianna had nothing more to do than stand to the side and watch.

"And good to see you as well." Powell clasped hands with Florence. "I heard there was some turmoil at the Alchemists' Guild shortly after your arrival."

"I heard so as well. Such a shame. Happened just after I left to come to Ter.0. I have yet to meet the new Vicar Alchemist . . ."

Arianna took another step closer as a few Ravens began to trickle in. She was honestly surprised they weren't late. The Ravens were notorious for it.

"And this must be the infamous Rivet."

Arianna knew when she was being spoken about and was pulled immediately back to the conversation.

"Yes, this is Arianna, Master Rivet under Master Oliver," Florence introduced them semi-formally.

Arianna clasped hands. "It's good to meet you, Vicar Powell." At least, she hoped it was.

"I owe a lot to Powell." Arianna took note when Florence dropped his title, and further notice that Powell didn't seem to mind. Arianna wasn't sure if it was a sign of some deep familiarity . . . or if Nova had ruined her when it came to reading into titles too much. "He was the one who helped me escape the Harvesters' Guild when the Dragon King attacked."

Arianna immediately saw the man with the circled sickle tattoo on his cheek in a new light. "Thank you, truly. If anything had happened to Florence . . ." She trailed off, barely able to bring herself to think of the idea.

"A decision that seems to be reaffirmed as wise with every passing moment." Powell looked only at Arianna now. She noticed a shift in him, from when he looked anywhere else to when he looked at her, as if she was *different* than the rest of the room.

These were the eyes of a man who knew what she was.

"And the best thanks you could give me is what Florence has already promised," he continued. "The Philosopher's Box."

Arianna nodded. She didn't have any other words. After all, she had spent most of her life pursuing the box in secret, then fighting to keep its existence carefully guarded. Now that people knew, she had to develop a new toolkit, and fast, for managing the topic.

"Vicars sit on the lowest tier." Florence had the insight to save Arianna from herself. "Then elder masters behind them, younger masters behind that, and every guild is allowed a handful of journeymen to sit along the back."

"I'll take my seat, then." Arianna started for the Rivet's section.

Florence grabbed her arm and her voice dropped to a whisper. "Sit on the edge? I may need you to speak . . ." She glanced around the filling room. "After all, I got them all to agree to come because of you."

"I understand, Flor." The last thing Arianna wanted was to cause Florence to lose esteem with those gathered.

She heeded the girl's advice. She sat four rows back from the floor, at the very end. She didn't want to be in the foreground. She was the White Wraith, a member of the last rebellion. Her whole life had been lived in secret—a quality she realized she no longer shared with Florence.

The room continued to fill and Arianna watched nonchalantly as various masters took their seats.

"You always preferred the back."

Arianna's eyes swung to an elderly man, smartly dressed in all black that blended with his coal-colored skin and accented his steely eyes and closely-cropped silver hair. A thin line of stubble covered his sagging cheeks.

"You always preferred being clean-shaven," Arianna pointed out.

"Well, the end of the world can do a number on one's hygiene." Willard chuckled and held out a hand. "Let me see you, Arianna."

She suddenly felt nine years old again. But this time there was no Master Oliver to stand by her side and do the talking for her. Arianna stood on command, walking down to the man whose filled and circled Rivet tattoo was nearly invisible.

"You have hands, now." He inspected the thin line around her wrists where her ashen Fenthri skin stopped and the steely blue of Finnyr's Dragon flesh began.

"A recent acquisition."

"How many organs are you missing?"

Arianna thought about lying. She didn't want to bare herself to the world. But Florence's attention was on her. Even while keeping up a conversation with Powell, she observed their exchange periodically; Arianna could feel her eyes on her face like a warm breeze.

"Now . . . only lungs."

Willard whistled low. "Only lungs . . ." He eyed her up and down, finally letting go of her hands. "It appears the Alchemists were right, too, about their postulations on Dragon magic affecting a Fenthri's growth. When did you get the blood? Seven?"

"Yes, seven." The memory was seared into her recollection with the fire of magic hitting her veins for the first time. Killing her. Resurrecting her. Time and time again until her blood ran black.

"And when did you become a Perfect Chimera?"

"Eighteen."

"Was it Oliver's work?"

Arianna couldn't stop a small grin. Willard and Oliver had always been friendly rivals of a sort, two who enjoyed mentally sparring with each other almost a little too much. They had needed each other to thrive, but couldn't stand the other's existence in equal measure. A perfect set of counterweights.

"No, no, the final box was not his work."

"Your own." Willard reached out a hand, resting it on the pin Arianna had affixed to the edge of her white coat by her collarbone. "And he gave you the circle for it."

"Just before he died."

For all the rivalry and competition, there was genuine sorrow to Willard's eyes at the memory of his deceased friend. "How did he die?"

"I killed him."

Arianna expected the reaction. She expected the look of shock, the probing stare for a lie where he would find none. Willard said nothing, no doubt expecting her to fill in the blank of the circumstances that led her to such an extreme action. But that was one line of history she wouldn't fill in, one unbroken stretch for the unrelenting passage of sands in the great hourglass of time to wear away.

They would have her knowledge, her schematics, perhaps even her body for their studies. But she would never give them that memory. She would never share the final moments she had with those she had truly loved. Other than her pin, and the box that pumped away within her, it was all she really had left.

"Well." Willard dropped his hand from the pin. "If what you say is true, then I expect you had a very good reason."

Arianna's mind was blank. She wanted him to rally against her. She wanted to see Willard rage for the death of one of the greatest minds of the last generation.

"Knowing Oliver, he likely commanded it." Willard shook his head with an ironic chuckle, heavy with sorrow. "There would be no way you could've done it otherwise."

She wanted to refute him. She wanted to tell him he was wrong. But it was the most truthful thing anyone had said in a long time, and betrayed the depth of the man's familiarity with her. Before Arianna could find any words, he dismissed himself, taking the seat on the lowest tier—the space reserved for the vicar.

If the Dragons' notion of gods were true, Master Oliver would be in some infinite beyond, watching Willard achieve all the goals they had ever competed over. Oliver would also be looking upon her. Were her achievements enough to bring a smile to his face?

By the time the Vicar Tribunal was called to order, the room wasn't even half-full. No guild, at any point, ever had more than about fifteen masters. The Ravens were almost at capacity; twelve lined the seats behind the vicar. The Rivets had seven, counting Arianna—all fresh faces she didn't recognize. The Alchemists had about the same count.

The most sorrowful sections were the Revolvers, who had four, led by a new vicar who very clearly had no idea what he was doing. And the Harvesters, who had five, including Vicar Powell.

Arianna looked around the room at the tired and unwashed faces. This was the best they now had. This was *all* they had.

"I suppose we should begin with introductions." Florence made her way to the center of the room when none of them did anything more than stare at each other. It seemed no one quite knew what to do at a Vicar Tribunal.

"Vicar Powell, Harvesters." Powell stood first at Florence's motion. The room went around clockwise after him.

"Vicar Ethel, Alchemists."

"Vicar Gregory, Revolvers."

"Vicar Willard, Rivets."

"Vicar Dove, Ravens." The woman with the long black braid put her hand on her hip, tilting it to the side. "And before any of you ask . . . Yes, the name is really Dove. Always has been. Was born before the family law. No, I didn't choose Ravens because of it."

Arianna leaned forward, placing her elbows on her knees. Dove was the only one among them who had an ease about her. She was also the only vicar to survive the attack. Willard was the next-most acclimatized to his role. But even he hesitated with a too-long pause when it came to using "Vicar" in association with his name.

Loom was a candle that kept being sliced into pieces from the bottom as it burned from the top.

"Excellent. Well, then . . . Since we're all introduced, we should begin by focusing on the issues of highest priority." Florence grabbed a ledger she'd been carrying all morning. Arianna wondered how many hours the girl had spent preparing. "Foremost, Vicar Powell informed me of concerns with regards to feeding such a centralized population on ground that has no natural resources. I shall concede the floor—"

"The issue of highest priority is the Philosopher's Box." Vicar Dove stood.

All eyes were on Arianna. Unflinching, unwavering, Arianna stared down at Vicar Dove who stared back at her, trying to draw whatever height she could in intimidation.

It wouldn't work. Vicar Dove may have every experience in functioning as the leader of the Ravens' Guild—the most reckless and freewheeling guild of the five. But the room had turned into a battleground, and no one had the gift of combat quite like Arianna.

"The Philosopher's Box will mean little if all of Loom starves before it can be made." Powell remained on his feet as well.

"*If* it can be made," Dove retorted.

"It certainly can be made." Willard pushed off on his knee, bringing himself into a standing position and fighting for the floor. "I knew Arianna as a girl, and knew her teacher. If there would ever be someone who could make such a thing, it would be her."

She just loved being spoken about as if she weren't there. Maybe if Arianna let them continue, she could actually sneak away and no longer be on display like some prize pig. Her fingers twitched, magic curling around her pinky. It'd be easy to illusion the room in a fog. They'd be none the wiser until she was already on a trike.

"If it so easily can be made, how did none of your guild make it before?" Dove didn't back down. "Or have you? And did you sit on the knowledge for years, locked away in your ticking halls?"

"If anyone had locked it away, it would have been an Alchemist," a master seated behind Dove remarked dryly.

"Certainly not a technology we have had in our possession." Vicar Ethel didn't rise to refute the notion.

"If it exists at all." Dove gave a look back to Arianna.

She knew when she was being goaded. The question was, should she let herself be? Arianna looked to Florence, who was allowing the volley of words from the center of the floor. Florence stared up at her with what Arianna hoped she read correctly as an expectant look.

Arianna rose to her feet.

"When I was seven, I left Ter.0 under the tutelage of Master Oliver. We travelled together around the world and ultimately back to the Rivets' Guild."

"I didn't ask for your life's history." Dove folded her arms over her chest.

"Let her speak." Powell, unnecessarily, came to Arianna's defense.

"Master Oliver, as some of you may or may not know, was the one who occupied the seat of knowledge for the Rivets on the Council of Five for the last rebellion," Arianna continued, as though Dove nor Powell had said anything. There were some whispers at the mention of the Council of Five. "If you think talking on the Council of Five is still taboo, you should leave the room now. You're all complicit in this new rebellion, and that will carry a far greater punishment than speaking on the last."

No one moved, but the room was thoroughly silenced.

"Was the box developed for the last rebellion?" Powell asked.

"Indeed." The metallic contraption that occupied her chest, for the first time, seemed loud, as if it wanted to drown out her words—to conceal itself forever under her skin and harness and coat. Arianna pressed onward. She would utter this once, and then never again. "I worked with other guild journeymen in the rebellion on the box. We struck close a few times, but the difficulty lay in finding a way for the blood to remain clean, and the Fenthri body free of rot.

"That was when Eva—" Arianna touched her wrist where Eva's link mark was dated in ink underneath her skin. "—a fellow Alchemist in the rebellion . . . made a discovery.

"We worked with a Dragon then, one who claimed to seek Loom's liberation. Who claimed to be on our side. He brought a flower from the sky world of Nova."

"A *flower*?" Willard clarified.

"Just so," Arianna affirmed. "Eva noticed that her reagents didn't deteriorate in the presence of the flower."

"Why?" Of course the Vicar Alchemist would be the one to inquire.

"I confess . . . I never fully understood it," Arianna admitted. "But, together, we found a way to temper gold with this particular flower." She withheld the name for now; it was too early yet to give them key details. She and Florence still held power as long as they held pertinent information.

"And how does all this relate to the box?" Dove asked.

"Don't you see?" Willard couldn't stop himself. "A metal that purifies the blood by merely being in its presence." He looked back to her. "Do the qualities imbued by tempering wear off?"

"They haven't yet." Arianna saw his somewhat confused look and knew it was time to elaborate. "It was critical for all blood to pass through the box continually, to be purified and prevent rot. All blood passes through one location."

Arianna brought her thumb to her chest.

It was a dark sort of amusement seeing who in the room could follow the relatively simple logic she was presenting them. Willard was the first to get it, followed by the other Rivets. Dove seemed the first, and one of only two, to get it on the Ravens' behalf. It gave her some faith that all the vicars seemed to put it together.

"Eva performed the surgery, both to implant the box and the subsequent organs to test that I would not fall." Arianna drew the sharper of the two daggers crossed at the small of her back. "Naturally, I cannot show you what the box looks like at this moment, as I vitally need it where it is. But I can assure you that the operation continues to be a success."

Arianna wrapped her fingers around the blade and drew it quickly across her palm. She held up her hand for the room to see. Blood, the color of molten gold, dripped from her palm and, in true Dragon fashion, quickly evaporated when exposed to the air. Her wound magically healed over; just like that, all signs of her being the Perfect Chimera disappeared.

All signs, excluding the shock in every set of eyes around the room.

"Traitor to Loom!" One of the Revolver journeymen was on his feet, finger pointed at Arianna.

That certainly wasn't the reaction she'd been expecting.

"You had this weapon and kept it from us? We could have been fighting the Dragons all along."

"I do not think a Revo should point fingers about concealing weapons from Loom." Helen's biting remark was thrown from the back corner but echoed throughout the whole room.

"Do not speak of what you don't understand, little crow," a master Revo cautioned.

"I kept it from Loom because I did not think we had the capability to unite together to use it effectively." Arianna didn't need to defend her decision, but she couldn't stop either. She looked to the vicars, rather than the boy. She didn't care if some little pistol understood, but the vicars must.

"And look at us proving you right . . ." Her Dragon ears picked up Powell's murmur. She was liking him more and more by the moment.

"Furthermore, Perfect Chimera would mean war—something I didn't think Loom could stand more of."

"That shouldn't have been your call to make." Vicar Ethel gave her a wary stare. "It should have fallen to the vicars."

"And what tribunal? I created the box following the One Year War. There was no effective communication among the vicars, especially none that wasn't monitored by Dragon ears." Arianna met the other woman's gaze. "Furthermore, the Dragon we worked with . . ." Arianna couldn't bring herself to say Finnyr's name. And she wouldn't, not so long as there was any likelihood that they would need to work with House

Xin. She wouldn't taint the relationship out the gate. "He was working for the king all along. We had spies from every angle, and that was before the box was even well known.

"He was the one who infiltrated the rebellion and brought the Riders upon us. It was the dying wish of Eva, of Master Oliver, of every other Rivet, Revo, Raven, Harvester, and Alchemist involved that the research we produced be destroyed, rather than sequestered by the Dragon King."

The room was silent, an instinctual mourning toward the mere idea of destroying information.

"But you didn't destroy it?" Willard asked hopefully.

"I did." Arianna stared down at them all. She was only midway up through the room, but felt as though she stood from the parapet of judgment itself. "I torched it. My work, theirs, every last bit of it is gone. And then, before they could fall from over-exposure to magic from imbibing to fight off the Riders, or before the Riders could get their claws on them… I killed them. Every last one."

The air in the room was changing. It was charged with their shock and fear. And Arianna was the conduit for it all. She fed off it. She gleaned power from it.

Below her, Florence wore the smallest of smiles.

"And the box?" Willard seemed to be the only one who could find his voice.

"Just the one." Arianna tapped her chest. "And the schematics for it are here." She moved her fingers up to her temple.

"You're a monster," the Revolver from earlier whispered.

"I am." Arianna made no effort to deny it. Let them be so fearful of her that they left her to the shadows and obscurity she much preferred. "I am not Fenthri and not Dragon. I am not limited by the confines of what Loom knows as a Chimera, either. I am a creature of my own creation, and that is why, if I am to share this knowledge with Loom, it will be when there is a plan for how it will be used."

"What do you have in mind?" It seemed Vicar Dove had come around.

"I—"

"There's only one." An Alchemist was on his feet, a journeyman of little importance, judging from his seating placement in the back row. "There's only one box and it's in her."

"Leo—" Vicar Ethel gave a cautioning tone.

"We just cut her open and see how it works." The Alchemist looked to Willard. "You Rivets can take it apart. If she won't give it to us, we take it from her."

Arianna was not about to feel threatened by a child who looked no older than Helen and had half the manners.

"We are not going to take it by force." Willard defended her. Arianna didn't know if it was because of his instinct as her vicar out of respect for her work. Either way, she appreciated the gesture.

"He has a point." Vicar Gregory finally spoke up. "There is little time before we can expect whatever the Dragon King has next for us, especially grouping like this. We need to defend ourselves."

"A defense will be planned." Florence reminded them all that she was there, raising her voice above the din. "It is why we are here." She turned to the Alchemist journeyman. "Now, take your seat."

"You can't command me."

"Take your seat, Leo," Vicar Ethel ordered with a glare that almost swung to Florence after, for ordering one of her students.

"No, he has a point." The Revolver from earlier stood. "I say we kill the traitor to Loom." He drew his gun, leveling it at her.

"Let's say you can kill me. Which is hard. Trust me, it's *hard*. And you *can* quickly reverse engineer the box." Arianna tilted her head to the side, her mouth curling into a grin. "I haven't told you what type of flower you need from Nova. I haven't told you the process to temper gold to get its properties. I haven't explained the principles of the box. How long do you think Loom will last?" She held out her arms. "Fire, if you think you can discover those things before the Dragon King kills us all."

The journeyman's hand shook, the barrel of the revolver making tiny swings through the air.

"Or sit down, and let the adults figure out a way to make sure there is a Loom for you to inherit." She dropped her hands to her sides.

For a brief moment, the Revolver had sense. But Arianna gave the situation too much credit. She now lived in a bent and broken world, where tensions where high and trigger-happy Revo initiates were elevated to journeymen before their time out of sheer necessity.

The boy took his shot.

Her ears rang, magic quickly healing the hearing damage from the gunshot in the small room. Dust plumed from a pockmark in the stone of the tier behind her. Arianna opened her mouth to speak, but all that came out was the sound of another revolver firing.

Smoke disappeared from the barrel of Florence's gun as the Revolver journeyman's body hit the ground hard, blood pooling around his face from the bullet hole between his eyes. The entire room was silent. Arianna looked at the young woman who had been her apprentice. The girl she had pulled out of the Underground.

One shot, and those images were gone.

She didn't know the woman who stood where Florence had been a moment ago. This woman moved the same as Florence, dressed the same as Florence. She even sounded the same as Florence. But Arianna saw her as if for the first time, and couldn't help but wonder how long she had been there.

"Now is not the time for dissension," Florence spoke softly, holstering her gun. "We stand together, or we don't stand at all."

No one spoke. No one moved. It seemed the whole room held its breath.

"Do you agree, Vicar Gregory?" Florence turned to the vicar of the man whom she had just slain in a blink.

"I do," Gregory spoke after a long pause. "The Revolvers need to remember that for every shot we take, there should be two we hold back. With the power to kill comes the responsibility to protect life."

"Well put." Florence looked back to the room. "And protect life is just what we will do, with the power of the Perfect Chimera. But first, I believe the Vicar Harvester wanted to cover some matters of supplies . . ."

"Y-yes, thank you, Florence." Powell cleared his throat, and launched into a lengthy discussion on their current resources.

Everyone else seemed engrossed, but Arianna's focus was entirely on Florence. She was avoiding Arianna's stare, even though she must have felt the weight of it.

Arianna hadn't questioned the idea of throwing her loyalty entirely behind Florence.

But for the first time, she wondered just what, and *whom*, she was supporting. For the first time, she didn't feel like the most dangerous person in the room.

CVAREH

He'd somehow managed to avoid Finnyr for the rest of the evening following his brother's arrival. Cvareh didn't make himself too scarce, at least not obviously so, but the gods looked after him and put his brother elsewhere at all times. When dawn came, he soaked in his bath until the water was cold, changed his clothes several times, and took the longest breakfast he could out on his terrace.

But just as Lord Xin came for all men in time, he eventually had to make his way to his brother.

Cvareh wasn't sure if he was surprised that Finnyr had yet to send for him. Surely, they had much to speak on. Petra had been the brave one of the three of them, the one who tackled problems head on—no situation too uncomfortable or frightening. Now, it was Cvareh's turn to be brave.

So, adorned with bronze pauldrons and a swooping blue cape that covered his left arm as he walked, Cvareh made his way to his brother's quarters.

Servants eyed him cautiously along the way, clearly not sure what to make of the youngest Xin sibling heading for the Oji. He could tell by the wariness in their eyes that they wanted him to challenge, while the hurt and betrayal there revealed that none of them expected him to do so.

Cvareh kept silent, his strides brisk and long. What had become Finnyr's domain was the third wing on the lower floor, comprised of only a handful of interconnecting rooms. By far the nicest of what Petra had designed to be guest and Kin chambers. It was good enough, Cvareh appraised as he took in the decor and careful woodwork.

It's too good for Finnyr, a treacherous little voice crept up.

His ears picked up voices several paces before the door. Cvareh stilled, trying to catch the words when the door was suddenly opened from within.

"See, I thought I smelled your brother," Fae said to Finnyr, but kept her eyes on Cvareh.

"Forgive me, brother." It was already hard to speak. His jaw was aching from the anger that kept it clamped shut. "I didn't realize by not taking breakfast with you that you would be forced to break the morning's bread with Rok."

Finnyr looked over dully from the table. It was a very different look than at the one he'd worn at his arrival the day prior. Now, he held the advantage. So he looked on Cvareh only apathy and ambivalence, as though he was appraising his own brother to be worth little and less.

"I have had many a meal with Rok. You would do well to find their company enjoyable also, brother." Finnyr looked back to his plate, ripping through a small, seeded loaf and smearing butter on it liberally.

"I had not meant to imply otherwise." Cvareh looked back to the woman who was still eyeing him with a gleeful grin. "I know better."

The woman strolled back into the room, leaving the door open. With all the hip swaying of a brothel madam, she paraded over to the bed, lounging back on it as though it were hers.

Could he have read this wrong? Was Finnyr merely bringing back a lover? It would make sense for him to find someone to confide in throughout the years he had spent on Lysip. A displaced Tam made as much sense as anything else . . .

Finnyr barely regarded the woman, instead watching Cvareh warily as he entered the room. "What do you want?"

"I wish to speak with you." Cvareh cut right to the chase. Finnyr's tone made it clear that they were not going to find themselves on friendly or casual footing.

"Speak, then." Finnyr shoved a wedge of melon into his mouth, chewing like an animal. Juice dribbled down his chin as his teeth chomped into the pale yellow flesh.

"May we have privacy?" Cvareh glanced over at the woman who was inspecting her claws. Cvareh understood the message clearly: She was ready to strike at any moment.

"Anything you say to me can be said before Master Rider Fae."

It was as though his brother had begun speaking Fennish. No, it was something more confounding than the whispering tones of the gray peoples below the God's Line. He was going to allow a Rok Rider to sit in on House Xin conversations?

"Finnyr, I would—"

"That is Finnyr'Oji, Cvareh." Finnyr demanded Cvareh use his title, yet still kept stripping Cvareh of his. It was equal parts confusing and alarming, and Cvareh had no intention of letting it go for a moment longer.

"Finnyr'*Oji*, I would like to know if I am nameless now?" That wasn't what he'd intended to say originally. But this was the path Finnyr was choosing—one of difficulty.

"I have yet to decide." Finnyr returned to his meal.

"What? Who is the Xin'Ryu then?"

"Presently, no one."

"Who do you intend to ask to be the Xin'Ryu?"

"I have yet to decide."

"Finnyr'Oji—" Spitting out the title of Oji in conjunction with Finnyr's name was like spitting up glass. "—I must encourage you to pick a Ryu. If not me, then *someone.* I could even put forward some names of those who are in the House who have proven their loyalty."

"Typical Cvareh," Finnyr snarled quietly, looking up from his meal like a dog protecting a bone. "Always so worried about *loyalty* for House Xin." Finnyr slowly put down his utensils, punctuating the movement by folding his fingers. "I am House Xin now. Do well to remember it."

"I am merely trying to give you counsel, as your brother, if nothing else."

"My brother?" Finnyr scoffed. "We are no more brothers than I am Tam."

The words blindsided Cvareh, hitting him so hard he nearly staggered. Not brothers? No Ryu? No Petra? His world was collapsing one cornerstone after another.

"Were we brothers, you would have sent for me years ago."

"I could take you from the Dragon King no more than Petra could." Cvareh glanced at Fae, who wore the smallest of smiles. She looked like a sea sponge on the beach's shore, lapping up every wave of words, absorbing them into her memory until it filled to capacity.

"Petra, she was an even worse example."

"Stop." Cvareh wouldn't hear it. He couldn't hear it. It was a load too heavy to bear so soon after her death.

"She spoke of family and usurped our father—"

"Stop."

"—sent me away—"

"Finnyr . . ."

"—used you like a tool—"

"I said stop!" Cvareh punched a fist into the doorframe. Anger escaped through heavy exhales and his heaving chest. Wood splintered into his knuckles and the smell of woodsmoke filled the room from his wounds. Cvareh didn't notice; his eyes were only on Finnyr.

There was the fear he expected to see from his coward of a brother. It was all talk. There was no greatness. It wasn't until the shadow of the giant green woman pulled herself off the bed with a sigh that any resolve returned to Finnyr's stare. He was only brave as long as he sat under the protection of Yveun.

Cvareh slowly pulled his fist from the doorframe, regarding the woman and her claws warily. He raised his hands, showing that his claws had yet to be exposed.

"Forgive me, Oji." He spoke to Finnyr, but looked at the Rider. It was apparent who the true Xin'Oji was. "I am merely emotional given the present trials. I shall work on composing myself."

Fae looked to Finnyr, and Cvareh's gaze followed. Finnyr continued to look at him with that same detached, cold stare.

"See that you do, Cvareh," he cautioned. "If you want any hope of keeping any sort of title to your name."

Cvareh gave a small nod. The meeting had been a failure from the moment the door opened and at the rate things were going, it wasn't impossible for him to wind up dead. It made complete sense to turn his back and leave, and yet, something compelled him to hover a moment longer.

"Remember, brother . . . For however much you hated Petra, and hate me, you are still Xin, and we are Dragons. Your blood flows from Lord Xin. Build your own legacy as you see fit, but at least make it truly yours."

Finnyr's mouth was shut so tightly, his lips weren't even visible. "Get out of my sight."

With pleasure, Cvareh barely kept himself from saying as he departed down the hall and away from that miserable room.

Cvareh strode through the Xin Manor with the look of a man on a mission, but it was all a carefully crafted illusion. He had no direction to go in, and what seemed like fewer options available to him by the second. His mind and heart both were heavy with a frustrating, infuriating ache.

He found himself walking up a long staircase. It was a narrow offshoot from one of Petra's lower halls, and wound upward into the heights of the manor. When he was lost, there was one place he'd always gone to for answers.

The viewing chamber was empty and that, for some inexplicable reason, surprised him. Cvareh stared at the far edge of the dais, where his sister had sat facing the large windows that looked out across the Ruana mountains toward the temple of Xin. He sat heavily in that same spot, looking for answers he didn't think he'd find.

It wasn't long before footsteps broke the silence, and Cvareh knew who stopped at the top of the stair without having to turn. He knew it by the smell of the man and the sound of his gait, and because there was only one other Xin Dragon who would dare venture up to one of Petra's most personal and private spaces.

"Sit with me?" Cvareh spoke without turning.

Cain didn't speak. He did as he was told, but in the wrong way. He walked around to the far edge where Cvareh sat, sitting next to him.

Cvareh didn't have it in his heart to correct the man. "How did you know I was here?"

"Dawyn told me," Cain answered softly. There was something about the space that made lowering one's voice in reverence natural. "She saw you headed this way."

Cvareh vaguely recognized the name. "One of my sister's attendants?"

Cain shook his head. "She actually helped see to the Fe—to Ari while she was here." He stopped himself mid-word with a glare from Cvareh at the slur for the people down on Loom.

"What is she doing in Petra's wing?" Cvareh felt protective of the space. He wasn't ready to see it turned over to Finnyr, to anyone.

"Paying her respects . . . looking for answers . . ."

Cvareh heard his friend's meaning without needing it spelled out for him. "I don't have the answers."

"I suggest you find some," Cain said firmly. "House Xin needs you."

"Finnyr has not said if I am to remain Ryu." Cvareh shook his head. "Even if he did, this is not what was intended. I was to help Petra, not become Oji myself."

"Pull yourself together. We need a leader." Cain sighed, looking out through the windows. "Plus, life is made of missed intentions."

"Poetic."

"I heard it at a tea parlor in Napole."

Cvareh chuckled and shook his head. With his friend, he should've known. "I think he will avoid appointing a Ryu." Cvareh whispered what he had been too afraid to even think. "If there is no Ryu, he's less likely to be assassinated from within Xin."

"Because if it's not in a clear duel and there's no Ryu, succession isn't assured." Cain cursed under his breath. "Damn that Yveun."

Cvareh was inclined to agree.

"What's worse is that Finnyr will get away with it. Because he knows you love this house too much not to keep functioning as Ryu, with or without title."

Once more, Cvareh's silence was his agreement. He'd always gone along. He'd spent every moment and every breath in devotion to his house. He'd only done what others had set out for him. But what should he do now, when there was no clear path?

"This is wretched."

Cvareh sighed and leaned back, wishing he had his sibling to lean against.

"What is it?" Cain made note of his shift in demeanor.

"I wonder how much could have been avoided if Petra had just given him some favor."

"Turn sympathetic to Finnyr and I will duel you myself," Cain threatened.

"Twenty gods, no." Cvareh shook his head. "Merely wishing things were different."

"Wishing gets us nothing. We need action." Cain folded his arms over his chest, beginning to pace. "We need to show Yveun that we won't tolerate these slights."

"We need to bide our time." Cvareh tried to use his words as a mental block to slow Cain down, but they only seemed to make him pace faster.

"Until what? Until Rok decides to pick us off one by one?"

"Until we hear from Arianna."

Cain spun to face him in one fluid movement.

"You know I'm right." Cvareh preempted whatever the other man was about to say. "If we are to stand a chance against Rok, we need the help of Loom. We bide our time until then."

Cvareh could almost feel Cain's anger bubbling to the surface. He braced himself for the moment it would explode. But Cain took a slow breath, and his whole demeanor shifted.

"How do you plan on making use of them for House Xin?" his friend asked, finally.

"The same way Petra intended: to make us an army." Cvareh wondered how much Petra had shared of her mind with anyone beyond him. Judging from Cain's almost confused frown, he guessed the circle was small, if it existed at all.

"Make us an army? Of people like *her*."

"Arianna is the first of her kind, a Perfect Chimera. They will make more and stand with us. With that much power, we will defeat Yveun."

"I hope you're right . . ." Cain shook his head, starting for the stairs. While Cvareh considered it a success that his friend could even stomach hearing mention of Loom and Arianna without exploding, it seemed the fuse of tolerance was still quick to burn. "Because if you're not, we're all dead."

"I know I am," Cvareh reassured Cain.

"Then I will leave it to you. Fetch me when I'm needed in your master plans, Cvareh'Oji." The final vowel of the honorific echoed back up to Cvareh, ringing in his ears several times over before it finally faded.

Cvareh . . . Oji . . .

He'd never thought of the idea before. That had always been Petra's mantle, Petra's mission.

Now, House Xin expected him to bear its weight—him, who had wanted to carry it least. Cvareh knew the esteem would honor many a Dragon, and it was something so many lusted over. But the notion sat uneasy with him. So uneasy, that he wondered if anything could ever make it settle.

FLORENCE

Just once in her life, Florence wanted a well-stocked workshop. She didn't want to buy supplies on a budget, or scavenge in secret, or scrape bottoms of barrels. She wanted a workshop with perfectly level tables, cabinets full of all manner of powders—even some she didn't quite know how best to work with—and a door with a lock that prevented people from entering whenever they pleased and nibbing through her work.

"So, this is where you've been holing up." Will ran his hand along the dusty countertop. "A bit dirty."

"Helping run a rebellion severely limits one's ability to clean." Florence looked up from the one surface she had scrubbed to shining perfection. Gun parts were carefully set upon it in meticulous order. Every screw was lined up, the springs sorted by size—it was an organization unique to her, which meant she'd know instantly if one of her items was missing.

"You always did like to keep things tidy." Will walked over to the table, assessing her layout. He touched nothing, an unspoken respect for another's guild ministrations.

Florence paused, her rag hung off the gun barrel she'd been cleaning. "One thing I could control," she said, finally. "When your life's a mess, it feels a bit better to tidy *something*. Even if it's just a bit of laundry, or a countertop."

"Or all of Loom." Will swiped away the dust on the empty secondary table in her room, hoisting himself up to sit on it.

"Loom is still a mess."

"We're getting better. That last meeting of the vicars was *almost* productive."

Florence couldn't keep in a groan. "I came to my workshop to escape that nonsense."

She'd been all but silenced for the meetings subsequent to the first, relegated to sit behind Vicar Gregory and say as little as possible. Florence knew she didn't have a leg to stand on when it came to actually leading the meetings, so she wasn't sure why she still felt frustrated.

"No rest for the weary."

"What do you want, Will?" Florence picked up a wire brush, working out some caked-on gunpowder from her gun barrel.

"I can't just call on a friend?"

"Are we still friends?" Florence flashed him a small grin. "And here I thought you liked Louie more than me."

"The man flies a few feathers short, that's for sure."

"I think you just said I'm not crazy enough for you." Oh, the stories she could tell him to prove otherwise.

"We're all afflicted with a different sort of madness." Will shrugged. "Louie's sort is more similar to mine and Helen's, though."

"Ravens." Florence had suspected Louie's actual guild for some time. The man was restless, wandering, driven to something unseen just over the horizon, just a few more steps away.

"You think so?"

"Birds of a feather." Florence dipped her rag in gun oil, the familiar tang filling her nose.

"Helen wants to take over his work. The man's on death's doorstep."

"What 'work' is that even?" Florence didn't have the foggiest what Louie considered his magnum opus to be.

"There's always something to steal, someone who will pay for it, and the people who need to broker the transactions." Will put his elbows on his knees. "Plus, it's pretty handy we're here with this rebellion of yours."

"We'll see . . ." Florence had ideas for Louie, but none that had paid out dividends yet. The man was like a rare canister—very few occasions to use it, but when you found one, the resulting reaction was magnificent.

Speaking of canisters . . . Florence began reassembling her gun. She should have just enough time to make some additional ammunition.

"We got Ari to you."

Her hands paused. *Ari.* The woman had been the kind of quiet Florence wasn't sure she wanted to break. She'd attended every meeting, sat as directed, said what made sense and anything needed to reinforce the idea that Florence had been right to call the Tribunal. But there was a distance between them, rendering the woman untouchable.

"That was chance." Florence tested the hammer and trigger of her gun, unloaded, with satisfying tension and clicks. "She would've gotten to me without you."

"She was in bad shape."

"I have no doubt." Florence re-holstered her gun. "But you don't know Ari like I do. She would've made it to me."

Will hummed, opened his mouth to speak, and was interrupted by a familiar ghost in the doorway.

"Will, I think Helen is looking for you." Shannra made her way into the small workshop.

"What does she need?" Will half-jumped off the table, waiting for Shannra to pass before he started for the door.

"Who knows? Something about a map?" Shannra shrugged.

"She with Louie?"

"Passed her in the hall." Shannra paused where Will had been sitting, the small of her back against the high workshop table.

"Right, thanks."

Florence set out four hollow canisters in a line, looking up at Shannra expectantly. The other woman's mouth spread into a coy little smile.

"Helen is looking for him?" Florence repeated.

"I may have lied." The woman's face lit up with a wide smile. She shook her head and laughter escaped.

"I hardly get to see you since everyone arrived." Shannra straightened and stepped over to Florence's table. Delicately, her fingers fell like fall leaves onto the surface; not a grain of powder was blown out of place or a canister disturbed.

"Help me," Florence asked, her eyes traversing the line of the woman's fingers, up her arm, to her face. "I could use an extra set of eyes on this."

"With pleasure, Flor."

Shannra was a capable teacher. She explained things thoroughly and kept her expectations both high and reasonable. It made Florence want to learn, want to earn her esteem. It also helped that she was a Revo as well, a journeyman at that, and contained a wealth of knowledge Florence had only just begun to scratch the surface of when she had last worked with a Revo teacher.

Florence watched the woman's hands carefully, her eyes drifting upward when she knew Shannra wouldn't see, to admire her face. Another beautiful spirit in her life. But beauty didn't change that the woman was one of Louie's minions, a fact Florence had been careful not to forget. Helen, Will, Shannra . . . all had to be kept at arm's length.

"... and then just fill it to top as you would normally." Shannra finished her instruction on the canister.

"Is this standard Revolver knowledge?" Shannra was one of the few Florence felt comfortable asking such questions around. She knew the woman wouldn't belittle her odd guild situation. Anyone in Louie's company was in no position to speak down to others for odd choices.

"Fairly so." Shannra nodded and then tapped Florence's bottle of sulfur. "But you add your own twists to it."

"Have to keep things interesting." Florence shrugged.

"Never a dull moment with you, certainly."

"Speaking of . . ." Florence tugged on the chain connected to one of the buttons of her vest, producing a simple pocket watch. "Almost time for the Tribunal. I should start down."

"You got it working again," Shannra appraised.

Florence had discovered the watch among the ruins of Ter.0, a remnant of some bygone days. The front of the watch had an odd design that was almost reminiscent of a wing and some kind of semicircle, but it was too dented to make out the full image. No doubt it had been some Raven's precious trinket before the world collapsed.

"Arianna," Florence answered simply.

"You two don't seem as close as you'd made it sound." Shannra fell into step.

"Are you probing for Louie?" Florence grabbed her top hat from its peg. "Peg" being a generous descriptor for the bit of gnarled iron that was sticking out from a crumbled section of wall.

"Not this time."

"This time." Florence huffed. "How often do our conversations make it back to that Endwig of a man?"

Shannra played with the ends of a handful of hair in thought. "Wait, you think he looks like an Endwig?"

"Most certainly." The resemblance was a bit of a stretch, if Florence was being fair. But she wasn't inclined to be fair toward Louie. "White, thin skin. Beady eyes. A taste for living flesh."

Shannra's laughter bounced between the walls and straight between Florence's ribs. She had a beautiful laugh. "A nightmare given form?"

"Yes, describes him well, don't you think?" Florence tipped her top hat at a passerby, a more frequent occurrence as they continued to descend the tower toward the Hall of the Vicars—as it had become known.

"Don't be cruel, Flor."

"I'm being truthful," Florence insisted. "It just so happens the truth is also cruel."

"I can't be too upset with him."

"Why is that?" Florence asked delicately. Shannra hadn't spoken much about the circumstances under which she'd come into Louie's service.

"Well, if I'm probing you for information on his behalf, it gives me an excuse to see you." Shannra shrugged, back to playing with her hair. "An excuse to talk."

Her movements combined with her words put a pang of longing in Florence's heart for something she didn't quite comprehend. The woman before her was deadly and beautiful, strong and sturdy, yet possessed a vulnerability Florence couldn't help but be drawn to.

It was all a lie, however. Shannra was Louie's. Florence knew how the old king of Mercury Town enlisted his help—extreme loyalty or death. So when the cards fell, she would do Louie's bidding, not her heart's.

Florence found herself at an impasse, the in-between that seemed to define her life. None of that changed the fact that Shannra was still dodging her question, and Florence had every intention of pointing that out. At least until Arianna appeared.

"Headed down, Flor?" Arianna emerged from the hallway, her violet eyes darting between Florence and Shannra.

"It's about that time." Florence patted the pocket where she kept the watch. "Thank you again for fixing it."

"It was honestly a nice distraction for the evening." Arianna was wearing her white coat and harness—always armed to the teeth, even among friends. It was a trait Florence admired and was already attempting to embody.

"I will let you know if I find any other such distractions." Florence flashed her teacher a smile that was reciprocated, however briefly.

"Were it up to the Vicar Revolver, I would have the distraction of manufacturing the Philosopher's Box." Arianna's expression quickly soured. "The man doesn't seem to understand that creating things is a lot more complex than destroying them."

Florence coughed softly and it served to remind Arianna that she was no longer in the company of Rivets.

"I didn't mean to imply that making explosives and ammunition wasn't complex," Arianna quickly backtracked, only mildly apologetic. The day Florence saw Arianna genuinely apologize for her thoughts was the day the world had, indeed, ended. "Merely that it is not as instantaneous as pulling a trigger."

"Especially not when we have still to sort procuring something from Nova," Florence agreed.

"I heard Louie was asked by the Vicar Raven to look into that." Arianna looked across Florence to Shannra.

"And how did you hear that?" Shannra arched her eyebrows.

"Louie isn't the only one who has his ways." Florence's chest filled with an odd sort of pride for Arianna's ability to uncover information. But there was also a twinge of frustration at the fact that she was only *just* hearing about it. Arianna continued to stare down Shannra. "Well? Does he have a solution for it?"

"Sounds like an excellent discussion for the Tribunal." Shannra smiled at them both. In a display of boldness, she grabbed Florence's hand, squeezing it tightly before stepping away. Then, speaking only to Florence: "I'll see you later, yes?"

Florence could feel Arianna's stare creeping between her vertebrae. "Perhaps. We'll see."

Shannra nodded, and strode ahead into the main atrium.

"Florence . . ." Arianna's voice was full of caution. "We have to be careful about her."

"I know, Ari."

"She's one of Louie's."

"Ari, I know." Florence rearranged her words so maybe they'd sink in better.

"What sort of things has she been asking you?"

"Don't worry so much. Louie is on our side."

"Flor—"

"Ari, let it drop," Florence demanded with a hard stare. Arianna opened her mouth to protest but quickly abandoned the idea. "I know what I'm doing. Trust me."

"I do trust you."

But I don't think you know what you're doing, Florence finished silently. What did she have to do to prove she was capable of organizing herself and others, of defending Loom, of being an active contributor to their future? The more time that passed, the more Florence began to feel like nothing would do it.

She would forever be a student in Arianna's eyes—a ward.

Florence adjusted her top hat and tilted her face downward. She needed this time to compose herself.

The tribunal room was mostly full by the time she arrived. Florence tugged at her pocket watch as she descended the stairs, popping open the repaired latch to look at the hands within.

"Ah, Florence, what time were we supposed to start again?" Powell asked from where he sat.

She pulled out the pocket watch again. "About another two minutes."

"Like I told you." The Vicar Revolver folded his arms where he sat. "Don't know why you felt the need to ask her."

"Just getting another data point, Vicar Gregory, no need to get so bothered." Powell waved off the other man's short fuse.

"Florence, take your seat," her vicar demanded.

"I had a question about today's agenda." Powell still hadn't sat down.

"A question you can ask me, as another vicar," the Gregory insisted.

Florence glanced between the two men and finally ended with a long look at Powell. She hated the feeling of being relegated to the corner when she had something worthwhile to contribute. At least, she thought she did.

"Very well." Powell spoke as Florence stepped up the risers to where journeymen Revos sat. She should be grateful; technically, she shouldn't even be in the room. "What are we talking about today, Vicar Gregory?"

"There's only one thing we need to discuss." Gregory nodded in Arianna's direction. "The lack of schematics in her hands."

"Perhaps we can discuss the lack of a manufacturing line that would necessitate the need for schematics." Arianna's remark was dry.

"You will need to share them with us eventually." The vicar grew more relentless by the day. Florence could only do so much to quell Arianna's frustration at the fact. If only Gregory would *listen* to her . . . and if not her, then Arianna at least.

"In all my years, I have never seen a Revolver so interested in a Rivet's work," Willard jumped into the fray as he entered the room. "Warms my heart to see you taking such an interest. Now that we are reverting the guilds back to a system of choice, perhaps you wish to come have a seat in the back behind me, and allow another Revolver to assume command? You seem to have a promising student with a talent for uniting us, just there in the back row."

Gregory looked over his shoulder directly at her. Florence leveled her eyes against him and fought every urge to look away. She was not going to be submissive, not when she'd done nothing wrong, and especially not when another vicar was standing up for her.

"Ah, Vicar Dove," Powell spoke loudly the second Gregory opened his mouth, cutting off whatever remark the man had been ready to levy against her. "Not a moment too soon."

The Vicar Raven waved her hand, assuming her seat with a yawn. "Don't wait on my account."

Florence resisted the urge to point out that it wasn't much of a Vicar Tribunal if all the vicars were not present at each meeting.

"Well, I have a question for you, so waiting was a necessity. It's with regards to harvesting these magical flowers . . ." Powell started.

"As I have said previously, the Ravens are glad to assist."

Assist how? Florence wanted to ask. She expected some resistance; not everything would go smoothly. But she had foolishly believed that all those present on Loom would band together. It still seemed that the selfish nature of mortals won out from time to time, even in the face of certain devastation.

"I'm a bit curious on the details surrounding the *how*, Vicar Raven?" Florence asked from the back of the room, drawing all eyes to her. She wanted to hear if Arianna was right, and she'd play dumb if she had to. "After all, I left the Ravens' Guild. I'm not sure how it all works, getting something from Nova . . ."

"Florence—" Vicar Gregory's tone had been getting harsher by the day.

"I'm curious about these details as well." Powell came to her aid. She didn't know what she'd done to earn such esteem in the man's eyes, but having the favor of a vicar was priceless.

"Well, since a vicar is asking now . . ." Dove gave Florence a look from the corner of her eyes. "We are currently working on the infrastructure between Loom and Nova, to find a consistent means of transport. Without the ability to pilot a glider, we will need to rely on Dragon intervention. But finding Dragons willing to work against the Dragon King while not endangering our own by drawing attention is difficult."

Florence rightly didn't care if Louie was in any sort of danger. That was the line of work he put himself in. But since Vicar Dove was, for whatever reason, keeping Louie's involvement quiet, Florence couldn't call out the fact.

She turned to Arianna expectantly. If they needed Dragons, surely House Xin would come to their aid. Florence met her teacher's eyes, and the other woman remained glued to her seat—and silent.

"Perhaps the Harvesters have some inroads with the Dragons that we could use?" Vicar Dove continued to speak with Powell, but the words were distant.

Why wasn't Arianna saying anything? She looked over to the Vicar Alchemist, and promptly realized that Cvareh had held his meetings with Sophie, not the vicar that Florence had ushered in by creating a sudden vacancy in the position. No one else really knew of the depth of Cvareh's involvement beyond her and Ari.

"Perhaps," Powell replied. "But most of our organ seeds—" he didn't even acknowledge the Dragons as people, Florence noticed. "—were given to us to cultivate legally by the Dragon King. An avenue I do not think is available to us any longer." He turned to the masters behind him. "Would any of you . . ."

Arianna still was immobile. Florence stared down at her teacher, but Arianna was doing an excellent job of ignoring her probing gaze. Why wouldn't she speak? It was for the good of Loom. They had the solution neatly. They could move on from the topic.

What exactly happened between her and Cvareh on Nova? The question from the first time she had laid eyes on her teacher again crept back to her. Now, more than ever, she was sure of it.

Frustration found its way like a billow of steam up the flue of her throat. If Arianna wasn't going to say anything, then she would—Vicar Gregory's growing ire toward her be damned. Somewhere in her, Florence felt bad for outing Arianna, but there wasn't any other choice. If Arianna wouldn't do what was best for Loom, Florence would.

The doors to the room were pulled open and a breathless man ran halfway down the stairs before loudly proclaiming, "Rainbows in the sky!"

No one breathed.

Then, chaos.

"What do we do?" Vicar Powell asked no one in particular. Typical Harvester.

"Revolvers, arm yourselves and to vantages!" Vicar Gregory jumped into motion. "Masters, summon the other journeymen. All Revolvers are to take to positions!"

"Vicar Gregory, can my Ravens assist your guns in flying to their stations?" The prior hesitation to work together melted away from Vicar Dove in a moment.

"Yes, while masters convene." Vicar Gregory gave a firm nod to the other vicar and then continued to bark orders.

Florence stood. She hadn't been given a position, but she was going to fight anyway.

"Where are you going, Florence?" the Vicar Revolver demanded.

"To where I can be of use."

"Just stay here. Only Revos were informed of what to do in such a contingency," Vicar Gregory called back, leaving and taking half the room with him.

Only Revos. The words echoed and Florence scowled. She adjusted her hat and started for the door.

"He said to stay here," Powell called after her.

Florence spun in place, looking at the three of the five guilds who had yet to move. "I am not going to sit here, waiting to die, while we are under attack." She drew her gun, pointing it to the doorway. "We all thrive, or we all perish—together. There's no other option for us now."

"You received an order from the Vicar Revolver," one of the still-lingering masters with a revolver chamber tattooed on his cheek cautioned her.

"Good thing I'm, apparently, not a Revolver then." Florence grinned, tapped her own cheek, and left the room behind her.

A pair of hasty footsteps caught up to her, slowing to fall into step with her own strides. Florence looked to her right, instinctively tilting her head upward so that the brim of her hat didn't hide Arianna's face. The other woman gripped her shoulder, stopping her in place. Florence's appreciation quickly melted into the frustration from earlier.

"What will it be, Ari?" Florence looked to the doors before them that led to the waste of Ter.0 in all its crumbling glory. "Are you my enemy or my ally? Will you try to keep me from fighting as well?"

She gave a huff of amusement and lightly took off Florence's top hat. People moved around them, rushing, shouting, cowering, drawing weapons and steeling their resolve. But for a brief moment, everything seemed to slow.

"You'll shoot better if you don't have to tilt your head funny to look up." Arianna deposited the hat on the window ledge of one of the inner stairwells. "You'll be upset if it gets damaged, too. Not too many hatteries around here."

It was madness. The world could be moments from ending, and Florence wore a smile at the gesture of her teacher and friend.

"Let's go fight some Dragons." Florence began moving again.

"Let's hope we don't have to." Arianna murmured under her breath. And, just like that, Florence was once more confused by the woman. Did she want to protect Dragons now? *What had happened on Nova?*

They emerged from the doors of the five-towered hall and into the rubble and chaos of the ground below. Men and women scampered to find places to hide. Revolvers held their backs against stones and beams of steel, loaded guns in hand. Florence looked up behind her at the tower, seeing the glint of gun barrels sticking from windows.

The Vicar Revolver stood atop the sloping road that led into the Hall of Ter.0. His arms folded across his chest and his eyes squinted at the sky. He was not the same man who had occupied the tribunal. Gregory was gone, and only the vicar remained in his place.

"You don't listen, do you?" The man glanced over his shoulder at her.

"I think my petulance is endearing." Florence grinned, selecting a few canisters she had made that morning.

"At least someone does." Gregory frowned disapprovingly. "Get back inside. I can't have you being a liability."

"Don't worry about me. I'm only here to help." Florence drew her gun. She knew she was pushing the limits. But she wasn't about to be ordered away and pushed around. She squinted up at the whitewashed sky, speaking before the vicar could. "What're they doing?"

"Flying out of range," Arianna responded, sparing Florence from having to endure another response from Gregory.

One glider broke away from the other two, veering down and away from the wide loop it had been making. The vicar rose a hand as it descended about halfway, just within range. The world was suddenly so heavy with silence that she could hear the collective chorus of guns cocking.

"Listen to me, girl," the vicar muttered. "Don't get us all killed now."

Florence barely refrained from pointing out that she may have been the one who saved Loom by uniting them all. It was a hard line to walk, being a nobody but aspiring to be a someone.

The Rider looped around a few times, looking down at the terrain, each time a little lower. It started its final descent on a trajectory that had them landing with an explosion of color on the dusty ground as the glider touched down lightly. The Dragon didn't move. She stayed exactly where she was, hands on the golden handles of the glider.

It was those handles that funneled magic strategically through and around the Dragon's body, into her feet, and the gold platform on which she stood. A shimmer of gold, like the scales of one of the great southeastern sea snakes, lit up across the Rider's body, forming a corona. It was only the second time Florence had ever seen one, the first being the last time Riders had descended on Mercury Town and brought chaos with them.

It was a field metal and bullets could not penetrate—a field only broken by the strongest of magic, more than any Fenthri had ever mustered. And just like that, it made them all helpless before the Rider.

Arianna took a half-step closer in her direction. Florence watched with equal parts fascination and discomfort as claws grew from her fingertips. The skin of the Dragon hands she had acquired on Nova was so pale that it could almost be mistaken for gray, and there was a sort of willing blindness Florence had mustered toward them.

She couldn't determine if the blue was identical to Cvareh's color or not.

"Arianna," the Rider finally said. The Dragon did not call for a vicar or the leader. She called for Arianna. "Our king wishes to speak with you."

"Yveun is here?" Arianna's voice was nothing more than a whisper. A whisper that could well be the voice of death.

"Yveun'*Dono*, knave."

"He is not our king." Florence raised her gun. She didn't care if her shot would be pointless. She would distract the woman while Arianna attacked. She would catch the corona the second it exhausted. She would have the satisfaction of *finally* pulling the trigger on a Dragon, if nothing else. "He is yours. And he is not welcome on Loom."

"Florence," the vicar hissed. "Do not act out of turn."

Florence didn't move, keeping her stance. Someone had to threaten the Dragons, had to show Loom's claws.

The woman tilted her head with an unnerving jilt to sweep her eyes from Arianna to Florence. Her mouth spread wide, like a crescent moon, and gleamed with razor-sharp teeth. "What a bold child."

"I am not a child," Florence insisted.

"Spoken like a child." The Rider scoffed and looked back to Arianna. "Tell your warriors to put down their weapons."

"Not my call." Arianna still held up her hand, claws out.

"Interesting . . ." The Rider's attention turned back to Florence, rather than the vicar at her side. "Is it yours?"

"It's mine." Vicar Gregory took a step. Sure, *now* he wanted to be threatening.

The Rider tilted their head in the other direction and made a noise that could be interpreted as a snort at the vicar. "What is your name, girl?"

"Florence." She hated answering to "girl" but the sooner she gave the Rider a name, the sooner she could hope for her to use it.

Without warning, the glider sparked back to life, magic flashing through the air with an array of colors. The Rider took to the sky once more, quickly ascending to where the other two gliders continued their wide, slow loops overtop the guild hall. Florence looked back at the men and women stuck on the ground.

A Dragon could fight against three, four Fenthri without the help of anything. Enabled by a glider, protected by corona, and bolstered by any weaponry pilfered or given from the Revolvers, and Florence suddenly knew why Loom had fallen so quickly—why it took so little for the Dragons to keep them under their thumb.

"Coming back . . ." Gregory muttered.

Sure enough, all three gliders were descending now. The main road was only wide enough for two to land side by side, so the third touched down just behind.

To the right of the Dragon Florence had just been speaking to was possibly the largest Dragon she'd ever seen. Easily twice her height, he was made of pure muscle—if muscle was sculpted from rocks. The Dragon King—or so she assumed—wore next to nothing, so Florence and every other Fenthri could see every stretch of skin across the bulging curves of his arms and legs. His flesh was the color of fire, his eyes molten steel, and his shoulder-length hair as red as Fenthri blood. She hadn't been a Chimera for very long, but he radiated ten times the power she had ever felt, easily double the most powerful person she'd ever known—Arianna.

"Yveun . . ." Arianna whispered.

"Good to see you again, Arianna." The Dragon King pulled his lips back into a smile that was half-snarl. "I have come to offer peace to Loom."

"Peace?" Florence repeated. "You?" She'd never known an anger so vicious. "You who destroyed our world is offering peace?"

His head shifted to look at her. A piercing pang shot right between Florence's eyes the second his met hers. It was a dull ache in the back of her mind that spread like venom. Her whole body felt stiff, succumbing to the pressure. Her jaw locked.

"You are Florence, yes or no?"

"Yes."

"You lead this rebellion, yes or no?"

"Yes," she spoke on command like a trained animal, the word drawn out by force from the well of truth deep within her.

"*What?*" She barely heard Gregory whisper at her audacity, even though he stood right beside her.

Florence tried to peel her eyes away from the Dragon King, but she couldn't. She couldn't do anything unless he told her to first. Even breathing without his blessing was currently laborious.

"Of course," the king chuckled, sending sparks of magic off his corona like raindrops that dissipated before they hit the ground. "It would be a child who would have no memory of the last time Loom fell." Yveun shifted his attention to Gregory. "But you, you're old enough to remember."

The vicar was afflicted with the same sort of rigor mortis that had overcome Florence. She saw the panicked look in his eyes, the stiffness in his limbs. Florence knew the sensation was like taking a visit into a nightmare, but she made no motion to release him from it. Her relief at the Dragon King's attention being off her was too great.

"Tell me true: as Loom is now, can you stand against us in another war?" the king continued.

"As we are now?" The words were forced between tight lips. "No."

The whispering she heard on the wind was the sound of Loom's resolve wavering. She saw Fenthri look to each other in confusion.

"What happened the last time a resistance stood against me, Arianna?" The king turned his attention off Gregory.

Arianna looked off to the horizon. She remained still and easy, her breathing even. *Eyes*, Florence realized. Yveun had magic in his eyes—mind control as long as eye contact was maintained. She put it together faster than Gregory, who was once more under the king's thrall.

"You tell us, then. What happened the last time a resistance stood against me?"

"They were destroyed completely," the vicar responded automatically.

Gun barrels began to waver. A man stood to get a better view, giving up his vantage and his fighting position. Florence looked over the field of lost Fenthri, desperate for a home, longing for the logical order they all craved. They had been broken by the man before them, and, for some reason, they looked to that same hand now to fix their world.

"How many perished?" the king pressed.

"Countless. Loom was never the same," Gregory responded.

Eye contact—she had to break the eye contact or the vicar would undo the threads of Loom's resolve himself. Without warning, she gave the vicar a strong shove. The man was much larger than her in all directions, but he was unbraced and stumbled before falling.

"Don't look him in the eye," she offered by way of explanation at the vicar's scowl.

"Foolish girl, the truth should be heard." The king drew her attention again, but Florence made it a point to look just above his head. His magic kept out of her mind and off her skin as a result. "Every man and woman standing here, brandishing their pathetic weapons at my greatness, should know only death awaits."

"It does not!" Florence took a bold step forward. "Arianna is proof of that."

"Florence, I am not the example to use," Arianna hissed.

She knew Arianna hated having the attention on her. But that was what Loom needed right now. And for all Florence loved Arianna, she loved Loom even more.

"You are right. We cannot stand against your Dragons as we are now. But as Perfect Chimera we are even stronger than your Riders. We can be more complete than even you. We can have all magics, fly gliders, and use corona." Florence took another step forward, raising her gun once more at the giant of a man. She could see in her periphery his muscles twitch with rage. Was it too much to hope she could goad him enough? To cause him to release the glider, relinquish his corona, and lunge for her? Even if she died the most horrible death, someone would get the shot on his head.

"And there are a lot more of us, than there are of you," she continued. "We outnumber you. It's why you regulated our breeding, killed us off."

"Foolish Fenthri. You regulated your own breeding long before I did," he snarled. "I was saving you by regulating your ridiculous expenditure of resources."

"The Harvesters would have seen that soon enough." Florence had every faith as long as men like Powell were in the guild. Plus, it wasn't as if she could be proven wrong. No one could ever know what would have happened to Loom had the Dragons not intervened. "And then, when you caught wind of a Perfect Chimera, of the Philosopher's Box being made, you tried to steal her work and kill them all.

"But she survived." Florence pulled back the hammer of her gun. "And no matter how many times you try to kill her, you just can't seem to land the final blow." She spoke as loud as she could. She hoped everyone would hear her words. Because it was well possible that she was about to die. "That is the power of *one* Perfect Chimera. Now, what do you think will happen if you face an entire world of them? Perhaps you're right in wanting to talk peace, but you shouldn't be offering it—you should be asking us for it."

His mouth twitched, his snarl widened, and for one brief second Florence thought she had him.

But the Dragon King hadn't lorded over them for so long by being clumsy. He eased back on his glider, hands still firmly on the handles. "Shoot me, child. Let it be known to the world that it was your gun that heralded Loom's ultimate demise."

He was bluffing. He had to be. Florence locked her elbow to make sure her hand didn't shake. The revolver felt heavier than it ever had. *All I have to do is squeeze the trigger*, repeated over and over in her head like a mantra. It wound up strength that flowed into her forearm, then her hand, then her fingers.

She didn't know what she thought she would really accomplish. At the very least, she'd show everyone that she did not back down. That Fenthri no longer cowered before Dragons.

"Don't shoot, Florence."

All her focus was broken, and Florence whipped her head around to stare down Arianna.

"You offered us peace?" Arianna addressed the Dragon King.

"No . . ." Florence breathed. What was Arianna doing? Would she even think of handing over Loom to the Dragons?

"Take heed, Fen. Even the woman you deem 'perfect' wishes to talk before war." Florence felt the weight of Yveun's stare as he spoke. But her eyes were on Arianna. She didn't look anywhere else. "Yes, I offer you peace as long as you subject utterly to me."

"Give us three days to destroy our weapons and return to our respective guilds. When you return, you will see us ready to serve you."

This was *not* the Arianna Florence knew. Rage shot through her mind like a cannon ball.

"Very well. Let it be known that I am a most merciful god! You have three days. And should I not find all of you back where you belong, ready to serve, I will burn your world to the ground. I will give no quarter. You will all perish."

From behind, she heard the glider take to the sky again. Florence was aware the Dragon King had left as keenly as she was aware that she would forever regret not taking the shot, not trying everything possible to kill him at the one opportunity she may ever have.

Florence stared at the woman who had been her mentor, her role model, her friend . . . and saw someone she no longer recognized.

ARIANNA

er whole body felt heavy. Phantom pains ached in her joints at the mere sight of Yveun. Her mind echoed with the sounds of her flesh tearing under his claws, and howls of rage at the man she wanted dead more than she wanted to draw breath, more than she wanted to tinker and invent.

Arianna was too eager to turn away from the space the Dragon King had just occupied.

No one impeded her short progress back to the guild hall. Part of her wanted to collapse under the weight of all her memories, every misfortune in her life that the Dragon King had orchestrated. Part of her wanted to personally wait where she had just stood for three days until she could tear apart the Dragon King limb by limb.

If she even could . . .

Doubt tightened around her throat in the shape of Yveun's claws and Arianna didn't know how to dislodge it from her neck, where it was slowly suffocating her.

"Arianna!" Florence's voice was the only thing sharp enough to pierce the shell that encased the vortex of her thoughts.

She turned to see the girl sprinting toward her. Florence skidded and half-skipped to a stop. Her fist shot out, grabbing Arianna's coat, jerking her away from the staircase she'd been about to use for escape. It felt like being thrown back on a stage she had been trying to avoid for days.

"What in the five guilds was that?" Florence panted.

"Let me go, Flor." The machine of her mind was clanking loudly; too many wrenches had been thrown in it from different directions. Arianna couldn't be sure what the output would be if she continued to be pushed.

"No, not until you give me some explanation."

Arianna stared down at the girl who was holding her in place. In half a second, she could wrest herself free by breaking or severing Florence's arm in the process. But Arianna would never intentionally hurt Florence.

"Explanation of what?"

"Why did you tell me not to shoot? Why did you offer peace?" Florence shook her head. Arianna knew she wouldn't like the next words out of Florence's mouth by the look the girl gave her. "Whose side are you on?"

"I'd like to hear this answer as well." Gregory and two other vicars stood with a small but growing group who had made it in from the outside.

"I owe none of you an explanation." They were putting her under a dangerous amount of tension with their demands and their idiocy. "If you can't see the logic behind my actions, then none of you are fit to lead Loom."

When he spoke again, Gregory's voice was loud enough for all those assembled to hear. "How dare you. You've been nothing but unhelpful this entire time. If you're on our side, help us."

Arianna stared stubbornly back at him, her mouth pressed shut.

"As the Vicar Revolver, I want to know why you told a Revo not to take her mark."

Florence's eyes were torn away from Arianna at being called a Revolver by the vicar himself.

"Don't call her a Revolver when it suits you to do so," Arianna sneered. Her rage compounded. "That's low, even for you, Gregory."

"Excuse me?"

"Do you really want to have this conversation? I know the rumors about the shots you take in practice. The faulty canisters you'd claim were made by your colleagues." Arianna had carefully vetted Revolvers from the moment she knew Florence would need a teacher, and Gregory's name had come up as a master with some flexible perceptions of morality—especially when it came to Dragons. He'd been a little too flexible for Arianna's comfort then, and now.

"Lies . . ." the vicar whispered.

"Say it a bit stronger so maybe someone will believe you." Arianna shook her head at the sad little man. "If Florence had fired, it would've done nothing but provoke the king's wrath."

"Something we already had."

"And now we have something more: three days assured when we don't have to worry about a Dragon attack." Powell, ever the voice of reason. Arianna liked him more and more by the second. She used the distraction to jerk free of Florence's grasp. The girl didn't make a move to recover her. "We have a timeline for when our preparations need to be complete."

"'Ready' may be a generous word," Willard interjected. "Nothing can be made in three days with regards to the Philosopher's Box."

"Three days to plan, fortify." She'd have to spell it out, apparently.

"Fortify with what?" Gregory snapped back. "There are no weapons."

Arianna sighed at the lot of them acting like children.

"Let us resume the Tribunal," Florence announced suddenly. She looked around at the crowd that had filled the hall, journeymen and initiates watching the vicars bicker like children. Arianna took a step away and Florence caught her as she was about to turn. "You too."

Arianna was picking her battles, and she chose not to fight the girl on the matter.

Once more, the doors closed on the meeting hall. But the room was significantly less full. Only the vicars—who all stood—and a handful of masters clustered around the lowest floor. Arianna sat herself on the edge of one of the higher rows by the door, more than ready to make her escape at the first possible opportunity.

The vicars continued to squabble. Ethel withdrew from the conversation entirely, whispering to the other Alchemists. Willard tried to appeal to everyone's collective sense of logic; Dove preached action, backed up by Gregory until she refused to agree to let him train all Ravens with a weapon. Powell looked lost and frustrated every time he failed as a peacekeeper.

Arianna rested her elbow on her knee, her chin in her palm, watching the chaos unfold.

"None of this would be an issue if she—" Gregory threw a finger in her direction and with it reminded everyone else that she was still in the room "—had merely given us the schematics for the box from the beginning." Arianna wondered if his accusation was reason enough to kill him where he stood.

"How many times will you take that shot at me before you realize it's missing?" Arianna quipped.

Gregory's hand was at his gun. Let him fight her. She'd taken down Dragons twice his size and skill.

"Even if she had—" Willard started.

"Even if I had we would be in the same spot." Arianna spoke over the man who was well her senior in years and experience. But she had no remorse. She didn't want to be at the forefront, but if she was to be thrust there, then she would speak for herself. Gregory opened his mouth to speak, and she spoke over him as well. "If I had given you the schematics from the first day, it would have taken weeks to set up any kind of manufacturing to roll out on the scale we need. And that's ignoring the fact that a key component cannot even be found on our world. A problem that the Vicar Raven still has not solved."

The room had been effectively silenced, but Arianna didn't want to stop.

"This, this here, is the reason I have held the box for years. This is what I tried to caution you against." Arianna looked down on them all like the children they were. "From the first minute, it was all you focused on, to the neglect of other necessities." She gave a nod to Powell, who seemed surprised to be addressed directly. "The Philosopher's Box is powerful. I can't deny it. Likely more powerful than any of you realize. But the box is a *tool* that strengthens *people*. Loom can have all the power in the world, but if we are divided and squabbling, it will matter little as the Dragon King makes sport of our disorganization. Even a Perfect Chimera can be picked off with little issue by a trained Dragon. There has to be a system around making Perfect Chimera, training them to fight, giving them as many organs as possible. Systems we just don't have."

"She's right." Florence was finally on the same page, and the relief of it was like cool water on fiery flesh. "Here we are, proving her right. Vicar Willard, how long to set up some kind of manufacturing for the box?"

The vicar looked back to her, but Arianna stayed silent. If they wanted her input, they'd have to ask. "Well, Arianna said weeks, so I would estimate . . . two months? But only after we have the flowers. And only if we can use the remaining machinery in Ter.3."

"Vicar Dove, you have three weeks to figure out a secure way to get us flowers, and hopefully some stock."

"Three weeks?" the vicar balked at Florence. "I don't know—"

"I'm not asking you, I'm telling you." Florence silenced the vicar from further objection with a look that Arianna didn't know she could make.

"Vicar Gregory, are there *any* weapons left?" That was the moment Florence's voice softened and the whole atmosphere of the room with it. It would take some time before the mere mention of the Revolvers' Guild would not fill every man and woman on Loom with pangs of loss and sorrow.

"No. Not beyond what every Revolver carries on their person or had stashed in some alternative location." Even the vicar lost some of his anger in reporting the fact. "Not unless there were any in transit through the Ravens' routes?"

"It's possible. There'd be a record at the guild hall."

A record. Speaking of, she needed to get the copy of Louie's ledger to Florence.

"Good, we're all headed there anyway." Florence continued in the wake of everyone's surprise. "The king expects to find us here. He knows all of Loom has assembled. I have no doubt that when he comes back, he will do so with force, ready to attack the instant he finds us noncompliant."

"So, we move." Willard finally sat, a hand on his knees as he eased himself down.

"We take Loom underground."

"Underground?" Vicar Dove repeated. "Florence, you cannot possibly mean . . ."

"The Dragons are a threat to us as long as they can use their gliders. If they cannot do that, our bullets can reach them."

Arianna thought back to Leona's glider crashing into the entry to the Underground they had escaped into months ago. It was solid logic grounded in proof, even if no one else knew it.

"That's assuming the Dragons even know the entry point . . ." Vicar Dove murmured.

"The Ravens' Folly? You can't possibly expect us to go there." Willard wiped sweat from the back of his neck.

"I don't expect *you* to. You will go down to Ter.3 and begin to set up manufacturing for the box. It will be faster to use whatever remains at the Rivets' Guild than start from scratch. And we can use the existing train lines for transport. They should mostly be intact."

"Alchemists will be the first to go." Vicar Ethel turned away from the masters she had been whispering with. "Train us to implant the box, and we can complete the organs for each Chimera, should we have enough of a farm to harvest from."

"Can you harvest from Perfect Chimera?" Vicar Powell asked.

Arianna grimaced at the idea but answered anyway. "You can. My organs regrow as a Dragon's would."

"That's convenient." Vicars Ethel and Powell said at nearly the same time. Arianna was no longer going to allow herself to be in a room alone with either of them.

"Who are you to order us?" Vicar Gregory's tone had lost some bite, but the question was still pointed enough.

"Do you have a better idea?" Florence held out her hands, as if to receive some great insight from the vicar. "If so, I'd love to hear it."

Gregory looked to the other vicars and masters. None came to his defense. "It will be easier to fortify the Underground with less," Gregory finally murmured. "Even if we'll be fighting on two flanks. Don't know what I want to tangle with less . . . whatever could come from above, or below."

The other vicars voiced their agreement, each one deferring to Florence. Arianna leaned forward again, inspecting the woman who stood in the center of the room. There it was, that same aura she'd sensed before—the one that showed the shaking girl she'd pulled from the Underground was no more.

And if that role was no longer needed in Florence's life, what did that make them?

As if sensing her stare, and thoughts, Florence turned. They shared a long look full of questions that neither of them could answer.

"You will head to Ter.3 with Vicar Willard."

Arianna knew it was coming because it was logical, and because logic could be used more effectively than the sharpest dagger. She wanted to object, to tell Florence that under no circumstances was she going to let the girl out of her sight again. She had gone to the world above and fell back to Loom below just for Florence.

"Go home, and make sure you know whose side you're on." Florence turned her back to Arianna and focused on the vicars once more. "We begin now. There's no time to waste."

None spoke for her and none objected. Arianna didn't really expect them to. One of them saw her as a weapon foremost, another a traitor, and now two more saw her as their new harvesting experiment.

Arianna stood and excused herself without a word. She wondered if she was the only one who had just witnessed the true leader of the rebellion rise.

COLETTA

The Gray Room was progressing nicely. Coletta ran her hand along the back shelf, where all manner of wicked-looking tools had been laid out in careful order. A knife was one of the most beautiful creations that had ever come from a forge. It could kill, it could save—it was both famine and feast. She picked up the item, inspecting it by the firelight of one of the two braziers.

"Will all this do?" she finally asked, turning to the man who stood next to Ulia.

"It should be enough, yes." The Fenthri, Thomas, blended in with the room around him—rock-colored and bland.

"What else will you need to conduct the surgery?"

The man brought his eyes upward from their respectful downward cast. He took one more long look at the shelf in quiet thought. "Nothing more comes to mind. But again, I've never done this before."

"So you repeat to the point of disgust." If she didn't desperately need this little man, she would do away with him on the spot. Coletta had only interacted with him a handful of times, but it was already too many.

"I want my queen to be aware that it is possible there will be failures before we see success," he said. Coletta could appreciate one thing about the Fenthri: Their logical minds didn't allow things like emotions to cloud their resolve, usually. Thomas didn't so much as blink when he said the word "failures," when what he really meant was "deaths."

"*You* will not see success," Coletta said softly. "Any success is mine."

"Forgive me for speaking out of turn, my queen." Gold glinted threateningly from around the man's neck, but the collar was tempered to Yveun, not her. Nevertheless, Coletta could kill him in a second if she so desired. "I merely do not wish to disappoint you."

"Well, that is wise. You shall have some room for trial and error." Coletta set the knife down. She didn't want to give him that leeway, but even she could recognize it was unreasonable to expect otherwise.

The Alchemist Coletta had brought from Loom years ago was, indeed, deceased. Topann had done well, finding a suitable substitute. He was older, but his black hair was only sprinkled with salt, rather than completely white. Thomas was old enough, however, to be born before the segregation of guilds, and he had spent time in his early years studying with the intent to become an Alchemist. When that no longer interested him, he'd switched to the Rivets. Between his knowledge and the information Coletta could acquire through her contact on Loom, she had faith that their research would yield fruit. How hard could it really be to stitch up some organs in a Dragon? There was no need to worry about decay, and they had ample power to heal.

"When will we begin?"

Coletta eyed the man. The question was awfully bold, almost bold enough for her to give him a warning shot. But she permitted it because she believed it mere curiosity rather than an indication of the false notion he could schedule his own timetable of events.

"Soon." Coletta waved him and her flower away. "Ulia, take him to his room."

"My room?" Thomas repeated, looking between them.

"Yes, I have prepared a room for you." Coletta enjoyed the look of shock on his face.

"M-my own room?"

"Indeed. Ulia will show you there."

His mouth gaped open and he looked between them many times over, as if waiting for one of them to correct the statement and inform him that he wasn't getting his own quarters after all and it was back to the squalor he had known his whole life.

"Of course, my queen." Ulia bowed and escorted the man. Coletta's flower avoided touching him, for which Coletta didn't blame her.

The Fenthri were dirty, rotten creatures that smelled and looked of death. Plus, if he tried to run, any Dragon would be twice as fast and kill him three times more horribly than he could ever imagine. By working with them, he now had his own room away from the cramped quarters Nova's Fenthri were confined within. Any Dragon would look at his accommodations and think them barbaric, but after spending most of his life in the darkness of the Fen barracks, Coletta suspected Thomas would find them palatial.

With her business concluded, Coletta started back through the estate to her gardens. She looked out the windows as she passed them, her eyes scanning the skies for traces of rainbow.

Yveun had left early that morning and now the sun was halfway through the sky with still no sign of him.

Coletta didn't want to think of the Fenthri as being able to slay her mate. But with numbers alone, they had him. One mistake, and that would be the end of it.

The garden was catharsis. Her flowers and their many concoctions kept her hands busy through the afternoon and into the evening, when the sun hung low and the sky began to fade into Lord Xin's hour of death. Coletta knew the moment the gliders approached, rainbows arcing through the air with a flash of brilliance.

She finished her careful slices of the plant bulb and wiped her hands on the appropriate rag—one of four set out. Her laboratory was such a dangerous place that even a gesture as small as this, done carelessly, could cause a reaction that might kill her. One of the many reasons why she had been so diligent over the years with poisoning herself and building her immunities.

Coletta tapped on a golden panel embedded in the wall that made up one side of her outdoor laboratory. Not so far away, a discharge point flashed; soon enough, Yeaan appeared on command.

"You summoned?" She gave a deep bow.

"Yes. The Dono has only just returned. Tell the chefs to stop preparing dinner for him. He will need his space before he is ready to eat. They should resume when all light has left the sky. It is possible he will insist he is not hungry. Should he do so, I would like for you to deliver the food personally and inform him it's at my request."

"Understood." Yeaan turned on her heel, quickly departing to execute Coletta's orders.

Yveun would no doubt go to his tiny claw-scratched room and pace for a while. He would act the child and refuse food, thinking this a reasonable way to avoid his failures. She would give him space, and a peace offering, to show that they still stood together, even if his effort to bring Loom neatly under their rule did not go as well as he'd planned.

Coletta continued to clean and tuck away her laboratory. Everything had its place, and everything stayed in pristine order. Success wasn't found in mayhem, but a strict maintenance of structure.

She looked up expectantly, her ears picking up the click of the door that led to Yveun's quarters and the main part of the Rok Estate. Sure enough, Topann appeared from around the corner. Coletta quickly assessed her from head to toe, her eyes falling on the small bound book in the woman's hands.

"Yveun?" she asked first.

"The Dono is well," Topann reported. "In a less-than-pleasurable mood. But there were no shots fired."

"And Loom?"

"He gave them three days to decide if they will agree to peace, or if it will be war, at which point he will wage his first attack."

Coletta sighed. Yveun was growing distracted by daydreams of fanfare and an arrival on Loom met with love, where they cherished him for all his contributions to their industrial world. He didn't just want to be the king in function; he wanted to be it in form as well. He wanted the same affection and devotion that he enjoyed on Nova, which, simply, he would never find from an oppressed people.

"Then it shall be war." She had no doubt.

Loom would fight until the only ones left of their abysmal race were chained in gold and kept in perfect servitude to

Dragons who guided them with a firm hand. It's how it should have been done from the start, but there wasn't enough space on Nova for all the Fen. The best solution would be for the Dragons to colonize Loom and manage those that remained. But finding Dragons willing to live on Loom may be just as hard as squelching the spirit of rebellion.

Coletta let go of the thoughts, for now. That was all planning, which needed to occur later, when Loom was once more under their thumb. Now, she needed to remain focused on getting matters firmly in hand.

"Is that from our Fen King?" Coletta held out her hand for the journal.

"It is, but it's . . . odd." Topann's voice was hesitant, but she wasted no time imparting the journal to her queen. Coletta knew exactly what her flower meant from the moment she opened to a page at random. "The little man said it was Raven code. Can you read it?"

She couldn't. Coletta had many areas of expertise, but every manner of language from the Fen was not one of them. She snapped the ledger closed.

"What other information did you get from him?"

"The rebellion is being led by a child named Florence," Topann began. Coletta knew that Loom was in a dire state, but it must be truly on its final threads if they were appointing children as their leaders. "A very petulant girl. She brandished a weapon at the Dono himself."

"Did she?" If the name hadn't been imprinted on her mind previously, it was now. Coletta wanted the satisfaction of orchestrating the girl's ultimate demise herself.

"As I said, the Dono is fine. He did not step off his glider, so his corona protected him the whole time."

But the girl no doubt wanted him to. Knowing Yveun, the Fen's affront had made his kingly blood boil so hot that he was tempted to do so to wring her neck. She could not afford to let Yveun off Nova again, Coletta decided then.

"And Arianna?"

"She was there, but did little." Topann thought a moment. "I heard the Riders say she actually called off Florence."

"Interesting . . ." Perhaps the fall back to Loom had knocked the inventor down in more ways than one.

"The king says weapons are scarce since the Revolvers blew themselves up, but I'm not inclined to believe him."

Coletta wasn't either. *After all* . . . She opened the ledger again. Even if she couldn't understand it, the ledger was a record of where gold was being kept on Loom, moved from secret storehouse to storehouse. If Loom had squirreled away gold, Coletta was certain they'd done the same with weapons, and that meant Yveun should brace himself for a greater attack than anticipated.

"There was one more thing." Topann summoned Coletta's thoughts back from the ledger. "The Fen King was grateful for the organs you provided in exchange for the ledger. But he mentioned something new he would be negotiating for: Flowers of Agendi."

Coletta paused, closing the ledger and setting it aside. Her mind pegged the information as important instantly. It was oddly specific and necessary enough to risk the request. The flowers grew only on Nova, and Coletta didn't think it chance that the man who had only dealt in organs for years was suddenly asking for something new mere weeks after Arianna had returned from the sky world.

"Why these flowers?" They had no medicinal properties and no poisons—that she knew of. They weren't even especially beautiful. Some Dragons held that their pollen made their magic feel stronger. But surely that wouldn't be enough to help Chimeras stand against Dragons?

"He didn't say." Topann bowed her head. "Forgive me, my lady, the gliders were leaving and I had to be subtle."

"Rise, Topann." Coletta extended her hand and the woman scooped it up, kissing it firmly, no doubt grateful to still be in her queen's favor. "You have done well to acquire this information. Now we must act upon it."

Coletta looked out over the leafy foliage that surrounded her outdoor laboratory. "I have none of this particular flower. Head to the fields on the north side of the estate where they grow, and bring me ten."

"Ten, yes."

"Then, when you have done this, I need you and Yeaan to collect all offshoots of our great vine." Coletta herself was the "great vine" and every offshoot was where a tendril crept in the form of one of her flowers. "You will find everywhere this flower grows, and you will destroy them all."

"How would you like them destroyed?" Coletta appreciated so very much that such was the woman's only question.

"Uproot them, and take them to some remote place to burn. Do it with as much discretion as you can muster."

"Always, my queen."

"One more thing, Topann." Coletta thought aloud. "Have them bring wine to my chambers this night. No food. I trust you to pick a worthwhile vintage on my behalf."

"Understood."

"Go now, make it so."

By the time Coletta finished cleaning up her laboratory, the wine was waiting for her on a bronze platter in the central room of her quarters. None dared go beyond that point. For if they did, it was well whispered that they weren't long for service to House Rok—or the world.

Coletta picked up the glass, strolling into her study. The room was rectangular with towers of bookshelves filled with all manner of odd knowledge she'd acquired throughout the years. Some volumes were rare, some commonplace, and some would only be important to the authors whose hands had scribbled the words, believing they would never be read.

At the far end, past a chaise and table with a single chair, was a large desk that matched a second in Yveun's side of the estate. Coletta set the ledger down there, but kept wine in hand as she walked over to the wall of windows. Far beneath her, the God's Line was a swirling sea of gray, masking Loom and all its secrets.

She took a long sip, allowing the crimson nectar to sit on her tongue—one of the few things she could still taste. She debated if she would crack this Raven code, or learn all about the Flowers of Agendi first. Coletta turned back into the room with purpose, heading toward her books on plants and herbology. It didn't matter where she started; it would all be torn apart, secrets exposed, by the time she was done.

FLORENCE

I t seemed as though she had just managed to gather everyone
together, only to see them scattered to the wind once more.
At least everyone was moving as a unified force rather than
blowing in, one rogue tumbleweed at a time.

Her goal for the Tribunal had been accomplished.

Even still, it was exhausting to take all of Loom—who
had only just been transported en masse to Ter.0—and move
them again. The Vicar Raven was no doubt no more annoyed
than she let on about the great exodus, but if the woman was
disgruntled, she did a good job of not betraying the fact.

"Are you really going to stay here?" Shannra asked.

"Only as long as it takes to clear Ter.0," Florence replied.

She was so very tired of cleaning out her laboratories, one
after the other. But having done it multiple times in her life
made it pretty short work. The experience equipped her to
make simple decisions on what was most important to take
with her, and what could be left behind, if needed. It was simple
logic where everything went, and Florence knew it all by heart
by now. Every canister, vial, gun part, and jar went in its place
easily.

"I'll wait for you."

"No, you won't." Florence didn't know if it was Louie's influence on the girl, or if she genuinely wanted to stay. It was a question she was unexpectedly afraid of asking—or rather, she feared the answer. "I need you to help organize defenses at the Ravens' Guild."

"There are plenty of people who can help organize defenses. I want to protect you."

"There are not plenty of people, and in fact there are precious few Revos left. Furthermore, I can protect myself. Despite the tattoo on my cheek, I am no Raven."

"I know that better than anyone, but it doesn't mean you couldn't use someone's help."

"The Dragons won't attack for three days. By that point I will be long on my way to Ter.4. I'll be nothing more than a speck on the map; no Dragon will find me and no Fenthri would attack me." Florence was fairly confident that at this point she had solidified her reputation as one of the deadliest people on all of Loom. How many others could challenge the Dragon King himself at gunpoint? Of course, that was a decision Florence had yet to fully unpack now that the initial fight-or-flight response had left her. Her hands had a tremble since the Vicar Tribunal.

"Florence, why won't you let me help you?" Shannra rounded the table. She rested a gentle hand on Florence's shoulder.

She moved away subtly from the offending touch, using the opportunity to stretch for a high jar and shake Shannra's hand free. But her distractions were growing limited, and soon she would be forced to focus on the other woman in the room.

"Do *you* want to help me? Or do you want to help me because Louie asked you to?" Well, there it was. The question was out and there was no taking it back.

"What kind of question is that?" Shannra almost seemed offended. She walked around the table to position herself between Florence and a narrow set of shelves she had been clearing. "Do you think I have been at your side this whole time because of Louie?"

Florence thought about it for a long moment. Was this woman nothing more than a pawn in the greater scheme? And if she was, why did it matter to Florence? "Have you not been?"

"Five Guilds! That's all you think of me, isn't it?" She seemed torn between laughter and anger. It was a combination that fit her. Light and dark. Happiness and sorrow. Anger and joy. Shannra was all of it wrapped into one.

"I don't know what to think of you," Florence answered honestly, at last looking her in the eye.

"Florence." The woman's whole demeanor changed. "Yes, Louie asked me to come here. I told you that from the beginning. I've never kept my affiliation with him a secret." Shannra shook her head. "And I have no doubt that he asked me specifically because he knew I could be of help to you, because he knew you would want to learn from me. But Louie has been here for weeks now, and I spend more time at your side than with him or any of his other . . . employees. It doesn't matter how I came to you; it matters what we do going forward."

She wanted to believe it was all true. Shannra's silver eyes shone brightly in the fading light of the day. Florence wanted to believe they hid no secrets, that there was nothing within them that could even be the seed of a lie. But she wasn't sure— couldn't be sure, maybe ever.

Still, arguing with the woman would do her no good. If her suspicions were founded, Shannra would never admit to them. If they were unfounded, she only risked alienating a friend.

Was it better to risk having a false companion than having no companion at all?

"Even still." Florence sighed softly and let go of the argument. Her focus had to be on other places, her energy devoted to more important things than unpacking the true depths of her feelings for the silvery beauty. "You are far more useful to me getting a head start on fortifying the Ravens' Guild and the Underground than offering protection I won't use and don't actually need. I will not be long behind you; all of Ter.0 will be on the move in two days' time and I will be out with the last of them. All this is for only a day's difference."

It seemed like Shannra was going to put up one more fight, and Florence braced herself for whatever the argument may be. The truth was, neither of them owed the other anything.

"Do me one favor." Shannra paused and reached for Florence a second time. This time, she didn't move away. "Okay, *two* favors . . . One, don't store this powder on the edge of the box. Rattle it too much and it could go."

"Really? But I thought that was why we cut it with sulfur?"

"We did. We cut it enough to prevent it from being a danger when mixed with other chemicals for canisters. But the whole thing in a jar? It's a rather pointless risk." Shannra took the jar and nestled it between some of the others toward the center of the box. For good measure, she even wedged in some leftover rags around the various vessels.

"Okay, and this other favor?"

"Seek me out when you arrive at Ter.4?" Shannra gave a small, delicate smile.

If she was being honest with herself, Florence had planned to do so immediately anyway. "I think I can manage that."

"I'll take this ahead for you." Shannra started for the door with the box still in her arms, speaking over her shoulder, "Think of it as collateral, to make sure you come looking for me."

"Collateral? It looks a lot like theft." Florence leaned against the table.

"Well, as you so aptly pointed out, I *am* on Louie's payroll. Who really knows when I may decide to just up and steal something?" Shannra gave a small wink and left the room with a satisfied swing of her hips.

It was one odd relationship to the next.

The halls were washed in shadows, and every footstep she took toward Arianna's room was elongated by a quiet echo. All the chaos was happening downstairs, people uprooting themselves from what fragile peace they had managed to scrape together in a few days since everyone had amassed at Ter.0. But up here, there was only silence—silence and Florence's thoughts.

She wondered if she should feel guilty for how she had treated Arianna.

Because she didn't.

Florence wanted answers. The uncertain world that surrounded her owed her nothing. She feared that if she did not take the chances that presented themselves, as they presented themselves, they would be forever lost. All of life's events, loaded into the chamber of a gun, and it all came down to having the courage to squeeze the trigger before the shot was lost. She would not lose this opportunity to speak with her mentor one more time. She would not be relegated to silence, like when Arianna had up and left for Nova, giving Florence no other choice but to swallow her curiosity and hope not to choke on it.

But Arianna was not in her room, leaving Florence to wander the tower in search of her wayward mentor.

As expected, Florence eventually found Arianna in the remnants of one of the Rivets' workshops. Unlike her own workshop, this one was filled to the brim, all manner of gears and tools lining the walls. The tang of metal was sharp on her nose, cut with the warmer scents of grease and oil.

Arianna looked up promptly when she arrived, her Dragon ears no doubt anticipating her arrival for some time now, which explained the lack of surprise on her mentor's face.

Florence leaned in the door frame, folded her arms over her chest, and waited. Arianna stared back, and neither said anything. Time stretched on and, as much as Florence didn't want to be the first one to speak, she wanted to waste her time a lot less.

"Ari, we should talk," she said with a sigh.

"Do you really think I am not loyal to Loom?"

Another sigh. "No. May I come in?"

Arianna motioned to the stool across from her and Florence accepted it. She didn't touch any of the various tools and parts scattered across the table, keeping her hands folded in her lap instead.

"Why did you tell me not to shoot?"

"You know the answer to that."

"I want to hear it," Florence demanded.

"There will be people, at times, you cannot demand answers from." Arianna was hesitant, but acquiesced to her demand anyway. "Because a shot would've done nothing against his corona."

"You don't think I know that? I was trying to coerce him off the glider. If I had, with that many guns on him, we could've taken him down and then . . ."

"Then what?" Arianna pressed when Florence's thought trailed off. "Then we would win? The war is ended before it begins? Freedom reigns on Loom and we celebrate?" Arianna put her gearbox down, which was open to reveal the guts within. "No, Flor. I told you about the Dragon houses when I first arrived. If you had killed the king, there is another who would inherit his throne. And if you killed her, there is another after that. And another, and another . . . All of Dragon society is based around the idea of someone always being in power. One man or one woman always being on top. It's a pyramid you can't topple."

The words were a bitter potion of truth and they turned Florence's thoughts sour. "Then what are we supposed to do? Roll over and accept them as our masters and oppressors?"

"We must work with them."

Florence's stomach churned at the idea, but she forced herself to think logically. She'd been rash since the moment she'd seen the king. Calmed now, she could see that it was Arianna's composure that had kept things from splintering too soon, that had given them time to organize and flee. Again, it came down to Arianna; she still had much to learn from the snow-haired woman.

"You mean Cvareh and his sister?"

Arianna nodded. "His family, the Xin, is fighting against the Dragon King as best they can. But like Loom, they aren't strong enough."

"Why?" Florence wasn't keen yet on the idea of allying with another faction getting crushed by the king. They needed strength.

"There are three Dragon families," Arianna began, and Florence settled into her stool, listening intently. Everything Arianna said sounded vaguely familiar, but Florence listened as though she was hearing for the first time. "Tam, Rok, and

Xin. Rok has remained the leader for hundreds—thousands—of years. Tam seems to be in the middle, their mantra favoring balance over upset. So, as long as the Rok family doesn't do anything too heinous, they work to maintain the status quo and do little else."

Florence instantly knew she would not get along with a Tam Dragon. "And Xin?"

"Houses Xin and Rok seem to be constantly fighting over who will be on top. With Tam de facto in the middle, one of them is always in power with the other in the weakest position on Nova."

"The weakest position? Poor things," Florence remarked sarcastically.

"None of them really see us as anything worth fighting over," Arianna admitted.

"So why would we ally with them?" Cvareh had seemed good enough, but if his family didn't see the value in Loom, then she would no longer see the value in him . . . even if it was his blood in her veins.

"Because they *don't* care about us. Cvareh's sister, and the leader of House Xin, only cares about ruling over Nova. If we help her get to that point—"

"Then she'll let Loom be free?"

"Killing the Dragon King means nothing. It's like severing a Dragon's hand. It *will* grow back time and time again. Not only must we sever the hand, but we must replace it with something that suits us better. Only then will Loom be truly free."

Florence let the information soak in. She took off her top hat, brushed off dust that had settled on the brim while she was cleaning out her laboratory, and returned it to her head. "If everything you say is true . . . we must work with House Xin."

Arianna was quiet, prompting Florence's attention. The woman had that same faraway look.

"Ari, what happened up there? The Dragon King knew you by name." She tried to be gentle, but it was a topic as sharp as a scalpel. "Why?"

Still, Ari was silent.

"How did you crash-land with a glider in Dortam?" Florence pushed a little harder.

Nothing.

"Arianna, please, I need to know." *Why?* Why did she need to know so badly? Why did it keep her up at night and draw her patience thin to think Arianna was keeping yet another secret?

"Yveun captured me. I escaped on a glider. I crashed."

It was the most unsatisfying explanation ever. "Yveun, the Dragon King, captured you?"

Arianna picked up her gearbox again. Florence was on her feet, reaching across the table to put her hand between Arianna's tool and the box. The woman brought her violet eyes to Florence's.

"Why didn't you fight?"

"You don't think I did?" Arianna scowled. "You don't think that, succession be damned, I wouldn't have killed him if given the chance?"

"What did he do to you?" she whispered.

"He made me weak." Arianna cursed, throwing down her tool. It was a fit of passion Florence had never seen from the usually reserved woman. "He made me feel weak, and vulnerable, and helpless. *Again.* Again, I could not stand against him or his agents to defend what and who I love." Arianna looked back to Florence; for the first time ever, her eyes beseeched her student for answers. Answers that no one had. "I am loyal to Loom and our fight with every breath I have. I am loyal to *you,* Flor. But no matter how hard I try, I cannot kill him. If I face him again, I will fall. I fear I will take Loom down with me."

Florence felt a dull ache of sympathy for the woman who clearly harbored so much pain and self-loathing. Slowly, as though she was trying not to startle a wounded animal, Florence stood. She rounded the table and reached to clasp one of Arianna's tall shoulders. Under her fingers, she knew there was a tattoo, a mark signifying the day they'd met, and a bond that would exist no matter what paths they traveled.

"You do not have to strike him down, Arianna. Go to Ter.3. Go home and realize that your strength has not left you. And when you see the truth of that, as I do, give me the greatest canister this world has ever known. Give me the Perfect Chimera, and I will hone it as a weapon to deal the final blow."

Arianna's hand clasped Florence's opposite shoulder.

"And give me House Xin to see that this chain of succession the Dragons so value puts someone we want on their throne," Florence continued. How could Arianna think she needed to have the strength to vanquish their foe when she was already the lynchpin holding the entire fate of Loom in place? The woman who wanted nothing more than to sit locked away in a workshop had saved them time and again. "Load the gun, Arianna, and then rest. I'll pull the trigger."

Florence saw hesitation in the woman's eyes, or maybe it was nostalgia. But it hardened like molten steel into a resolve that would hopefully last long enough for them to abolish the scourge of Dragons that plagued Loom once and for all.

"I will, Flor. I will do this one final act of rebellion, for you."

Florence knew the most important thing was that Arianna had agreed to do what they needed. Which made it all the more confusing that her heart clenched at the notion she was doing it all for her alone.

ARIANNA

rianna leaned back against the upper deck windows on Louie's airship. Checking the magic discharge was unnecessary now, but it gave her an excuse to be away from everyone. Up here, there was nothing more than a gray sky, the wind, and the earth slowly changing below.

The last time Arianna had traveled this route, it had been by train. She had sat next to Master Oliver, pressed up against the window of the train car, watching Loom unfold before her in a way it never had before. She had pressed forward, hungry for the vast unknown the world seemed to offer.

But this time was different. This time she watched the spiraling trails of magic fade away into the dusky morning over the back of the airship. The world wasn't unfolding before her but collapsing in her wake; it slipped away like a ribbon running wild, and the spool was nearly out.

She knew her body had changed from becoming a Perfect Chimera at such a young age. It was obvious before any others had pointed it out. She could run faster, endure more injuries; her bones were thicker and her height dwarfed most Fenthri. After being on Nova, she knew she was built more like a Dragon than one of her own gray-skinned race.

Arianna looked at the line that ran around her wrist where the soft blue skin of her hands met her natural, steel-colored flesh. These hands had tried to dismantle her world. She would use those same hands to be that man's downfall—to annihilate all who sought to oppress Loom.

The door to the deck opened.

"Am I taking your spot?" Will asked, from where he hovered on the threshold.

"Yes." Arianna turned her eyes forward, pointedly ignoring the child.

"Sorry about that." He clearly wasn't sorry, and sat down next to her. Will drew his heavy coat tighter around him, pulling up the collar to shield his face from the wind that whipped around them. "How are you not freezing to death out here?"

"If it's too cold for you, perhaps you should return indoors?"

"I just may."

Victory, Arianna thought.

"I'll wait just long enough to lose him." Will peered over the window ledge and looking into the upper deckhouse before ducking down again.

"Okay, I'll bite." Wasn't as if she had anything else to do. "Lose who?"

"Vicar Willard. The old man just won't shut up about how to make the engine run more efficiently."

Arianna laughed. "Oh, to be young and stupid—"

"Hey!"

"—and not capitalize on the opportunity to learn from a vicar." Arianna adjusted her goggles. Granted, she had some mixed feelings about Vicar Willard, but she was allowed—they had history.

"At first I did." Will was instantly defensive. "But he corrected *everything*."

"That's because everything in this rig is wrong."

"No, it's not. It runs just fine, thank you," the boy insisted.

"It could be better and you know it." He made it too easy for her to push right on his soft spots. "You've been away from the Ravens' Guild proper for a while. Getting sloppy, Will."

"Sloppy? You're one to talk." Will breathed on his hands, looking out at the magic discharge. "Thought you were supposed to be some great White Wraith, master thief, super sneaky."

Arianna arched her eyebrows, not even dignifying him with a response.

"I overheard you and Florence. I know what you gave her."

"I don't know what you're talking about." Arianna looked him in the eye, challenging him to call her on her bluff.

To her frustration, he did. "Sure. Well, then I heard *some other* Arianna through a crack in a wall talking to *some other* Florence about *some other* copy of a ledger she made of something she stole in Ter.3 before leaving the five-tiered hall."

"You were sent to spy on me?" Arianna mentally cursed herself for not inspecting more carefully the rooms surrounding her laboratory.

"Louie likes to know what's going on."

"That he does," she agreed, training her expression to be void of emotion. "Too bad any reports he gets would be from a bored Raven with an overactive imagination."

"Be careful, Ari. I wasn't the first and won't be the last."

"The irony of you telling me that." She'd been in dangerous situations longer than he'd been alive.

"Fine, ignore me." Will shrugged. "Just saying that if it had been anyone else in Louie's crew, you would've been outed."

"*Anyone* else? Including Helen?" Arianna wondered if she was hearing between his words correctly.

"Helen has her eyes on inheriting all of Louie's operations. She'll do anything to suck up to him." Will had the tone of a friend who'd been chapped by some rather cold treatment.

"Why are you telling me this?" Helen and Will were a matched set. In no world could she imagine Will doing anything that would separate them.

"Because when she *does* inherit Louie's kingdom, we'll need a champion. I hear he has a pretty good one he's been working with. Don't want to see Helen burn any bridges we may need to drive over."

Arianna snorted with laughter at the idea of taking orders from either of the children. But still, fair was fair. The warning he gave her was valuable, almost adult-like, and she appreciated it. "Play your cards right, and maybe you'll be so lucky. If you can pay."

"The business is pretty lucrative." Will glanced through the window into the deck cabin.

"Have you heard anything else?" Arianna asked when they both confirmed no one was observing their clandestine meeting.

"Anything else?"

She didn't know if he was being coy, or just stupid. "Why did Louie want the ledger in the first place?"

Will's mouth turned into a frown. "I don't really know. But I know he speaks to someone on Nova with the red-eared one, Adam."

Red ears. Arianna's instincts went off again as they had the first time, apprehensive at anything that resembled Rok.

"Do you know who?"

"That's all I know . . . for now."

"For now?"

"Like I said, I want to work with you." Will shrugged again. Arianna didn't know what she'd done to endear herself to the boy, but she wasn't going to challenge it. The fact that he hadn't gone to Louie—or at least claimed he hadn't—was good faith enough. "Except, can we please do this in the future where it's not freezing? I think I'll brave the vicar and his corrections over losing my fingers."

"It's not that cold."

"Ari, my fingers are turning blue."

Before she could even comment on where, when, why, or how he thought it was acceptable to refer to her as "Ari," Will had pulled open the heavy door to the top-deck cabin and disappeared within. She looked back down at her own hands and realized she wouldn't be able to tell if her fingers turned blue.

Even out of his element, Louie could still be a problem . . . She needed to tread carefully and learn what game he was really playing.

It was, in total, a two-day ride from Ter.0 to Ter.3, thanks to Arianna's contributions with magic, Will and Willard working together on improving the engine, and Helen's keen insights on charting their course.

Thick palm fronds branched out overtop each other. Stronger trees that preferred dryer climates quickly disappeared as the land became more marshy and wet. The bogs in the forests to the south of Garre held dark waters, caged by tree roots.

Garre itself was known as the clockwork city.

Tethered by her cabling and winch box to the heavy door behind her, Arianna crouched atop the cabin roof for the best vantage the airship could offer. She dug her knees and fingers into the metal grooves for stability, but the wind threatened to rip her away. The city of her childhood grew from a speck in the distance to the towering mechanical marvel that rivaled any in the world.

The capital of the Rivets was entirely the guild hall. There were no other elements to the city itself; there were no visitors without specific business for the Rivets.

Even late in the year, humidity crept beneath her coat and made her hair cling to her neck. It was an omnipresent citizen of Garre, rising up from the marshes under the city's stilts. A mechanical haven built atop water, destined to fight an endless war against rust and corrosion. It was the worst place possible for the Rivets to have attempted to build, and it was all the more perfect for the fact.

The airship banked and began its descent.

Closer up, the movements of the guild could be seen. Slowly rotating upper walkways ticked around cores like odd-faced clocks, counting down to something unknown. Steam billowed in jets, piped from the depths of the all-metal guild hall. Giant gears showed their teeth proudly on the outside of walls, perpetually churning against equally sized counterparts within.

Arianna had never seen her guild from the air before, and it was quite the sight. There was an undeniably breathtaking quality to its spectrum of metallic colors and carefully constructed pathways and structures that formed one tight, singular city. A city that changed before her own eyes on their descent, as walkways moved with the groaning of gears and various windows and doorways opened and closed.

It was also a vantage by which she could clearly see the remnants of the Dragons' attack—wounds that could not be healed with the limited hands available. An entire wing seemed to have been hit hard, the metal jagged and oddly bent, pulled apart by blasts that Arianna could still imagine the echoes of.

The whole of Garre was spotted with such damages, but it persisted.

The airship looped three times before finally finding a landing that would fit their wingspan. As soon as they touched down, Arianna leapt from the roof, tumbling into the metal below with a clang. She sprinted for the doorway into the guild.

Locked.

This was not like the usual locks she faced. She was back in the Rivets' Guild. Here, everything was designed as a challenge—a mental puzzle where success often hung opposite bodily harm. Right now, she suspected that harm took the form of a collapsing platform beneath their feet if she couldn't open the door in time.

Arianna ran her fingers along the lock. There were a series of pictures and numerals on its spinners. She could either solve the puzzle, or break her way in. The Arianna of the past would have delighted in the former . . .

But she was too old for games.

Arianna unclipped and unrolled a bag of tools from her belt, quickly selecting a narrow, flat-headed screwdriver. Fortunately for her . . . the designer of this particular lock expected her to revel in solving the puzzle, not dismantling the thing entirely. Its seams were well exposed and screws easy to access. Arianna had the box apart in a mere minute, manually unlatching the heavy curved bolt that affixed the lock to the door.

The room within crackled with electricity. Arianna could hear it humming in the wires that draped from the ceiling like moss off swamp trees. She flipped a switch next to her, funneling that energy into a bulb in the center of the room. Arianna blinked at the light. The last time she had been at the guild, electricity was new and only in a few areas.

She looked around the room, finding a series of levers on one of the side walls, nestled between two bookcases.

"Lock, raise, release . . ." She read the labels scribbled on each of the handles. Arianna tugged on the one labeled *lock*. The release lever raised slightly in reply, a soft click engaging it in place.

"You're much faster than I," a weathered voice spoke from the doorway.

"I should be." Arianna turned to face Willard, rolling up her tools. "You have a good fifteen years on me, old man."

"You're back in the hall; you'd think you'd show a little more respect to your vicar."

"Just honoring what would've been the wishes of my Master." Arianna couldn't fight a small smile at the idea of being back in the Rivets' Guild, but her face fell at the thought of Master Oliver. He had never been able to return.

"Your work alone honors him."

Arianna didn't have a chance to comment one way or another, for the door to the inside of the hall opened, revealing a man with a filled bolt and wrench tattoo on his cheek. The journeyman crossed his forearms in an X—a gesture of respect within the guild, for the vicar. Willard promptly settled them in what would become their new quarters.

"Should they require anything, see that they receive it, within reason," Willard said after Louie and his crew had been closed away behind the doors of their new rooms. Arianna appreciated the vicar's foresight to add the final caveat. "And go tell Charles to meet me in my office in one hour."

"Understood, Vicar." The journeyman departed promptly.

"This way, Arianna." Willard motioned for her to follow him.

She ran her fingertips along the metal walls that encased her. They pulsed with the omnipresent movement of the hall itself. Behind every wall there were gears churning, shifting, pushing something into a new design. Every panel could be removed and tinkered with, and every Rivet was encouraged to leave their mark by doing so.

"What is it?" Willard paused, noticing her palm flat against the wall.

"It's unlike Holx," she observed. "The Ravens' Guild was so quiet from everyone being gone . . . How many people are still here?"

"I believe about fifty journeymen stayed behind, and I left one Master, Master Charles, to oversee them."

And in case something happened to you, Arianna finished mentally. "Nearly empty, and the guild still moves, still lives."

Vicar Willard outstretched his gnarled and age-spotted hand, placing it next to hers. "And it will continue to tick, long after we all are dead."

That much was true.

As they continued, the paths became more and more familiar. It was like an old toolkit, where every wrench and screwdriver was remembered the moment it was seen once more. Ghosts were their only company in the empty halls.

"Wait, Willard, my room is that way." Arianna pointed down a hall at one of the forks.

"Your room has long since been given away." Willard progressed forward, and Arianna did the same, ignoring the stab of pain she felt at his words. She knew there hadn't been a home for her to come back to for some time, but to hear it articulated so clearly wasn't easy. "And even if it hadn't been, you no longer belong in that wing."

Instead, Willard led her into a great hall. Square skylights dotted the ceiling, letting in natural light to blend with the electric sconces that dotted every column of the main stretch. Between the columns, down the center of the room, were sturdy wing-backed chairs, high tables—impromptu meeting areas and spaces to sit and think. On the perimeter, between the columns and the outer walls, doorways adorned with nameplates lined the room.

Arianna adjusted her harness, which suddenly felt too tight and tightening with every step.

The Vicar Rivet led her back to the far corner. Her feet weaved her among the couches and chairs, familiar with the path rutted into the plush carpeting. This was the hall of masters, a place she had visited frequently to consult with a man whose door she now faced.

"You kept it?" Her voice was stunted, and she couldn't quite figure out why. Her eyes fixated on the plaque that read *Master Oliver.*

"In a way."

"Oddly sentimental for a bunch of Rivets." Arianna buried her hands into her pockets and told herself that Oliver's untouched old quarters meant nothing.

"Sentimentality only had little to do with it." Willard tapped one of the two door locks.

Every master's door had its own lock fused with the metal door. But Oliver had conceived a second addition that he welded into the doorframe himself. It was the most complicated lock Arianna had ever had the privilege of seeing crafted, with multiple tumblers and no clear seams or screws.

"You can't open it." She grinned knowingly. "Why not break the door down?"

"Perhaps that was the sentimentality—violating a master's workshop like that. But now . . ."

"You want me to open it?" Arianna arched her eyebrows.

"Well, of course. You know the combination, don't you?"

"I do." Arianna thought briefly about concealing the fact, but she'd have much more fun watching Willard squirm as he pined for access into the physical manifestation of his rival's mind.

A long moment stretched on. "Well . . .?"

"I'll have to think if I want to open it or not."

"This is going to be your chambers, now." He stopped her with a sentence as she turned away. "Everything within is yours."

The words buzzed between her ears louder than the electricity that hummed throughout the guild. "It's not mine to have," she whispered without facing the vicar.

"It is." Willard patted her shoulder, passing by her and heading for the exit.

"He did not give it to me." She wasn't good enough for it. Arianna knew she was ten times more brilliant than most other Rivets and she was still only half as smart as Oliver was.

"I think, in his way, he did."

"Don't you want to see what's inside?" she called across the room.

"Oh, more than anything." The old man stopped. "I've wondered what things Oliver was working on behind that door for years; I've fantasized over his brilliance. But he imparted his master status to you. He gave you the key to that door. He gave you his tutelage. Whatever is in there is meant for you, not me." The conversation shifted before Arianna could formulate a reply. "In an hour I will meet with Master Charles to discuss outfitting a line for your boxes. I'll need you in attendance. I trust you still remember the way to the vicar's quarters."

She remembered it well, as if she hadn't left the guild at all. "I do."

"I will see you then." Willard nodded and departed, leaving Arianna alone with what suddenly felt like the most important decision she would ever make.

COLETTA

oletta was an excellent judge of other's pain.

She had seen men and women die in combat countless times. She had seen Yveun inflict agony with the grace of a dancer. She had watched hordes of nameless, worthless test subjects die under the influence of her experimental poisons.

So, she knew, from the moment she walked into the Gray Room, that Yeaan was not faring well.

"He has poisoned me." Yeaan pointed a long finger in the direction of a cowering Fen. "He has cut me open and he has poisoned me."

"I highly doubt he would be the one poisoning you." Coletta couldn't resist the bit of levity. Who could blame her? The agony of others put her in such a good mood.

"I did not poison her," the Fen insisted.

"Then why is she in such pain?" Coletta approached Yeaan. The woman was nearly doubled over, clutching her stomach.

"I-I don't quite know."

Coletta ignored the incompetence and pulled Yeaan's hands from where they clutched her gut. Sure enough, there was a long, angry line down her abdomen. The red skin was

222 — Elise Kova

oozing gold, a pale, almost puss-like color from where the skin was visibly rippling with not quite right magic—the body not quite able to mend itself.

"Why isn't it healing?"

"I don't know that either."

"What do you know?" Coletta asked quietly, letting her whispering tones express every ounce of discontent she felt.

"I tried to implant a stomach, as you asked. I used the organs you provided me." He eased some as he spoke. "I implanted them, clumsily perhaps. But I did everything right. It's fairly straightforward actually. And unlike a Fenthri, I didn't have to adjust other organs' positioning to make the size fit . . ."

Coletta frowned at the incision. "Take it out of her."

"My queen, if I do, she will have to regrow her own."

"I would rather that than this agony." Yeaan bared her teeth in a snarl.

"Do it. She's useless to me like this." Coletta cupped Yeaan's cheek gently—comfort amid pain. *Cling to me*, she wanted the touch to say, *let me be your rock in this storm*. For the more her flowers saw her as their foundation, the less likely they would stray. "I will find you better organs next time, from among the sun. I will not try to force lesser scraps of meat from underneath the island into you."

"Thank you, Coletta'Ryu, thank you." The woman took Coletta's hand from her cheek, bringing it to her mouth, kissing it gently.

"Stay strong for me, my flower." Coletta turned to the Fen. "See that she is stronger than before."

"I—"

"No excuses," Coletta snapped, punctuating the demand with a forceful slam of the door. Her day was filled with flowers.

The wilting one that needed attendance had consumed her morning and now she returned to her garden, full of life in many forms. Topann patiently waited by her laboratory, hands folded and back straight, poised.

"How is your progress with the Flowers of Agendi?" Coletta asked, headed right for her work table. There was no time for pleasantries.

"We have almost finished burning all of Lysip," Topann reported. "We shall move to Gwaeru to look for any next."

Coletta paused at the mention of the island where House Tam made its home. "See it done with the utmost caution." If they played their cards right, it shouldn't matter if the flowers of Agendi were on that island or not.

"I will."

"That's not all I need you to see, Topann. I require your attentions elsewhere."

"My queen?" She stood when Coletta motioned for her to approach.

"I have taken the time to translate this ledger for your benefit." She placed the book Louie had acquired on the table between them. "Head to Loom with the Riders Yveun is sending to suss out the location of this resistance, and bring gold back with you."

"How much?"

"All of it."

"All of it?" Topann repeated, surprised.

"We require it." Coletta tapped the table in thought. The last missive from House Tam had not gone well. They were growing impatient, and the refineries on Nova were a grand idea by Yveun but an utter failure in practice. They didn't possess enough resources or manpower to make them effective.

"Then I shall bring as much as I can."

"Leverage the Riders and anyone else you see fit."

"Should this be my priority? Above the flowers?" It was a fair question.

"Yes. I'll see that Yeaan assists with them."

"Very well. I shall begin my preparations with haste." When Coletta said nothing more, Topann gave a bow and departed.

FLORENCE

She was back in the Underground once more. It was a place she couldn't escape no matter how hard she tried or how far she ran. The force of it was too much; she kept being drawn back in.

The oppressive blackness and heavy feeling of stone all around her were now almost like familiar friends. That may have been too strong of a word, but at the very least, the Underground had become a familiar acquaintance that Florence was required to interact with by some unspoken law.

Returning this time felt different. This time, the Underground was filled to the brim with life and noise.

Activity echoed through the caverns, filling every available space and making the unseen terrors lurking in the shadows slightly less terrifying. Those terrors were the first thing Florence had asked after when she had arrived at Ter.4—had there been any Wretch attacks? She had been surprised to hear that the answer was no. Usually, the Wretches used sound to track easy prey.

The Fenthri that now occupied the tunnels and pathways of the Underground were anything but. They were armed to the teeth and settling in better than Florence could have expected.

If anything, she wondered if the Wretches were afraid of *them*. After all, she reasoned, the influx of Fenthri might sound to a Wretch like one giant beast. If they could be fearsome to Wretches, then perhaps all of them together might add up to something strong enough to slay Dragons, too.

Florence started up the sloping walkway. The new inhabitants of the Underground had made fairly quick work of setting up the rocky tunnels and antechambers as home. Most of the main tunnels had been outfitted with a patchwork of illumination—from glovis eyes to bioluminescence.

She had been given a lantern that now guided her through the dark tunnel. Those building out the infrastructure—no doubt Rivets—hadn't made it to this corner of the Underground yet. Florence suspected it would take some time, if they ever reached this far at all.

The eerie glow of another lantern winked into existence from the darkness before her. It grew into the shape of a man with a Revolver tattoo on his cheek. He nodded and continued onward; it was the only assurance Florence had that she was headed in the right direction.

After what seemed like forever but was likely only about three minutes—darkness distorted time in weird ways—the tunnel opened into a large cavern. The ceiling was obscured by blackness that clung to it like heavy clouds, but Florence was struck by a sensation of spaciousness above her—a rare commodity in the Underground. In the center of the room there was a giant metal basket, within which countless glowing orbs rested. Florence tried to make sense of what the basket contained—not glovis eyes, nor typical bioluminescence. Whatever it was gave off enough light to bathe most of the cavern in a pale, bluish-green glow.

Light and shadow carved out silhouettes of people hunched over faintly glinting gun parts. Some lay out on bed rolls, perhaps sleeping, or just wiling away the boredom that accompanied waiting for an attack from above or below. A few took notice of her, but none seemed to recognize her. If they did, they didn't seem to care.

Florence progressed through the room, looking for someone familiar. A few of the faces she recognized, though none by name. In that moment, Florence made the decision to move in with the rest of the Revolver journeymen, rather than the more comfortable accommodations above she'd been offered by the vicars. While it was true that her status was unofficial, the Vicar Revolver had called her one of the guild. Even if he'd only done so to manipulate Arianna, she'd twist it to her advantage.

In the far corner, separate from everyone else, torchlight painted a head of white hair a soft blue color. Shannra had set out her own lantern, hunching over it to work on her weapons.

"I'm sorry I'm late for today's lesson." The other woman jolted as if she'd received a physical shock. Her head whipped around and she looked up at Florence. "Careful you don't break your neck."

"Or have a heart attack. Neither are implausible when one sees a ghost." Shannra's mouth cracked into a smile. The woman with the moonlit hair stood, embracing Florence without hesitation. "I was worried about you."

"I told you: You have nothing to worry about." It was awkward to leave her arms by her sides, so Florence wrapped them around Shannra's waist.

"So it would seem," Shannra admitted. "How was the journey here? No issues?"

"No, no issues." It was easy to get lost in the concern so evident in the other woman's eyes—a mix of both elation and relief.

"I have something I need to ask you."

"It sounds important." Shannra sat, motioning for Florence to join her.

"I would like you to tell me if it is." Florence debated where to start. In her satchel, she carried a notebook—one Arianna had meticulously transcribed for her. It was the copy of a ledger Louie had her steal from Holx, a ledger containing information on gold storage across Loom. Florence thought about going directly to the Dove with the information, and she still might. But she first wanted to see if Shannra knew anything about the matter. "How much do you know about Louie's . . . operations?"

"This again?" Shannra's mouth fell into a frown. "Is it too much to ask if you will ever be capable of putting aside my affiliation with Louie?"

"For now, yes," Florence answered honestly. "But how much you help me can only quicken that process."

Shannra sighed. "Very well. What is it?"

"Louie wanted something stolen in Holx, and I want to know why."

"Louie steals lots of things. I can't claim to know the reasoning behind every one." Shannra ran a hand through her wild white hair. "Maybe if you're more specific . . .?"

"He took the most current ledger from the Ravens' Guild that contains information about all the gold storage locations across Loom." Florence studied Shannra's face. Her surprise seemed genuine. "Do you know why he would want this information?"

"For Louie . . . it doesn't seem abnormal for him to go after gold." Shannra shrugged. "I have no doubt that he saw an opportunity and capitalized on it."

The same idea had crossed Florence's mind. While she wanted to believe that Louie would not use the current situation to his advantage if doing so would be detrimental to Loom, she had all evidence to prove otherwise. Still, the request sat uneasy with her. Louie had always been obsessed with organs and magic; he had never once shown much of an interest in gold. Reagents, surely, but never gold.

"Very well. But I will still bring this to the attention of the Vicar Raven."

Shannra sighed. "Do you really want to risk alienating Louie? After all, the Vicar Raven herself knew who she was getting into bed with. She went to him personally to ask him to acquire organs and these magic flowers Arianna seems to need."

"Arianna can take care of herself. And unlike Louie, I believe her when she says she's on our side."

"Very well." Shannra waved away the unappealing notion. "It's not my business anyway."

"Are you still in touch with one of Louie's men through whisper?"

Shannra merely shrugged. The lack of answer was the distance between them embodied.

"I'll take that as a yes." She didn't know what she expected from Shannra, but apparently, she harbored more optimism than she cared to admit.

"One more thing," Florence said as she stood. She needed to go somewhere else to cool down. "By the time you report to Louie, I will have already informed the vicar of his actions against her guild. So, you may want to use whatever means of communication you have at your disposal to let him know. That way, you can try to remain in his good standing."

"It's not like that, you know," she muttered. "I'm not constantly looking for an opportunity to betray you to him."

Florence arched her eyebrows.

"I'm not," the other woman insisted.

"Why does he have your loyalty at all? Why are you involved with him?" Not that it mattered. Whatever her reasons, the fact remained that Shannra was one of Louie's. And that meant Florence should stay well away.

"You wouldn't understand."

"Try me," Florence pressed.

"I was frustrated with the limitations the Revolvers' Guild put on their students." Her voice had dropped to a whisper. "I had all these ideas for projects, but none of them would get approved. They were all deemed too radical, too dangerous."

"So, you found someone who would fund your ideas."

It wasn't a question but Shannra nodded anyway. "By the time I fully realized how he was using my work, it was too late."

"He had enough information on you to get you thrown out of the guild." Under Dragon law, being exiled from your guild meant death. Florence finished the story in her mind, a simple, cautionary tale central to the Revolvers' Guild itself: just because one could, didn't mean one should.

"It doesn't really matter now. The vicar knows of my involvement with Louie because of all this. I suspect the only reason he hasn't kicked me out yet is because Loom is so short on manpower. Especially the Revolvers."

"So why stay with Louie then?" Florence crouched down again so that way she could speak in the quietest voice possible.

"He doesn't have anything on you anymore. And even if you do get kicked out, the guilds are reverting back to what they were before the Dragons. There are no more death sentences. There's nothing keeping you to a single guild or location."

"Yes, that may be true. But if I'm kicked out, I have nowhere else to go." Shannra picked up her gun parts, slowly assembling her weapon once more. "And if that's the case, I would rather stay in the company of someone who will actually appreciate my work."

Florence had always thought of Louie's lackeys as greedy bottom-feeders, hungry for the payout that his jobs brought. Or people with such wretched histories that they had no other option than to associate themselves with the gremlin of a man.

But Shannra's story was relatively benign; if anything, it made her association with Louie borderline normal. For a moment, Florence wondered if, under a different set of circumstances, she would've ended up in Louie's service, too.

For all that she'd thought those on Louie's payroll were loyal because of the money, she realized now it was because he offered something far more valuable: a place for wayward souls to call home.

"I appreciate your work." Florence grabbed Shannra's hand. "And many others will, too."

Shannra stared at the initiated contact and gave a small laugh. "You have no idea how good it feels to hear someone say that."

Florence did. In that moment, she was veca away from the dark cavern and back in her and Ari's flat in Old Dortam. She heard Arianna's first praise of her work keenly, felt her chest swell with phantom pride.

"I do, actually," Florence whispered.

"It feels good to hear *you* say that." Shannra turned her head, their noses almost touching. "I want to always be there to appreciate your work, Florence."

It's not your appreciation I want, Florence realized suddenly.

She was shaken to her core by the revelation, but in the same instant, so was Loom's fragile reprieve. Gunshots echoed from some faraway location.

Florence was on her feet, ready. The Dragons had made their first attack.

ARIANNA

She had an hour all to herself.

There was no one around her, nowhere to be, no one to interrupt her. Arianna laid out on one of the couches, worn to the perfect softness by countless hours of occupation over the years. She closed her eyes and breathed deeply.

The smell of leather, the size and shape of the furniture, vaguely reminded her of what she had procured for her and Florence's home in Old Dortam. She'd chosen those beaten-up sofas more carefully than she'd ever admit. The hours they'd spent on them, discussing, debating, reading quietly.

Arianna opened her eyes, returning to the here and now. *Here* was the masters' wing of the Rivets' Guild. *Now* saw Florence no longer a girl, nor a wayward student in need of an educational guide and protector.

Sitting, Arianna looked back to the corner where she could still read Master Oliver's name clearly on the door. He, too, had taken in a girl curious about the world and educated her. But Arianna hadn't been ready to give up his tutelage; she would still accept it now if she could.

After the events on Ter.0, she had little doubt Florence did not quite feel the same.

A door down the hall opened unexpectedly. Arianna's feet were on the floor, a hand on her dagger hilt, before the echo of squealing hinges faded from her ears. She coaxed her hand to relax, reminding herself that she was once more around friends and allies.

After spending so much of her life in secret, it was an odd feeling.

"Oh, hello . . ." The coal-skinned man seemed as startled to see her as she was to see him.

"Hello, Master Charles." The name plaque on the door confirmed her suspicion. But it was an easy deduction; Willard had said there was only one other master in the guild presently.

"And you are . . .?" His body was still tense. His light gray eyes scanned her face, no doubt making note of her lack of guild mark.

"Arianna."

"Arianna . . ." he repeated, bringing his fingers to hook his chin in thought.

"Master Arianna." The title was odd on her tongue, unfamiliar. "I was Oliver's pupil."

"Oh . . . *Oh*." Comprehension lit up the man's eyes and he crossed the room to her. His hair was cut short, and shone like an oil slick in the light. "I've heard about you."

"Whatever you've heard, I'm sure it's greatly exaggerated." Arianna leaned back into the sofa.

"It is fairly fantastical to think I'm in the presence of someone who supposedly created the Philosopher's Box."

"I did create it."

"I believe that's what's to be discussed with Mas—Vicar Willard soon." Arianna didn't miss how his instinct was still to refer to Willard as "Master," rather than "Vicar."

"I believe so."

He produced a watch from his pocket, clicking it open. "It's early yet, but I doubt the vicar has many other priorities right now. Would you care to walk with me?"

She stood and fell into step behind him as they wandered through the guild hall toward the vicar's wing. "So, what's been all the rave at Garre while I was gone?"

"Automations along the line," Charles responded easily.

"Sounds interesting."

"It is." Rivets and their "get to the point" nature weren't exactly known for small talk.

"And what happened to Master Oliver?"

"I killed him."

Few statements could stop a conversation as abruptly.

Vicar Willard was in the lavish workshop attached to his private residence. His hands were occupied when they arrived, focusing on making space on the long central table.

"You're early," he observed. "Well, since you're here, help me clean this off."

Arianna and Charles set to work moving the various parts and tools back to their supposed places around the room. Taking over someone else's workshop was like slipping into someone else's shoes. Nothing fit right about it.

"So, I was thinking we would start with building a working model of the Philosopher's Box that we can use to design the line for mass production," Willard started.

"It really is true?"

"Yes, she has supplied—"

Arianna grabbed one of her daggers and drew it across her palm, showing Charles the same stream of gold she'd displayed to the Vicar Tribunal. Showing was always better than telling. "Proof enough?"

Charles's eyes darted from her palm to her face several times. "Yes."

"As you build, Charles can sketch schematics and I can take notes," Willard instructed as they finished clearing the table. "That'll make it easier to pass on the information to the initiates and journeymen who will be working on and overseeing the line."

Arianna could only nod. The idea of making the Philosopher's Box again put a lump in her throat.

"Let's begin, then."

If she allowed herself to think about how her hands were moving, she risked error. Arianna pushed all else from her mind, beyond the numbers that gave structure to her creations. It had been a long time since she had last made the box, and there were parts that came more slowly to her than others. Still, she worked through them logically; after all, the only other option was allowing Willard to take the only other prototype in existence and build a model based off reverse-engineering. Ari wasn't about to let that happen.

They worked well into the night, tinkering until the box had mostly taken shape—minus one or two essential parts that could be manufactured with ease. Arianna looked at her work, a nearly identical replica of what sat in her chest and kept her alive.

"So now what?" Charles asked.

"It's implanted in place of the heart."

"This . . . it's just a glorified pump. How does it create a Perfect Chimera?" he asked skeptically.

"It's unfinished until it's tempered." Arianna leaned against the table, ignoring what she had just produced. Her eyes swept over the detailed notes and skillful schematics the men had drawn. The greatest thing she had ever done, reduced to a few sheets of paper.

"Tempered?" Charles's confusion reminded her that he hadn't been privy to the Tribunal and that Willard hadn't had time enough to fill him in.

"There's a special flower from Nova that has magic properties. It cleans blood of rot." Judging from Charles's facial shift, she didn't need to explain the rest.

"So, when do we get our hands on it?" He looked to Willard.

"Louie, the man whose airship I arrived on, has been asked by the Vicar Raven to procure it, along with the necessary organs."

Arianna folded her arms over her chest as a physical reminder to keep things close. She wasn't ready to expose her whisper link with Cvareh yet. Not until she had to. Purely because it was an advantage, and those were best kept as secret as possible for as long as possible. There were no other concerns, Arianna assured herself. She'd see if Louie could do it first, and then step in as necessary.

"I see . . ." Charles hummed. "Well, if it's what the Tribunal decided . . ." The man chuckled, shaking his head at himself. "Things I never thought I'd say or hear."

"Indeed, friend, indeed," Willard agreed. "For now, it's been a long day. We'll resume tomorrow, setting up the journeymen on building out a manufacturing line for this. Can the metal be tempered after the fact? Or is it a high-heat tempering that will warp?"

"It can be."

"Good, then we'll produce as many as we can while we're waiting for the supplies to finish them. Rest well, you two. We have a lot of work ahead of us."

Dismissed, she and Charles wandered back through the empty guild. He made no attempts at conversation until they were back at the masters' hall.

"What you said, about killing Oliver . . ." She'd commend him for holding in the need to clarify for as long as he had.

"It's not a lie." Arianna sighed when she saw the spectrum of emotions run across his face. "But it's not entirely the truth, either."

"Why?"

"I had my reasons." *That I will not divulge.* She'd had enough of baring her soul to strangers.

"Well, if the vicar is unconcerned, then I am, too." Charles let the matter go. "After all, no one held Oliver in higher esteem than Willard." Before Arianna could ask him to elaborate, he started for his chambers. "I'll see you in the morning, Master Arianna."

"In the morning, Master Charles," she murmured.

Arianna looked toward the back of the room for a door that was now completely shrouded. She wondered if in that darkness, the ghost of her former master still lingered, watching, waiting. She started for the door.

"I'm here, Master," she whispered. Her fingers hovered over Oliver's lock. "Sorry I'm so late."

Without a second thought, she spun the dials on Oliver's lock in a succession that required a series of clockwise and counterclockwise rotations, pulling on the different dials, and unlatching small parts of the lock itself to reveal secondary push buttons. After a long minute, the lock eventually gave with a *click*. It was a code he hadn't decided to tell her until she'd made the Philosopher's Box.

Now, Arianna wondered if the man had somehow foreseen their betrayal by Finnyr. How much had he accounted for?

Inside, the musty air of the room hit her like the first yawn of a long-slumbering beast. It smelled of oil and grease, metal, aging paper, cracked leather, and the faint tinge of a floral note that was in Oliver's blood, one that Arianna could never quite place. Nostalgia attacked her from every corner.

Understandably, the room hadn't been fitted with electricity. But Arianna knew exactly where he'd kept his oil lamps and matches. Illumination did little to scare away the lingering memories clinging to every wall, book, and unfinished piece of creation that still sat out, waiting for its master to return.

She walked over to his desk, drawn by a familiar set of scribbles. Arianna lifted up her own schematics, done in a rough hand years ago when she was little more than a child.

"Why did you keep these?" she whispered. Her heart knew the answer. It was the same reason why she would always carry a canister marked with the notches of a clumsy Revolver-in-the-making.

Speaking of Revolvers . . .

"Letters with the Vicar Revolver . . .?"

She pushed papers aside, skimming through about a month's worth of missives. They went back and forth about ideas, about Dragon bone density and how coronas worked. The words "in a purely hypothetical question for intellectual pursuits" were scrawled multiple times over, safeguarding each page against potential accusations of treason.

"Intellectual pursuits." Arianna scoffed at the idea. This was talk of methods to kill Dragons. She'd always known Oliver to be a revolutionary, but it seemed to extend into his entire history.

Her hand shifted a letter to the side and exposed a very different schematic than the childish one she'd held earlier. This was done with a graceful, steady hand, lines built on each other, coming together to form what Arianna could only describe as a masterpiece of death. And just perhaps, Loom's salvation.

FLORENCE

If there was some test in the Revolvers' Guild that involved running through pitch-black corridors towards certain danger, gun in hand, and nothing more than a makeshift plan—Florence would have already achieved master status.

Nothing good ever comes of the Underground, she couldn't stop repeating to herself. It was still the most logical place to have collected the majority of Loom. But that didn't change its innate nature: a gaping black hole, filled with nothing but misfortune and bad luck, especially every time she was in it.

More gunfire echoed as her hands counted the canisters that ran along her belts and shoulder harness. She had a good twenty made, ready to go. Those, combined with the one disk bomb she also had tucked away, *should* be enough ammunition. *Should be.* If it wasn't, she would just have to improvise as she had done so many times before.

"All noncombatants," one Raven stood at a crossroads shouting, "head down to the lower halls. This is not a drill! All noncombatants should retreat down to the safety of the lower halls. This is not a drill! Do as you were instructed."

Florence broke free of the startled and cowering masses, and continued to head upward toward the gunfire. The potent smell of sulfur in the air guided her, like a hound attracted to the scent of its quarry. But when she emerged at last into one of the uppermost tunnels—a rare exit topside—ready for a fight, she found none to be had.

A Dragon lay prone on the floor. Gold blood still oozed from his gaping chest and from the forearm that had been torn off at the elbow. Four Fenthri lay dead, scattered around the Dragon. Two Chimera nursed slowly healing wounds; they bled black, which was lucky, but would be out of commission for however long it took their bodies to mend.

"Press forward," Vicar Gregory ordered from just ahead. "Reseal the doors."

Florence strode past the deceased Dragon, toward the vicar. Just around the bend where he stood, Florence saw two heavy steel doors warped open. Wedged between them, like tree limbs through walls after windstorm, were the remnants of a glider.

"The bloody Rider slammed right into them," Gregory explained unnecessarily.

"Are there more?" Florence asked, trying to catch a glimpse of the sky through the sliver of an opening.

"Likely."

"How did he even get through?" The doors were thick and sturdy. There should have been no way to penetrate them, even sacrificing a glider. What was more, the Dragon shouldn't have known about the entrance at all. Florence only recognized it as the one major access point to the Underground because it was fairly infamous in the Ravens' Guild. But because it was so notable, no one ever used it.

"Came out of nowhere. We didn't even see him until it was too late." Her confusion still apparent, Vicar Gregory continued, "I had taken a small party out through the gates in an effort to help fortify them."

"Oh, the irony." Did it not go without saying that they should not be opening gates and letting the Dragons know of their location?

"Florence, I don't know what you're aspiring for, but do be mindful that I am still the Vicar Revolver," Gregory said in a cautionary tone.

"Yes, you are, and I am grateful that you hold yourself to the highest standard in order to prevent oversight that leads to accidents like this." Her remarks earned some looks from the other Revolvers, but Florence held her ground. Let them see; she wasn't in the wrong here.

"You only just arrived, so I realize you have not yet been informed that the vicars have agreed to collapse tunnels to protect from below and fortify the entrances above." Vicar Gregory ground his teeth. "I think you should head back into the depths of the caverns for safety. With the other noncombatants."

"I don't think that's necessary. After all, you said it yourself: I'm a Revolver, right?" Florence had no inclination to be dismissed and was ready, at last, to use Gregory's words against him. She looked back to the Dragon, then returned her eyes to the sky. There were no rainbow trails, and the sensation of magic did not prickle against her skin. "Plus, I think he was just a scout."

"Why would the Dragons merely send a scout? They made it perfectly clear their attack would come in three days."

"Three days were up two days ago. I'm sure the attack came, but they went to Ter.0 first, expecting to find us waiting and insolent."

"Scouts," Gregory repeated. "They're sending scouts to see where we ran off to."

"That would be my guess. And we can only hope that this Rider was the first."

"And why is that?"

Florence wanted to think his aim was a lot more accurate than his intellect. "Because when this Rider doesn't make it back to Nova, it will be fairly logical for the Dragon King to assume he was killed. And the death of this Rider will lead the Dragon King and his agents directly to us."

"And why would we want that?"

Florence forced herself to sigh mentally, rather than heaving it outward in frustration. "Because we are relatively protected here. And as long as we don't go showing our faces, or get careless, the Dragons will know where we are but not how to get to us. The Rivets' Guild, on the other hand, is not so fortunate."

"We must get a message to them." Gregory had finally caught up with her logic. "I believe Vicar Dove has a means to communicate."

Florence sincerely hoped so, because if they didn't, there was a real possibility that Garre could still fall.

ARIANNA

rianna didn't know what to do with herself when nothing was going catastrophically wrong.

The peace was nearly unnerving. Whenever it became too much for her, she retreated to Master Oliver's quarters and tinkered with the various projects, the original intentions of which she could only guess. She had yet to figure out how to contact Florence unnoticed about the gun schematics Oliver had been working on. Her solo attempts to complete his renderings only yielded uncertain results.

A Revolver's insight on the mechanics of weaponry would be imperative to finishing her late master's great work. Still, she continued to hope against hope that she would find some way to communicate with Florence privately, rather than involving all the vicars and half the remaining Revolvers.

Arianna wiped soot off her hands from the charcoal pencil she preferred for drafting schematics. It was a pointless gesture, as she was just about to head down to the factory floor that had occupied most of her time in the past week. The factory bustled along with all the impressive noise of a fully operating manufacturing line, but any Rivet who looked upon it would know that it was anything but.

They were grossly understaffed for the technical nature of what they were trying to produce. The tooling workshops had only completed one out of three specialized machines required. And while she had heard from Victor Willard that more Rivets were on the way, Arianna didn't want to sit on her hands and wait.

So, every day she went down to the factory floor to meet the other journeymen and initiates who had stayed when everyone else had departed for Ter.0.

When she was younger, every initiate of the Rivets' Guild was required to spend a certain amount of time on the factory floor each week. Young Rivets were taught the basics of their trade, and learned that essential quality of a tinkerer: humility. Working the floor inspired respect for how things can come together with elegant sophistication.

But the pedagogy had been abandoned in the wake of the Dragons.

Young men and women—children, really—with soft delicate hands, who had never seen a manufacturing line before, stood before Arianna each day at dawn. Each day, she critiqued their work from the day prior. Even though they had yet to produce a fully functional Philosopher's Box to her specifications, she permitted the better prototypes a place of honor on the shelves along the back wall of the factory for a day or two before getting dismantled and smelted. The gesture served both as an opportunity to raise the spirits of her workers and function as a red herring for Louie. Arianna had no doubt that upon seeing all the yet-imperfect boxes lined up on the shelves the other day, Louie immediately assumed the Rivets were further along in production than they actually were.

It was this assumption that she would use against him. For if knowledge of stockpiled Philosopher's Boxes was to make its way to any third party, Arianna would know immediately who the false information came from. It wasn't as though any of the initiates spoke to Louie; Arianna had gleaned great pleasure so far at seeing the haughty man on the edge of all interactions, never able to penetrate closer.

She glanced up at the catwalk where Louie had appeared the other day. Today, like most days, it was empty. Arianna put it from her mind to focus on the floor. The boxes wouldn't become perfect with her mind busy elsewhere.

They worked until lunch, breaking to head to the mess hall on the floor above.

The food wasn't glamorous, but it was consistent, and it was what Arianna was accustomed to from her childhood.

"It seems like you're doing well with them." Charles sat across from her, startling Arianna from her thoughts. He usually sat with the young Rivets.

"With Louie?" Arianna couldn't imagine what about her relationship with Louie looked remotely positive, let alone qualified as "doing well." It was a sort of peaceful tolerance on the exterior, at best.

"No, no." Charles shook his head as if remembering for the first time in days that the skeletal man and his ragtag followers even existed. "I mean with the initiates. They're doing well learning the line. It's something that many were resistant to, but now they're all taking a liking for it."

Arianna scoffed softly, and refrained from making a comment about how "in her day" all initiates were required to spend time on the line. Instead, she capitalized on the fact that she had someone familiar with what had evolved in the Rivets' Guild while she was away.

"Why is it that the initiates don't work on the line anymore?"

"Ah, that . . . That was a change the Dragons imposed about six years ago. They wanted most initiates focused on refining." Charles shook his head, expressing in a single gesture that he felt much the same as Arianna on the matter.

"Shortsighted creatures," she muttered. The Dragons had the most use for gold, and they put high value on the difficult-to-craft resource. Converting all manpower to its creation made sense. It was, after all, nearly impossible to produce without a lot of time and manpower.

Well, made sense if a child was the one calling the shots.

Yveun's face appeared in the forefront of her thoughts, and Arianna shook her head to relieve herself of the memory. The Dragon King may be formidable, and may even have had smart insights for Loom—at least regarding the Harvesters—but it seemed he would have driven the true value of the Rivets into dust if he had remained in control much longer. So, a child in only some ways, perhaps.

A giant dais protruding from the ceiling of the cafeteria turned with an audible *click* that silenced the entire room. Everyone looked up at the transformed signal, interpreting it at the same time. Down the tracks not far from Garre, an engine had triggered the pressure switch. Just as Vicar Willard had promised, more Rivets were on their way.

"Well, I suppose lunch is going to be cut short for us." Charles stood, taking note of how little Arianna had eaten. "Have you had enough? I can always greet the newcomers with Vicar Willard alone. You are not required."

"I don't need that much food." Arianna stood as well. "There are a few benefits to being the Perfect Chimera, after all."

"A few? I think I could name several, and I have only known you for two weeks."

The train station for Garre was slightly north of the main guild hall. Steam engines were quite particular about the ground they ran on, and the soft, marshy earth beneath Garre did not do for a train station. The Rivets and Ravens compromised to create a station just beyond the guild hall proper. It was accessible via a short light rail that gently sloped downward to the station. On the way out, the small ferrying rail was powered mostly by gravity and momentum. On the way back in, when it was mostly uphill, the trains were powered by steam—or magic.

Arianna looked with interest toward the large engine that bellowed down the winding track leading from the northern Territory. On it would be extra manpower to set up her manufacturing line, and hopefully new ways to communicate with the rebellion locked beneath the ground of Ter.4. And, in particular, one Raven-tattooed Revolver.

They arrived just before the train did, and the three present leaders of the Rivets' Guild stood alone on the long platform as the engine slowed to a stop. Amid the steam billowing over the platform, the shadows of men and women emerged. They all immediately headed for the light rail without hesitation. All of them were Rivets—knew where to go, what to do. Arianna scanned their cheeks for some sign of any other guilds. But there were none.

"We may want to address our own protection sometime soon with the other vicars," Arianna said to Willard.

"Weaponry is quite tight right now," the old man replied.

As if she didn't already know that. "Yes, and I realize that the majority of it must be used to fortify the Underground and the majority of Loom. But there will be no Loom, should we fail to produce the Philosopher's Box. I doubt it will take long for the Dragon King to check all the other guilds when he returns to Ter.0 and finds no one."

Willard stroked his chin in thought. "You do raise a fair point. I will whisper to the Vicar Raven this night; perhaps we can see some Revolvers on the next train."

Arianna sincerely hoped they would see a next train, period.

A young man jumped from the engine, a filled Raven on his cheek. He looked utterly exhausted, but still determined. "Vicar Rivet." His eyes scanned the three of them, waiting to see who responded, as though he wasn't entirely sure who he was looking for. "I have a message."

"Let me see it." Willard held out his hand.

"It came by whisper a few days after we left Holx." The man produced a hastily scribbled letter, depositing it in Willard's palm. "That's all there was."

"Thank you."

Most of the platform had cleared and, when it was apparent that the train held no more, Charles started to make his way toward the rail as well.

"What does it say?" Arianna wasn't sure if she wanted to know, but when the vicar's face fell, she knew she had to ask.

"What is it, Vicar?" Charles pressed gently, stopping.

Willard looked up from the letter, his attention darting between his companions. Arianna knew she would not like the outcome when his eyes settled on her.

"The Dragons have attacked Ter.4."

CVAREH

His knees ached, and his feet had gone numb.

Cvareh knelt before the statue of Lord Agendi in the Temple of Xin. The statue was a spitting image of the mischievous, happy lord; he held his silver box, outstretched, cracked halfway, but his crown of flowers was hidden under a stone veil, the edges of the petals barely protruding from beneath the sculpted fabric.

The temple was the only quiet place he could retreat to now. The only place he could sit and think without his family's questioning eyes, Fae's unyielding presence, or Finnyr in general. But Cvareh's peace was abruptly interrupted when another worshiper knelt beside him.

"Cvareh'Ryu," the man said with a bow of his head. Judging from the man's sky-colored skin and lack of tattoo, he was Xin— though Cvareh didn't recognize him. "I thought that was you. What an honor to kneel before my patron with the Xin'Ryu."

Cvareh did not have the heart to correct the man.

"Simply terrible, isn't it?"

"What is?" Cvareh asked cautiously.

"The flowers. I made it out there today, myself. Sure enough, it's as they say, almost half the island gone."

"Flowers?" Something resembling horror dressed in the trimmings of panic threw its arms around Cvareh's shoulders. The Flowers of Agendi were the one thing Arianna needed from him and his world. The one thing that could offer Xin the future they so desperately needed.

"Is that not why you're praying? So that the dying Lord may find peace?"

"Please, explain. I have not heard this news," Cvareh demanded quickly.

"Oh, no? I suppose not . . . I imagine the manor is still in mourning. It was just rumors at first—that all the Flowers of Agendi had disappeared from the isle of Lysip. Sure enough, there were whispers that Gwaeru was the same. I didn't know what to think, but Agendi is my patron. Perhaps I didn't worship at his temple enough . . ."

"Gone?" Cvareh tried to keep the man on track as his heart began to race. "What do you mean, *gone*?"

"I didn't believe it myself either. Thought it was just gossip with a supernatural twist in the parlors at Napole. But I went out to the lord's temple today and sure enough, half the flowers on the island were missing."

Cvareh jumped to his feet. His knees had turned to gelatin from kneeling for so long and his toes started prickling up to his shins, but he ignored the discomfort. The man blinked up at him, surprised by Cvareh's sudden movement. "Your house needs you. Go to the Xin Manor, and tell Cain Xin'Kin to meet me on the isle."

The man pulled himself to his feet, confused but obedient. "Anything else?"

"No, that's enough." *For now*, Cvareh added in his head.

He was working on a plan as he went. He had been silent in the face of Arianna's demand—holding back, waiting for her signal. It was a natural role for him, the same one Petra had carved for him. But, Arianna was not here. Petra was not here. Which meant if he didn't act, no one would.

Cvareh mounted Saran, who had been perched on one of the high ledges around the Temple of Xin, and took to the skies.

The small pebble islands that floated between outposts and tethered the three main islands of Nova together whizzed under him, blurring into a line. Cvareh squinted ahead, looking against the setting sun for the island he knew well. Even among the howling wind, the buffet of wings, and his own racing thoughts, his heart reminded him that the last time he had flown to this island, Arianna's arms were around him.

A dark speck appeared in the distant sky. Cvareh pushed the boco harder with a short, urging shout. He wanted to be wrong. He wanted to get to the island and see that the man's report had been nothing more than tea parlor gossip.

His shadow crossed over the edge of the island, soaring over greenery until—

Nothing.

The island, once filled completely with the tall stalks of the Flowers of Agendi, was nothing more than bare earth on one side. Cvareh landed his boco on the platform that was now only halfway surrounded by foliage. He dismounted, crossing to the dirt in a few long strides.

The cry of another bird distracted him and Cvareh turned on instinct, claws ready. But he recognized the creature, as well as its rider.

"Raku lets you ride him?" Cvareh phrased it as a question to Cain, but the answer was obvious.

"He does." There was an apologetic note to Cain's voice. "He came to me the other day and began roosting on my balcony..."

"I'm glad he returned home, and I'm glad you're the one to ride him," Cvareh said honestly, hoping to allay the guilt Cain clearly felt over being chosen by Petra's mount.

"What is happening?" Cain looked around the island, the question layering in more ways than one.

"Rok." Cvareh scowled.

"Why would Rok attack the Temple of the Lord of Luck? To get back at you?"

"No, Rok isn't quite so small-minded." *Unfortunately.* "The resistance needs these flowers."

"The resistance? On Loom? Needs . . . *flowers*?"

"There's something about them. They're used to make Perfect Chimera." Arianna could've explained it far better than him, but the point seemed to be made well enough. "I didn't want to move for them too early, for fear of identifying them as important. Furthermore, they're needed fresh; if the rebellion isn't ready, we waste this resource."

"Damn Rok is wasting them for us. Yveun must have discovered something during his trip below." The parlors in Napole had been abuzz with rumors of the Dragon King descending to parlay with the Fenthri, but no rumors had mentioned flowers.

"We have to save as many as we can."

"How?"

"We have to move them, replant them somewhere on Ruana where Rok won't find them, but they still can grow." Cvareh was formulating plans as he spoke.

"Do you have an idea for where?" Cain gripped Raku's feathers and Cvareh could sense the ripple of movement about to turn into a wave of feathers.

"No, but it seems you do."

"I'm going to return with help," Cain vowed.

Cvareh gave a solemn nod. "See that you do."

Raku took to the skies and soared higher and higher before becoming nothing more than a speck. The boco was almost as fast as a glider, and they needed that speed now.

Cvareh dropped his eyes back to the earth.

Divots where the flowers had been rooted nestled between ridges of upturned earth. They'd been uprooted, not trampled, not burned. Why? Why would Rok remove them? Why waste the time, when total destruction was so much more efficient?

Cvareh tried to make sense of it. Was it possible that Arianna had negotiated with someone else? He suddenly imagined the flowers already in her possession, acquired via whisper link with some *other* Dragon. He couldn't stop himself from looking to where they had made love on the stone steps of the temple before his patron and the pantheon above.

"She wouldn't," he whispered, needing more than anything to believe it was true. "Saran, take to the skies." Cvareh gave a whistle and gestured the command. The bird took off.

Cvareh raised a hand to his ear, still staring at that spot. She had given herself to him, and he to her.

He uttered a specific, magic word, and felt the tension spring up between them.

"I told you not to contact me." The snappish words were the first he'd heard of her voice in months and somehow, despite their edge, he found them lovely.

"I know. Don't break the link."

The subtle hum of magic filled his ears. There was no retort and the connection between them didn't drop. Cvareh took a deep breath.

"It's important."

"It must be." Her voice had already softened.

"The Flowers of Agendi are being uprooted."

"What? By whom?" Her surprise reassured him that there was no auxiliary method she'd used to acquire them.

"Who else?"

"Rok?"

"I think so. I'm at the temple now. I'll wait and see who comes." Cvareh leaned against one of the pillars at the top of the stone steps, looking over half the barren earth. "Do you know anyone who could've betrayed us?"

There was a long pause that said more than her actual answer. "I'm not sure."

"But you suspect."

"I do."

He was impressed at how well their conversation was going, though everything in him told him not to push things too far. "I'm going to do everything in my power to protect the flowers, but you need to get them sooner rather than later."

"Understood."

There it was: the end of their interaction, the moment when everything was going to drop. "One more thing," he added hastily.

"What?" He was relieved to hear more curiosity than annoyance in her voice.

What was he going to say? *I love you still*? Cvareh knew better; she had no interest in such professions.

"Be careful."

"You too."

The connection ended.

Cvareh walked under the shade of the temple's roof, proceeded to the far wall, and wedged himself in the corner behind the statue of Lord Agendi. He would wait there to discover what force was disrupting the flowers that were so special to them both.

ARIANNA

He contacted her.

She had asked him not to. She had told him that if he valued anything about them, he would not.

She had excused herself from the manufacturing line when she felt his whisper and now stood in a small side room adjacent to the floor. Arianna stared at the line through the window. It was beginning to run well. Their defect rate was almost low enough now to call it a proper line. But it would be worth nothing if they didn't have the flowers.

Her Dragon had paid attention to that. As dense and inept as he was at a great many things, he truly understood how critical the flowers were for them. A smile crept on her lips.

She shouldn't be smiling. It betrayed all reason. After all, he'd done what she'd explicitly asked him not to, and the flowers they needed were being destroyed. Not to mention there was still the matter of the Dragon attacks and the schematics she needed to send to Florence.

But her heart was pounding. Her mind was alert and ready. Even as Arianna the Rivet, she experienced the acute sensations normally reserved for Arianna the White Wraith—those that meant something big was coming.

"Charles!" she called, storming back toward the line. "Charles!"

"Yes, here!" A hand waved from the far end of the line and Arianna sprinted to the other master. She gripped his elbow and pulled him to the side. Over all the noise of gears churning and machines whirring, they could barely hear one another, let alone be overheard by anyone else.

"Charles, where do the Rivets keep gliders?"

"Excuse me?"

"I know you keep them here."

"There's a hangar, just outside of Garre proper . . ." His voice trailed off and he gave her a look likely intended to be probing. When she remained silent, he came outright with it. "What do you need it for?"

"Tell Willard I've gone to get him the flowers we need."

"From Nova?"

"The same. We have enough boxes ready; we can begin stage two." Arianna paused, thinking of the gun she'd been working on for weeks. "I'm going to leave out some gun schematics in the masters' hall. See that they're sent to Florence."

"To Florence? Not the Vicar Revolver?" Charles seemed confused. The demand was unorthodox.

"Yes, to Florence—only Florence," she affirmed without hesitation.

"When will you be back?" He glanced nervously at the line.

"When I can," she said. "You're fine. You understand the box."

"The code to the hangar is red, thirty-two, five, orange."

"Heard." Arianna quickly stepped away, betraying the urgency of the situation.

He caught her elbow. "And be careful."

"I—"

"Truly, Arianna, be careful." Charles gripped her arm tightly a moment before letting go. "The world needs you alive right now."

The words "right now" stuck in her mind as she ran up through the halls, back to Master Oliver's room. They echoed like a quiet promise as she grabbed the gun prototype and laid out the schematics for Charles to find later. They continued to replay as she sought out one of the gliders in the far hangar with as much speed as she could manage.

Right now, the world needed her as Arianna the inventor and crafter of the Philosopher's Box. But when the fighting was over, when the rebellion succeeded, she could retire back to obscurity. She could be whomever she wanted and answer to no one, as she'd done all her life in the years leading up to this rebellion.

But before she could slip back between the cracks of time and memory, she needed to see Loom's victory secured. And that meant going back to Nova.

CVAREH

He had been waiting for an hour that felt like eternity when Cain arrived.

His friend and a female Rider unknown to Cvareh landed, dismounted, and started down the path toward the temple. Cvareh stood, emerging from the late hour shadow into the remaining sunlight.

"Send away your boco," he called to them.

"What?"

"Send away your boco," Cvareh repeated, softer now that they were near.

"Why?" Cain asked skeptically. "Aren't we moving flowers?"

"Not yet." Cvareh looked over the horizon for anyone approaching. "We're going to wait to find out who is taking them."

"Cvareh, we should try to save some first."

It was sound advice, but the idea of leaving the island and possibly missing the perpetrators behind the flowers' disappearance was unthinkable.

"We will wait," Cvareh said, weighting the last word with a note of finality. To really drive the point home, he looked to the woman who had been otherwise silent, and changed the topic. "Who are you?"

"Dawyn Xin'Anh Bek," the sapphire-skinned woman answered. She had long golden hair that cascaded in waves, not unlike Petra's curls, but just different enough that it didn't hurt to look on her.

"Do you know why you're here?"

"Cain told me it's to preserve some of the Flowers of Agendi before they all go missing." She kept her eyes down out of respect, but her voice was strong.

"Look at me." Dawyn obliged. Her irises were the color of honey poured into water—yellow on the edge and blue around the iris. "How long have you been in the service of the Xin Manor?"

"All my life."

"How old are you?"

"Thirty-five." She was quite young, but not a child.

"If you are involved in these affairs, I cannot promise your safety."

"Can you promise my safety at the manor?" Cvareh didn't have an answer for her so he remained silent and she continued, instead. "No, you can't really, not anymore." Dawyn looked to Cain, then back to him. "I don't know everything, but I know that Rok killed our Oji and is poisoning our halls as they poisoned our wine. I am not afraid to die, Cvareh'Oji."

There was that title again, chasing him like a beast he didn't want to admit was gaining ground behind him. This time, he didn't outright refute the notion.

"Come, let's talk while we sit." Cvareh wanted to get them out of view. He didn't want the thieves to know that anyone was waiting for them until they landed, until it was too late. The two followed him in, sitting along the back wall. "Why you?"

"Why did I ask for Dawyn's help?" Cain sought clarification and Cvareh nodded. "Because she's as loyal to Xin as anyone could ask, and her family owns a winery on the west coast of Ruana."

Her mention of the poisoned wine made a lot more sense. Cvareh met the woman's unusually colored eyes. This was loyalty to her house, and it was also personal. He didn't need to ask if her family's vintage was some of the wine that had been tampered with.

"There are plots of land at the vineyard where the flowers will thrive," Dawyn explained. "My family will see to them personally with the utmost discretion."

Cvareh hoped she was right.

The conversation kept on with relative ease until it naturally died out. Both the tension and impatience of waiting consumed their focus. Cvareh could hear and feel Cain beginning to stir. But he kept himself still. He would wait days if he had to, and they would wait with him.

When the moon was high in the sky, and wispy clouds cast the world in on-and-off twilight, boco cries cut through the stillness. Cvareh crouched forward, ready to spring into action. Cain and Dawyn did the same.

"Don't move until I do . . . Keep your magic pulled in tight."

Even in the pale moonlight, the approaching Riders' red skin shone brightly, as if by their own light. Three women dismounted their boco. Two went for the flowers, but one stopped mid-step. She held out a ruby-colored hand.

"Come out." She squinted into the temple.

Cvareh stood, and with him, Dawyn and Cain. He walked forward, stepping into the moonlight and stopping on the top stair of the temple.

"Cvareh Xin, you seem to have a habit of being where you shouldn't be and meddling in Rok affairs."

"I don't know what you're talking about," he dead-panned. Why bother trying to mask a lie everyone already knew was false?

"Yveun'Dono will be delighted to have proof of your treachery."

"Yveun'Dono cannot bar me from worshiping at my patron's temple."

"He can do whatever he pleases." The woman narrowed her eyes. "Now, by his order, leave."

Cvareh didn't move. The smart thing to do was to leave. Doing so would be consistent with the role Petra had carved for him: keep his head down, acquire information, be forgotten, be underestimated. She would be the one to plan and execute the attack later. But she was gone, and he had to fight for himself. For Xin.

"By his order? Or Coletta'Ryu's?" Cvareh didn't expect Dawyn to speak, but now that she had, he wanted to hear the answer as well.

"I don't know what you're talking about." The woman's lips curled back, exposing her teeth. "If you do not leave, it will be a refusal of an order from the Dono. We are permitted to kill anyone who demonstrates such impudence."

"Are you?" Cvareh assessed them. "You have no beads, so you're not Riders. I've never heard of anyone but the king's Riders operating with enough authority to duel and kill on his behalf."

"Go, wayward Xin, and you will live out the rest of your god's hour."

"You go, and leave the flowers." Tension rippled through his muscles. "Or I will be forced to defend them on behalf of my patron."

He didn't know if it was excuse enough for a duel, but it was all he had, and the women before him seemed even less concerned than him with the idea of keeping things respectable.

"You, the weakest of the Xin children? Fight us with your pets . . .?" The woman laughed. "Leave, Cvareh."

He didn't need to endure any more disrespect.

Cvareh lunged.

The woman was ready for him and darted forward, claws out, taking the first swipe as they met halfway. Cvareh dodged widely, forced to step back and avoid a second attack from one of the other women. Cain and Dawyn weren't far behind, however, and quickly engaged the other Rok fighters one-to-one.

"This won't last long." The woman before him thrust a clawed hand out. Cvareh side-stepped and quickly pushed off his other foot. A woman's scream rang out nearby; Cvareh turned, expecting to see Dawyn in need of assistance.

"You wretched girl!" The Rok Dragon was on the ground, hand covering a shoulder pouring blood.

Dawyn spat flesh from her mouth. "Look out!"

Cvareh turned back in time to dodge the point of a hairpin slicing downward in a vicious arc.

"Don't let it touch you!" Dawyn shouted, even though they were not very far apart. "They're Coletta's women. Expect poison!"

"Coletta'Ryu, Xin scum." The woman Dawyn was fighting regained her footing and lunged.

Cvareh lost track of Dawyn and Cain, focusing on the fury of attacks at his front. The woman was good, better than she had any right to be. She fought as Cvareh would expect a Rider to, every attack precise and fearless. Her long claws gleamed in the moonlight as Cvareh laced his fingers with hers, gripping her hands in place.

"What do you want with the Flowers of Agendi?" he demanded.

"Wouldn't you like to know?" She kicked out her feet, tumbling backward and pulling Cvareh with her. Her claws dug into his skin as they rolled, swiping at his face and neck, seeking a blow that would incapacitate him long enough to go for his heart.

He twisted, scrambling, and a claw came out of seemingly nowhere, shooting straight through his jugular.

"I will kill you," she snarled, leaning in toward his face.

Cvareh looked at the woman over him, gurgling blood onto the earth as her knees pinned him. He sunk under her weight as though the soft, upturned ground itself was going to engulf him whole. Cvareh saw one imperfection in the moonlight's outline of her hair as she pulled back.

"I will watch you die, just like I watched your sister die."
Petra.

Blood spewed from his neck as he mustered a roar that gave voice, at last, to the rage he felt boiling inside. He pushed into the ground until he found something firm enough to brace against and pressed upward. She may have the advantage, but she was off-balance with his sudden movement and he had height on her. His arm, barely long enough, whipped upward.

Her hand caught his wrist, knowing what he had been going for.

Cvareh fought against her. Magic pumped through his veins and fueled his muscles with an energy he shouldn't possess. But she had leverage still, and used it to keep the poisoned hairpin at bay.

Just when he thought the bones in his wrist were about to snap from the woman's grip, it slackened, and her head whipped skyward.

Everything on the island seemed to still as a glider landed, and a large, strawberry-colored Dragon stepped off.

"Yveun'Dono has requested your return," the Rider announced. There was something undeniably familiar about her accent.

"Who are you?" The woman had yet to ease off Cvareh.

"Lesona'Kin."

"I know of no such person."

"Perhaps you are not worthy of such information." The Rok Rider shrugged. "Leave, now."

Finally, the woman eased away. Her claw extracted itself from Cvareh's jugular, but it didn't recess entirely. He felt his tendons beginning to knit . . . but did he dare attack in the presence of another Rider? Looking around, it seemed Cain and Dawyn had the same hesitation.

"I will not be leaving, imposter!" Cvareh's attacker lunged.

The Rider moved with a rustle of clothes she didn't appear to be wearing. Seemingly from nowhere, a gun unlike Cvareh had ever seen materialized. The strangeness of the thing, combined with its presence in a Dragon's hand—and on Nova nonetheless—made Cvareh's brain stutter to find context.

"Die."

He knew the newcomer instantly, the moment he heard the whispered word.

The gun fired, but the discharge exploded by the grip rather than the barrel. What had been a Rok Rider moments before was now a Fenthri woman, clutching the side of her face, doubling over. But she used that motion to grab for the daggers at the small of her back.

Cvareh lunged to action. He sprinted for the Rok woman and the Fenthri—no, the Perfect Chimera—in her sights. She was several steps ahead of him, but his legs had never stepped so wide, his muscles never felt so strong, as they did in when he was working to get to her.

Whoever the Rok woman was, she was not a Rider, because she made a critical error. Cvareh sprung for her, tumbling head over heels. In the process, the hairpin she'd forgotten he still held found its way into her neck.

Cvareh quickly let go, watching as the woman's yelp was cut short by her eyes rolling back in her head. She shuddered violently, collapsing open-mouthed and wide-eyed. Cvareh watched in horror as foam bubbled from between her lips.

He tore his eyes to the Fenthri in their midst. The earth seemed to quiet; he trusted the silence to mean that Cain and Dawyn had won their respective battles, and now stood in as much shock as Cvareh.

"Well, that rescue really blew up in my face." Arianna rubbed her knitting skin, washed white in the pale moonlight.

Cvareh couldn't stop his mirth and roared with laughter for the first time in what felt like forever.

ARIANNA

Her Dragon had finally snapped.

Arianna picked the remaining shrapnel out from her shoulder, flicking it to the ground. Cvareh was busy laughing like a fool and she waited until he stopped to take a breath.

"Are you quite done?" Arianna muttered. "The joke wasn't that funny."

"It was and you know it." Cvareh steadily approached. She could smell him more keenly, see him more clearly, with every confident step. Arianna regarded him warily.

Half of her screamed for him, the other half against. Cvareh was exactly the same as he'd been, the same as he'd always be. He was a Dragon. A few months apart was a not-so-insignificant portion of her life as a Fenthri; for him, it was a blink.

"Cvareh, what're you—"

He cut her short with arms around her, wrapping her up with bone-crushing force. Arianna felt every ripple of his muscles as he tensed against her. She breathed him in as his mouth covered hers. He tasted of daydreams and foolishness. He smelled of sweet nostalgia. The combination silenced the irritated voice trying to remind her that she should be cross with him.

He made her so soft.

"Enough," she whispered across his mouth when he came up for air. Cvareh pulled his head back, noses still touching, questions in his eyes. "That's enough, for now."

"For now?"

"For now."

At that, he finally pulled away, leaving a hulking vacuum of space where his Dragon form once was.

Arianna instantly recognized the two other Dragons in their midst. It had been some time since she'd last seen Dawyn, but she remembered the woman's name keenly from her first affair on Nova. Cain—now there was a face she'd never forget.

"Been awhile." Arianna was nonchalant, confronted with Cain's anger and Dawyn's outright confusion.

"Why are you here?" Cain growled in her direction, looking accusingly at Cvareh.

"He didn't know I was coming either. Heard you might need some help with the flowers, and we can use them on Loom now." Arianna looked to the Dragon corpses. One still frothed bubbles from lips frozen and parted with death. "Poison? Fighting fire with fire now?"

"No." Cvareh turned away from her and looked to Dawyn. Arianna fought the urge to pull his face back to her. She wasn't done having him look at her yet. "Dawyn knew they were Coletta's, because…"

"I found out spending some time on Lysip." Dawyn answered the unspoken question.

"On Lysip?" Arianna narrowed her eyes at the girl. She didn't have much reason to love her, and now she might have a reason to hate her.

"It's not like that." Dawyn shook her head and added hastily, "I went there after the wine incident. I wanted to know what happened and wasn't getting anywhere on Ruana. So, I went to spend time with a relative."

"You're Rok?" The Dragon in front of Arianna was as blue as the sky.

Dawyn shook her head. "My mother's sister mated with a Rok; their son, my cousin, came out red, so she stayed there and joined Rok."

"I'm sorry." Cvareh sounded sincere. Arianna withheld comment that this was the danger of the whole idea of families on Nova. It was so much simpler on Loom without them.

"The situation proved useful enough." Dawyn shrugged but her magic had the sour note of regret all around it. "I heard the rumors of Coletta'Ryu's flowers there. Yveun has his Riders and, while most think she's a disgrace of a Ryu, she has her flowers to act out her nefarious plans."

Arianna looked to the poisoned Dragon, prone on the ground. Sure enough, a lacquered flower sat around her neck. "Who would've thought flowers of all things would be so important," she muttered, and Cvareh hummed his agreement. "We should dispose of the bodies."

"Dispose of them?" Cain looked to Cvareh. "You heard what this wench said." He pointed to the Dragon foaming at the mouth. "She just watched as Petra died. I say we leave their bodies as a message that—"

"We will dispose of them," Cvareh interrupted firmly.

"You're taking her side?" Cain was aghast.

"I'm taking the side of reason. The only message would be that they need to wage war against Xin and now have cause to do it."

"No bodies, no deaths, and no stupid duels," Arianna finished with a nod of affirmation from Cvareh.

Cain looked as if he still wanted to object, but he had the sense to keep it to himself.

One by one, they carried the Rok corpses to the edge of the island, tossing them over like a great offering to the world below.

"The boco, too," Arianna suggested when they were finished.

"The boco?" Dawyn repeated with surprise.

"No trace they even made it to the island tonight." Cvareh unsheathed his claws in agreement with Arianna's suggestion. "We kill the boco, send them over the edge, then we take as many flowers as we can back to your family's vineyard before dawn."

Dawyn and Cain shared a look, then nodded in agreement.

"Whatever you say, not-Oji."

Arianna gave a sideways glance at Cvareh. Of course he wouldn't be the Oji; that role fell to Petra.

"I'm going to take you somewhere safe." He clearly mistook her look as an expectation of attention.

"I was fine on Nova last time." Arianna pressed her fingers together, summoning the guise of Ari Xin'Anh Bek for emphasis.

Cvareh radiated pure happiness. It fluttered from him and soared through his magic. Arianna wasn't used to feeling so much joy from one person, and especially not at the sight of her. She was unsure how to process it, so she ignored it entirely. "We need to move the glider, too."

She hopped back onto the piloting platform, gripping the handles. "If we fly with the dawn, we may be able to hide the trail in your watercolor skies."

"My thoughts exactly." Cvareh brought his fingers to his lips and gave a sharp whistle, summoning his boco. "Follow me, and fly low."

The boco took off with a hop and a flap of its wide wings. Arianna sparked the glider to life, following behind as the bird tucked its feathers and dove toward the clouds below at Cvareh's command. The rising sun lightened the sky from a pale, ethereal gray to the colors of spun candy, brightening almost to white by the time they directed themselves upwards and toward the isle of Ruana.

At first, Arianna thought they were headed for the Xin Manor. But they were too far back; Cvareh pointed at a waterfall ahead of them, pouring between the massive towers and structures carved into the underbelly of Ruana. Whatever he shouted to her was lost, so Arianna was left curious, but followed dutifully behind.

The waterfall was attached to a massive opening into the earth itself. Cvareh went ahead unhindered, but Ariana slowed as she crossed into the vast unknown of the cave beyond the falls. The magic of her glider lit up the darkness, just enough in combination with her magic eyes to make out the path ahead.

Pulling right, pulling left, weaving between columns of stone, stalagmites, and stalactites, there was only one course for her to go and Arianna for once found herself struggling to keep up with Cvareh. He charged ahead with the dexterity of a Raven and just as much disregard for the dangers of how he progressed. Arianna gritted her teeth. Her back felt as though it was going to snap in half from tension.

Light filtered into the blackness, and Arianna breathed a sigh of relief as she heard the squawking of the bird ahead and felt the buffet of wings that usually signaled landing.

The cave had opened up into a small cavern with a wide-ledged mouth. Arianna parked the glider and mentally forced every white-knuckled finger to uncurl.

"Are you trying to kill me?"

"Was it hard to navigate?" Cvareh seemed genuinely concerned.

Arianna sighed heavily. It may not have been hard for a suicidal Raven like Helen or Will, but Arianna had come to start valuing her life, as insane as the notion was. "It'll be fine as a transport route. If I can do it, a Raven can make it twice as fast."

"Careful, Arianna—that sounded like humility." Cvareh extended a hand to her, offering to help her off the glider. Arianna stared at it, but stepped off unassisted thanks to that remark.

"So, where are we?"

"We are at the refinery of Ruana."

"Refinery of Ruana?" Arianna repeated, utterly dumbfounded.

"This way."

Curiosity propelled her to follow Cvareh without further comment around a lip of stone and into a narrow passage that quickly opened up into a cut staircase. The walls transformed from rough and natural to carved, as they ascended into what was clearly a Dragon-built structure.

She watched the back of the man ahead of her, as if the skin between his shoulder blades had some secret to reveal. Not for the first time, Arianna found herself studying him, wondering just what it was about Cvareh that drew her. It was not the depth of his mind, nor the muscle of his frame. Their pull to one another was indescribable; the features she would not usually find her eye drawn toward attracted her like the sheen of a freshly oiled gearbox.

At least, until her eye was pulled in a different direction.

The stairway leveled into an icy hall. Glassless windows welcomed the high snowdrifts of the mountains through their thresholds. Flurries danced on unseen currents, crunching underfoot as they traversed to a large room.

She found herself in a spacious antechamber overlooking an even larger space. Ahead of her, a window of tempered glass— slight imperfections rippled through it—looked down at the core of the refinery. A large vat was suspended by a massive hook off to the side of a grounded tank. They were surrounded by machines and long belts, all cold, waiting for molten steel to be poured down them.

"It's a refinery," she whispered.

There was an odd disconnect between her mind and body. Her eyes told her mind that she looked at a refinery, albeit a small one. But her mind argued back that such a thing was impossible, for she knew she was up on Nova, where paragons of industry did not rightly exist.

"I told you it was." Cvareh was at her side.

"Why?" Arianna was trying to process the idea.

"Yveun is—or at least was—setting them up on Lysip. Started the project a decade back and put Petra in charge of oversight. Naturally, she seized the opportunity to build one here as well."

"So, is your sister here now, then?" Arianna's voice was still a whisper, matching Cvareh's tone. She'd felt a somber shift in Cvareh's magic when he mentioned Petra. Warning bells and alarms sounded in Arianna's mind.

"No. Petra is dead."

Cold.

Detached.

Arianna felt the muscles around her lungs contract and her breathing grow shallow. A feeling deeper than reason and stronger than logic ruled her—empathy. She clutched his hands as though she was pulling him from the unbearable riptide of grief, grabbed him like someone should've grabbed her after Eva.

"You will make it through this," she vowed, acting entirely on impulse.

Cvareh tilted his head to the side and his mouth cracked with a tired smile. He leaned forward and Arianna's eyes closed of their own accord. They, like all other parts of her body, moved in the ocean of this man. He didn't kiss her, but merely rested his forehead against hers and breathed.

"I know." Cvareh took a slow breath. "I have you."

Why did those words make tears prick her eyes? She felt so frustrated by them, so angry, yet so happy. It was like drinking chocolate and licking salt.

"Are you the Oji now?" She had to focus. She couldn't let herself be distracted by the things she'd given away years ago.

"No, but I will be." Arianna opened her mouth to speak, but was interrupted by his movement. "I must go now and see to that. But I will return to you. Make yourself at home until then."

Oji. Cvareh as the Oji. Her mind tried to wrap itself around the idea. The prone Dragon she'd found on Loom, leading the rebellion on Nova. He would be pulled from her to change the world, just as Master Oliver had been, just as Eva had been. As Florence was.

The space before her had never felt more cold.

FLORENCE

Dragons were annoying. They weren't scary, they weren't dangerous, and they certainly weren't the fearsome creatures they made themselves out to be.

More than anything, right now, Dragons were simply a nuisance.

Florence sat in an abandoned building on the outer edge of Holx. From her vantage, she could see Dragons swirling around the Ravens' Guild. Every now and again, one would land and its Rider would disappear inside for a few hours. Then they'd eventually return to their glider, having accomplished nothing, and take to the skies again.

She leaned against the wood paneling of the room she'd made her temporary home. Watching the Dragons, recording their movements, keeping track of how far they seemed to get in the guild and how long it took them to do so was a convenient excuse to spend extended time outside the Underground. It had been almost a month since the first Dragon attack, the first unsuccessful one of many, and a month was too long to spend in the dark. Florence felt sorry for the Fenthri who had no other options beyond spending their days confined below. Not sorry enough to pass up the chance to escape the ever-oppressive gloom herself, but sorry still.

Here, her window was cracked. She didn't open it fully because she didn't want her magic to betray even the slightest scent on the wind. But that same wind tickled her cheeks as it whispered of the outside world. Here, Florence could stare up at the sky and watch day turn to night and, more important, night turn to day.

When the Dragons weren't flitting around the guild hall—their forays grew less frequent by the day—she would invent stories about the people who had lived in the apartment she now occupied. When her stories lost their luster, she would wonder how she and Arianna would have redecorated to make things more comfortable. When thinking of Arianna was too painful, or frustrating, she had Shannra to smooth away the rough edges of annoyance.

Shannra was in her arms now. Florence loved the way the light painted the woman's dark skin in graphite hues, like a page from a Rivet's sketchbook. These schematics drew what could be argued as the perfect female proportions.

A soft rapping at the door jarred Florence back to reality. No matter how nice it was to daydream, this was not her home and she was not spending a lazy afternoon with the woman who had somehow become her unorthodox lover. Florence tugged the blankets around them as Shannra began to stir. She loathed disturbing the woman, but the second set of knocks did just that anyway, and Florence worked to preserve their modesty.

"Come in." Florence didn't have to speak loudly to be heard. They were as quiet as possible due to the Dragons' keen hearing.

The door cracked and another Revolver poked her head in. She seemed unsurprised to find Florence and Shannra together.

"I was told to fetch you."

"Fetch me to where?"

"There was a letter for you on the last train from Ter.3. Vicar Gregory wishes to see you regarding it."

"I'll be there in a moment." Florence dismissed the other Revolver with a small nod.

"A letter?" Shannra repeated.

"I know no more than you do." Florence began to button up her clothing once more from naval to neck.

"From Arianna, I'd bet." Shannra straightened and leaned against a window frame. The wind ruffled her hair slightly as Shannra stared at the few Dragons in the sky.

Florence could sense the tension whenever Shannra spoke of Arianna, though they'd never spoken of it, not outright. Florence didn't even know what she'd say if Shannra pressed for clarity. What had she and Arianna been to one another? What were they now? Some questions were best left unanswered or better, unasked.

"Perhaps." Florence leaned forward and kissed Shannra's cheek lightly. "I'll be back as soon as I can. Keep an eye on things for me."

Shannra merely nodded as Florence moved for the door. But before she could reach it, Shannra spoke. "Flor, when all this is over, how about we get a nice little flat in New Dortam, right by the guild hall?"

Florence's mind immediately went to the home she'd shared with Ari in Old Dortam and a melancholy ache filled her chest. "There is no guild hall," she murmured.

"They'll rebuild it." Shannra finally turned her head, her eyes searching, begging. "What do you think of that idea?"

"I think I love sharing my days with you."

Florence left before she could soak in Shannra's reaction and affirm her suspicion that the response was not the one her lover was looking for. Right now, the only thing Florence could let herself think about was seeing Loom survive another day.

Through a back door into a narrow alley, Florence slipped from above ground to under in a mere moment, dropping down through what looked like an open sewage grate. It led her into a tunnel, straight to one of the still-open passages for what had become Loom's unofficial capitol.

She found all the vicars gathered in Ethel's makeshift receiving room, just outside the Vicar Alchemist's sleeping chamber.

"Ah, Florence, thank you for coming." Powell was the first to notice her.

"A Revolver always heeds their vicar's call." Florence wasn't quite sure if Gregory was speaking to her or Powell.

"I heard there was a letter?" She cut right to the chase.

"Yes, here." Powell shifted, passing a carefully sealed envelope. Its thickness was more like a folio than a letter, and Florence looked at the curious marking on its front.

To Florence
From Arianna

"Vicar Gregory suggested that we open it, but since it was addressed to you specifically, I wanted to make sure it found its way into your hands foremost."

"Thank you, Vicar Powell." Florence could feel the curiosity burning off Gregory to the point that the temperature in the room might have been rising.

Wasting no time, she broke the seal and slid out the papers.

Every leaf was marked over in many places. Layers of text betrayed years of work from different hands. Some, Florence recognized as Arianna's scribbles. Others were foreign to her.

"Don't hold us in such suspense," Vicar Dove practically yawned.

Florence read over the notecard twice. She knew what she was looking at without Arianna's hasty explanation.

"It's schematics for a gun . . . that could fire through a corona."

"Does Arianna now fancy herself a weaponsmith?" Gregory seemed amused, dismissive.

Florence didn't even bother to combat her scowl. "Given what she's accomplished to date, I wouldn't put it past her. Furthermore, it looks like the work wasn't started by her, but the late Master Oliver and the Vicar Revolver I believe you replaced."

Gregory clearly was not pleased with her tone. "Let me see those," he demanded.

Florence had little option but to pass them over.

He read over the papers once, twice. Everyone in the room was attentive, waiting for his assessment.

"Ethel, let me use a pencil?" Gregory dropped to the ground, scraping away pebbles and dust to lay out the schematics on what had now become his work surface. The Vicar Alchemist produced the requested utensil and he set to making hasty smudges and drawing lines across the notes.

"Could such a weapon actually exist?" Powell was the only one who risked breaking the silence.

"I would've said no a few minutes ago. But this . . . this should work."

Florence stepped over, looking at Gregory's sketched calculations. She followed his adjustments, the accounting for an extra feedback of magic, using a canister for priming . . . Her eyes stilled on one line he'd smudged out.

"I think I could make these modifications to something I have currently. It'll make the gun quite large, but I shouldn't need anything too special."

"But that's . . . what about—" Florence tried to point at the spot she'd gotten stuck on.

"Thank you, Florence," Gregory said curtly. "In the future, please inform Arianna to send such things to me directly, as the vicar. Now, we need you to return to your post."

Florence stared at Gregory for three long breaths. She thought about speaking up. She wondered if she should try to make him listen. But this was Loom, where your failures were your own, and you bore the burden of them.

"Should any of the vicars require anything else, you know where to find me."

Florence gave a tip of her hat and left the room, saying nothing about the explosively critical error she'd noticed in Gregory's calculations.

CVAREH

Something about that woman changed him. All was right with the world when she was near, yet she made him want to alter everything for the better.

Arianna had come to Nova for him. His boldness had not pushed her away, had in fact brought her to him. Cvareh gripped the feathers of his boco and stared toward the horizon as he raced back toward the Temple of Agendi.

She needed him as the Oji, to fulfill Petra's promises. Petra's memory needed him to defend House Xin. All of Xin needed him to work with Loom. So much rested squarely on his shoulders, and it was time he got to work—starting with arranging transport of the remaining flowers to Dawyn's family's plot.

He didn't even spend half of a day on the task, but when he arrived back at the Xin Manor many hours later, it felt as if he'd been gone an eternity. He had scrubbed himself to bleeding at Dawyn's, but still imagined he could smell the combination of Rok blood and Loom on his skin.

Oddly, Cvareh found it difficult to muster concern over the fact. *Let Finnyr and Fae smell their fallen kin and Loom rising to defeat them*, his mind whispered dangerously.

As soon as he landed his boco, a servant rushed out to greet him.

"Cvareh . . ." There was a long pause following his name, proof the man clearly had no idea how to address him.

"What is it?" The lack of formality suddenly seemed more obvious than it had before—a matter long overdue to be settled.

"I was asked to send you to your brother the moment you returned."

"Did he say what for?" Cvareh had half a mind to ignore the request and attend Finnyr later, just to send the message that he did not jump at his brother's every beck and call.

"No, just that he would be waiting for you in the main hall."

Cvareh trudged down through the manor, exhausted from the lack of sleep and still recovering from combat. But instead of finding every step harder than the last, he found it easier. Life returned to him in the form of anger, frustration, and a small bit of hard-earned triumph. He had shed Rok blood, hidden the fact, and thwarted what was no doubt a very clear plan to put a swift end to Loom's rebellion—and with it, Xin's hopes.

He had done it all before Finnyr had likely even woken for the day.

That anger reached its peak when he entered the hall and his eyes fell on Finnyr, seated on Petra's throne. Where Petra commanded the seat and it cradled her in return, Finnyr was dwarfed by the stone chair. For the first time, Cvareh wondered what he would look like in such a seat.

"Seems an uncomfortable place to wait."

"You did keep us waiting," Finnyr replied curtly.

"I may not have returned at all, and what then? You were planning to sit here all day?" To think, he could have been spending time with Arianna in the refinery *and* making his brother wait. It was truly a missed opportunity.

"Where were you?"

"Worshiping at Lord Xin's temple."

"Do you honestly think that will work on me? I know better."

"I have alibis." Cvareh was glad he had spent so much time there throughout the days prior. "Ask several witnesses, if you'd like." He strode forward before his brother could get in another word. "And you know better? You know *nothing* about me, Finnyr."

"That's Finnyr'Oji." The emerald-skinned Rider stepped forward, her magic blowing like an uncomfortably hot wind. Cvareh ignored the all-too-familiar scent of honeysuckle in it.

"Sorry, *Finnyr'Oji*. New title and all, it slips." Cvareh smiled and didn't even try to make it look sincere.

"You should be more respectful before your Oji." It was a normal thing for a Dragon to say, but the woman looked like she could burst out laughing at any moment. Perhaps she found the idea of Finnyr as Oji as comical as the rest of them.

"And you should be more respectful of the Xin'Ryu, Fae *Rok*'Kin To, and stay out of Xin matters." Cvareh snapped back, rising up onto the lower step.

"The Xin'Ryu? I don't recall Finnyr ever appointing you such." She looked between the two men.

"Finnyr'Oji," Cvareh corrected as he took another step, assuming his position where Petra usually placed him. He looked down at his brother, who seemed utterly stunned to find his little brother standing toe to toe with the Master Rider.

"Perhaps he doesn't tell you as much as you'd like to believe?" Cvareh wasn't backing down now; he'd come too far. "Isn't that right, brother? Tell her, tell this Rok Rider that she is an excellent protector you are most grateful to have, but she doesn't know everything about Xin."

Finnyr seemed at a loss for words, looking between them for something to say. If he wanted lines, Cvareh would feed them to him.

"Tell her that I am the Xin'Ryu."

Finnyr's mouth opened and nothing came out.

"Tell her." Cvareh's hand curled into a fist as he stared down his brother. He searched those familiar golden eyes for any shred of the man Finnyr could have been, for any remaining love he might harbor for his house. Finding none, Cvareh scraped the bottom of Finnyr's pathetic personality for a lingering scrap of self-preservation, and found it.

"He's right. Cvareh is the Xin'Ryu."

Cvareh felt as shocked as Fae looked. Her surprise quickly turned to anger, and she stared down a now-cowering Finnyr. But Cvareh was done; he'd gotten what he wanted, and so had his brother—the oversight of House Rok and all the joys that came with it.

Cvareh walked away, leaving Finnyr alone, and not feeling a speck of regret for the fact.

COLETTA

Yveun never sought Coletta out in her garden unless something had gone catastrophically wrong.

"Cvareh is moving to gain control of House Xin." Right to the point, her mate wasted no time.

Coletta wiped her hands on a delicately embroidered rag, giving the declaration some thought. "How have you arrived at this conclusion?"

"Fae has whispered this afternoon that the youngest Xin has begun to show signs of ambition. Cvareh, out of everyone, shows ambition! What is this world coming to?" Coletta wasn't sure if he sounded impressed or frustrated.

"It was only a matter of time, and we knew it." Coletta had long suspected there was more to Cvareh than Petra let on. The schematics, and then the events on Loom, followed by the Crimson Court, all confirmed it. This was more of the same, and therefore nothing to be worked into a panic over.

"I would like to bring Fae back to Lysip."

Coletta turned to her ledger, feigning attention to its contents.

"If Xin truly decides to wage war, she will do little alone and—"

"—and we risk losing her," Coletta finished, looking up from her notebook. "I do not disagree with you, Yveun. Fae is far more valuable to us alive. Her presence at Xin would always come to this end."

Yveun nodded. Coletta wondered how much he understood about the delicate play of keeping Fae at House Xin. An opportunity to ensure the house's loyalty just a little longer while they attempted to weaken Loom through demoralizing attacks and weaning their gold, as well as an opportunity to further their organ research.

Even failures could be part of a plan.

"After she has returned and you have had your fun, send her to me," Coletta instructed.

"Have you found more success yet with your experimentations?"

"Not yet," Coletta admitted.

"Then I would not have us carving up our prize stock." Even Yveun referred to the woman as little more than an animal. To them both, Fae was a bitch on a chain, poised to attack, or satiate whatever desires he could conceive.

"She will be fine. Despite our setbacks, there has been no lasting weakness in Yeaan. Even now, my flower seeks out the resources the rebellion on Loom requires, and destroys them." Yveun seemed unconvinced, so Coletta continued. She didn't really need his approval, but things were easier when she had it. "Furthermore, Fae is far stronger, wouldn't you agree? She'll manage without issue, I'm sure."

"I hope you're right, Coletta." And just like that, the hulking monster that was Yveun gave in to his Ryu.

"I usually am." It never hurt to remind him. "Summon her back before House Xin descends into anarchy. Then, contact Tam for a meeting."

"Tam?"

"With Fae gone, I have no doubt Finnyr will be dead within the month. As soon as that happens, we should make sure we have the loyalty of House Tam secured."

"Their tithing?" Yveun asked grimly. Coletta knew he hated Tam's demands; she held no love for them either. But there could be no half measures. Anything less than absolute loyalty to him was a foreign concept.

"I have acquired enough for them to make all things equal in the matter of their assistance for the battles ahead."

"I am a wise man, to leave such important acts in capable hands."

Coletta could not stop the swell of pride that came at his words. "Trust me, Yveun, and I will see us through to a bright future where Rok reigns the worlds above and below unquestioned."

"If anyone can, it is you."

"It is *us*," Coletta reminded him. They would either live together in victory, or perish in failure. No half measures.

ARIANNA

"Nevertheless, I don't know how you stomach them," Arianna muttered, having the oddest conversation she'd ever conceived.

"They treat us better than House Rok did." The man across from her, a Fenthri with the Alchemist symbol on his cheek, continued to fiddle with the tubular object they'd been passing between them for the better part of the afternoon.

"So you've said . . ." Arianna mumbled, though she just couldn't imagine it. Fenthri on Nova—not just Nova, but *Ruana*—the whole time she was there. There had been a taste of home hidden right under her nose while she was isolated in the Xin Manor, and Petra never told her. It was almost enough to make Arianna resent the deceased Dragon. "Didn't you want to come home?"

"Of course, but it wasn't an option."

Arianna chewed on her lips and flipped one of her daggers in her free hand. She felt restless, uneasy. Was Xin any better than House Rok if they kept Fenthri? Surely, if conditions were so good, Petra would've mentioned it. Had she been conspiring to put another Yveun in power?

The idea quickly evaporated. Petra was dead and whatever kind of king Cvareh would be, he wouldn't be anything like Yveun.

"Did you try to escape?" She wanted to find a way to make herself feel better about the whole situation.

"To what end? Escape would, at best, require a sympathetic Dragon. I've met Dragons I'd dare call kind, but sympathetic enough to just let me go? Certainly not." The Alchemist, Luther, sighed and leaned back in his chair. "I've been here thirteen years." She believed him, judging by the white streaks in the slate hair running back from his temples. "I don't have that much longer left."

"Hush."

"It's true and you know it." Arianna kept her mouth shut, rather than argue against a fact. The man smiled tiredly at her silence. "I wouldn't know what to do if I returned to Loom. From what you tell me, I doubt I'd recognize it."

"Or maybe you'd know it better. It's moving back to what it was before the Dragons."

He held out the tube and Arianna took it, popping off the bottom and inspecting his work, making her own modifications. "I can't believe you're happy here . . . you *want* to be here."

"I want to be here more than I wanted to be at Rok. I've had my own room, proper food, the ability to work. What more does a Fenthri really want?"

She withheld the word "freedom" for his sake.

"I'm not crammed in a single room like livestock," he continued. "None of us are. None of us are beaten or debased. The ones Petra got out were the lucky ones."

Arianna felt anger rise in her. Anger at herself, at the world she lived in, at the people she'd made into Loom's allies. No matter what happened Arianna was beginning to wonder if Loom was trapped in an endless cycle of subjugation at the hands of Dragons.

It was a dark moment—perhaps one of her darkest—and the least ideal for her to see a Dragon, any Dragon. Naturally, Cvareh rounded the corner of the laboratory at that very instant.

"Ah, I see you've made a friend." He beamed.

Arianna didn't know what expression her face had, but it was enough for Luther to stand from the seat he'd been comfortably occupying for hours and make a swift retreat.

"Xin watch over you, Cvareh'Ryu," the other Fenthri muttered as he passed. Arianna wondered if it had been drilled into him by force or if a Fenthri could actually believe such superstitious nonsense.

Cvareh didn't even motion at the display of respect. His eyes stayed locked with hers, searching. He opened his mouth to speak, but Arianna had already decided she would not give him the liberty of having the first word.

"Were you going to tell me?" She carefully set down the tube she and Luther had been working on to transport the Flowers of Agendi past the clouds without damage.

"Tell you what?" Cvareh frowned.

"Tell me your sister was no better than Yveun."

"*What?*" Cvareh hissed. "You know well and true Petra was not Yveun. Not by any stretch."

"Then what of you?" She practically leapt from the chair. "What of you, Cvareh?" She rammed a finger into his chest, though she couldn't recall crossing the room to get to him. "Are you any better than Yveun?"

"Arianna, what happened?" Cvareh clasped her hand with his. There was no reason why she couldn't wrench herself away;

she had the strength. But every part of her suddenly felt weak. Arianna couldn't place why until she felt her eyes burning at their corners.

"Petra, you . . .you kept Fenthri as slaves."

Cvareh's head whipped from her to the door Luther had just exited through. Emotions swept across his face, beckoned by the winds of a truth undeniable to either of them.

Arianna stepped away.

And was tugged closer.

His cheek was against hers, staving off the first prickle of tears by pressing his flesh to her own. His mouth was on her ear, and he uttered promises she didn't know if her heart could hear.

"We never saw them that way, Ari. We couldn't get them home."

"You lie." Her mind knew better, but her heart begged to believe him. It ached for him despite herself.

"I never saw them that way," he clarified.

"Set them free, then."

"Is this your boon?"

"No, this is what you will do for me if you truly care for me."

"And care for you, I do." He moved the corner of his mouth against hers, and then the whole of his lips.

She leaned into him, matched him touch for touch. She hated herself for it, for needing it, for wanting it, for wanting *him*.

Eva forgive me.

"Free them," she repeated. It was the only thing she could cling to. She'd lost all other dignity the moment her fingers curled around his.

"I will. When I am Dono, I will," he uttered.

And then, the tears fell.

Not since the death of her master and her last lover had she cried. For what Arianna had just heard was the decree that would separate them; it was the utterance that would tear them apart as the great machine of fate continued to roll over the world.

He would be Dono, and she would be no one. That would be the end of them.

So, for now, she indulged herself. Arianna cast aside all pride. She pulled him by the scraps of fabric he called clothing and pressed herself against him. She felt the curves of that all-too-familiar chest, the swell of his pectorals before they fell to the dips of his abdomen.

Cvareh's hands moved to her face, held her mouth to his, and they breathed together for a blissful moment.

"I will be leaving soon."

"When?" The word was more of a gasp—part groan, into her neck.

"Soon. I must return to Loom. I must bring flowers with me. There are boxes ready for tempering; we shouldn't dally."

"*When?*" he repeated.

"Tomorrow? Soon." She had to return to her world and leave him to his, or else they would fall into that contented state that dulled the pressing needs of all they had become responsible for.

"Then give yourself to me now?"

Like he had given her a choice. "I demand something in exchange."

He laughed darkly against her shoulder. "Of course you do."

"I want your lungs."

"My lungs?" he repeated.

If he were to give them to her, perhaps she could make time stop. In those frozen moments, she could let go of her own harsh judgment for loving such a man. She could savor him, as though he wasn't about to step into a role that prohibited her from standing by his side.

It would be the only part of him she could keep forever.

"Give them to me. Make me Perfect."

He paused and pulled away. His brow furrowed as he inspected her thoughtfully. His long, blue fingers ran through her snow-colored hair and swept it from her brow in thought.

"Arianna, you were perfect long before the Philosopher's Box."

If only it were true.

"Give them to me. Please."

"If that is what you want of me, then it is yours." He kissed her again. "I am yours."

Cvareh crushed her lips with his and encircled her waist with his arms, and Arianna forgot about all reservations as he pushed her against the wall.

FLORENCE

"With this, we will be able to fight Dragons head-on," Vicar Gregory addressed the Revolvers' Guild. In his hand was a weapon he hoisted up to his shoulder with ease. It had the look of a rifle, only shorter and fatter through the barrel. Wires connected disk-like multipliers, covered in the scratches of Alchemical runes, along its length. "With this, we will no longer be forced to rely on imperfect alchemy or failed negotiations."

"Will there be a Philosopher's Box?" an initiate asked from Florence's left.

It was disturbingly easy to take stock of the guild. All of them now fit into a single cavern in the Underground. There were about twenty-five journeymen, thirty initiates, three masters, and the vicar. Florence would guess the Revolvers were at one-fifth of their previous size, maybe even less.

"The Rivets are still working on the Philosopher's Box. But in the meantime, this will give us a real chance to escape the Underground and fight against the Dragons out in the open." Gregory was back to showing off the weapon. "In fact, the preliminary work on the gun was done by the Master Rivet who designed the Philosopher's Box herself."

As murmurs flew between people assembled in the room, Shannra caught Florence's eyes. There was no mention of Florence, which she could stomach since she hadn't done much other than receive the letter; but there was no mention of Master Oliver—which Florence knew would not sit well with Arianna—or the last Vicar Revolver either.

She wanted to ask herself how such a selfish man could have landed as the head of the Revolvers. But then she remembered they hadn't had many options to choose from. Knowing Gregory, he'd likely strong-armed his way into the position when the rest of the guild was still reeling from grief and terror.

" . . . so I will be taking a select few with me topside this very day. We will go, and we shall use this to cut a Rider from the pack and take them down, so the Dragons know we are working on a weapon that their gliders and coronas won't protect them from."

"I volunteer." An eager journeyman jumped to his feet.

"Take me with you!" A woman joined him, standing tall and resolved.

"I want to see the gun fire!" An initiate was not going to be left out. The Revolvers were nothing if not recklessly curious.

"The masters and I have already decided on the team." Gregory motioned for them to sit down. "It shall be composed of Master Joseph, journeymen Thomas, Willie, Shannra . . ." There was a long pause, audibly separating the last name from the others of journeyman status. " . . . and Florence."

Florence's ears perked up at her name. She rose to her feet, seeing that everyone else who had been called had done so. Shannra's eyes squinted slightly at her. She knew they were both wondering the same thing: What was Gregory up to?

That question was the first thing out of Shannra's mouth as they prepared to go topside in the hour that followed.

"Why would he invite you?" she mumbled, checking her guns for the second time.

"Perhaps he's using me to help navigate the guild hall?" Florence was already on her third check.

"Did he even ask if you could?" Shannra asked. Florence shook her head. Truth was, she wasn't even confident that she could, beyond broad strokes. It'd been so long since she was last there.

"I don't like this, Flor."

"Maybe it's his way of thanking me for giving him the schematics?" Florence's mind immediately jumped back to the vicar's hasty calculations. "Share the glory of its first use?"

Shannra hummed, unconvinced. "Sharing isn't something our vicar is known for." The woman glanced around, but she had maintained her corner away from all the other journeymen. "What Arianna said about Gregory on Ter.0 is true. He's a good Vicar Revolver, but not because he's a renowned teacher."

"It's because he's cutthroat." Florence had figured out that much on her own. It was a strong front for the guild to have right now, especially when the world had gone to pieces and they needed the Vicar Revolver to be a beacon of strength. What was good for the guild, however, was not necessarily the best for Florence.

"He was only ever tolerated because he was effective." Shannra harnessed her weapon.

The word *effective* stuck. Florence grabbed the other woman's wrist, arresting her complete attention. Florence dropped her voice as low as possible.

"When I gave the schematics to him . . . he did some quick calculations, called the problem solved."

"I hear a 'but,'" Shannra whispered, evoking a solemn nod from Florence.

"I noticed the error. He ignored me when I tried to point it out." Shannra's scowl deepened. "He may have since fixed it."

"I doubt it. Gregory was never much known for theory."

"We'll just have to be extra careful."

They each packed an additional box of canisters before setting off to the arranged meeting point. It was a narrow room that had a ladder leading into the Ravens' Guild hall. Vicar Dove had spared one Raven to guide them, inadvertently proving that Florence was not along to navigate. It was a young man who was looking very uncomfortable with the whole idea of what they were about to do.

"Our objective is simple," Gregory instructed the small group. "We will head into the hall and up to a waiting point and wait for a whisper from a lookout. When Thomas gets the signal that a Dragon has landed, we will run to intercept, dispose of the Dragon, and return." He said it as though doing so would be the simplest thing in the world. If Florence had learned one thing, it was that nothing was ever easy when it came to Dragons. "This is nothing more than a test run for the weapon."

"Do you have any reason to believe the weapon may not work?" Florence just couldn't keep her mouth shut.

"Are you questioning my work?"

"Is it not the nature of a journeyman to question?"

"It is. But you are no journeyman."

"What am I, then?" Now was not the time to make such a demand, especially not when they were about to enter a dangerous situation. But Florence didn't hesitate. "You said I was a Revo on Ter.0."

"The masters have not yet discussed your official status, Florence." Master Joseph stepped in to play damage control. "Perhaps that is something we can look into after this test."

Gregory looked at Florence the entire time Joseph spoke. Florence didn't take her eyes away. She refused to allow anyone to think they could intimidate her.

"Let's go." Gregory motioned for the Raven to lead up the ladder.

Florence had entered the Underground through the Ravens' Guild, but this was a different pathway than last. She tried to make sense of where she might be, dredged up old memories of her childhood in the guild, but it wasn't until she saw a level marker along the main helix that she knew. They had a long way to go before they could even be seen by a Dragon, and that assumed any were currently flying around.

"It's odd to see it so quiet," Florence mused softly as they stepped onto the main track.

"I could grab us a trike?" the Raven offered, clearly compelled to fill the space with the sounds of engines churning and wheels spinning.

"Best to keep it quiet," Gregory shot down the idea. "Don't want to draw too much attention."

They continued up the track on foot. Florence adjusted her grip on her gun, peering around corners as they passed. She had seen Dragons landing on the guild hall for stretches of time before taking off again. But it was entirely possible that they had begun to set up operations as they cleared different portions of the building, working their way downward in search of their prey.

There were no markers of Dragons anywhere, however. No markers of any other life, and the silence quickly became uncomfortable. Florence swallowed hard, looking around the group. There was no reason why they should all be so silent. The path they walked had every appearance of being safe and no one—not even Thomas with his Dragon ears—had any reason to believe there were enemies nearby.

Nevertheless, their lips had been sewn shut with invisible strings.

"We're here," the Raven said finally. "Halfway."

"Take us to the closest room with one exit and no windows," Gregory demanded. "We'll wait there."

The Raven led them to a small interior room that was little more than an access for the back panels that supplied electricity to the guild. It was a good thing the Alchemists had been hard at work developing alternatives to electricity, because the generators had long since stopped running and the room would've been completely dark without each of their torches.

"How long do you think it will take?" the man named Willie asked.

"However long it takes." Vicar Gregory settled into a seated position, his prized weapon across his lap.

Florence used the opportunity to inspect it more closely. She scanned the wires, the multipliers, the gold channels that ran along the outside and peeked out from the inside. There was something about it that seemed *off,* but she couldn't quite put her finger on what it was. As a result, she couldn't even be sure there was anything wrong. Perhaps Gregory had seen his error after all and fixed it. Maybe that was why he'd let her come along—a silent nod to her help, however little credit he'd actually give her.

"So, does it use a canister?" Master Joseph made the Revolver's equivalent of small talk.

"Only as a primer to get the reaction going. The rest is magic, after that." Gregory seemed much more inclined to discuss the logistics of his weapon with someone he deemed his equal.

"So the wielder must be a Chimera?"

"Yes, though not a Perfect one."

Florence couldn't deny the merit of the idea. Making Perfect Chimera already felt like it was taking too long, and she was likely the person who would be the most patient with Arianna on the matter. It was also resource-intensive and mostly untested.

But making a gun . . . Most of those still alive on Loom were Chimeras—the healing powers of magic helped many who might not have otherwise survived the attacks on the guilds. If they could perfect this weapon and mass-produce it . . . Between that and Perfect Chimera, Loom would be unstoppable.

The conversation had faded and several of the party were dozing by the time Thomas sat up straight. Florence felt the familiar crackle of magic in the air that heralded a whisper link. Thomas brought his hand to his ear.

"Yes?" Thomas asked the person on the other end of his magical tether. Everyone in the room roused swiftly. "Middle floor . . . landing area . . . by a large crane . . ."

"Airship test pad." The Raven knew the place instantly.

"Is it far?" Gregory stood.

"Not very, up a bit more."

"Master Joseph, you focus on protecting the Raven as he leads us," Gregory commanded. "I will be up running point with them. I want Thomas and Willie watching flanks. Florence and Shannra, take up the rear."

It was an important and sometimes life-saving position, but no Revolver wanted to be put in the back, away from the front line and all the action. Yet again, Florence had no doubt this would come back as some slight against her.

They all voiced their agreement and set off as Gregory had instructed. If the tension was heavy when they ascended the tower, it was multiplied several times over now that they knew a Dragon was present. Everyone kept their breathing low, weapons drawn. Florence wished, not for the first time, that she had sought out an Alchemist for Dragon ears. Not having them suddenly felt like a severe limitation.

Shannra glanced around warily; Florence put her trust in the other woman's magic and long pointed ears. Her head jerked and the Master Revolver held up his hand, looking in the same direction that Shannra was fixated on. Magic pulsed. Thomas raised his hand to his ear.

"Two more have—"

"One incoming!" Shannra announced, leveling her gun in the direction of a side hall. If Florence could feel the pulse of magic from Thomas's whisper link, then surely any Dragon would've been drawn to it.

"I have the bastard in my sights," Gregory proclaimed, hoisting his weapon.

Florence watched as the vicar's gun slowly lit up. She felt his magic spike and the metal began to glow. Magic sparked off the gold in rainbow fractals that shone like embers and disappeared before hitting the ground. Alchemical runes shimmered. Power continued to build in the multipliers, lighting up the gun like a beacon to all Dragons nearby.

All at once, Florence knew why the gun had seemed so *wrong* to her.

She remembered the weapon she had made at the Alchemists' Guild hall. It too had a series of runic multipliers, a series that Florence now knew had been flawed. That, combined with the magic discharge . . .

Florence looked to the door that everyone else had leveled their weapons against. She could hear the footsteps now, closing fast. She was torn between what she ought to do, and what she wanted to do. She wanted to get back at Gregory for every rebuff. She wanted him to bear the responsibility of his haste and hubris. But Florence wasn't inclined to put herself above the best interests of Loom. Not even now.

"Gregory, put the gun down! There's a mistake! The runes are wrong!" Her voice rose, as if to convey the severity of what she was saying.

Gregory did nothing. His eyes remained on the door, his magic pouring into the weapon. It was too late. The proverbial bucket holding his magic had tipped too far into the gun, and there was no way he would be able to disentangle himself from it now.

"Everyone, get back!" Florence could still feel the shrapnel and daze from the gun exploding in the skeleton forest. "It's going to blow!"

Florence ran away. She didn't care how it looked. She didn't give two canisters about Gregory. All she knew was that she had to survive.

The door they had been watching slammed open, but Florence didn't even turn. She threw herself down the hall, hands over head. Her ears filled with the sound of a Dragon's snarl and then the explosion of magic.

Metal and concrete groaned; Florence was slammed into the ground. She tumbled, allowing the momentum to carry her further away along the shock wave. Another body rolled beside her, wheezes betraying life. Florence forced her eyes open and her hands under her shoulders. She pushed upwards, raising her head.

Willie slumped, dazed, against the wall to Florence's right. She would've presumed him dead from the streak of blood that led down to his head, were it not for his groans. Thomas rolled in pain nearby, his lower half burned to a crisp. Even with magical healing, it would likely scar, but the man would live. Shannra was also finding her feet, about as bruised and scraped as Florence. Their position as the rear guard had likely saved them both.

Dragon and Fenthri guts lined the walls, floor, and ceiling out from the epicenter of the blast. Had Florence not known the men who had been standing there moments earlier, she may not have been able to piece together enough flesh to identify them. Gun parts littered the floor.

"More are coming," Shannra warned. "We need to retreat."

Florence stared at Willie and Thomas. She had no attachment to these men, no kinship with them. Most of the journeymen hadn't even given her the time of day while she'd lived among them in the Underground. So, it was surprising to feel her lips form the words, "We can't leave them."

"What?" Shannra hissed. "This is the life of a Revolver; they knew—"

"I won't leave my guildmates behind!" Florence sprung forward into a sprint. She collected up the largest pieces of Gregory's weapon, pulling them together and flicking aside scraps of flesh.

"What are you doing?" Shannra followed her.

"Leave us . . ." Thomas groaned.

"I know what was wrong with it. I saw a similar weapon once before. Riders used it to shoot down the airship Ari and I were on. The magic . . . We think that magic should be colored, split, but if you put all the colors together you get white. The discharge should be white, not rainbow. It's not an airship that diffuses and breaks magic apart for lift . . ."

"What are you going on about?" Shannra was utterly lost.

"I knew this before . . . But I was wrong on the Alchemical runes to multiply without splitting. Gregory made the same mistake, but in a different way, which means . . ." Florence began to frantically sort out the parts.

"Florence, there's no time for this."

"I can fix it." Florence laid out her revolver. The barrel would be shorter. She'd have to account for that when it came to how many multipliers she stacked, and the range it would be effective in before the magic beam unraveled. "I can make it work."

"We're going to die if we stay!"

"Two more, incoming . . ." Thomas moaned.

"Go on without us," Willie wheezed.

"No!" Florence's hands continued to move so quickly that she hardly had time to think between motions.

"Florence, is this about saving guildmembers? Or saving your pride?" Shannra grabbed her elbow. "They knew the risks. Don't insult them. Save yourself. Fix it later."

"I will not be like her!" Florence shouted, tearing her eyes away from the gun parts and bringing them to Shannra's face. "I will not treat my guild like it's expendable!"

"Her? Who? *Your* guild?" Shannra shook her head, standing and letting go of Florence. "What do you think you are?"

"I'm the woman who will save Loom." Florence bent and heated gold, connecting parts with seams that would likely only hold for one or two shots. One or two shots would be all she needed. "Before anything else, I am a Revolver, and I will not let the death of my vicar—however much of an idiot he was—go to waste."

Florence finished etching the runes she needed and stood. The footsteps were close enough now that even she could hear them. She leveled her weapon.

A Dragon bounded around the corner. One or two shots, that was all she had. She couldn't miss. Florence kept her magic even, pouring it in slowly. Consistent, not a burst of power, but a steady stream, like a rope spun from runes and gold and steel.

Gunshots echoed as Shannra panicked. The bullets sheared off the haze of a corona. Florence adjusted her grip slightly and widened her feet. She had to wait until the last moment.

Another female Dragon rounded the corner, gaining speed.

Florence squeezed the trigger.

It wasn't like a normal shot—fire and done. Florence continued to feed her magic into the weapon. *Stay together, stay together,* she repeated in her head as the beam shot out straight and true. The magic impaled the Dragon straight through the chest, his corona cracking and splintering off like an eggshell made of light.

The man fell dead, and Florence already had the other Dragon in her sights. Her magic was depleted from the first shot, and she locked her knees to keep them from buckling. Still, her hands were steady.

Florence waited two breaths after she thought the Dragon was in range.

It felt like the gun demanded every ounce of her, down to the very breath she drew to live. So Florence gave it that, and let the world go black.

CVAREH

is chest still ached. There was a sort of phantom pain scraping against his ribs long after his lungs had grown back from where the Alchemist's knife had raked against them. Cvareh rubbed his chest again and thought of how many of his own he had condemned to harvesting. Cvareh had never lost an organ before and, now that he had, he was having a hard time seeing it as anything more than a deeply barbaric process.

For now, the ends still justified the means. But he wondered if the Alchemists in all their madness and wisdom couldn't think of a way to grow organs in their tubes, or harvest from the dead. Something, *anything*, to prevent Dragons from enduring what he just had.

Suffocation. Death without death. Repeating again and again until his tissues had grown and mended enough to hold air again.

He said nothing of his pain. He was the rightful Xin'Oji, the man who would win the war for them all and become Dono, and he had made the choice willingly. Furthermore, Arianna had to endure much the same—at least half of what he had gone through, as she didn't have to regrow—and she had yet to speak a word of discomfort.

It was moments like this one, when he looked at her readying her weapons, not more than one day from undergoing a major operation, that he was ensnared in awe at what she was—something more than he could ever aspire to be. Something different from anyone he'd ever met. And none of it had anything to do with the fact that she was now a true Perfect Chimera.

It was a fundamental construct of her nature, of *her*, that made her an unstoppable enigma. It was the same thing that allowed her to take organs and make them her own, like her hands, or ears, or now his lungs—motley parts that seemed so naturally incorporated into her body, like they'd yearned to be there all along. It was that nature which gave her the wisdom of Dragons four times her age, and kept her going with a profound, insatiable drive.

Cvareh wondered if it was something that could ever be lost. Or if she would forever pursue her ends with the march of a soldier to battle until Lord Xin finally came for her immortal soul.

It was something he wanted to embody as well, something he needed to possess to be worthy of her.

"When will you be back for more?" he asked, picking up the golden tube that would be used not to transport reagents, but flowers.

"I don't know just yet," Arianna said without looking at him. "As I mentioned, the Rivets were growing competent at making the boxes when I left. It's been a few days since then, but there may still be just a few ready for the flowers.

"It may not be me, however, who comes back up." That thought hadn't occurred to Cvareh until the moment she said it. "If all goes according to plan, I won't be the only Perfect

Chimera in the world. Whoever comes, I'll have them use that river passage through the island to hide the glider trail."

"Will *you* come back?"

Her motions stopped. She must have heard his heart more than his words, the quiet panic that came at the thought of her leaving him and not returning.

"I'm sure you'll need me to fight at some point." Arianna sheathed her dagger behind her back. "The Perfect Chimera will take some time to train."

"I need you for more than that." He stood over her, looking down. If she could hear that nervousness in his soul at the idea of her trying to vanish from his life again, then she could also hear the truth of his words.

"Are all Dragons this insatiable?"

"Only the ones in love."

Arianna huffed in amusement, shook her head, and stood. She collected her things and carefully loaded the tubes in her bag. But none of it was a gesture of her own feelings toward him, and Cvareh was keenly aware that she had never told him if she reciprocated his affections to the same degree.

"I should be leaving."

He knew it was true. They'd kept each other for three days from the world. Cain had been covering for him, but Cvareh knew it was time to return to the Xin Manor. It was time to assume responsibility for his destiny.

"Whisper to me whenever you come. I will escape the manor to see you."

There was a moment's hesitation when Cvareh rightfully feared she was about to refuse him. But Arianna merely said, "Very well."

"When you return, I will be Oji," he swore. "And I will free them."

Arianna's expression looked as surprised as he felt in that moment. Cvareh had never said anything so bold, never uttered the slightest treason. Furthermore, it was faster than he'd first promised, originally saying he'd keep that vow when he was Dono.

But it felt right.

Right enough for him to know that he had to act on it before the day was done, before he risked losing his resolve.

"You will kill Finnyr?"

"I must." He knew her, and he knew where her mind was.

"I'll consider the lungs a trade for the kill that should be mine." Arianna gave him a stern look, as if warning him not to argue. He wouldn't have anyway. And he would have given her whatever she asked without a trade.

"I will end him," Cvareh vowed.

"Make it terrible. If you let me down in this, I will never forgive you."

Cvareh had never felt more motivated.

The feeling stayed with him the entire ride home. Cvareh knew he would be seen approaching the manor, and word would get back to Finnyr. He made a direct approach for Cain's balcony. It was smaller than his own, and Cvareh ended up making the short leap from his bird as it perched on the ledge before swooping back to the sky.

"The prodigal son returns." Cain opened the doors leading out to the balcony.

"I need you to do something." Cvareh wasted no time. The idea of challenging Finnyr, of assuming the role of Oji, of putting his house knowingly in harm's way by outright starting war against House Rok, was already planting uneasiness in his stomach. If he didn't do this now and seal it in blood, he risked losing his nerve.

"What is it?"

"I need you to find Fae, and keep her from Finnyr and me." Cvareh somehow managed to keep his voice level despite the fear and apprehension that wanted to seep out with every word.

"Cvareh, does this mean—"

"I'm going to challenge him, Cain." Cvareh clasped the shoulder of the man who had been like a brother to him. "I am going to take back House Xin from Rok. But I wish to do it by the laws of the gods. Even if Rok fights with shadows and deceit, I will challenge my brother in a forum befitting the title he claims to hold."

"Then I will distract Fae. I will challenge her if I must." The conviction was unsurprising, but also unwelcome.

"That is the one thing I must ask you not to do. I need you alive, Cain. I need you as my right hand, as my Ryu, should all this come to pass."

He wasn't prepared for the mix of surprise and emotion that crossed his friend's face. But what did Cain think would happen? There was no other choice, as far as Cvareh was concerned, and he wouldn't have chosen another under other less dire circumstances.

"I will do as my Oji commands."

COLETTA

Fae had returned, and Yveun had indulged in his dark delights.

There was an easiness that settled over the estate when the king was pleased, not unlike the afterglow of the man himself. It was a collective sigh of relief for them all, none more than Coletta. Yveun wanted results. But he didn't want the practical kind that careful planning and hard work yielded. He wanted fanfare and the kind of victories that would have minstrels singing for centuries to come.

Coletta merely wanted to see their longevity secured.

Fae's arrival set in motion a series of carefully planned steps on Coletta's part. Yveun knew he had his time with the woman. Ulia knew to wait and observe until the Dono was finished with his conquest, and then spirit Fae away to the Gray Room—the room in which Coletta now waited with an Alchemist and a long, glistening tongue centered on a tray like some new delicacy.

"My queen," Ulia announced as she entered the room, Fae trailing behind. The green-skinned woman did little to demonstrate reverence to the Ryu, and Ulia could not contain a disdainful little side-eye. Coletta had the time to deal with neither, so she permitted both.

"Thank you for bringing Fae here. You may leave." Coletta had yet to allow Ulia to watch any of the experiments that went on in the room, and it was an intentional play.

She wanted the youngest flower to fantasize about the possibilities and mull over the potential horrors of the procedure. Even though Ulia would never utter secrets, Coletta knew no one was perfectly tight-lipped. And she wanted just enough truth to seep into the bedrock of Lysip to know that something of a great and terrible nature was happening at the Rok Estate.

"Do you know what is about to happen?" Coletta did not want to mince words with Fae.

"I have some vague idea." The emerald woman combed through her hair, still a nest from Yveun's hands.

"We will begin with your tongue."

"My tongue?"

"I do not believe you have magic there?"

Fae shook her head and sauntered over to the operating table as though she was doing little more than sitting down for a meal. Coletta admired the total lack of self-preserving instinct. It made the woman an ideal warrior to have in her arsenal.

"This will hurt some." The Alchemist regarded Fae warily. She was nearly twice his size.

"Your tiny knives can't hurt me, Fen."

"Open your mouth, then." It was almost as if he had accepted a challenge.

Coletta would never tolerate such boldness from a Fenthri herself, but there was something almost adorable about watching the gray people try to muster strength against their superiors.

Fae obliged and the man set to work. She didn't flinch as he pulled out her tongue with a long pair of metal tongs, the flat paddles at the end indenting the organ he set about removing. Coletta didn't avert her eyes from the moment the scalpel first cut into the flesh of the tongue to the last second before it was entirely severed.

The Alchemist tilted the Dragon's head, allowing blood to pour from the corner of Fae's mouth. Nothing more than a rough stub protruded from where her tongue had been, already beginning to ripple with magic to regrow the absent tissues. Even still, Fae's breaths were even, unlabored, and Coletta was forced to admire her monster yet again.

She watched as the new tongue was stitched into place. Despite having searched for the best organs on Ruana, she could make none take to Yeann or Topann's bodies. They all formed festering, agonizing wounds that her flower's body refused to heal.

But Coletta wasn't one to give up, not when there was so much to explore. It was the one thing she could count on the Fen agreeing with, and the man continued to carve up Dragons at her request.

The Alchemist pulled away, looking at his handiwork. Coletta could tell from his expression alone that something was different this time.

"What is it?" she demanded.

"I can't be sure . . ."

"Out with it, or it's your tongue that will be cut off next," Coletta drawled, not even mustering the energy to threaten him properly.

"This was a success."

"You can tell already?" He nodded. She knew almost instantly when a poison was right and when it was not. But the man's mouth still formed a grim line. "What have you discovered?"

The man looked from Fae to her, as if jarred from thought. He swallowed hard. "I think I know why the other organs didn't take."

Given the amount of fear radiating off the Fen in that moment, Coletta was certain that she was not going to like whatever the explanation was.

CVAREH

ain had gone ahead to distract Fae. Cvareh paced his friend's room for what felt like forever, though he knew it couldn't have been more than a few minutes. When he could wait no longer, he stepped into the hall.

The halls of the Xin Manor seemed alive once more. Even though Cvareh didn't see another soul for the first half of his walk to find Finnyr, the air seemed to pulse with an energy that he hadn't felt since before Petra's death. It was like House Xin was waking up from the grips of mourning at last.

Finnyr wasn't in his room, and neither was Fae. So Cvareh went to the main hall. Again, Finnyr was nowhere to be found, but Cvareh ran into a servant, her hands laden with laundry.

"Have you seen Finnyr?" Cvareh intentionally left off "Oji," an omission that did not go unnoticed.

The woman's eyes widened. "I have not."

He cursed, wheeling for another wing of the manor. Perhaps Finnyr had gone to claim Petra's quarters as his own. Killing him there would be its own kind of pleasure.

"I did, however, hear two men who work with the bocos saying that the Oji had requested a flight. They could not decide which mount to give him."

Cvareh stopped, only sparing a second. "Thank you."

"Good luck," the woman whispered.

If Finnyr was looking for a boco, there was a chance Fae had been called away and he was fleeing until his bodyguard could return. Perhaps he somehow had the instinct to know when death was coming for him. And it *was* coming.

Cvareh paused, turning. He saw the woman at the far end of the hall still, and called back to her. "Leave your task. Round up everyone you can to go to the departure platforms. I need witnesses. And I need to make sure he doesn't escape."

"As you command!" The woman practically threw down her basket of laundry, sprinting away so quickly that Cvareh almost felt a wind kicked up by her feet.

Cvareh thought of Finnyr, his cowardly slip of a brother. If he were Finnyr—which was rightly near impossible to imagine—where would he go? He would want to flee back to the safety of Rok's arms until Fae was no longer indisposed. But he would do so as he did everything else—with a coward's weakness.

So Cvareh headed down through the back passages and thoroughfares to a modest platform. Unlike the one Finnyr arrived on, this had no sculpture, no foliage or design. It was primarily used for quick trips, deliveries, and trysts that were not to be observed by the watchful eyes from the manor.

Here was where he found his brother pacing back and forth, wringing his hands. Cvareh hated that his brother's hands, of all people's, were attached to Arianna. Finnyr didn't deserve the honor. Maybe it was the gods above working in some weird way to see Finnyr's hands put to good use. His brother would have never created anything meaningful with them.

Cvareh waited in the archway leading out to the platform. He knew he didn't have time to waste, but he hadn't thought about what he was going to say. He had to challenge, but he felt there should be more gravity to the situation, more impact.

"Where is my boco?" Finnyr snapped when a servant appeared at the door, two others in tow.

The servant said nothing, looking from Finnyr to Cvareh. That was what finally drew his brother's attention. Cvareh wondered if he was having a waking fantasy, seeing his brother's lip tremble slightly.

"Cvareh, good, I'm glad you're here." Finnyr tried to draw up his height, to make his voice stable. Both failed. Had he always been such a tiny man? "It seems as though we have an issue. They have not yet brought my boco as I commanded. Perhaps as the Xin'Ryu, you can sort this out?"

Three more people appeared from another doorway. Cvareh didn't recognize any of them, but they all hovered with purpose. Their eyes carried a sharpness that seemed to pick at Finnyr with every glance.

"I will not sort it out as the Xin'Ryu."

"I'm your Oji." Finnyr looked around at all of them now, as if to search for someone to affirm the fact. "I'm your Oji!"

"Finnyr Xin'Oji To." It was the one time Cvareh didn't mind saying his brother's name in association with Petra's title. It was something that must be done if he was going to take it. "I challenge you."

"On what grounds?" Finnyr squeaked.

Where should he start? "Neglecting House Xin."

Everyone's eyes volleyed from brother to brother. The outcome would affect each of them in a way that would be forever irreversible. Cvareh's victory would mean war, but his defeat would mean centuries of oppression under House Rok.

"I-I have not—"

"Finnyr, do you accept my duel?" Cvareh pressed.

"Of course I do not!" Finnyr began laughing. "Do you think I'd let you duel me on such unsubstantiated grounds?"

"On what grounds did you duel Petra?" His sister's name was forced out as a snarl. When his brother said nothing, Cvareh asked again, "What grounds, Finnyr? What did you charge her with? Did she cower even though it was a fool's challenge? Or did she stand for it?"

"She challenged me." There was truth in Finnyr's affirmation.

Cvareh took a step forward. "She challenged you? And you killed her?"

"It was a duel!"

"Did you have help?" Cvareh continued his advance. He didn't know what he was going to do yet, but that first step had crossed him over the point of no return. This would end now. One way or another, there would be only one Xin sibling standing when the next morning came.

"N-no."

"Did Rok help you bring down Petra?" Cvareh's claws shot from his hand. "Did you see our sister die a coward's death?"

"Someone stop him!" Finnyr pointed. "He's threatening your Oji."

No one moved.

"Did you kill her?"

"I killed her!"

"Was the fight fair?" Cvareh's voice rose. More people continued to arrive, no doubt drawn by the shouting.

"It was a rightly charged duel," Finnyr insisted.

Cvareh sheathed his claws and reached out for his brother's neck, drawing the man to him with both hands. Had Finnyr always been so weak?

"Don't lie to me," Cvareh growled, pressing his fingertips into Finnyr's squishy flesh. At any moment, his claws could extend right into his brother's pale blue skin. "Don't lie to us."

"I—" Finnyr gasped.

"The eyes of Xin are upon you. Did you kill Petra fairly? Are you the Oji of this house?"

"Help me!" Finnyr's eyes lolled about, looking for salvation. But no one moved. "Fae, help me!"

"She's not coming." Cvareh didn't know what Cain was doing to distract the woman, but it seemed to be working so far.

"What will you do? Kill me without a proper duel?" Finnyr hissed. It only made Cvareh want to squeeze tighter. "Will you be Oji then? No."

"Are you Oji now?" He returned to his earlier line of questioning.

"House Rok recognizes me as such, and they're all that matters in this world."

Cvareh threw his brother aside. Finnyr rolled, scrambling to stop himself before he tumbled dangerously close to the ledge.

"House Rok is all that matters? Your cheek is unmarked, but you are one of them, aren't you?"

Finnyr clambered to his feet, shifting his rumpled clothing back into place. He smoothed his vest over his narrow chest. "House Xin, I command you to slay Cvareh, for assaulting your Oji."

No one moved.

"That's an order!"

"Are you our Oji?" a woman asked.

"Did you kill Petra in a fair duel?" another chimed in.

"W-What?" Finnyr looked around in confusion. "Don't question me. I'm your Oji!"

"Finnyr, you don't understand, do you, what it really means to hold that title?" Cvareh stepped forward.

"Take another step and I-I'll attack you myself."

Cvareh opened his arms, welcoming the first blow. "That's what I wanted from the beginning. If you are our Oji, defend your title. Lord Xin should be on your side."

Finnyr's claws shot out.

It was the final mistake in a lifetime of poor decisions.

Cvareh lunged.

Finnyr tried to guard himself, but the movement was slow and telegraphed. Cvareh swatted the defense away with one hand and plunged the other into his brother's chest. He would waste no time. He would not draw out the fight. As satisfying as the act would be, he had more important things to focus on than bloodlust. It served all of them, even Arianna, for his brother to stop existing as quickly as possible.

Finnyr coughed in shock. "Y-you really did it," he wheezed.

"Salvage her memory." Cvareh's fingers closed around Finnyr's heart. "Did you kill Petra?"

"I did . . . but she was already poisoned." His brother leaned forward, whispering in his ear. "You will never beat her. She is stronger than you all."

"Coletta?" Cvareh asked. It had to be.

Finnyr grinned, grabbed Cvareh's shoulders, and pushed himself away. Cvareh had never seen a Dragon take their own life, but it was a coward's death befitting his brother's existence.

Finnyr stumbled backward. One foot had nothing to fall on, and he tumbled lifelessly into the empty air beyond the edge of the balcony.

Cvareh brought his brother's heart to his lips, taking a bite out of it. It was stringy and tough. Even though he knew Arianna had Finnyr's organs, he couldn't find the taste of her in the man himself. It was a relief, and Cvareh cast the unwanted scrap of meat after its owner.

He turned to those gathered, wondering what they thought, what they felt. It was an anticlimactic end that put the title of Oji on a man who had never wanted it and hadn't been trained for it. Were he one of them, he wouldn't feel very confident.

"What now, Cvareh'Oji?" a woman was bold enough to ask.

"Now, we fight." Cvareh took a deep breath. "We fight to end Rok's tyranny."

"How are we to stand against them?" The question wasn't asked to undermine him, but as a genuine concern—a warranted one, Cvareh understood.

"As Xin, we have always placed the end before our ideals. Our patron teaches us that the end is all that matters, for all things march toward the ultimate end—death." Cvareh hoped they would understand, and that his first action as Oji wasn't about to be defending his plan for saving their house from annihilation. "We shall rely on Lord Xin's guidance. We shall set aside our ideals, the pride as Dragons that blinds us from what we must do to gain our victory. We will ally ourselves with the Fenthri on Loom, and we will achieve victory."

The long silence that followed did not encourage him in the slightest.

ARIANNA

She hated that Dragon.

She loved him, too.

Cvareh was nothing but raw emotion and conflict that gnawed at her fresh lungs from the inside out. Arianna flew the glider with reckless abandon, plunging into the God's Line and speeding for Garre as though nothing else in the world mattered.

Nothing else did.

She was going to lose the chance to kill Finnyr. She was going to lose the chance to kill Yveun, too, for Cvareh to become Dono. And when he did assume that title, she was going to lose him as well.

Arianna had never wanted to want him in the first place, but now that she did, it was hard to even breathe, thinking about him marching down a path with more conviction than she had ever seen—a path that would ultimately separate them. Just as Florence had found her place in the world, so would Cvareh. And neither of them required a Wraith.

It was night by the time she landed the glider in the far hangar. The room was still, icy with winter, and her breath curled in the air as she relaxed her magic from the glider.

"Good to see our wayward inventor return," a weathered voice spoke, as cold as the darkness itself.

Arianna turned in the direction of the sound. Magic pooled in her eyes and goggles until she could make out the living skeleton lurking in the shadows.

"Garre needs to work on its welcoming committee." Arianna stepped down and started in his direction. Louie stood in front of the entrance to the guild, and there was little else she could do. He didn't budge as she approached. Goggles of his own covered his beady little eyes; Arianna could only assume he stared up at her. She sighed heavily. "What do you want?"

"You don't seem pleased to see me."

"I will never be pleased to see you and am not in the mood for your games." The single sentence used up all the patience she could muster for the man. "Now, step aside."

"We need to speak."

"We have done so. Step aside." Arianna wondered if he was heavier than the tube-filled satchel at her side. She could just lift him up and move him.

"No."

"Do you have a death wish?"

"Not in the slightest. Quite the opposite, actually. The question is, Arianna, do you?"

"Do not threaten me." One warning—that was all he would get.

"The vicars may consider you a threat."

"*What?*"

"Since your little experiment as a weaponsmith blew up in the Vicar Revolver's face." Arianna was instantly reminded of her prototype on Nova. She'd sent the schematics to Florence and—

"I heard Florence was there, too. Fighting Dragons with faulty weapons . . . it's so sad, the outcome."

"Is she alive?" Arianna snapped. She was going to lose Cvareh and Florence; she had accepted that. But she would lose them to their choices and watch them thrive from her place in the shadows. She pushed the small-framed Fenthri against the door. His head banged dully against the metal. "Louie, do not play games with me."

"Then do not play games with me," he growled. "You went to Nova. You conspired to cut me out of the equation. You have yet to produce the schematics for the box . . . And after all I've done for you? After all I am willing to risk to secure your flowers, when Dragons would see them systematically destroyed?"

There was a moment of clarity that cut through the confusion and anger. "What did you say?"

"I will gladly secure the flowers for you." Louie smiled his wretched little grin, thinking he had a leg up on her, not knowing what she carried in her bag.

Arianna's hands loosened their hold, smoothing over the wrinkles thoughtfully, almost gently. She had not told him, or anyone on Loom, about the flowers being destroyed. "How far does your influence reach?"

"Straight to the Dragon Queen."

Those five words sent her into a blind rage. Coletta'Ryu, the woman who had drugged Arianna with her dagger, who had put her under the claws of Yveun—this was who Louie had been in bed with. Leave it to worthless slime like him to deal with such a revolting creature.

With a shout, Arianna swung the frail man to the ground, *hoping* she broke him. Her ears twitched eagerly at the sound of his body breaking and tearing. Arianna was on him, her knees pinning down his arms—as if he needed to be pinned. Louie couldn't put up a fight even if he tried. She felt his bones snap like twigs under her weight.

But Louie didn't cry. He didn't beg for mercy. He didn't even grimace. Instead he grinned like a fool, his crooked yellow teeth winking up at her like dying stars.

"Yes, yes, White Wraith, show me your claws," he urged. "Kill me, go ahead, and never know what I have told her."

"How dare you!" Arianna was glad they were far from the guild, because she was screaming now. There was no reason not to let the dam break, because the only person who could see this jagged, destroyed side of her would be a dead man. "I always knew you were the worst of the worst but this, *this*? You have sold out our world for profit!"

"Indeed," he replied with equal fervor, managing to keep his voice strong despite his position. "And I will do it again, time after time. I'm loyal to the highest bidder. So, you better make your offering more appealing, Arianna, for all of Loom."

"How long?" She couldn't even look at him straight. "How long have you been working with her?"

"*Years.*" It made so much sense. The king of the underworld, the man who could seemingly get anything, who always happened to have organs to trade. Of course he did! He had sold his soul to a queen of death for them. "She trusts me, Arianna, and we can use this to our advantage. We can use this to save Loom if—"

"If what?"

"If you do not dare undercut me again," Louie finished.

Arianna reeled back, rolling from the balls of her feet to standing.

"I offered you an opportunity to work together. You went back on that deal."

"We make a new deal, right now. I don't kill you—"

His laughter interrupted her. "You think I care about death? You think I have people I love whom you can threaten? Arianna, you are the most idealistic fool of them all." Arianna watched with disdain as the man continued to lay there, his magic slowly re-growing his muscles and bones, popping his sagging flesh back into place. "If you kill me, you won't have the organs the Alchemists need for the Perfect Chimera. You won't have a means to get those precious flowers off Nova."

Arianna tilted her head to the side. How the tides shifted . . .

"Oh, Louie, *that's* your bargaining chip?" She drew her dagger. She didn't want to do this with Dragon claws. She wanted the tool that took Louie's life to be Fenthri-made. "That queen you so adore has betrayed you. She failed to inform you that her plans have been thwarted and her minions have been killed. That Xin has saved some of the flowers for themselves." Arianna crouched down as Louie's eyes widened with surprise. "Yes, my sweet King of Mercury Town. My friends have not sold me out, unlike yours. And they just so happen to be able to provide organs as well as any other Dragon."

Arianna pointed her dagger at his throat again, thinking back to Cvareh. She wondered if he had killed Finnyr yet. "You know, for most of my life, I've wanted to kill a king. You weren't the man I had in mind, but I think your death may be just as satisfying. Let's find out, shall we?"

"Wait, Arianna, let's not be hasty, I can still—"

"Still what?" She nearly purred with delight. He'd really come alone, thinking his contacts could protect him. He was an old knife, one that would snap if she even tried to put it to whetstone. Only one solution for such a worthless thing. "Be useful? I think there are a few Ravens who have just as much use as you, and they happen to know most of your network."

Arianna leaned forward, sliding a hand around his shoulder. It was an odd sort of embrace. She could feel the pistol he carried in his vest, but he didn't reach for it. He must've known it'd do nothing against her. Even if it alerted someone, he'd be dead before they arrived.

"Did you know it would end like this for you?"

"I couldn't imagine a better death than at the hands of the best thief and killer I've ever had the pleasure of working with." Louie spoke softly, as if to a lover. Arianna wondered if it was the first time the terrible man had been touched by a woman. "Eat my heart, after you cut it out."

"No," she whispered against his ear. "I know it'll taste rotten."

Arianna plunged the dagger between his ribs. She twisted it, the chorus of shattering bones and ripping tissue harmonizing with his final breath. Louie spit black blood that oozed down her shoulder—a stain on her white coat that she'd wear as a badge of honor.

Arianna plunged her hand into his chest, ripped out his heart, and cast it aside.

She stood, leaving the body of the King of Mercury Town oozing black onto the cold floor of the hangar. She left it as a clear warning to any who found it that the White Wraith had returned to Loom.

She slammed open the door Louie had been blocking with a *bang*, not caring who heard. The passage back to the guild was a blur that ended with her yanking another door open without warning. Will and Helen jumped to attention, wide-eyed and startled. Arianna leaned against the doorframe, flipping her knife, blood on her shoulder.

"All of Louie's men—bring them here, now," she demanded cheerfully. "Try to run and I'll flay you alive."

"What?" Helen stuttered.

"We need to do as she says." Will grabbed Helen's arm and dragged her from the room. The boy gave Arianna a sidelong look that she reciprocated. She hadn't forgotten his attempt to warn her on the airship. It may not be enough to save him, but it was enough to keep him alive for the time being.

They returned with three men in tow. Arianna closed the door behind them, appreciating the looks of apprehension each of them wore. She leaned against it, making it clear that no one was getting out without her blessing.

"So, let's talk about loyalty." Arianna pointed her dagger to the man with the red ears. "You first."

"My name is Adam."

"Fantastic Rok ears, those are. They're a whisper link, right?"

"To a woman named Topann."

Continued cooperation would earn him minutes, maybe even hours of life. "And that woman is in the employ of Coletta Rok, the Dragon Queen?"

"Yes."

"Would you sever the whisper link now if I demanded?"

"Yes."

"What's going on?" Helen demanded. "Where's Louie?"

The child wouldn't let herself see the obvious. "I killed him for crimes against Loom."

"You can't do that!" The girl seemed genuinely distraught.

"Occupational hazard for operating outside the law. Louie knew what he was about." There were few laws on Loom—

Fenthri laws anyway. Most were unspoken, at that. "Don't commit treason" was a fairly obvious one. Louie's protégé seemed stunned still, so Arianna pressed the point home. "Helen, I am *not* the Master Raven and will never turn a blind eye to treason against Loom. As loathe as I am to kill talent, I dislike those who work against Loom much more."

The child pressed her lips shut.

"Louie liked deals. So how about this? I won't kill you all, and you—and everyone else who was loyal to Louie—work for me now. Whatever he paid you, I'll pay."

"Sounds more than fair, boss." Adam was the first to speak, crossing his arms over his chest and leaning against the wall. The idea clearly didn't bother him the slightest.

"Count us in." Will spoke for himself and Helen. The girl seemed to have a moment of protest, but she had the sense to swallow it.

"Cross me and die—"

Adam held up a hand. She arched her eyebrows at being silenced but permitted him to continue. "We all know what you can do. Would rather work for the Queen of Wraiths than the King of Mercury Town anyway."

Queen of Wraiths. That was new. But she'd killed Louie, which meant she'd get his title according to Dragon law. Arianna didn't bother hiding a smirk.

"First things first, then. How was Louie communicating back to Ter.4? I demand word on Florence."

CVAREH

The streets of Napole were empty.

Restaurants were quiet enough to lure the rats out in search of food that had been left at tables—unpaid for, uneaten. Gaming parlors were still, decks unshuffled and wheels unspun. The tasting rooms for both wine and tea were, for the first time in the history of the capital city of Ruana, void of patrons.

Cvareh appreciated the reprieve from the chaos that had raged through the night. Hundreds of people, his people, had relocated up the river that ran down the center of Ruana. The order to flee was met with trepidation, but he was surprised by how many people gave him their faith and trusted in his orders.

"Now what?" Cain whispered. There was no need for discretion, but it suited the stillness that pressed in around them.

"Now, we go home." Cvareh took one last look at the building before them.

It was the old Xin Manor, the estate that had once been the most prestigious structure on all of Ruana but had languished in Petra's time as her focus had shifted to the new manor along the Western ridge. This had been his home when he was a boy.

It was where his father died; in the calm before the calamity, he could almost pick up the scent of his father's blood from where Petra had ripped his beating heart from his chest.

"That's it?" Cain balked as Cvareh turned away from the old homestead. "You're turning tail and running?"

"Yes," Cvareh affirmed.

"No." Cain grabbed Cvareh's elbow and held his ground, practically yanking him back into place. "I will not let you hand Napole to them. You became Oji to fight."

"And fight I will," Cvareh vowed.

"How do you figure? You're leaving our capital, the Xin jewel, ripe for the taking." Cain snarled at the mere thought. "As your Ryu—"

"As my Ryu I need you above all others to trust me, Cain. Napole is not in the ground, or the buildings. What makes it shine is not the revelries or cafés. It is the people, Cain."

"They will come here."

"I know." Cvareh was counting on it. If Yveun let him down and didn't make a show of taking Ruana, he was in very real trouble. He'd only had time enough to come up with one plan, and this was it.

"You mean to ambush them!" Cain had yet to wrap his mind around not fighting. "The streets will run gold with Rok blood."

"No." Cvareh took Cain's hand, removing it from his person to clutch it tightly in both of his. "I will rob Yveun of his conquest. There will be no victory here. He will land on Ruana and be met with nothing more to claim than dust and rotting food."

"And then you will fight him?"

"I will not duel him yet." Cvareh shook his head and started again for his boco.

Cain fell hastily into step, his feet no doubt trying to make up for the slowness in his mind. "He will certainly challenge you."

"I know."

"You can do it here without fear of others' involvement."

"I know."

"But you won't do it anyway . . ." Cain's voice trailed off, trying to process a concept he had never heard of before. "What are you doing, Cvareh?"

"I am focusing on the end." Cvareh mounted his boco, taking up the reigns and looking toward the breaking dawn. "We've played along with Rok's world order for too long, and for what? If our goal is to build our own, we only have ourselves to answer to."

"This will be war on Tam as well. They will come to Rok's aid," Cain cautioned, finally understanding but still two steps behind.

"I know. So it must be if Xin is to lead. We must earn our victory over both of them." Cvareh squinted, wondering if he imagined the outlines of boco on the horizon. Not wanting to take a chance, he spurred his own mount to the skies. Cain did the same. "We will soon have Perfect Chimera. Only then will we strike."

"And what if she doesn't send them?" Cain called over the wind and flapping of wings. "She will."

"I hope you're right, Oji. All bets are on the table." Cain looked uncertain, but still he followed. Even when his doubts were at their peak, he followed. He had earned every shifting shade of blue his skin took on in the lightening dawn.

"With stakes this high, we have to go all in."

Cvareh gripped the reigns, leaving a city he loved dearly behind him to be ransacked in frustration by Rok and the

Dragon King. Instead, he headed for the refinery that had just enough gold to produce the first new glider of what he hoped would be many.

FLORENCE

In her mind, she was in that oversized bed in Old Dortam she'd foolishly lamented having to make every morning. The noise around her was Arianna's. It was a lazy day, one where there was no job and no one in Mercury Town—the sort of day where she could wake slowly and leave the room a bit of a mess. They would quietly sip something hot while their throats woke up, before bundling up to brave the icy winter wind that swept down the mountains, as they set out in search of something more substantial to put in their stomachs.

Florence would ogle the hats on pedestals in the window of her favorite hattery and walk slowly by the one confectionery in all of Old Dortam. It would be Arianna who would insist that they had to keep going. They could stop another day . . . but for now, they had to keep going.

I have to keep going.

She cracked her eyes open. The light shining from the other side of her eyelids was not evidence of a bright winter morning, but a buzzing electric bulb. The noise around her was not Arianna, but an Alchemist. The chill was indeed from winter, but it was magnified by the depths of the Underground.

"Shannra? Willie? Thomas?" Florence whispered.

"They're all fine," a familiar voice replied. "Varying states of fine, but all fine, nevertheless."

Florence knew who she was speaking to the moment his face appeared in her vision. "Didn't know you made it to Ter.4, Derek."

"I was one of the last to make it out of Ter.2. You'd already moved by the time I got to Ter.0 and by the time you settled in here . . . Neither Nora or I knew how to approach the infamous Florence."

"Infamous? Has a nice ring to it."

"You would think so." Without warning, he plunged a syringe into her arm and a warm sensation flowed up through her veins.

Silence passed between them as Florence waited for her mind to clear. Things were different now. Perhaps it was because she'd gained "infamy" that she hadn't set out in search of them either. After all, there was a time when he and Nora had been everything to her.

That time was over.

People changed, the world changed, and everyone moved right along.

"How long was I out for?" She looked at her arm, and the large bruise formed around the injection site that her magic had yet to heal.

"Only a day." The Alchemist shook his head. Just like that, their relationship had finished settling into a friendly, but professional comfort. "We could do more if we had access to proper reagents and medicine, but we'll have to let you mend up the old-fashioned way, with magic alone."

Florence wondered how quickly something became "the old-fashioned way" since there had only been magic on Loom for two decades.

"I'm going to fetch the masters."

Derek left, and shortly after two master Revolvers entered the small, makeshift medical room. Florence recognized them as Bernard and Emma. These were the last two Master Revolvers alive and one of them was—or would soon be—vicar.

"Don't bother trying to sit up." One of them raised a hand to stop before she could move. "Save your strength."

If the room wasn't crowded enough, the door opened again and the three other vicars entered. Florence felt like she was some sort of feast laid out for the powerful to devour. It didn't help that her "hospital bed" was an actual table.

"What happened up there?" Dove demanded.

"Give her a moment to catch her breath." Florence appreciated Powell coming to her aid, even when she didn't need it.

"I'm fine, thank you, Vicar Powell." Despite what the masters had told her earlier, Florence pushed herself upright. Her body felt more fatigued than anything else. Her muscles had a dull ache, but it seemed the medicine Derek had given her was taking effect and the pain was a distant whisper in her mind. "Vicar Gregory assigned a group to go into the hall to test the weapon based off the schematics Arianna had discovered in Master Oliver's office . . ."

She tried to summarize everything as succinctly as possible without leaving out any important details. Most important, she tried to expunge the general disdain that she still found herself harboring for Gregory and the incompetence that led to his death—and the deaths and injury of others.

"Why didn't you retreat?" Master Bernard asked when she had finished her story. "Thomas corroborates that he asked you to leave him behind."

Florence thought about it for a long moment, folding and unfolding her hands in her lap. How could she tell the truth without also outing herself as the woman who killed the last Vicar Alchemist? "I know what happened in the Alchemists' Guild." She didn't feel guilty for Sophie in the slightest, just as she didn't feel guilty for not pushing Gregory harder about his mistakes. But she remained intentionally ambiguous. "I know that Vicar Sophie made the decision to leave behind a portion of the guild to die." Florence looked right at Ethel. If anyone knew the truth—it was her. But the vicar's face betrayed nothing. "It has never sat well with me. And there's precious little talent left in Loom."

"You killed a Revolver point-blank in the first Tribunal," Dove pointed out.

"I did. But that was different."

"How so?" Master Emma asked, more curious than threatening.

"Because he made his choice. He stood against Loom, and I stood back. But Thomas, Willie, Shannra, Master Joseph . . ." Florence looked to Dove. "The Raven you sent to guide us." She felt guilty she couldn't remember the lad's name. "They were all following orders. It was a mistake they had no share in making that would cost them their lives."

"How did you know you could make the gun work?" Master Bernard asked. "I saw the equations and details you gave Gregory. How did you arrive at the correct conclusion when he and the rest of us could not?"

Florence wanted to say it was luck, but that wasn't true. "I've worked on magical weapons for the better part of my tutelage. I was the gunsmith for the White Wraith, after all." It felt like such an odd thing to confess now. "I once saw a weapon fired that I can only assume was experimental, possibly stolen, used by a Rider against an airship I was on. I worked on my own guns, tried to recreate what I saw without the benefit of 'proper' guild teaching.

"So, I made up the difference in my lack of education with creativity. Plus—" Florence couldn't stop a small smile from gracing her lips, one that quickly faltered from the severity of the situation. "I know how a Rivet thinks. I know where their minds run into walls and how to step around them."

"Can you recreate it?" Powell asked. "Do you remember what you did?"

"Of course," Florence confirmed. "But I'd want to properly run it by Arianna. She may have improvements to offer."

"With this, we can truly fight back," Bernard murmured. "Regular Chimera can join the fight here on Loom, and we can send the majority of the Perfects directly to Nova."

"More than that, we can *win*." Florence let there be no room for doubt.

"We can win with a strong leader at the helm of the Revolvers." It registered to Florence as a weird thing for Powell of all people to say. The man looked at the two Master Revolvers and wondered who he would pick from between them.

"We are far from a quorum." Emma glanced uncertainly at the room. "I will vote for myself."

"As will I." Bernard side-eyed the woman who was now his competitor. "Perhaps the other vicars can help break the tie."

"I'm not sure I'm qualified." Leave it to the Vicar Alchemist to retreat from the world and its decisions.

"I cast my vote for Florence." Her ears rang as though Powell's words were gunshot.

"What?" Dove squinted her eyes at the Vicar Harvester.

"She is strong because she has learned from many guilds. She is what Loom is working to return to, and what students should strive to be—better versions of themselves through the acquisition of knowledge."

"There's no precedent for this," Ethel cautioned.

"There's no precedent for living in the Underground either." Dove shook her head and pinched the bridge of her nose. She sighed heavily. "I vote for her, too." The Vicar Raven looked to the two shocked Revolvers. "Nothing personal, I just already have a rapport with the girl and I *hate* getting to know new people."

"Do you think the Revolvers would support it?" Ethel was the only one focused on how the guild would receive the news.

"We haven't even heard yet if Florence supports it." Bernard crossed his arms and looked to her.

Florence wondered if she stared down another Gregory, another powerful man who saw her as less because of her age and experience and tutelage. Even if he wasn't, there would always be people like Gregory, seeking to undermine her at every turn.

Florence looked back to Powell. He had risen in an unconventional way as well, and she had witnessed it. Now, she wanted to show him that he had made the right choice in saving her from the wreckage of Ter.1. She wanted to make her life mean something.

"I support it," she affirmed.

"How do you think you can lead the Revolvers without ever truly being one?" Emma asked skeptically.

It's not an outright no, Florence thought hopefully. "Respectfully, I have been a Revolver from the day I was born."

The room went silent. Florence wondered if she should say something more, but she let those gathered chew over their own thoughts. It gave her time as well, to think about the position she was about to put herself in. The more she considered, the less afraid she became.

"I change my vote, and cast my support for Florence."

"What?" Bernard gaped at his counterpart.

"She did something the last vicar couldn't do. You saw the gun."

"That's not reason enough to make someone a vicar!"

"She did something more than that," Powell interjected. "She united Loom." The Vicar Harvester held up his hand, drawing a circle in the air around his palm. "Five guilds, once separate like fingers, united once more as a singular entity." He curled his hand into a fist.

The five guilds of Loom—Florence had always imagined them like one great chain, but perhaps they were more like a hand. They could move separately, but their strength came from banding together, from seeing that they were one unified force.

"I support her." Vicar Ethel finally made up her mind. All eyes fell to Bernard.

"I'm outvoted." He shrugged. "My opinion hardly matters."

"It matters to me." Florence waited to continue until she was sure the whole of his attention was on her. "You are one of only two masters. I will need your help, leadership, and insight. I will not take up this mantle surrounded by bad blood."

He squinted at her, and Florence wondered what he was searching for. She knew nothing about the man, so she didn't know what to portray. Even if she did, she was too tired to fabricate anything.

"Had it been you and Gregory alone and you knew his gun was defective, would you still have tried to warn him?"

"Yes." Despite her honest answer, Bernard's eyebrows rose and he looked even more skeptical. "He was the Vicar Revolver. I would have tried to save his life even if it meant pointing out his mistake."

"And if he still didn't listen?"

"Then I would have let him die. As the Vicar Revolver, he must be held responsible for his own mistakes, even if they cost his life."

"And you? Will we hold you accountable with your life?"

"I would have it no other way." A bit of her Raven shone through, and Florence smiled wildly. "Isn't that the way of the Revolver? Taking life in your hands and accepting what happens if you drop it?"

Bernard continued to scrutinize her, but finally gave a nod and left the room. On his way out, he said, "You have my support."

There was a gravity to the way the door clicked closed. It was as if the matter was deemed finished before Florence had even wrapped her mind around it. *Had that really just happened?*

"Let us hold a tribunal tomorrow, when you're feeling stronger," Powell suggested. "We need to go over the status of the Philosopher's Boxes and how we can manufacture your guns, in addition."

"Right. Send me Shannra." Florence tried to keep her voice strong. She felt a tempest of emotions, but none of them was hesitation at being named the Vicar Revolver. "She can whisper to Arianna for me."

The room cleared and Florence found herself alone for one very long minute. She could do nothing more than stare at her hands in shock. Somehow, she'd managed to keep herself level, composed, in control, but now her bones felt like they were trying to rattle her flesh into gelatin.

She curled and uncurled her fingers into fists, thinking of Powell's metaphor. If the guilds were like hands, then she, too, must be. There was a part of her that was scared and it was no less or more than the part of her that was thrilled. Nerves flourished within the confident woman who knew she was about to step into the most important role of her life.

She inhaled through her nose and exhaled through her mouth. Her hands balled into fists. Like the competing parts within her, she would bring all of Loom together as one.

The door opened and Shannra practically bounded in with excitement. "I just heard!"

"News travels fast." Florence smiled faintly.

Shannra sat on the edge of the low table Florence had been laid out on. "I'm sure you wanted to be the first to tell me."

"So don't be upset, hm? Especially because now that you *have* been told, I need you to whisper to Arianna. I must tell her what's happened with the gun."

"I am at your service, Vicar Revolver."

She very much liked the way Shannra purred the words "Vicar Revolver." Florence reached up a hand and cupped the curve of the cheek she so adored.

"I do like the sound of that."

"There's something else you should know." Shannra sat on the edge of her bed, brushing Florence's hair from her face. "There was a whisper while you were out. You're not the only one with a new title."

"What?"

"It seems she's killed Louie. We're all reporting to the Queen of Wraiths now."

"Killed Louie?" Florence repeated, wondering what could've possessed Arianna to go so far. "Don't we need him?"

"She seems to think otherwise."

Florence struggled to make sense of what she was hearing. Just what was Arianna doing?

Shannra raised her hand to her ear, but Florence tugged it away before she could activate the whisper link to one of Louie's—Arianna's—lackeys.

"It can wait one more second," Florence said, pulling the other woman toward her. She claimed Shannra's mouth and felt her lover relax into the kiss. Florence herself relaxed for what felt like the first time in ages, despite the weight of all her new responsibilities. That was Shannra's power, or perhaps the power of them coming together.

Florence would tell Arianna—she must. But vicars did not jump to associate with those who ruled the underworld, and she—Florence, the runaway Raven who had been decreed to die—was a vicar now.

PART TWO

ARIANNA

Her golden cabling whizzed through her harness with a precise *zip*.

The clang of gold on metal as her clip slid along the railing came to a hard stop, Arianna swung around a low smokestack at breakneck speeds two seconds after the initial churning of gears ceased. Three seconds after that, a glider whizzed around one of the giant main houses of the refinery hall. To make the jump to the glider, Arianna had to know the glider's approximate rate of speed, her terminal velocity mid-swing, and the cusp where the two would meet.

Numbers like those were all child's play.

She soared through the air on a collision course with the glider. A shining corona coated the Dragon's skin, so Arianna's daggers were sheathed. During her first stint on Nova, a Dragon had pointed out something pivotal to her: The corona was designed to protect from harm, and it was designed by Fenthri. So, the Fenthri engineers—who were geniuses to develop such a magical field— did so to protect from Loom's weaponry: metals, bullets, blasts.

There was never any accounting for bone.

Bone was just what protruded from both of Arianna's fingertips—bone in the shape of giant talons, forged by magic and hardened by the Dragon hands she'd stolen from a man who had worked against Loom until his dying breath. Now, she'd use that same magic to sculpt Loom's future from the flesh that shredded beneath her palms.

The Rider had only a moment to look up in shock as Arianna landed atop him. Her claws dug into his shoulder and neck, shearing flesh from muscle and muscle from bone. Tendons snapped; she savored his look of shock in the moments before he released the handholds, sending them both tumbling through the air.

Wind gusted over her ears, and Arianna knew she had mere breaths before they would both be plastered on the next metal cropping. *Live to fight the next battle*, instinct cried. Arianna relinquished the Rider to the sound of the crashing glider behind her.

She unclipped the golden clip from her harness. The Dragon snarled in rage and flailed his arms, attempting to strike her, or cling to her—whichever he could manage. Her gold line was impervious to his strikes, so she cast it without hesitation. Her stomach was in her throat and shot back down to her lower abdomen as the line snapped to tension.

The Dragon's claws sunk into her calf and Arianna swiped at him with a snarl. She shredded the tendons in his wrist, his hand going lax, and he continued to fall without her. His body met the refinery's rocky foundation with a calamitous *clang*.

Arianna tapped her winch box.

She slowed her descent to nonlethal speeds, keeping the line loose enough that the cabling spun freely off its spools and her stomach shot back into her throat. When she was two pecas from the ground, she pulled the lynchpin on the box and fell the rest of the way.

Dazed and barely conscious, the Dragon Rider blinked up at her. Fools hesitated and sympathizers died. Arianna plunged her claws into the man's chest, perforating his lungs and surrounding his heart. She twisted, ripped, and ended the Dragon's life.

The door to her right burst open.

Arianna sunk her teeth into the soft tissue of the Rider's heart. Blood exploded in her mouth—the taste of blackberries, tart yet sweet. With that sweetness was something all the more savory. Magic flooded her senses. It pulsed within her, bolstered her own. Her wounds healed, her skin regained its strength, and, with a snap of her fingers, her line returned itself to its coil as she turned to face the next enemy.

The Dragon levied a gun against her—one of the reasons she was here to begin with. Arianna dropped into a crouch, ready to dodge the shot. The Dragon snarled and pulled the trigger at the same time as she lunged.

He tried to anticipate her movements; his gun swung right as Arianna pushed forward. He thought she'd move to the side. But Arianna went straight for the jugular.

He swung back. The Dragon pulled the trigger again and Arianna heard a familiar click. She drew her dagger and plunged it into his throat.

"With that style rifle, you need to reload a canister with every shot," she chided softly.

The Dragon threw aside the empty weapon with a shout of frustration. He had fight in him as he gripped her shoulders, making a play for her throat. Arianna tumbled, slid into a crouch, and prepared to lunge anew.

"Witch!" he shouted at her before swiping with his claws.

"Scientist!" Arianna corrected, dodging his slash. She thrust with one dagger and the Dragon moved left, completely ignoring the second blade attached to a golden line at his back.

He fell, and another appeared.

The Dragons here were bleary from sleep, shocked into sluggishness, out of their element in narrow industrial halls. There wasn't a true combatant among them—at least not by the standards of the Queen of Wraiths.

She tore through them, one after the next. Golden daggers floated at the ends of her lines like barbed tentacles shooting from her hips, carving out the hearts of all who dared to oppose her. Arianna killed without question. Man, woman, young or old—if they stood before her, they would be struck down.

Dawn broke over the horizon to find her bathed in slowly evaporating gold. Arianna's chest heaved and her eyes were blurry from exhaustion. She ran on the magic of her conquests, shoving hearts into her mouth in the same unreserved way Florence would indulge herself on an unattended plate of cookies.

Magic from deep below prickled at her senses. Arianna knew what she'd find before she arrived at the heavy, bolted door. Still, when she pulled it open and looked at the squalor within—the men and women blinking nervously at her—her chest felt heavier than all the metal and stone of the refinery that surrounded her.

"I can't save you all." It was where she had to start. "But I can try to give you each the power to save yourselves."

"Who are you?" a woman stammered.

"The Wh—The Queen of Wraiths." Arianna sheathed her daggers. "And I come from the rebellion on Loom."

Shocked rumors rose among the Fenthri slaves.

"House Xin is standing with us, and together we will overthrow the Dragon King and save Loom." For all she believed in Florence and Cvareh, uttering the words was hard. How many times in her lifetime alone would she espouse the end of Yveun's rule? "Help me dismantle this refinery, then flee, hide. Stay out of sight and stay alive until Rok has fallen."

They looked nervously at each other. No one moved. She wondered if Florence would have been able to inspire them to action. Arianna was not meant for rousing speeches or motivating the masses. She was the hired blade in the dark.

"I can take one of you with me," she continued anyway. "Loom needs knowledge of the weaponry and whatever else they're having you make here. I will let you decide who it will be. This is the Fenthri way."

The slaves looked among themselves, and still, no one moved. Then murmurs, speaking, a consensus. Arianna watched them use their minds for themselves for the first time in what may have been decades. They selected one man with the circled symbol of a Rivet on his cheek. He was young enough that Arianna didn't recognize him from her time in the guild, but old enough that she had no doubt he'd spent most of his life on Nova.

"I'll bring the information back to Loom."

"Good." Arianna gave a curt nod. "Now that that's settled, let's get to work making Rok's life as difficult as possible."

COLETTA

E ven when the world was at war, Lysip was a beauty to behold. The brown winter grasses against the brilliant reds of the estate created an ethereal elegance that was capped with a bright sky, its blue almost washed into a soft off-white. It was not uncommon for the clouds above the God's Line to deposit rain or snow onto their island. But the winter had been dry so far.

Coletta preferred it this way. She didn't like getting the hems of her clothes muddy, and the only damp she ever wanted to feel on her hands was the blood of her enemies.

As much as Tam flaunted their island's perpetual jewel tones as some kind of superiority, Coletta found the world in stasis several times more stunning than the lushest of gardens—with the exception of her own garden, of course.

It was a day for thinking of Tam, as she'd greeted the viridian house just hours ago. She played the part of the Rok'Ryu they expected—a mysterious woman whose presence often heralded death, but it couldn't be of her own doing, for she was much too frail for that. She didn't have the spine to kill someone; she didn't have a spine at all. Or so Coletta imagined them whispering.

The entourage would take the rumors back to a hungry Gwaeru, where the nobility would eat them up like dogs fighting over the juiciest scrap to bring some satiation to their meaningless lives. House Tam represented balance, "all things equal," as their motto stated. But balance, Coletta found, was a close sibling to complacency, and complacency was the lover of sloth.

While the Dragon in her thought it was always a shame to see her race reduced to something that glorified excess, Tam's taste for finer things and the time to enjoy them suited her. It made the house easy to control, and fairly simple to work with. If there was one thing that didn't suit the comfort of luxury, it was the chaos of rebellion.

The woman walking next to her was one of the few Coletta did not expect to deceive. From the first moment Doriv Tam'Ryu To arrived at the Rok Estate, she saw Coletta as a force to be reckoned with. Coletta saw much the same in her fern-colored counterpart. They each knew who was really in charge at the respective households. So, while the majority of the attendants and upper nobility of both houses sat in on a meeting with Yveun'Oji and Cashi'Oji, the real decisions were being made by the two women who strolled the estate with only a few handpicked attendants many steps behind.

"Lysip in the winter is stunning. The way the sun shines on the browning grasses that adorn your hillsides makes the whole of the island look as though it has been dipped in gold." Doriv'Ryu made no effort to further disguise the remark on their dead foliage as a compliment.

"Gwaeru is equally stunning this time of year. All of your large flowering trees endlessly dumping their petals is quite the spectacle to behold—or so I hear." Coletta responded in kind.

"I didn't know you thought of Gwaeru with such fondness, Rok'Ryu." Doriv'Ryu adjusted the chiming earrings that pulled needle-eye holes into the lobes of her long ears. "Perhaps we'll conduct one of our future meetings on my homeland. Rather than dragging the entirety of House Tam's nobility across the sky."

"Ah, I know how so many speak with fondness of the opportunity to come and try Lysip beef and see the Rok Estate. I'd hate to deny them the opportunity."

"You are a truly charitable woman. I don't know how you give so much away to others while still having enough for yourself, such that you can create the flamboyant lodgings where you house guests." Doriv motioned to the gilding on the columns that supported the roof covering the walkway, which wound through the wild outer fields they roamed.

"It is important to make sure we both take care of our people, while continuing to display Rok's might."

"Indeed . . ." Doriv stopped and half-turned, looking out over the sea of slowly dying greenery between carefully placed statues. Coletta stopped as well, angling her body to mimic the other Ryu.

Neither of them cared about the flowers, or the grasses, or the sun, or the end of the boco mating season, or any of the other pointless topics they had spent the morning discussing. They cared about one thing alone: how close they were to any other living, sentient creature who was not one of their most loyal vassals.

"You like this spot," Coletta observed. "You usually stop here."

"This scuff here—" Doriv answered, running her fingers over an unassuming etching on the column beside her. "—

marks the point at which our conversation officially becomes private."

"Indeed." Coletta smiled. She enjoyed the reaction her scarred, gray gums and knobby teeth evoked in other Dragons. It was its own type of terror. "This was a meeting you called. What is so important that you needed to speak with me in person?"

"The wine turned sour at the Crimson Court . . ." Doriv began walking again. "An odd affair, that . . . I don't believe there has ever been a case of deadly mold on wine casks before."

"An odd affair, indeed. Perhaps it was Lord Xin requesting a tithing of his people."

"I certainly hope so." Doriv's hand was back to playing with her earring. "I've heard whispers of some nefarious designs."

"Have you?" Coletta asked earnestly. It was imperative that, at any given time, she knew what the world knew about her. The moment the masses actually saw her as a threat was the moment she lost the vast majority of her effectiveness. Yveun was the visible menace, she the invisible hand holding the dagger from the flanks.

"Only rumors, nothing more, and nothing worth heeding past the gossip parlor doors." The answer wasn't satisfying for Coletta, but she saw no avenue to pursue the matter. Furthermore, she had to trust her alliance with Doriv; if there was something to consider alarming, the woman would tell her. Doriv immediately proved Coletta right. "However, if they are true . . . It would be a grave offense. Ending a Crimson Court before the majority of grievances could be heard would be the least of it, really. To slay Dragons outside of proper duels or cause death on such a mass scale . . . the idea is unprecedented."

Coletta skillfully refrained from pointing out that Xin's mere existence gave her cause to wipe their blue faces off the earth itself.

"And then, there's the matter of Petra Xin'Oji," Doriv continued. "Her death is not sitting well with House Xin. They think that, too, has some darker truth to it. The new Oji dueled the late Finnyr on such grounds. If these accusations prove true, in addition to the other oddities . . . House Tam would need to evaluate, and potentially work to remove a power that acts so far out of Nova's structure."

She heard Doriv's warning clearly. "Well, if such terrible things were to have transpired, it seems the persons involved would have acted with the utmost cunning, if there are only floating rumors. The Xin can hardly be trusted to be unbiased, or logical for that matter. They all have so much to grieve for now. They act like children in their time of mourning."

"One would hope it is just the lunacies of a grieving house . . . It would be a shame to have to forcefully shift the world back into balance so that all things are once more equal."

"Indeed. After all, doing so could result in many of the Tam nobility being forced to give up the titles and the luxuries that come to them from the graciousness of House Rok."

"Rebellion is good for no one," Doriv agreed. "All one needs to do to see it is look at the Fen in the world below."

"Something that should be alleviated soon." It was the only topic Coletta wasn't utterly sure of. The Fen were agents of chaos; no matter how carefully she planned and plotted, the wretched little creatures were determined to prove their insolence. Yveun did the situation no favors, either.

"Let us hope. It's such a nuisance."

"Yes, well, we can only hope the nuisances of the world are put to rest sooner over later."

"I make every effort." Even if half of Coletta's efforts were thwarted by idiocy or incompetence or the foolishness of the system she was forced to navigate.

"Speaking of efforts . . . I hear there is a disgraced Tam babysitting House Xin?"

"There was. Fae Rok," Coletta affirmed.

"How fitting that Rok requires a wayward Tam to keep the balance with House Xin. It is in our blood, after all."

"Rok name, Tam blood—together it's a powerful combination," Coletta answered carefully. She wanted to drive her point with the Tam'Ryu deep. "Our families making a stable balance, equal force . . . We both have much to gain, and much to lose if that balance is disrupted."

"Tam will continue to defend the balance so long as House Rok continues to abide by Dragon law." *Tam and their bloody obsession with the law*, Coletta thought as Doriv spoke. "And so long as we continue to be appropriately compensated for the assistance we give."

They stopped again, now at the apex of the large loop that swept around the outer fields. A pathway split away through the hills, still paved but no longer covered. Usually, their conversation would shift back to veiled threats and jabs as they rounded the curve back to the estate proper.

"How lovely it would be to have some precious gold to adorn Tam's castle." The Tam Ryu turned in a different direction than normal, headed away from the estate.

"Perhaps some could be spared, as a gift between our families—a gesture of thanks." Coletta heard the request clearly. It was a request that all prior conversations with the Ryu had prepared her to hear.

"I said it before, Coletta'Ryu—you are much too generous." Doriv smiled, showing her razor-sharp teeth.

Coletta did the same.

Doriv folded her hands before her. "I hear rumors too that Yveun's refineries are taking shape."

That was the greatest lie of them all. The refineries were a failure. Difficult to maintain, difficult to feed with resources. They were glorified houses for the gold she had stolen from Loom, a façade and nothing more.

"Would you like to see one?" Coletta knew better than to deny the woman, which would only raise suspicion. She knew the request was inevitable, but trusted that her carefully crafted plans would yield the expected result.

Coletta knew something was wrong the moment the wind shifted around them. The air smelled sweet, rather than sharp with the metallic tang of the refinery. She couldn't demand they turn around; to do so would be admitting something had gone awry. But as the refineries nestled in the hills beyond the Rok Estate came into view, Coletta wasn't prepared for what she found.

"It's quiet."

Damn Doriv and her observations. "We run it on alternate days, so as not to draw too much attention to it."

The Tam Ryu gave a small hum of amusement.

"I can see the gold transported to you from here," Coletta offered, trying to arrest their progress.

"I'd like to see these operations—temples of industry from the world below."

Coletta had no grounds to object, so she didn't. She continued onward and downward to the main entry. The tangy sweet smell became overwhelming; Coletta had no option to brace herself.

"We'll head straight to the storehouse." Whatever had happened here, Coletta would deal with later. For now, she'd show the gold she'd stolen from Loom, keep the illusion of a strong House Rok, and get Doriv out as quickly as possible.

"Lead on." The woman's smile was knowing, frustratingly so.

Coletta walked through the still passageways, trapped in by lattices of steel and iron, to a small storehouse not far from the outer edge of the refinery grounds. Coletta took a breath, unbarring the door.

Were it not for the dozens, hundreds, thousands of people she'd killed over the years, her face might have cracked. The room that she'd filled to the brim with gold from Loom, stolen from storehouses revealed to her by the self-styled Fen King's notes, was completely vacant. A large pennon hung over a pile of hearts, dull and fraying already with rot.

Coletta read over the brief message, painted with the grease pencils the Fen used to mark various machines and walkways in the refineries.

After a long moment of silence, Doriv was the first to speak. "Coletta'Ryu, who exactly is the Queen of Wraiths?"

FLORENCE

"I don't call the shots, just deliver them." Helen shrugged at a fuming Vicar Dove.

"We sent one hundred men and women to be made into Perfect Chimera, and you bring us only three back *and* ask for fifty more."

"Again, just delivering the message."

Florence looked at the delivery summary in question. She knew, better than Powell or Dove, what the request meant. They had precious few Revolvers as it was; to ferry them by the tens to Ter.3 was putting a strain on their ability to defend themselves in Ter.4.

"What are Willard and Ethel thinking?" Dove turned her attention to Powell and Florence.

It was a question Florence knew the other vicar didn't really want to be answered, but answer she would. "They're trying to encourage us to consolidate."

"Then they should outright say it." Dove pushed away from the table where the papers lay strewn, as if she was too disgusted by them to bear another moment in their presence.

The Alchemists had been sent ahead to Garre to learn how to transplant the boxes, and then become Perfect Chimera themselves. At first, due to "tempering issues," the process was painfully slow. But, as was the case with most new technology, things improved quickly and efficiency increased exponentially. From the whispers, it seemed the Alchemists were content to stay in Garre for a while; it was a hard point to argue when that was the site of the boxes.

"I'm fairly sure they have." Florence picked up the letter from Ethel that encouraged the rest of the guilds to come south. "It's not an illogical proposition."

"We cannot keep moving people," Dove objected.

"And there's the issue of Dragon attacks," Powell added.

"If we hadn't already sent so many Revolvers south, that wouldn't be an issue," Dove seethed.

"What's done is done. There's little point in arguing now." Florence couldn't believe she was younger than them both, especially not when they acted like squabbling children. "We should heed Ethel's suggestion and relocate."

"We *just* got to Ter.4," Dove needlessly reminded Florence.

"We arrived at Ter.4 nearly eight months ago. And this move will be far less tedious with established rail lines. We can leave right through the guild hall. It's a fairly straight shot south from Holx."

"But we did just finish fortifying the Underground." As weak as the objection was, it was still an objection and Florence couldn't remember the last time Powell spoke against her. She hoped it wouldn't become a habit.

"Fortifications in the form of blocking tunnels and building some doors," Florence countered. "Hardly any significant investment of time or resources."

"And turrets," Vicar Dove reminded.

"We set up *two* turrets. Though I realize you may have gotten the number confused, since it doesn't directly relate to your Ravens." Florence was almost proud of how nonchalantly she delivered such a scathing remark.

"Careful, Florence, or one might think that you are fostering separation between the guilds."

"I would never." Florence returned them to the topic at hand, not wanting to risk further ire. "In any case . . .we cannot ignore these two attacks on Ter.3. The Dragons have finally realized our manufacturing there."

"Took them long enough," Helen mumbled.

"If only it took them longer," Powell remarked with a pointed look.

"We must protect the factories at all costs," Florence continued, unbothered by the exchanges occurring around her. "They are a far greater priority than staying holed in the Underground."

"We can use those same lines you mentioned earlier to transport what we need here," Dove insisted.

"You can't possibly mean that." Florence was beginning to suspect that Dove was just fighting her for the sake of fighting now.

"I do very much. The trains—"

"The trains run on tracks easily targeted by Dragons." Florence shook her head. "They can destroy the tracks and separate us. Remember the whole reason we banded together?" Florence held up her hand by her shoulder, palms out, fingers upward, mimicking the symbol that had come to represent the sign of their rebellion. "Five guilds, separate but connected, and together strong."

Powell sighed a sound that had a distinct tone of resignation to it. "There *are* more resources in Ter.3 than the Underground. We're running thin on food."

"The Ravens' Guild has storerooms."

"That have all been exhausted."

"Fine." Dove threw her hands into the air. "We shall move again. But we do it slowly, one group at a time."

"No." Florence shot down the idea immediately. "We take out all locomotives at once. We run them one after the other. And we move together, as one unit, safe and strong. That way, if the Dragons should take notice, they can't find a way to block the lines and separate us on opposite ends of the continent."

The room was silent for a long moment. Florence took silence to mean victory, and she turned to Helen and Will. She barely recognized her old friends now. They had gone off to be emissaries of the seedy underbelly of Loom and Florence had become the Vicar Revolver. She wished them well, but there would be little more than that between them as the years progressed—if the years progressed.

"Return to Garre with the requested manpower. Inform Willard, Ethel, and Arianna that we will be moving to Ter.3.2."

"Not Garre?" Powell interrupted.

"No." Florence shook her head and looked back to the edited schematics she and Arianna had been passing between them by way of Helen. "Garre needs to stay focused on making the Philosopher's Box. We will set up in Ter.3.2, close enough that we are nothing more than a stone's throw away and can exchange information, resources, and men with ease. But far enough that we can retrofit our own factories to make the guns. Are there any questions?"

Silence.

"No? Good. Let's get to work."

COLETTA

She was particularly grateful for Ulia's help in undoing the intricate clasping on the front of her jacket that night. Coletta wasn't sure if her hands had ever felt so shaky, and it took all her focus to keep them even, her voice level.

"Is there anything else I can do for you?" Ulia asked as she slung the garment over her hand for proper cleaning. Even the girl, one of the most loyal among them, was nervous now. She had seen the refinery and the look on Doriv's face when the pennon was discovered.

"No, leave." Ulia hovered for a half second, debate written on her face. This was not the night to be insubordinate. But Coletta had every faith that she knew as much; whatever made her falter was of the utmost importance. "Yes?"

"It is perhaps nothing . . ." Ulia kept her eyes downcast. "I do not claim to know the greatness you weave nor would I ever dream of passing judgment—"

"Out with it." Coletta had no patience for floundering. Ulia jumped at the unusual strength in Coletta's voice.

"I noticed that Yeaan's room has been empty for a few days now . . . I merely thought it odd that there has been no sign from her. I wondered, perhaps, if this 'Queen of Wraiths'—"

"How long has it been?" Coletta interrupted, formulating her own theories. She had merely assumed Yeaan had been focused on the eradication of the flowers. But now that she thought of it, it had been some time since one of her more favorite flowers had come before her.

"Since I last saw her . . . a month, maybe more?" Ulia shook her head. "I apologize, my lady, it's merely an estimate."

"You did well to tell me." Coletta forced out the praise. Taking out aggressions on her most loyal for the faults of others was a very certain way to lose that loyalty. "Now, get out."

"Yes." This time, Ulia did depart.

There was truly no rest for the weary. Before Coletta even had a breath to think about Yeaan and the last update she had received on the Flowers of Agendi, another invaded her space.

"Coletta!" Yveun roared.

"I am here." She kept her voice calm, almost monotonous. One of them had to keep it together.

"What happened?" It was such an odd sight to see Yveun in her chambers that Coletta almost overlooked the fact that he was pacing like a wild animal newly freed from its cage. "Everything with the Tam'Oji goes well and then, just as they depart, Doriv'Ryu offers me her condolences for our loss? That there is no gold?" He stopped, and squared off against her. "You assured me there would be gold."

"There was."

"Then what—"

"It was stolen."

"*Stolen?*" Had someone told Coletta what she was currently telling Yveun, her reaction would've been much the same. "Who would dare?"

"The Queen of Wraiths."

Emotions swept across his face, one after the next, swirling until they reached peak speeds, turning the Dono into a twister that was prepared to kill everything in its path. "Queen of Wraiths? I told you that Arianna was dangerous. I told you she was the one we needed to hunt." Yveun drew a finger like a Fenthri gun, casting it at her. "You cautioned against it, sent Fae to Xin. Now see what it has wrought."

Coletta's mouth twitched and she fought to keep her face passive. It was hard to say if Yveun was right, but she also couldn't assert that he was *wrong*.

"These are unfortunate events, but—"

"But? *But?* We are thwarted at every turn on Loom." Yveun snarled out some nasty series of words and set to pacing once more. "Even on Ruana, we are struggling to hold Napole on resolve alone. Our men are dying of skirmishes in the night, or of boredom."

Napole. The "battle"—if it could be called that, as they were met with no resistance from House Xin—was over in a night, which Yveun had interpreted to mean that they could run through the island unhindered. Xin was, unfortunately, too smart for that. They had retreated into their forests and mountains, copying the strategy Loom had been embracing for months.

Hiding was shameful for a Dragon, but it kept them alive.

"That blue scum—" *Cvareh*, Coletta filled in mentally "— will not respond to my demands for a duel."

"Nor will he."

Yveun's claws shot from his fingertips. Coletta allowed the ripple of his magic to send shivers up her spine, dotting it with goosebumps. It was a sickeningly sweet smell, rage ripening her mate.

"He calls himself Oji! If he ever wishes to be recognized properly on Nova, he must respond to my challenge."

"Not if he seeks to topple Nova." Coletta moved with all the grace she possessed, easing herself down on the ottoman in the center of the room.

"He has no hope of toppling Nova. We shall win every duel!"

"There are no duels to be had." Nor would there be. Were she in Cvareh's position, she'd wait until she held all the cards before making a public stand against Yveun.

"This is unheard of. He's acting like . . . like . . . "

"Like a Fenthri." The statement drew Yveun's attention. Finally seeing his eyes clear from anger, enough to listen at least, Coletta continued. "The Fenthri care not for proper society, as we know. They will do anything to survive, and Xin is no better. 'The ends'—*their* ends—will justify the means used to achieve them, even if that means ignoring Dragon law. Why wouldn't they? If they don't, they die. If they do, they have a slim chance of victory."

"You must be truly mad to understand their twisted logic." Yveun shook his head slowly, as if disgust weighted down his movements.

"My madness is why you love me." Coletta stretched her mouth wide, showing her teeth and reminding him of all the poisons she had endured for the sake of their greatness.

"One of the many reasons." Yveun hulked over her like a great mountain casting a long shadow on the ground below it. But Coletta didn't mind being in his shadow—she thrived in it. She conducted her business in his wake, used his greatness to distract from her own, his massive frame her shield. "Our gray wards seek to overthrow us from beneath. The scourge of

Dragon society fights against us and is gaining ground. Our key ally has left this day on fragile relations. And yet, you smile."

"I do."

"Why?" At last he asked the right questions. But Coletta didn't know yet if he was ready for the answers.

"Because we, too, can build an army. Xin isn't the only house that can think like the Fen."

"Do you mean . . . ?" Eagerness hovered more potently than his words.

"Xin has looked to the Fenthri to be perfect. Rok, we make our own perfection."

"You have met success." It was not a question.

"Come, my Oji, and allow me to show you my Gray Room." Coletta started for the door, not even bothering to see if he was following. For she knew there was no way Yveun had escaped her mental tether. It was good that she had him enthralled for now. When he learned the bitter truth of her triumph, Coletta knew his rage would be uncontrollable.

ARIANNA

rianna nearly lost her breath pulling the glider upright. She landed it on a platform, albeit roughly, rather than going for the hangar on the edge of Garre. She was in and out so often by glider these days, it had become her own personal landing pad.

"After you."

Xavier, the Master Rivet who'd returned home with her, descended with wonder in his eyes. Arianna couldn't imagine what the homecoming was like for him.

"I never expected to see it again."

"I believe it." Arianna stepped heavily off the glider. Feeding on Dragon hearts was a way to sustain, but not thrive. She needed some time before she went up to Nova again.

There was a click inside the tower her platform was attached to and the entire structure groaned to life. Xavier held his hands out, working to balance himself, unaccustomed to the mechanics of the guild hall. Arianna could hear the grinding of massive gears as an entire segment of the tower turned, connecting with another platform that had been on the opposite side.

Waiting there was a familiar, weathered face.

"I'm beginning to think you have a death wish." It wasn't much of a greeting from the Vicar Rivet. Willard walked over, stopping when his eyes settled on Xavier.

"I brought a master home, liberated from our enemies," Arianna explained. Xavier was overcome with emotion and, given the glistening in his eyes, it would be some time until he could form cohesive sentences.

"I thought you were acquiring more flowers." Willard gave her a long, hard stare.

"Oh, I got those." Arianna patted the satchel at her side. "I just made a detour, working off some intel that Rok had built their own refineries and workshops."

"*What?* How did you find this out?"

"Our Dragon friends." It wasn't entirely a lie. Cvareh had mentioned the refinery project when he had shown her Xin's own structure. But what prompted her to actually investigate was when the Dragon Queen had asked Adam for two more ledgers from Holx, thinking the demand would be passed on to Louie. Arianna recognized the target ingredients as refinery resources.

"Dragon friends?" Xavier was brought back to life with the mention of Dragons. "It's true? Xin?"

"It is." Willard ushered the master toward him. "Come, come, we'll get you inside. I'll summon the Vicar Alchemist to look at you both."

"I'm fine, Willard." Arianna stretched. She knew the cure for her ailments—a good night's rest, rarer than gold now on Loom. "I'm going to head toward the workshops."

"The Vicar Alchemist is here?" Xavier asked, ignoring her. Arianna was hardly offended; she wanted to be forgotten by people as quickly as she appeared before them.

Willard gave Arianna a nod before ushering Xavier away.

"We've come to attend you, oh queen!" Helen burst through a door opposite the one Willard had just departed through. She gave a bow with a mocking flourish.

Arianna was weeks away from trying to fight the foolishness of her unwanted Raven chicks. Instead, she shrugged out of her coat. "Will, follow Willard and tell him that I still need to speak with him when he's done with Xavier." Arianna threw the garment at Helen. "And you, fix my sleeve."

"I am not a tailor!" Helen fumed to the point of nearly stomping her foot like the child she was.

"And I am not a babysitter. You want to remain in my good graces?"

Helen stormed off without another word, thanks to a look of encouragement from Will, who followed close behind. Arianna headed in the opposite direction.

The manufacturing line might be where the boxes were made, but the workshops were where they transformed into functioning Philosopher's Boxes that were then passed along to what had become the Alchemists' wing of the guild hall. They were implanted in Chimera, and after that . . . it was up to the Revolvers for training.

"I'd like to see everyone's progress," Arianna announced the moment she entered the room and set down the tubes of flowers in their storage spot. She was too tired for pleasantries, and focused on the task at hand. It was a mixed bag of successes that launched her into a familiar lecture. " . . . Extracting the properties of the flowers comes more from magic than mechanics. You need to heat the gold using magic, and then pull the magic that lives in the flower into it while it's near-molten.

"Try again." Arianna stood over one particularly focused journeyman and, at the risk of breaking his concentration, said, "Exactly like that . . .You know the magic is transferring properly because the gold will actually begin to cool again. It's very similar to tempering with blood."

"Oh." One journeyman said. "But we're not mixing the molten gold with blood here."

"No, just the magics are mixing," Arianna reiterated. "It's not *identical* to tempering with blood—fundamentally similar, but not the same."

A woman gave a grunt of frustration, hanging her head over like a wilted flower petal. Arianna didn't even need to touch the box in her hands to know that it wasn't tempered properly. She struggled with all her might to stifle a sigh and failed. She was too tired these days to expend much energy on patience.

"Put any boxes you think are successful on the table here." Vicar Willard's voice cut through the room, saving Arianna from herself. "The rest, bring back into the finishing room to be recalibrated so we may try again tomorrow."

Arianna gave the man a severe look, but managed to hold her tongue until they were alone—somehow. "There won't be a tomorrow if they don't get better at this."

"Exactly, so why stress them further and lessen our chances?" She ground her knuckles into the table next to her.

"You don't really take after Oliver, after all."

"Excuse me?" Arianna arched her eyebrows.

"Well, given how you were at first with the initiates, with Florence, I thought perhaps we had a new great teacher among us."

Florence. She knew the woman had departed for Ter.3.2, where they had begun manufacturing the new weapons.

"I just play favorites with the competent. In that way, I'm exactly like Oliver." Arianna shrugged, leaning against the table, completely unashamed of the fact. Willard chuckled at the idea but didn't contest it. "How's our master?"

"With Vicar Ethel, then I think some much-needed rest." Arianna let her silence be her agreement. She could not imagine what the man was going through, having spent his life on Nova until now. Willard returned his attention to the boxes. "Will you be able to do any today?"

Arianna glanced over at the boxes that lined the table. She'd already counted how many they had started with and knew how many more were in the other room waiting to be salvaged. Even more still waited at the end of the line on the factory floor beyond that.

"Ten, maybe fifteen . . ."

"Stick with ten," Willard cautioned. "You have been expending a lot of magic these days with your jaunts up to Nova."

"I'm not a child, old man. I don't need you cautioning me."

"I think you do." Willard stood his ground and Arianna didn't argue the point further. The last thing she wanted was him bringing up the last time she'd pushed herself too hard, and he'd found her completely passed out the next morning on the floor of the workshop. It was an embarrassment he'd spared her publicly, but Arianna was now tempted to tell all of Loom herself so the man couldn't hang it over her head. "We don't have that many flowers, in any case. We're somewhat limited until more Perfect Chimera can confidently fly gliders. We should preserve them for more practice."

"How are things with the Revolvers going?" There was only a small pack of them now, training what few Perfect Chimera had been made. But they were all hoping for more to come, since Loom had moved away from the Underground.

"Progressing. I will ask you to measure the progress of the first class. You know better than any what they need to stand against Dragons."

Arianna folded her arms over her chest. "Speaking of fighting Dragons . . . The refineries on Nova, while utterly pointless as refineries—"

"No resources?"

"No resources." Arianna affirmed. She found it amusing how any Fenthri instantly knew about the issue with refineries on Nova, but none of the Dragons seemed to have figured it out, or heeded the warnings. "In any case, they are making weapons there."

"Dragons armed with weapons. That is not ideal."

"No," she agreed. "But they're rudimentary, and the Dragons don't understand how to use them. We'll still overpower them with Florence's gun and with the Perfect Chimera."

"Oddly optimistic for you," he observed.

Arianna shrugged. "What other choice do I have?"

"A hard spot we've put you in, indeed."

"I don't mind the fighting."

"I didn't just mean the fighting." She stared at the old man, waiting for him to clarify. "You've spent your life in secrecy, Arianna. You've worked in the shadows, functioned mostly alone. Now, so much rests on your shoulders. Too much."

"I'm fine." Arianna herself didn't know if it was a lie. "As I said before, what other choice do I have? I won't abandon Loom."

"That's good to hear."

Arianna searched the vicar's face. Her eyes narrowed. "Did you suspect I would?"

"You were forced into the limelight. Your hand is forced to action. And you were forced to do what no inventor should—share your schematics."

"Sharing them was my choice." The four words were so familiar that Arianna almost believed them.

Willard spared her his protest. "Loom appreciates your loyalty. I, and every Chimera, appreciate you sharing the whole technology of the boxes, unaltered."

That was when she understood him. Arianna couldn't stop a snarl. "I may be a Wraith, but I would not harm my own people."

"You never wanted to share the boxes, and the idea of widespread Perfect Chimera was something you resisted. Forgive me for asking Arianna, but is there anything I should know about them?"

"They are as true as the one in me." Arianna scowled at the man.

"Very well."

"You don't believe me?"

"It doesn't matter if I do or do not. You have or haven't tampered with them. You will or won't. But this wave has crested, Arianna. There is no turning back progress now." He paused, and Arianna had nothing to fill the silence with. "Don't exhaust yourself. We need you alive." With that, the old man departed.

"No turning back progress," she repeated, staring at the boxes that lined the table. Was it really progress? Or was her creation the thing that would drive Loom to its demise?

COLETTA

long the narrow, depressingly unadorned passage away
from her Gray Room was another receiving area—a
collection of holding cells, really—where incoming Fen
would be tested on their worth. Rok only had room and
resources to support a select few of the wretched creatures, so
the pack needed to be thinned. This area had been re-purposed
as an observation room for the two women who currently
occupied the space.

Topann lay on the table in the center of the room, a book
Coletta had granted her open flat. The woman cupped her chin
with her palm, lazily flipping the pages as her foot, with a mind
of its own, rocked a chair slightly behind her back and forth.
Where she was the picture of serenity and patience, the other
beast in the room was not.

Fae crouched before the barred door to one of the cells that
lined the perimeter and grinned at the cowering Alchemist
inside. With one claw, she scratched away at the lock. A deep
groove had already formed underneath the harrowing sound
of her claw.

At Coletta and Yveun's arrival, the two women were on
their feet with varying speeds and levels of decorum. Topann

stood straight, head bowed, hands folded demurely before her. Fae leaned heavily against the door of the cell, causing a faint clanking sound as the hinges strained under her bulk. Her purple eyes drifted lustily over to Yveun, the foreplay between them beginning with a mere look.

"How many organs do you each have?" Coletta asked.

"All of them," Topann answered dutifully. "Save for lungs."

"What she said." Fae gave a mocking imitation of Coletta's flower.

"The sickness, the magic rejection . . . You worked through it?" Yveun walked straight for Fae. "I want to see."

"I'll let you see inside me, if it pleases the Dono." Fae made a show of leaning forward to whisper in his ear, but it was really entirely for the titillation of the man before her. Coletta, in turn, gave an approving look to Fae. She needed the woman to smooth over her mate's rough edges at the impending news.

"How did you do it?" Yveun couldn't seem to decide on which head he wanted to let govern his actions, and his body pivoted between her and Fae. Coletta knew his curiosity was great indeed if it pulled him away from the purring sex goddess before him.

"At first, we used like-organs." Coletta motioned to Topann. "A symbol of Rok's strength certainly required the best organs and nothing less. So I scoured the underbelly of Lysip, and then topside when that did not work."

"But you said none of them took," Yveun recalled.

"Indeed. Fae was the key." Having a recklessly accepting test subject had more than proved Fae's worth to Coletta. "She experienced no problem accepting Rok organs, even those from below."

"A particular Dragon, then?" Yveun theorized.

"I thought the same, but Topann still rejected them, even ones regrown from the same stock."

"You said you now have all of them but the rarest?" Yveun looked to her flower. "What did it take?"

Topann looked uncomfortable now. She folded and unfolded her hands firmly, working up her resolve. Coletta spared her flower the difficulty. The agony was needless.

"It took no half measures."

"What does that mean?" The slight edge to Yveun's voice from earlier was returning.

"Well, Fae as a Tam could accept Rok organs without rejection. I assume Xin can accept Tam organs . . ." Coletta wanted to see if he could put it together on his own. She had every faith her mate could, but hate blinded him too much. Prejudice was the true antithesis to progress. "Xin organs. A Perfect Rok Dragon requires Xin organs."

There was a long silence.

Then, an explosion.

"*What?*" Yveun turned his head to the Alchemist in the cage. Coletta knew he hadn't realized at the time that she was locking him in there for his protection. A kindness truly befitting a great ruler like herself. "Explain this, Fen."

"I-I can't!" He scooted away from the opening of his prison. Coletta could almost smell the sour aroma of fear oozing from his pores. "She's right, but I don't know why, it just is."

"Explain!"

Coletta let the exchange drag on a moment. It was good for the Fen to see Yveun in a fearsome role, to reinforce the image of their great and terrible ruler.

"I don't know. I'm not a proper Alchemist. I never received—"

"Do you want to give me excuses?" Yveun's voice dropped, low and deadly, as his hand gripped the lock. Coletta wondered if he could rip it off. She almost wanted to let the situation escalate long enough to see him try.

"Magic rots Fenthri. We know Fenthri bodies aren't made for it, so it rots us out ... It doesn't matter where the organs come from, it's a property of magic." The man swallowed hard a few times. "Perhaps there are different *types* of magic in different Dragons, in the different houses? There's no way we could've known because it's all magic for a Fenthri—it causes the same issue no matter who it's from, or what type . . . But perhaps it explains why some can have three organs before falling, and some only two. Perhaps different houses have different potencies, or certain organs are noncompatible in a single body . . . " The man trailed off into his own thoughts.

Yveun turned to Coletta. When his world was at its bleakest, its most unstable, he turned to her. It was their balance, their equal parts. "What does this mean?"

"It means that nothing has changed," she said easily. "We hunted Xin before, purely for their deaths. Now, we will hunt them for their organs."

Yveun was quiet a moment, but only just. With a half-snarl, half-roar, he buried his fist into the nearby wall, splintering and cracking the wood. "No, we will not."

"No half measures." Coletta shouldn't have to remind him of their house's motto, of how his failure to embrace it had only led, time and again, to their failure.

"This is not a half measure, this is a matter of our pride! We shall not lower ourselves to Xin for strength." Yveun swung his head toward Topann. For a brief moment, Coletta could feel him considering saying something, but he abandoned the notion, storming out of the room. Even when he was pushed past his limit, he knew better than to disturb her precious flowers.

"Fae." Coletta was unfettered. "Please go see to the Dono."

"With *pleasure*." The woman practically moaned the last word in her carnal excitement.

"Then you will head down to Loom." They didn't have time for dalliances and her mate needed to learn how to be placated without a toy to keep him occupied. If Coletta could teach him that one skill, how much easier would her life be?

"Yes, I remember the deal, what you gave me all this power for. Kill the girl, nab more gold."

"And another, after Florence."

Fae tilted her head as a display of her attention.

"Arianna, Queen of Wraiths."

"Yveun will be pleased." Fae bared her teeth. Clearly the name was already one Yveun had uttered, no doubt time and again.

"Good. Now go." She waited until Fae was gone and they were alone. Well, excluding the Fen. "And you—" she turned to Topann "—you will help me in acquiring Xin organs."

"Whatever you need of me, my lady."

Even if Yveun did not yet agree with her methods, Coletta would charge forward. If they could not find more gold, Tam could not be relied on. Without Tam, and with Xin allying with Loom, the future of Rok looked more uncertain by the hour. But Coletta liked dire situations; they made her creative. And when she was at her most creative, she was also at her most deadly.

FLORENCE

There were a total of four engines left in the Ravens' Guild hall, but only three slowly lurched to a halt at Ter.3.2. The compartments had been cramped, but in the end, there was only enough fuel left at Ter.4 to run three engines. It was a severe oversight on Vicar Dove's part, one that made Florence agitated for nearly the entire trip.

"I'm so ready to be off this train," Shannra muttered. The woman had been dozing off for hours but had perked up slightly when the train began to cut fuel in an effort to conserve their remaining supplies and coast into the station on momentum.

"The ride isn't so bad." Florence stretched her legs forward in the narrow compartment. Her status as vicar—*vicar*! The title still had yet to fully sink in, had earned her a bit of privacy that she shared with Shannra gladly.

"Five days!" Shannra groaned, sinking back into the narrow bed. The cabin was only wide enough for one chair and the bed that was tucked oddly into an alcove that jutted into the hall outside their door. "I forgot what fresh air feels like."

"Then open the window." Florence counted her canisters on a table that was little more than a window ledge and held back a small grin.

"You think you're awfully funny, don't you?" They had discovered the window was broken a day in.

"More than one way to open a window." Florence drew her revolver and brought her arm across her body, the grip exposed on the end as though she was about to smash the window with it.

"Florence, stop!" Shannra lunged, gripping her hands.

Florence grinned, wide and silly. No doubt stir-crazy. "Ask me nicely."

"Oh, I see how it is." Shannra gave a low chuckle that curved her cheek in just the way Florence liked. "You do think you're funny."

"What of it?"

"I'll wipe the smile off that mouth of yours."

"With what?"

Shannra leaned forward, half-laughing into the kiss that set free Florence's own laughter. Florence placed her palms over the other woman's hips, smoothing them against the bone that protruded from her narrow waist. Shannra had never boasted a sturdy frame, but she had begun to shrink before Florence's eyes and hands.

They all had. Being at war, living in hiding—it took a hefty toll on Loom, and rations were scarce as it was. All the more reason to keep moving, follow the remaining resources.

Yes, war was brutal, and it demanded a high price of them all. But Florence wouldn't let that price be Shannra. She indulged herself in what distractions the woman could provide and savored the moments they got to spend together not as Revolvers, but as women.

Instead of tracing the all-too-clear outline of Shannra's lower ribs, Florence kissed them. Instead of focusing on the bony jut of her hips, Florence gave careful mind to the woman's knee resting on the chair right at the apex of her thighs. She reveled in feeling the other woman's hands in her hair and nails on her scalp, and offered the same distraction.

Shannra's hands moved to Florence's back, gripping and smoothing the fabric forward before sliding forward to grace her chest. Florence conceded to the clear desire and rose without forfeiting her lover's mouth. Shannra was taller than Florence, as most were, and she had to crane her neck when standing if Shannra didn't slouch.

Florence carefully worked on the latches of her holster and Shannra was eager to assist. When it came loose, her lover handled the weapons with care, breaking the kiss to set them aside. Despite the fact that it resulted in Shannra's mouth off hers, Florence had never seen anything sexier than this mindfulness of weaponry.

With a soft hum rising in the back of her throat, Florence pulled Shannra back to her, using the height difference to sink her teeth into the woman's skin, scarred and rough with battle. Her white hair tickled Florence's nose and Florence closed her eyes. In the back of her mind, despite all will or conscious effort, another white-haired woman appeared like a dangling loose end, never quite tied off.

Florence pressed her teeth down harder. The flavor of someone else on her tongue was enough to clear her head again, and Florence pursued the distraction. Without much thought, Shannra was on the bed, Florence above her.

Sex had its own power and its own weakness, Florence had learned. It was gaining true vulnerability from another while giving it from yourself at the same time. But there was a guarded look to Shannra's eyes and an echo in all the woman's moans that came from the distance that still lingered between them. Neither was ready to give or take that power.

So they took only pleasure instead.

When the brakes of the train engaged some time later, Florence finally peeled her sweat-slicked body from the sheets. Her clothes hadn't gone far in the small cabin, but she was still stalled by the task of sorting them from Shannra's.

"What's the hurry?" Shannra yawned.

"How can you be sleepy? You've been dozing all day." Florence started with her underthings, dressing up to her skirt, shirt, and vest.

"You wore me out." The woman grinned, forgetting her earlier question entirely. Florence silently applauded herself for the effective distraction.

"Ah, well, that's not very hard." Her statement sent Shannra into a pout that transformed into a retaliation against putting on clothes.

"Where are you off to?"

"Train's almost stopped." Florence looked out their small window. The platform had begun to creep along the sides of the train. They were made of metal and wood, which echoed the architecture of a small town in the distance. Florence saw the marked smokestacks of a refinery and other buildings she didn't recognize.

Arianna's home.

It was Florence's first time laying eyes on a proper establishment of Ter.3, and she wondered how different it was from when Arianna was a girl.

"I'll need you to whisper to Arianna," Florence spoke as she adjusted her holster. "Let her know we made it to 3.2."

Shannra's mouth pressed together slightly. The woman was good at a great many things, but hiding her emotions from Florence was not one of them. It was as if Shannra could see through her, straight to that never-quite-defined aspect of her relationship with Arianna.

"Anything else you'd like me to tell her?" Shannra began moving for her clothes.

"No, that should be enough." Florence grabbed her top hat, the final piece of her ensemble. She hoped Arianna would have more to say to her—updates on the Philosopher's Boxes, suggestions for training, a remark on her cleverness for bringing all of Loom south . . . something.

"As you command, Vicar Florence." Shannra raised her hand to her ear.

Florence snatched the appendage by the wrist, quickly bringing it up to press a kiss against Shannra's knuckles. She searched the other woman's eyes. She wanted to offer reassurances, but she didn't quite know for what.

"Thank you, lovely," Florence whispered against Shannra's flesh.

Just like that, her steely eyes eased to wool-soft. "Anything for you, you know."

"Careful on what you offer me . . . I just may take it," she cautioned.

"I hope you do." Florence gave a small smile and moved away. Shannra added, "All of you."

Florence merely nodded, adjusted her hat, and left. She heard Shannra's meaning more clearly than she would've liked, but wasn't inclined to address it. Not yet. There was always tomorrow. For now, she had more important things to focus on than pesky matters of the heart.

For now, she had Loom.

Florence stepped off the yet-moving train, one of the first on the platform. Shannra was right; it had been too long since they had proper fresh air. Florence filled her lungs as if for the first time and relished the filtered sunlight of aboveground Loom. She hoped she had seen the last of the Underground.

After all, she was the Vicar Revolver now. Holx wasn't, and had never been, a place for her.

"Vicar Florence." She shouldn't have been surprised when Dove addressed her; the Vicar Raven would be the other to disembark first. Florence fell into step with the woman as they migrated toward the exit. "I trust your ride was good?"

"The Ravens do an excellent job of maintaining their trains, Vicar."

"They do indeed." Dove was completely oblivious that Florence's compliment held more than a bit of irony. "We should have more than enough coal here to see the rest of the way to Garre, a few routes between . . ."

Dove tried the door of the station master's office. When the handle didn't budge, she didn't even blink, smashing through the window with her pistol and reaching around to unlock it. She descended on the quarters as if she owned them, deftly locating the primary ledger for the station.

"How does it look?" Florence asked.

"More than enough coal . . . Should be a gold storehouse here, too, if I'm not mistaken. Perhaps we could even outfit one engine to focus more on magic and alleviate some of the draw on the resources."

"It'd certainly relieve Powell." Florence looked through the open door back out to the platform, seeing the man in question disembark.

"Anything to quiet him about draining resources," Dove muttered. Florence chose to ignore the remark. She'd seen just how impressive the Harvester's work to manage resources was.

"I'll whisper to Garre, have Arianna speak with Willard about outfitting the next train."

"And I'll look into that storehouse of gold."

Florence said nothing about the copied ledger she still had in her possession. Dove was almost too good at her job, remembering with ease where every outpost for the Ravens was along their trade routes. Plus, if Dove had concealed the state of their coal reserves, Florence could only imagine how she would handle gold. Thus, she kept the means to verify the Vicar Raven to herself.

"I trust you both had a smooth journey?" Powell asked as he joined them, referencing the last time they had spoken on the train a day ago.

"Indeed." Dove closed up the ledger and pushed past the Vicar Harvester. "If you'll both excuse me, I'm going to see to the state of our engines and manage my Ravens."

"Oh, right, very well . . ." Powell was left muttering to a woman who was already out of hearing range. "I don't think she likes me very much," he observed quietly to Florence.

"We don't have to like each other. We merely need to be effective." Florence shrugged and started for the door as well.

"Effective, huh? You like me though, don't you, Florence?"

"You know that's true." She gave Powell an encouraging smile. "We're both young vicars and need to stick together."

"No doubt."

The station had two platforms divided by a turnstile. Powell and Florence emerged opposite the side they'd arrived on, and found themselves on a covered stretch that descended into a cobblestone arc of road lined with small storefronts, completely void of life.

Florence's hand was on her gun before she was even conscious of the prickle up her neck. She looked along the road that led down the sloping hill into the downtown proper, where the smokestacks of the refinery and factories stretched toward the sky.

"It's quiet."

"I was just thinking the same thing," Powell affirmed.

"Revolvers!" Florence called over her shoulder back to the filling platform. The handful of her guild that still remained turned their heads in attention. "We move first, guns at the ready."

There were looks of confusion, but none objected. The Revolvers naturally ordered themselves in small squadrons based on specialization and available weaponry. Bernard was at her right.

"Bernard, I want you to set up roosts with the initiates, there and there." Florence pointed at two balconies down the road. Initiates weren't the best shots, but Florence hoped they could at least lay cover fire.

"Emma, you and I will go with the journeymen." Florence spoke loud enough for everyone to hear, but her eyes caught Shannra's. *Stay close to me*, they said.

"Vicar, we'd like to switch." Bernard spoke before Emma could even open her mouth, setting Florence's eye to twitching. "The Revolvers cannot manage the loss of another Vicar."

"The Revolvers can survive whatever comes our way," Florence said firmly. She'd not have men uttering words that would make the initiates weak. "Furthermore, I will be in good company."

"What are we defending ourselves from?" Emma asked the right question.

"I don't know yet." Florence looked back down the sloping, still road. "But something doesn't feel right."

They walked with guns at the ready down the center of the street. Florence felt the unease from the other Revolvers, but if there was fire to draw, she wanted to draw it. She wanted no chance of going unnoticed by lurking hostiles.

But the silence persisted and, other than its unnerving stillness, it was almost a pleasant walk. The air further south was slightly less bitingly cold and the wind was a gentle breeze. Still, Florence's concern continued to rise like molten steel coming to temperature.

The moment they arrived at the factory's entrance, where the Rivets had gone ahead early to begin manufacturing the corona-blasting guns, Florence knew every sickening concern was founded.

Bodies littered the ground, soaked in black and crimson. Blood formed small rivers in the grooves between the stones of the street. Fenthri and Chimera alike, most bearing Alchemist and Rivet markings, all had the distinct slash marks that came with Dragon talons. A startling few had guns on their person. It was a slaughter of noncombatants that set Florence's mouth into a grim line.

All movement had stilled around her and every living eye was on the large factory doors, pulled shut. Upon them, written with the smear of a large palm, was a message in blood.

"To Florence, with love," Emma read from her side. "What do we do now?"

Florence stared at the door for another long moment, as though it were the Dragon King himself. "We do what Loom is best at. We clean up the mess the Dragons have left us, and we get back to work."

CVAREH

"She would be impressed." Poiris folded his arms over his chest and looked out onto the refinery floor that wasn't much of a refinery anymore.

"Do you think so?" Cvareh rested his hands on the window sill.

Below, the floor that had been mostly dark since its creation now glowed with life as men and women flitted about from one machine to the next. His eyes tracked over each of the Fenthri, and he silently practiced each of their names. It was something small, but he hoped it would be enough to show Arianna that he had begun to take seriously the idea of Fenthri as equals on Nova.

"Petra wanted to see this place come to life. It was a grand vision that now means something. Yes, I think so."

"Thank you." Cvareh gave his friend a tired smile. His shoulders felt like they sagged a little deeper just from expending the energy to do so. "She wanted it to make gold."

"She couldn't have foreseen that we needed it for a much greater purpose. More than anything, Petra wanted it to be useful." Poiris had a working relationship with his sister that Cvareh had only glimpsed briefly. This had been Petra's pet project; were it not for Poiris, Cvareh would've had a hard time assuming the mantle, going in blind.

"Useful, it is."

"To think, we underestimated them for so long." Poiris's eyes were on the Fenthri. "Thinking them lesser. Thinking we had things to teach them and order to bring. We had a lot more to learn."

"I wouldn't say that . . ." Cvareh's eyes fell on one woman in particular, who nearly stopped all movement on the floor with her white-haired, nearly ethereal presence.

Arianna was a force to be reckoned with. Respected among Fenthri and feared among Dragons alike for her knowledge, she commanded loyalty with an ease Cvareh didn't think she even recognized. With him as Dono and her at his side, they could rule the world together.

Do I want that?

It had long since stopped being about what either of them wanted.

"Why is that?" Poiris pulled Cvareh from his thoughts.

"Why is—*oh*, because as much as we have to learn from them, they need to learn from us." Cvareh thought of Arianna when she first landed on Nova, the things she questioned. Was it fair for him to think that she was better off for having her world expanded beyond the cold logic that governed Loom?

"Well, call me greased," Arianna said as she opened the door. "This damn near looks respectable."

"Are you surprised?" Poiris asked, his chest puffing like a bird ruffling its feathers.

"With this one at the helm?" Arianna motioned to Cvareh. "Yes."

"I don't think—"

Cvareh merely chuckled and allowed the sound to diffuse Poiris's tension into confusion. "Poiris, all is well. Please excuse my mate and I."

Arianna arched her eyebrows, a silent question.

Naming her as such extended her all the respect and protections that came with his own status. But he couldn't deny the quiet thrill that hummed through him at the notion.

With Poiris departed, Arianna dropped her bag into a heap by the door, empty. The tubes it carried had already been handed off to be filled anew with flowers. "Your mate. Sounds serious."

"It's not," he lied.

"You're lying."

She could be very frustrating. "It doesn't matter. Nothing does unless we win."

"Until we win," she corrected and stared out down at the Fenthri. "They're doing a good job, seem happy enough."

"When the war is over, every Fenthri who wishes to return home to Loom will be ferried back. The ones who don't will be treated the same as any Dragon."

"None will want to stay."

She sounded as if she had every confidence, but Cvareh wasn't so sure. In the hybrid world that existed just beyond the horizon, there was a place for Fenthri on Nova to maintain the various mechanizations that would no doubt crop up across their landscape. The mere idea brought a smile to Cvareh's mouth.

"What?"

"What?" he echoed.

"That smile."

"Just imagining a Nova with Fenthri, and machines."

Arianna snorted. "The likelihood of that happening is about the same as the Alchemists giving up dissections."

"I don't think so." He leaned against the glass, following her stare. Even now, Dragons were beginning to walk among the Fenthri, work among them. "Plus, for the longevity of one world, we'd better hope that we get along enough to live on land or sky."

"Well, we will be living in both places soon, as Loom is about ready to ferry Perfect Chimera."

"How many?" Cvareh didn't even bother to hide his desperation.

"Ten."

Ten, the word echoed. "That's not nearly enough."

"It will have to be."

"Ari—"

"Loom isn't sending anyone who isn't ready to fight. If we send them up here prematurely, they will be slaughtered."

"It's my people who are being slaughtered right now." He knew it was a faulty argument, but he couldn't stop himself. Logic and emotion didn't always work well together.

"Loom could always, instead, just fortify ourselves and leave Xin to fight alone."

Shock started with his mouth and rattled up to his brain. "You'd condemn us to death?"

"That's not what I said."

"Isn't it?" Cvareh pushed off from the sill and stepped into her personal space. He stared down at her, working to ignore the familiar scents of her. "You'd leave me to die by Rok's hand?"

Arianna stared up at him. Her chin stretched forward, as though she was about to fight him. But then her brow softened. What looked like conflict overcame her features, and Cvareh no longer had any idea what was going through the woman's mind. He loathed the distance that had come between them, though he couldn't quite identify when the chasm had started to form.

Cvareh never had the opportunity to find out her answer.

"Attack on the western side of Ruana!" Cain skidded to a stop in the open doorway. His eyes narrowed at Arianna and hers narrowed in reply, the defensive expression instantly back on her face.

How the two most important people in Cvareh's life ended up on opposite sides of the coin, Cvareh did not know. But he appreciated that they could put it all aside for their common enemy.

"It's close to Dawyn's family's vineyards." Cain confirmed Cvareh's worst fear.

"I have to go," he said to them both.

Arianna pushed off from the window sill as well. Her hands went through their motions, an instinctual check of every tool of her trade. She patted her blades, her winch box, her breast pocket where there was, no doubt, some kind of gun or other weapon concealed.

"I will go, too."

"What?" both men said in unison.

She looked directly at Cvareh and he instantly regretted challenging her. For there was nothing more fearsome than an Arianna with something to prove.

"I will go, too," she reiterated. Her attention was solely on Cvareh. "And I will show you just how valuable one Perfect Chimera will be in your fight." Arianna turned to Cain. "Lead on."

Cain obliged and Arianna followed, her focus entirely on Cvareh's Ryu. Cvareh followed close behind, pushing his conflict from his mind. He needed to be focused for whatever battle awaited them. But for now, he felt some pity for whatever Dragons were about to face Arianna.

FLORENCE

The winter air pricked at her skin, turning it into gooseflesh. Florence rose from the bed she shared with Shannra, finally abandoning all hope of sleep. Instead, she tugged on a random shirt and skirt and padded lightly to the large window that overlooked Ter.3.2. Quietly easing open the latch, Florence leaned into the night air.

The world was still. Somewhere, a Revolver kept watch, ready to raise the alarm if gliders were spotted against the darkened sky. But they didn't make their hiding spot known.

Florence rested her elbows on the sill. The metal was like ice under her flesh and shot daggers right to her bones. She inhaled deeply, allowing the cool air to meet the sensation of her arms and finish numbing out her bare toes.

"You're going to catch your death if you let in this weather." Florence half-turned and was met with a blanket slung over her shoulder.

"I didn't hear you stir."

"I know." Shannra nestled herself under the blanket at Florence's side, closing it around them like a great cocoon. She'd thought she wanted to be alone. But Florence was proven wrong by the beautiful woman at her side. Her head gravitated toward Shannra's shoulder, and she pulled the blanket more tightly around them.

"How long do you think it will take?"

"How long do I think what will take?" Shannra followed Florence's gaze, looking at the factory in the distance. "The new weapons? Sooner over later, I'm sure. The revisions didn't seem too complicated, at least according to the Rivets."

"That wasn't what I meant."

"My mind reading must be rusty, then." Florence didn't even bother fighting a small smile at the woman's jest. "What did you mean?"

"All this." Florence nodded to the city sprawled beneath them. The fractured homes, void of occupants. The sloping streets, empty and quiet. "How long until the cities are full again? Until steam clouds the sky at all hours of the day? How long until Loom is alive once more?"

"Loom *is* alive," Shannra insisted. "In no small part thanks to you."

Florence didn't want to be placated. She wanted a real answer. She wanted to know if what she was doing would be enough or if she had only set the target for Loom's revival too far away for anyone to hit.

Ari would've understood what she was trying to say.

"I'm not enough," Florence spoke mostly to herself, to all the flaws she still had and everything that she still wanted to accomplish.

"Where is this coming from? Flor, you can't be discouraged by what happened here."

"I'm not discouraged, I'm motivated," she insisted. "All those people died because someone wanted to leave me a message." Florence scowled at the invisible killer who had laid waste to a factory producing a gun she had an important hand in designing. It was an attack on her even without the words on the doors. "I need to find the person who killed them and shoot them down for Loom. I need to be better for us all—"

It dawned on her in a rush. "I need to be Perfect."

"What are you saying?" Shannra's grip had relaxed some. Despite the blanket being around their shoulders, Florence felt very far out of reach.

"I need to be Perfect." Florence repeated. That was what she was missing. That was what separated everything she was, and everything she could become. It had been Arianna's turning point, the thing that had made her so strong for so many years.

"You don't need to be anything but what you are." Shannra squeezed her tightly again. "You're already enough."

Florence opened her mouth to protest, when the wind shifted and a familiar scent tickled her nose. It was faint, so much that she could've ignored it entirely. Florence looked for the source, turning her face toward the breeze. But Arianna was far away, and the scent was nothing more than a wisp on the wind.

"My mind is made up." Florence kept her eyes on the southwestern horizon, wondering if the smell was all in her mind. She would've known that aroma anywhere: Arianna's magic. Perhaps, it was her mind finally telling her that with Perfection would come an understanding of something greater. She would see the world with eyes like Arianna's and gain insights into all the corners of herself that she seemed to barely understand.

COLETTA

our Dragons snarled from their respective pens in the observation room. Things had changed since Fae and Topann's time. These were not loyal servants who deserved free roam, but bottom-dwellers. Dragons who had never seen the sun couldn't be trusted not to kill each other, let alone leave unharmed the Fenthri charged with observing them for any signs of magic rejection.

She watched as the Alchemist walked the length of the room, purposefully staying out of swiping reach of each of the cages. Coletta wondered what the world looked like to him. The only thing keeping him from certain death was her.

From where she stood, it was a gorgeous world order.

"And how are they?" Coletta inquired, growing impatient with the Fen's endless humming, pen-tapping, and pacing.

"None of them are showing the same signs as Yeann. It seems the Xin organs you have acquired work well."

"If only there were more. You said with one Dragon we could make another Perfect in how long?"

The Alchemist thought a moment. "We'd have to time regrowth . . . too many organs out at once and the body won't heal. One Dragon can make one Perfect Dragon in . . . I'd estimate two weeks? If all the organs aligned."

It was too long. She needed more Xin organs sooner over later. Coletta's eyes settled on the Dragons in their cages once more. Even if there were more to sort, a success would still be a success, and she would do well not to forget it.

Instead of allowing the limitations to frustrate her, she let them bolster her sails.

"My queen." Ulia appeared in the doorway. "Forgive the intrusion, but Yveun'Dono requests your presence."

"Where is he?" Coletta's voice was impassive toward the summons.

"The sun room."

"Continue as planned," Coletta instructed as a final note to the Fen. Even if they'd only found one Xin Dragon to harvest organs from, Coletta would still have him move forward at whatever snail's pace he could. It was better than nothing.

"Right . . ." The man's agreement trailed off as he looked at the other empty cells in the room, no doubt imagining what it would be like to have them all filled with swiping, snarling, rage-filled Perfect Dragons.

The Fen's greatest fear was Coletta's sweetest wish.

Yveun's temperament had not much improved from their last interaction. The balm of Fae's touch had done little, if anything, to soothe him, and her departure for Loom had only made matters worse.

Coletta dismissed Ulia halfway to the room Yveun had made his center of operations for managing the various battlefronts they faced. She adjusted the beads around her neck, then entered. Yveun sat behind a low desk positioned in front of a great vertical circle, atop a pedestal, overlooking a balcony.

Coletta saw it for what it was—fanfare. The real work happened in Gray Rooms and secret gardens.

"That necklace is new," Yveun observed with a glance.

"I thought it fitting." Coletta touched it delicately even though it was likely as sturdy as the bones in her fingers.

"Taking Rider beads for yourself?"

Sure enough, the necklace had been crafted from Dragon bone in the same fashion as the beads the Riders wore to mark their kills. "I think I have earned this many beads and more."

"It's the 'and more' I am most interested in." Yveun hoisted a folio and tossed it toward her feet. The papers scattered across the floor—transcripts of the reports from the Hall of Whispers. "I'm in need of much more from you, Coletta."

Coletta merely arched her eyebrows. "I'm not sure how making a mess of your notes helps me produce it." She folded her hands and stood tall, hoping to convey that she had no interest in collecting up his documents for him.

"We are thwarted at every turn on Loom, Perfect Chimera have begun to fight alongside Xin, and Tam's interest in struggling against the abominations seems to be wearing thin."

Wearing thin because there was no more gold to tip the scales in Rok's favor.

"And you, what have you done?" Yveun approached with purpose. "You have played Alchemist with your Fen toy, doing little for our plight."

"I have given everything for our plight." Coletta stretched her mouth wide, showing her teeth and reminding him of all she had endured for the sake of their dominance.

For the briefest of moments, he softened into the man she was accustomed to seeing when it was just the two of them, alone. Yveun reached out one of his massive hands and ran it almost tenderly across her necklace. "It suits you."

"Thank you. Now, with regards to Tam . . ." Her demeanor shifted and the moment evaporated like fresh blood. She had his levelheaded attention and she needed to capitalize on it while she could. "We do not need them."

"Coletta—"

"Yveun," she interrupted. He had to hear her; everything hinged on him putting aside his prejudice and truly listening to what she said. "You know what Fae has done on Loom. With just her and two other Riders, she took down an entire Fenthri stronghold."

"A feat my Riders could always boast," Yveun countered.

"There were casualties then," Coletta reminded him. "Fae thrives with not so much as a scratch. On Loom, a Perfect Dragon is the perfect predator. *Think* of what we could do with them here, on Nova."

"No."

"Without Tam's assistance we must do something to sway the tides back in our favor." Coletta had always known that pride made men stupid, but she never appreciated *how* stupid until that moment.

"Then acquire more gold and buy back their loyalty."

"There is no more gold," she said for what must have been the hundredth time. "We are sitting atop an army, yet you do not wish to mobilize."

"I will not see Xin organs in my house's Dragons."

"Defeat them with what they are." It would be glorious. The idea of thwarting Xin with their own organs sent shivers up her spine.

"No."

"Yveun—"

"Your Dono has decreed it!" Yveun roared. Coletta didn't even flinch. "You will not put any more Xin organs into Rok bodies. *That* is not perfection; it is an affront to Lord Rok himself."

Coletta started for the door.

"I have not dismissed you," he growled.

"I have dismissed myself." Coletta stood as tall as possible. She was shorter than him, smaller and frailer, yet she could still look down her nose at the short-sighted man who claimed to be her mate. "I will only speak to you again once you are ready to see reason." Her eyes dropped to the papers still scattered on the floor, nothing more than a pathetic list of failures. "I hope it will not be too late by then."

She closed the door gently behind her. Coletta would not give in to sudden outbursts or rage. She was not her mate, who, judging from the crash, promptly set to destroy what remained of his beautiful façade.

Let him ruin it, she thought, starting down the hall. Perhaps once he had made a mess of the illusion, he would be ready to face reality.

CVAREH

"Arianna, what are we?" he moaned against her mouth, pressing his hips against hers.

"You talk too much," she sighed back in reply. For all the brilliance the woman could craft with her fingers, they seemed to be thwarted every time by the clasps Nova's tailors could conceive.

"What are we?" he repeated.

"What does it matter?"

He heard the fastenings holding up his trousers click open and Cvareh knew there was little more he could do. He was helpless before her, trembling like a mortal before a god whose altar was a small bed in the back of the refinery-turned-factory.

Cvareh pushed her down and heeded her hands. His body swelled, enveloping hers. Arianna pushed and pulled, contorted herself to meet him until that moment when they both could breathe again, when he was fully immersed in her.

It was the greatest feeling he'd ever known, though it would be impossible to attempt to explain to anyone else why it was so wonderful. He didn't try. Cvareh kept them, and whatever they were or weren't, between them. He kept this feeling between them.

This blissful, all-too-short feeling.

It was the fourth time he'd had her in two short months and the wait between each time became harder than the last.

Every time was the same. Every time, she'd arrived to take flowers, bring resources. Every time, she'd ended up fighting alongside Xin men and women against Rok. Every time, she was met with the same apprehension from his people that Arianna would claim didn't weigh on her until the day she died and yet, there was something to it. Some kind of jealousy that came over her like a shadow when those same people praised Cvareh for his actions as their Ryu.

The more others learned of her, the more she withdrew. Her demeanor had even begun to earn praise from Cain, so much that the man had stopped pestering Cvareh at every turn about his fondness for Arianna.

He never thought he'd actually miss Cain's nagging. But at least when his friend complained, it meant things were as they had always been. His silence underscored the distance he felt growing between them.

Cvareh lay at Arianna's side, tracing the outlines of her ashen skin with a long finger. He graced over the scars of her body—the gash where her chest had been cracked open to allow room for his lungs, the ring on her wrists where the hands Finnyr had once carried met her natural flesh, the horizontal slit where her stomach had been scooped out. On and on, her body was pockmarked and flawed. But every curve, every gnarled scar, was *hers*. Her hands belonged to none but her. Even the lungs, still heaving from their lovemaking, he no longer saw as his own.

"Ari . . ." He leaned in to press his nose against her cheek, nuzzling it.

"I should go."

"You've barely caught your breath." He watched her get up, locating her underthings first. Cvareh was proud to say that this time he had not shredded them in his zeal.

"We can't afford time for things like this."

"I object," he said with a chuckle. "We've afforded time, every time."

"And we shouldn't." Arianna buttoned up the fly of her trousers—all seven needless, frustrating, delicate buttons.

"Why?" He watched as she shrugged on her shirt next, back still to him, as her form in all its beauty began to be shrouded from him once more. Arianna located her vest and was buttoning it before he pressed again, realizing she had no intention of answering him. "Why shouldn't we?"

"You're the Xin'Oji."

"Since when have you cared for Dragon titles?" He stood with a soft chuckle and gripped her shoulders, half-turning her to face him. Arianna's eyes were full of all the life and fire he loved in her, even when it was directed toward him. "You are right, I am the Xin'Oji. But that merely means no one will object to me—to us."

"When you kill Yveun . . ."

He appreciated her certainty. "When I kill Yveun, what?" he repeated. It wasn't like her to leave a thought hanging.

"What then?"

"Then I will be Dono." Cvareh searched her face, surprised to find pain there. "I promise you, Arianna, I will be a Dono for Nova. Loom will have their sovereignty."

"I have no doubt." She pulled away from him and snatched up her white coat. Arianna tugged it on with renewed purpose and went right for the door.

"Ari—."

"I have to get back to Loom," she interrupted him curtly, not even bothering to look back. "More Perfect Chimera are ready to sent, and guns will soon be ready to ship with them. I need to help train Ravens to run gliders."

Cvareh stared dumbly as she left him to wonder what, exactly, he had said wrong.

Certainly, he could've chased after her, but he didn't. He could've whispered to her in the days that followed, but he didn't do that either. The words that needed to be said, words he was still discovering, needed to be said to her face. And those he wanted to hear, he likewise wanted to see emerge from her mouth.

So, when she whispered a week later that Perfect Chimera were on their way, Cvareh vowed to be ready. He prepared his heart, only to have it sink when he discovered not Arianna making the delivery, but Helen in her stead.

FLORENCE

The Rivets' Guild hall was everything Florence expected after her brief time in Ter.3.2. The clockwork structure of patchwork metal—some dulled with time, greening with age, and other parts fresh like new skin grafts over old wounds—fit with what she'd come to learn was the Rivet sensibility. Steam hissed and gears churned in perpetual motion within the walls.

She was put up in very sensible chambers close to Willard. Florence could tell they were designed especially for guests, as they had different accommodations than usual. Even in comfort, there was something purposeful and methodological about the way the Rivets approached their existence. The whole place echoed of Arianna in the most nostalgic of ways.

Florence had been sequestered from the first moment she'd arrived. Willard and Ethel had greeted her at the platform and talks began almost immediately. How would they allocate their increasing numbers of trained Perfect Chimera? Would they outfit them with Florence's weapon, or would they save the weapon for regular Chimera in effort to double their effective fighting force? Would they be willing to supply the weapon directly to the Dragons? On and on the questions went.

They looked to Florence for answers that she wasn't sure she had. She was the Vicar Revolver, and hadn't ever set foot in the Revolvers' Guild hall—at least, hadn't set foot when she wasn't sneaking. She didn't know the first thing about how to properly train Alchemists to think like fighters. So she made it up as she went, and hoped it all worked out.

Yes, she was exhausted from trying to live up to others' expectations. She was tired of the world looking to her for answers she didn't even know if she had. But Florence knew she wouldn't sleep tonight.

Her mind was heavy, and her heart was knotted. It was a combination that kept sleep at bay and Florence knew better than to fight losing battles. So, instead, she attempted something she hoped would be productive.

She had set out to find Ari and, thanks to Will's help, she knew right where to look.

Master Oliver, the name plate on the door still read. She gave a few solid knocks before noticing it was slightly ajar.

"It's open, Flor."

The voice alone shot right to the heart of her. Florence suddenly wondered if she had the courage to enter. She'd done so much, but felt daunted by this small task.

Pulled by an unseen hand, Florence pushed through, and saw, for the first time in months, the visage of the woman she'd admired for years.

Arianna sat behind a large drafting table, where papers weighted by rulers hid under pencils worn down to nibs. Her coat was hung on a peg nailed into one of the bookcases, almost hidden by manuscripts draping half off the overfilled shelves like crooked teeth. Ledgers stuffed in-between threatened to spill out their secrets in protest of their treatment.

Florence's eyes drifted from the worn leather chairs around a table, to the bookshelves, to the doorway to the rooms beyond, and back to Arianna. Any frustration or apprehension she felt melted away the moment she saw the white-haired woman dressed in plain woolen trousers and a rumpled shirt, open at the collar.

It was like finally a piece had been slotted back into place. *This* was where Arianna belonged, not in some dingy flat in Old Dortam.

"So, this is where you grew up?"

Arianna looked around the room, as if with fresh eyes. "Sort of, I suppose . . . Willard found me at seven, and we left due to differences in ideology when I was about ten."

"When he joined the Council of Five and started the rebellion?" Florence helped herself to one of the seats facing Arianna.

"Indeed." Arianna's eyes drifted back to whatever it was she'd been working on and her hand reached for a pencil, no doubt on instinct more than command.

Florence let her work. She knew how Arianna was with an idea; there was no stopping her mind once it was coiled around something. If history had proved anything, it was that the world was better off for letting Ari's ideas run their course.

The chair wrapped her in a cozy embrace, inviting Florence to lean into it. So, she obliged, and tipped her head back. She was going to allow her eyes to flutter closed, perhaps even sneak in a moment of sleep in this tranquil oasis amid a sea of war and questions. But the ceiling captured her focus.

Even there, schematics and equations were plastered. Notes written in multiple hands layered on top of each other, fighting for attention and maybe even supremacy. There was no discernible order, yet Florence knew that if she tried to move a single one, Ari would know instantly.

"You didn't come to the station to greet me," Florence said when the pencil finally stilled.

"By design. I knew Willard and Ethel needed to speak with you."

"We needed you there, too." Florence's eyelids suddenly felt heavy, and she let them close.

"If you had, one of you would've called me." Arianna appeared in Florence's field of view the moment she opened her eyes. Her mentor's hair was awash in the pale orange of the dim lamplight that only stretched a peca away from the desk. "I didn't want to insult your status as a vicar."

Florence wanted to tell Arianna that she still needed her, no matter her title. But she knew that crutch was long gone. She'd been moving away from it for months. So why did she seem to ache so fiercely at the idea of Arianna letting it go, too?

"We may have been able to make an exception for the Queen of Wraiths." Florence grinned lazily.

Arianna chuckled, a deep, rich sound. She stretched out her long legs.

"A foolish moniker."

"An upgrade."

"Who really knows?" Arianna rested her head against the back of the seat in an almost mirror-image of Florence's posture. Florence couldn't help but wonder who had done it first . . . Was it her own habit and Arianna mirrored her? Or was it a trait she'd stolen while growing up with the Rivet? "Perhaps it'll be of use to me when Loom is finally free."

A free Loom. Florence had spent so much time fighting that she'd never thought of what she'd do when she had to live after. When the battles were won, what did soldiers become?

"Will you return to Dortam?" Florence was brave enough to ask the question and cowardly enough to fear the answer.

"Who knows?"

"I will be there."

"I assumed so." Arianna straightened with a sincere smile. "You are the Vicar Revolver now, after all. You, Flor! The Vicar Revolver!"

Florence stared at the kind, beaming face of her mentor. It was a gentleness that only she had ever seen, and all her life it had meant something profound. But it was in that moment when she looked into Arianna's brilliant lilac eyes, full of so many emotions—pride, admiration, hope, compassion—that Florence realized they had never seen each other in entirely the same way.

"Ari…" Her throat closed, trapping the words. Florence forced them out; even if the shot missed, she had to pull the trigger or she'd regret leaving the canister in the chamber forever. "I love you."

"And I love you, Flor." Her expression didn't shift in the slightest. Arianna continued to look at her the same way she always had—with the eyes of the proud mentor. Or as Nova would have it, an older sister. It was nothing more or less than that profound connection.

Not as I love you.

Surely Arianna knew. Surely she heard it in the crack in her voice and the odd jitter of nerves vibrating across her whole body. Arianna noticed the most minute details in complete strangers, so there was no way she hadn't seen it in Florence.

Which meant every action Arianna took was a careful and measured response. In her own way, Florence's mentor was attempting to communicate her desire for things to remain the same as they'd always been.

Florence didn't know if this had been the response she'd wanted. But it was the response she was going to get. So, she chose not to dwell on "what if" and, instead, focus on how having any response was freeing in its own right.

"Thank you, for everything you ever taught me."

"That is something you don't need to thank me for. What you have accomplished with the rebellion is all the thanks in the world."

"Hopefully, something I continue to accomplish," Florence sighed softly.

"You will." Arianna folded her arms over her chest.

"See this through with me, Arianna?"

"I think I should scold you for having any doubt."

Florence wondered if Arianna felt it, too, the split in their parallel paths drawing near. Florence didn't need a teacher any longer; she needed a partner. One like the woman waiting for her back in Ter.3.2. She couldn't lead if she was constantly following in someone else's shadow.

That night, her heart flipped the switch that would set them, eventually, on their separate paths. They reminisced of their time in Old Dortam, of grand heists and early failures, and Florence began to feel the last cloying hands of childhood and first love release from her soul. When she finally left, it was nearly dawn; Florence had not once brought up the idea of becoming a Perfect Chimera.

ARIANNA

It was almost as if Florence had never even been there.

Arianna's student-turned-vicar had stopped into the Rivets' Guild for a total of two nights, and they had spent both of them talking into the late hours. But by day, Florence was busy with Willard and Ethel, as well as setting up a new training program under a Master Bernard—one of the two Master Revolvers Florence had left, supposedly. But what were masters worth any more in a world where a Raven-born girl with nothing more than an outline on her cheek could become the Vicar Revolver?

She saw Florence off the morning of the third day.

"Take care of yourself." Florence embraced her tightly but briefly. Her arms didn't seem to linger around Arianna's frame as they once had.

"I should be saying that to you." Arianna righted Florence's hat after it was jostled during their embrace. "Vicar Revolvers aren't well known for their longevity."

"I've already survived longer than the last."

"As if that fact is supposed to make me feel better."

"What will you do, after it's all over?"

Arianna stared down at the girl, the question seeming to curdle time into a sticky weight there was no escaping from.

She could keep them here in this moment, if she wanted, but Arianna couldn't even seem to find a breath. Florence was leaving to continue her role as the Vicar Revolver. Cvareh was championing a cause that would make him King of the Dragons. And she . . .

"Will you stay the Queen of Wraiths?" Florence's mouth pulled into a smile. However well the girl knew her, there were still barriers and boundaries her mind wouldn't let her cross, where Arianna wouldn't permit her entry. She wouldn't let Florence know of the turmoil the future presented.

"Perhaps." Arianna tapped her winch box. "I am fairly talented at the whole affair."

"Vicar Willard tells me you're also talented at being a master and teaching students."

"Vicar Willard is a liar," Arianna retorted with mock sweetness, earning a laugh from Florence.

"Come back to Dortam," Florence offered. "I can see a place for you at the Revolvers' home. You could run the refinery there."

"You mean the one I used to steal from?" Arianna arched her eyebrows.

"Who better? You can make it more secure than ever before." The whistle of the train sounded and a Raven scuttled over, giving a light tap to Florence's shoulder.

"We're leaving shortly."

"Yes, I know." Florence tipped her hat, sending the girl away. "In any case, think on it, Ari. I still need you around."

And then she was gone before Arianna could formulate another word.

She disappeared into the curling steam of the engine amid a bustle of men and women loading up the short locomotive with supplies. Arianna, a good head taller than the rest, watched the dark-haired woman go. People parted for her out of respect for the circled Revolver pin she wore on the lapel of her coat.

Arianna was glad Florence hadn't pressed the matter further. *I love you*—she'd heard the girl. Arianna knew all too well the heartache clinging to a lost love could reap, and there would never be anything between them. If not because she was the mentor and Florence the student, then because the girl was a child of the future, and Arianna would always be shrouded in the shadow of the past. It was best for both of them to let go, move on.

Plus, Arianna had her own battles to fight.

"You actually let her go."

Arianna's head whipped to the young man who had suddenly appeared next to her. "Your reward for sneaking up on me is my not lodging a dagger between your eyes."

Will hummed in low amusement at the idea, but continued to drive on the path of his earlier sentiment. "I always thought there was more between you two."

"There was everything between us, in different ways, at different times." The platform had been cleared and Ravens began to shout to each other. The great gears inside the train ground to life. "She needed me, and I needed her. We're both better for what we got out of the arrangement."

"Arrangement?" Will crossed his arms over his chest. "How . . . clinical."

"I'm not an Alchemist."

"How precise, then," he corrected. "Will you go back to her?"

"Just how much did you hear?" Arianna finally peeled her eyes away from the vessel that was taking Florence from her.

"Enough."

"You're getting too good at this job." She was creating monsters left and right. Perfect Chimera and now a competent Will? What next? A tolerable Helen?

"Learning from the best."

She snorted at the idea.

"If you don't want to be Queen of Wraiths, give it to Helen. She wanted to take over for Louie; you'll endear yourself to her if you offer her the same."

"I don't care about endearing myself to her." The potentially harsh statement was void of real bite. She couldn't fault Will for looking after his friend. Nostalgia made her soft. Florence made her soft. All this sentimentality was really beginning to dull her.

"That much is obvious," Will acquiesced. "But she is trying to endear herself to you, nevertheless."

Arianna arched her eyebrows, prompting him to continue.

"She's returned from Nova."

"I was beginning to think she got lost up there." It had been two days since Helen left. Arianna had expected an extra day due to glider exhaustion—all the new Perfect Chimera were becoming accustomed to piloting the machines and managing their magic—but she was also expecting the little crow to be side-tracked by the vast and new lands of Nova. "Take me to her."

Will started for the end of the platform, where the light rail would take them back to the guild proper. "She brought back more flowers and is already preparing for another trip up. It seems the fighting has increased on Nova."

"The Dragons do enjoy their blood sport." Arianna's mind drowned her in images of Cvareh fighting—fighting and losing.

"Something about House Tam no longer assisting Rok—"

"*What?*"

Will repeated himself and, then, added, "Helen said to make sure you knew."

Arianna's eyes turned skyward at the battle that no doubt raged on just beyond the clouds. She'd learned of House Tam's influence on Nova as the silent enforcers; if they were no longer assisting House Rok, that meant power could shift—was, in fact, already shifting.

"Will, see Helen is outfitted with more guns, however many we have. Take the airship to Ter.3.2 and gather any from there as well." Her mouth moved fast, but not as fast as her mind. "Then, bring up all the Perfect Chimera who are ready and willing."

"All of them?"

"A constant stream." They had the manpower. If Tam was backing out from House Rok—for whatever reason—they had the numbers to overwhelm them. "It's time to strike."

"Where are you going?" Will motioned to the trolley approaching down the narrow rail.

"I'm headed up first. It'll be faster for me to get to the gliders this way." She paused on the edge of the platform, her clip already flying toward a far steam pipe. "And tell Helen that if she wants Louie's 'kingdom' then it's hers. But the title is mine."

"More than fair." Will gave a solemn nod.

Arianna returned the gesture a moment before her winch box sprung to life, pulling her in sweeping arcs around the outside of Garre to the hangar where gliders were kept.

FLORENCE

"Welcome back, Florence," Emma greeted her the moment she stepped off the train.

"I should take your presence to mean that something has gone wrong?" Florence asked, barely taking time to sling her bag over her shoulder before they began walking off the platform.

"Quite the contrary, actually. The first batch of weapons have all been tested and not a moment too soon. Will arrived not long before you to pick them up." Emma seemed pleased to report, and Florence was equally pleased to hear. Her tone shifted, however, on the next note. "It seems the timeline has been pushed forward to get as many Perfect Chimera to Nova as possible."

"I trust you facilitated this transaction to be as quick and smooth as possible?" Florence gave no indication that she had not heard of nor approved things happening faster. Either Bernard had been included, or he had been told. No matter, it was too late now to change it and Florence silently praised Willard and Ethel for being able to accommodate the change.

"I did."

"Good. I'm ready to see an end to this war."

"As we all are."

Florence gave a nod of agreement and produced a folio from her satchel. "I have new schematics here for the next round of manufacturing."

"Another round of edits?"

"I have no doubt that there will be some moaning over having to re-tool the line again." *And I don't care*, Florence left unsaid. "But there is no point in making something unless we continually strive to make it better, make it right."

"Agreed." Florence believed Emma stood behind her on the matter. It was the Rivets who would protest.

"Inform the Rivets that these modifications come from Arianna." Florence was still becoming accustomed to Arianna's name meaning something to random strangers, but she'd use it to her benefit without reservation.

"Right away."

"Take it on ahead. I'd like to put my things down and change out of my traveling clothes. I won't be long."

Emma gave a tip of her cap. It had a short, leather, rounded brim with a band over top and, unlike a top hat, the fabric sort of flopped over on one side. Florence had been admiring it since she'd stepped off the train and immediately regretted not asking Emma who had stitched such an interesting headpiece.

Later. Right now, her priority was elsewhere. It had nothing to do with changing her clothes or dropping her bag. No, she was on the lookout for a certain someone she had an insatiable urge to see in private.

The door to their adopted abode was unlocked. They had never made a habit of locking it, so Florence thought little of it when she entered the foyer. "Shannra?"

There was a long moment of silence and, just when Florence was about to leave, she heard floorboards creak from an upper floor. The building they had assumed as theirs was three stories. Foyer and living spaces on the first floor, workshops on the second, bedrooms on the third.

"Shannra, it's me." Florence called again as she rounded the first flight of stairs, not wanting to startle the woman if she'd somehow not fully heard the first time. Their respective work tables were vacant, which left the third floor as her only remaining option. She'd been hoping to get the woman in bed, and it seemed Shannra would make it easy on her.

Florence paused halfway up the second flight of stairs, when she heard the floor creaking again. The sound came with a second's worth of hesitation.

Something was off.

The floorboards weren't moving in the rhythms Florence had come to associate with her lover. Their syncopation, combined with the silence and . . .something else . . . something familiar. . .

Honeysuckle. It was unmistakable after being around Arianna. But where Ari's floral magic was mixed with other scents—there was always the soft hint of something woodsy—this scent was cloying and powerful against the nose. Florence put her finger on the difference immediately as she rounded the last step and into the doorway of the bedroom.

Shannra stood at the double window, just where they'd huddled underneath the blanket the night before Florence left. She turned, greeting Florence with a familiar smile. The fading daylight glinted off her white hair and she opened her arms invitingly.

"It's so good to see you." Florence spread a smile across her face with great effort at the visage that was every bit as familiar as it should be, yet incredibly off-putting. She dropped her bag at the foot of the bed, rummaging through it. "I was hoping I would catch you."

Every hair on Florence's body stood on end. Magic was thick in the air, potent and powerful. It was overwhelming and unlike anything Florence had ever experienced before.

She didn't quite know what specter was before her, but she knew it wasn't Shannra.

Right at the top of her bag, where they should be for any self-respecting Revolver, were her canisters and weapon. "Ari did a great job." Florence held up a canister, putting it on display. "They'll be manufacturing these soon, I'm sure."

Imposter Shannra kept her arms outstretched, motioning in a sort of "come hither" way. Florence popped her spare revolver into the empty slot on the left side of her under-arm hoister.

There was only one entry and exit to the room—the door she had come through. The creature would, no doubt, expect her to flee in the direction she came. Whatever magic this animal possessed, it was a safe assumption to think it could run her down. Until she knew what she was fighting, she wasn't going to waste ammunition fending it off.

Until she knew what she was fighting, she also wasn't going to give it the benefit of predictability.

Florence took a step toward the Shannra-shaped specter. She held out her hands as if to accept its embrace. Every muscle coiled with tension around her bones. At the very last moment, she let it spring.

The specter half-lunged forward, dropping her head. Florence drew her weapon and thrust it to the imposter's chin. Her hand disappeared straight through—an illusion. The muzzle of the gun didn't find the creature's head, as Florence had hoped, but she brought the hilt of the gun hard against its chest, firing in the process.

It roared, a feminine sound, but not like those she'd heard from any Fenthri or Dragon before. She took advantage of the creature's surprise, and bolted.

"Get back here!" Imposter Shannra grabbed for her wrist at the same time Florence's hand twisted the handle of the window. It swung open as she was grabbed back by a hand that felt much larger than what her eyes saw wrapped around her forearm.

Florence used the release of momentum to twist, crossing her arm over her, to draw her second gun. She pressed the muzzle into the air just above the creature's hand, meeting invisible flesh.

Florence pulled the trigger and gold blood flew through the air—a Dragon.

Even still, the monster didn't release its hold on her. Florence yanked her arm, once, twice; on the third time, it snapped free with the Dragon's claws raking across her forearm.

Florence was face-to-face with one of the most unnerving creature she had ever seen. The Dragon was nearly the size of the Dragon King, but lacked the stoicism and composure of the man. She had a hooked nose and narrow jaw, adding to the severity of her overall look.

The eyes were the only familiar part of her. Like the smell of her magic, the woman had a nearly identical set of lilac eyes to Arianna. But the similarities ended there, as these sharp and angry eyes were framed by the rich green skin of a Dragon.

Florence had no doubt this was the animal who had killed everyone at the factory. The one who had called for her demise.

She didn't spare more than that glance. It didn't matter what foe she was up against. She'd kill it, or perish.

Florence launched herself over the windowsill. The roofing over the entryway broke her fall with a clamor. Florence's knee popped painfully as she tried to soften the impact. The pitch of the shingles pulled her downward and she did a quick two-step, landing on the ground with a roll.

She didn't waste time looking back at the Dragon. She had no doubt it would follow, and the loud thud on the ground behind her affirmed the fact. Florence loaded a cartridge into her gun, whirling around a lamppost as magic pushed into her knee, mending the torn ligaments and knitting flesh brutalized in the fall.

With a straight and steady arm, she aimed true at the woman who did little more than jog behind her. *Arrogant Dragon.* She no doubt assumed that it would be a bloodbath like last time. Florence squeezed the trigger. The Dragon was in for a surprise; last time, the Vicar Revolver hadn't been in charge of protecting the factory.

The canister shot forward, the chemicals inside reacting to the sudden motion. It exploded halfway to the Dragon, a plume of thick purple smoke erupting from it. Florence heard coughing but could no longer see her assailant.

She loaded a different canister into her pistol and took aim toward the sky. This was another plume of smoke, but unlike the one before her, it exploded bright red and harmless—a signal, if the gunshots alone weren't enough to alert other Revolvers to her plight.

Just as she was readying her weapon again, the Dragon exploded through the smoke. Florence dodged backward but underestimated the Dragon's long strides. The woman was upon her in a breath, a clawed hand shooting straight for her face. Florence pressed the muzzle of the gun into the Dragon's emerald palm, and pulled the trigger.

At close range, bone splintered and tissue was practically liquefied, exploding in all directions. With golden gore smattering her face, Florence dashed away.

The Dragon didn't cry out in pain, didn't hiss, didn't curse. She began to laugh, so loud it echoed off every building and rattled Florence's brain.

"You are everything I hoped!" the woman screeched, lunging forward again.

A chorus of gunshots alerted Florence that her men and women had joined the fray, stalling the Dragon. The woman brought her hands together, smashing two golden bracelets on her forearms to form a shining barrier that made her impervious to the hail of lead. Florence was almost to the factory and ran as though her life depended on it, because it did.

"I need a corona gun!" she shouted ahead.

A woman with wind-swept hair emerged from the doors. She was a sight to behold—a goddess of weaponry. Shannra was clad in tight-fitting pants and a double-breasted military vest, lined in gold piping. Emma's hat wasn't the only upgrade the Revolvers had received.

Florence let out a small choking noise, relief catching in her throat. She hadn't given much thought to where Shannra had actually been, so she hadn't realized the full power of the subconscious terror in thinking her lover had perished at the hands of the beast.

"Florence, here!" Shannra called. With a grunt, she hoisted the weapon toward Florence.

Florence's hand almost gave out as she caught the gun. Her tendons were shredded still from the Dragon's claws. They'd knitted some, but her magic had been pushed in too many directions at once to have any one singular thing be perfectly mended.

It would've been easier if she'd become a Perfect Chimera. But as Florence rounded once more to face the charging Dragon, she didn't regret her decision. She didn't need Arianna's designs to find her ground and hold it.

"After my shot, you fire," she commanded the men and women who were quick to flank her. "Then hold."

Just as Florence issued the order, the sound of gliders roared through the skies.

"Right flank, to the airships after mark. We take down this one first, and then we take down the ones in the skies." Florence leveled the weapon.

The Dragon continued her rage-filled charge. It was as though she'd gone crazy, like a fallen Chimera.

Florence poured her magic into the gun. She remembered the Skeleton Forest, her early prototype all those months ago. This was different—smooth and easy. It was how a trigger should feel under a trained hand.

She shot a beam of pure energy.

The Dragon hadn't been ready for it, or had vastly underestimated the power Loom now wielded as the shot hit her square in the chest. Florence took a breath as the woman fell and then, the second her body hit the ground, shouted, "Fire!"

Gunfire pelted the ground around the prone Dragon, ceasing when Florence raised her hand.

"Right flank, to airships and higher marks," Florence repeated. "Take down the gliders!" Half the group ran, the other half remained as her cover. Florence charged.

She drew a golden dagger. It was cast in nostalgia— originally crafted as a replica of Arianna's own infamous knives. But this one was entirely her own. She wielded it as an homage—a testament to the woman she had been, and a tribute to the mentor who had helped her become something entirely new.

Florence mounted the dazed Dragon and cut out what remained of her heart, casting it far aside. Florence stood with a sway, looking to the skies. One of the three gliders had already been taken out and the other was under heavy fire.

Relief flooded her, and combined with exhaustion to make her suddenly dizzy. An arm wrapped around her ribs.

"Take it easy."

"Shannra." Florence turned, sloppy and half-delirious, but with all the purpose she'd ever had in the world. Her hand gripped the woman's face and she pulled it to her.

Shannra smelled not of honeysuckle, but of gun oil and sulfur. The tattoo on her face was raised slightly under Florence's thumb as she caressed the familiar lines. *This* was the woman Florence loved. This was her heart's aspiration now—to have a partner, an equal.

"You didn't become a Perfect Chimera." Shannra, still breathless from their kiss, observed Florence's wounds and their thin coating of black blood.

"I'm already the perfect shot; how much more perfect does one woman need to be?" Florence hoped her grin was playful enough to cut the arrogance of the sentiment. She hoped Shannra understood.

"My thoughts exactly."

Gunshots echoed above them, drawing both their attention. The final glider was falling from the sky. Something swelled in her at the sight. This was their turning point. This was the moment when Loom's revolution, at long last, finally took hold.

CVAREH

Lord Xin made no distinction between Rok or Xin or Tam, and so it seemed he had no qualms with Dragon or Fenthri.

Men and women littered the ground in shades of red, blue, and gray. But the hand of the Lord of Death wasn't the only thing that unified them. Every corpse oozed gold blood, regardless of skin color.

The age of the Perfect Chimera would be ushered in with blood.

Cvareh pulled on Saran's feathers, banking across the clouds, surveying the battleground below him. Rok continued to make attempts to push further into Ruana. But without the help of Tam, they were continually thwarted. It had been a stalemate for months, but he was beginning to see signs of the momentum shifting.

"Hold your position!" he cried over the winds, swooping low enough for the survivors to hear him. "Another wave comes from the west!"

In the distance, a swath of bocos cut their silhouettes against the skyline. At first, seeing ten to thirty attackers at once would have been cause for concern. But manpower made all the

Elise Kova

difference. Rok's numbers were dwindling, Cvareh was certain of it. Meanwhile, his numbers were only increasing with every transport of Perfect Chimera.

Cvareh rose higher, squinting against the afternoon light. He saw no rainbow trails. That had been another evolution—the decreasing number of Riders. But from what he heard of the attacks increasing on Loom over the past weeks, he had every suspicion that Yveun was refocusing his minions on the lands below.

The cry of a boco had him twisting in his saddle.

"You looked like you were thinking of doing something reckless," Cain remarked, flying close.

"Never."

"Let them reach the island. We can take them on land."

Cvareh nodded, realizing it to be true. As much as he wanted to cut his enemy right from the sky, they had the advantage on the ground. Perfect Chimera could pilot gliders, but the vessels were in short supply and were primarily allocated to ferrying more soldiers from Loom—not for fighting.

Like an explosion, a plume of clouds tangled in the rainbow tail of a glider breaking through the God's Line far below. It curled upward, chasing after the single-manned vessel that shot toward the sky.

"One of ours?" Cain squinted.

Cvareh didn't need to squint. He saw the tattered flaps of a white coat almost blending in with the clouds and immediately knew. Every muscle in his body tightened in response to the sight. "Arianna."

The glider moved with suicidal speed and reckless agility toward the Rok fighters. They noticed the Fenthri barreling at them like a bullet out of a gun and shifted course. Arianna didn't change her trajectory, continuing head-on.

"We have to help her."

"Cvareh, no." Cain tried to stop him.

Cvareh wasn't about to listen. She had come to fight. There was no world in which he wouldn't do it at her side.

Gunshots echoed over the wind as Arianna sped past the pack of Dragons. One man lunged from his boco at her, only to miss and whistle for his mount to catch him before he was swallowed whole by the God's Line.

"Arianna!" Cvareh shouted, wondering if she could hear him.

If she could, she ignored him.

In a maneuver that would make Helen both jealous and proud, Arianna continued her ascent, high above the pack of Dragons that were now pulling on their floundering boco to try to keep up with the more agile machine. She pulled on the handles, tipping it in a wide arc until she was facing down at the God's Line and the Dragons beneath her.

Arianna let go of the glider and Cvareh's heart went straight to his throat, blocking another scream of concern for the woman's wellbeing. He watched as she seemed to float in the air, falling alongside the vessel, a hair's breadth away. She hoisted a weapon that was strapped to her, holding it with surprising calm given that she was a puppet to gravity and pummeling toward fifteen Dragons all scrambling to kill her.

Cvareh couldn't stop his eyes from closing at the beam of bright light that exploded from the gun.

Another shot rang out and the column of pure magic that punctured through Dragon and boco alike lingered on the wind as though it was trying to draw a line in reality itself.

Arianna reached back for the glider. Another Dragon dove, intending to knock her off-course before she could recover the mechanical safety net.

Cvareh gave a roar and kicked Saran's sides. Faster, he willed the bird to fly faster. He let go of the boco's feathers, feeling the wind whipping his clothing against him as he straightened away from the diving bird. He wouldn't be fast enough if he relied on the boco alone.

His feet pulled from the stirrups, curling under him, and Cvareh launched from the saddle, claws out.

He met the Rok man in a tumble of feathers and blood. Cvareh sought purchase as his enemy's boco squawked and spun through the air, trying to catch the wind once more with the fighting Dragons on its back. He raked his claws across the other man's face as the Rok fighter desperately tried to cast him off.

Petra had always told him that once he used the gift of his lungs on Nova, there would be no turning back. Every Dragon on the entire island would feel the shock wave of his magic. It was his greatest strength, and when Petra had lived, it served her and Xin for Cvareh to never let it be known.

But Cvareh was the Oji now.

He hoped his sister was right in her assumptions, because he wanted every living soul to know that they were up against a force strong enough to command time.

Cvareh sucked in the air through his nose, filling his lungs, and felt the world slow. He looked over and almost lost time in his startle. Arianna's piercing eyes stared back at him. They seemed to look right at him, even though her hair was frozen in a windless world.

She'd recovered herself on the glider, pitched downward, parallel to him.

Trust me, those eyes seemed to demand.

And he did.

Cvareh sliced at the Rider's hands and legs with determined swipes. He peeled muscle from bone in deep gashes. He didn't hold time for more than a second—he needed to conserve his magic for the battles ahead—but that was all he needed.

Time snapped back into place as he breathed again. Cvareh was once more in free fall.

Now he spun through the air with a Dragon dazed, confused, and thrown from his boco. Cvareh gripped the man by the throat and plunged his hand into his chest. He took the warm Rok heart and let go of the suddenly still body.

Magic cracked through his mind with a sort of dizzying elasticity. For the first time, Cvareh felt what he'd done to others when he stopped time.

"Hold on!" Arianna cried, coughing blood into the wind.

He closed an arm around her waist, his feet cementing to the glider behind her. Cvareh tore a hunk of heart and shoved the rest into her face. Arianna ate from his hand, and they shared the spoils of their fallen foe.

His lover imbibed like a ravenous beast and turned toward the remaining Rok. With her face half covered in blood, mouth set in a grim line, he felt her lungs expand.

Cvareh watched in wonder as time slowed. She recovered faster, her magic responding to her whims with surgical precision. This was the power of a truly Perfect Chimera. She would always be more than what the Alchemists were splicing together now; she had been crafted by the magic her whole life; with his most recent addition, she had all the power that had ever existed. Arianna raised her arm and pulled the trigger, taking down two Dragons before she nearly collapsed onto the handles, gasping for air between outpourings of gold from her lips.

Cvareh forced the remaining heart into her mouth.

"Let go," he demanded, his hands over hers. "I'll take us to the mainland. There's more who will take them down on Ruana."

"Don't get us killed."

Cvareh felt her magic retreat as her hands slipped from the handles, barely enough to keep her glued to the gold platform beneath them. She turned, grasping him awkwardly, keeping herself in position as he assumed control of the glider.

He was not nearly as graceful as she was with the machine. But he was determined. With Arianna counting on him, there was no world in which he would fail to keep his word.

Cvareh sped past the tiring boco for mainland Ruana. They soared back up to the topside of the island, and he selected a landing spot behind what had become, more or less, the front line.

Perhaps he'd finally had enough practice with the gliders. Or perhaps battle had honed his senses just enough. But Cvareh was half-proud of the landing.

Arianna's magic gave out and she slumped, Cvareh quick to catch her. The sounds of boco on the wind combined with guns cocking; over it all was the ominous announcement from Cain, "More incoming!"

They panted together, and all the things he'd wanted to say and ask were suddenly meaningless. Nothing mattered until victory was assured.

No.

Nothing mattered because she was in his arms again.

"I'm going to help." Arianna stood on her own once more. He felt magic swelling in her, already returning at a rate his could not hope to keep pace with.

As much as he wanted to tell her not to, as much as he wanted to flee with her to a safe location to ride out the final throes of the storm, Cvareh knew nothing would stop her. She turned her eyes to the horizon, to their mutual enemy, and adjusted the hulking weapon—a new prototype similar to the guns they'd been sending, but different somehow, too.

"I will come with you."

"Are you sure?" She gave him a quick up and down, no doubt skeptical of the magic she felt—or didn't feel.

Cvareh gave a laugh, skeptical himself. "We are in this together, from now until Rok falls."

"Until Rok falls," she repeated with a solemn nod. "Together until Rok falls."

COLETTA

oletta could smell Ulia before she saw, or even heard her. The woman was coated in a fine gloss of sweat that Coletta knew to associate with fear or nervousness in weaker creatures. Her little flower did well trying to hide it, however. Her strides were even and her hands were still at her sides when she delivered her message.

"The Dono wishes to speak with you."

Coletta thought on the statement a moment. She carefully set down her pruning shears. It seemed today would not be the day she would get to conduct her second set of tests on the Flowers of Agendi. Whatever secrets they held, they did an excellent job of hiding them from her.

"And where is the Dono?"

"The Red Room."

"*Ah*," Coletta murmured softly. That was all the information she needed on the matter. "Thank you for delivering this message, Ulia."

"Is there anything else I can do for you, my lady?" She lowered her head in subservience.

"Not yet." There would be in the coming days; Coletta could feel it. The scales that held the world in balance had already tipped. Equilibrium of power and order had shifted too far out of neutral and now chaos was threatening to reign. The dawn of an age that couldn't be accounted for—that was where the real danger lied.

Ulia left her, heeding the unspoken command. Coletta briefly considered changing her garb before meeting Yveun, but decided to go as she was. Yveun had seen her in all states. He had lifted her up when the poison had wracked her body past the point of brokenness. He had kissed her mouth after her gums had turned black. What had always mattered more than their appearances was their presence for one another. They were there when the cards fell.

Perhaps, her plain attire and immediate attendance of his summons would remind him of that fact. The fact that she had come to him promptly at his command, despite their last disastrous encounter in his war room—a confrontation neither had yet made any motions to reconcile.

The Red Room was on the opposite side of the estate from Coletta's garden. As such, she had ample time to anticipate the mood her Dono might be in. Her general preparation was for bad, worse, and downright volatile.

A Rider posted at the door regarded her warily. It was an uncommon summons to be sure. Coletta gave a tilt of her head and a small uncharacteristic smile, just enough to see the man unnerved by his Ryu's unexpected behavior.

"The Rok'Ryu, Dono," the Rider announced as he opened the door for her.

"Thank you," Coletta said demurely, but still clearly dismissive.

The man nodded and promptly departed. Coletta listened closely to his footsteps, making sure they left his post. She waited until they faded. Only then did she turn her eyes to her mate to see what fate had in store for her.

"It's not enough," he growled.

"What isn't?"

"Everything." Yveun's claws shot from his fingertips. "None of it is enough."

So, it was to remain war between them. Her prompt presence had done nothing to smooth over the agitation of the past, or remind him of the natural roles they'd filled for so long and that had served them so well. "I offered you victory in this war. You would not take it."

"No, you offered me monstrosities made from the skin of our own family." He rose like a thundering god. "I am tasked with protecting House Rok."

"The success of House Rok is all I have ever worked for. It is all I have ever dirtied my hands for and manipulated the shadows for."

Yveun stalked toward her. Coletta wondered if he realized how weak, how out of control, it made him look. Kings never descended. Not for their mates, not for anyone.

"You lost our gold."

It was stolen.

"You lost the loyalty of House Tam."

A loyalty Coletta had bought herself over the years.

"You sent away Fae, splitting our power. There have been no reports from her for over a week. Coletta, if she—"

"Need I remind you that she is a tool, Yveun?" Coletta snarled, no longer able to keep her mouth shut. She was pushed to a rare point, and there was no going back now. "She was a distraction for you, I see now. She did not make us strong, but weak. Good riddance if the Fen have killed her."

"You would do well to not say such things to me." Yveun motioned toward her and Coletta grabbed his wrist with a speed that surprised her mate. His head reared back slightly, like a serpent ready to strike.

"Do not point your claws at me," she whispered dangerously. They sheathed on command. "Better." Coletta released him and Yveun spun away, setting to pace like the pouting child he was. "Fae's death would be tragic. But *we can make more of her* now. What made her strong could be as common as a cherry-skinned Dragon."

"Not this again." He stilled.

"Yveun," she pleaded. Coletta hated begging. But she would beg, bargain, steal, and murder for her House. "I have ten Perfect Dragons—"

"You continued, despite my direct order?" He looked at her with a gaze that was no doubt an attempt to make her feel small.

"I did." His stare had no effect on her. "And we can begin to shift the tides if we set them free. If you bring me three, two, just one Xin, I can produce them faster."

"I needed you to be producing gold for Tam."

"The refineries are a sham!" Coletta's claws plunged into the air. "All knew it from the moment they were commissioned. But I allowed you your fantasies. Refineries are effective on Loom because of their systems and resources. But their gold stores have been tapped dry and my contact tells me that they have not resumed production again with the guilds as they are."

"You." He pointed at her again, without his claws this time. "You told me, you encouraged me, to destroy the guilds."

"And it was the right choice." She stood by the decision without remorse. "But it is still the world we live in, the world we must adapt to."

Yveun growled and set to pacing again. "Tam is useless and disloyal. Xin fights like Fen. The Fen fight worse than Fen. We have three fronts and make headway on none of them!"

"We've made ample headway, if you would only see it as such." Coletta refrained from pointing out that he was making a fourth front by stoking a rift between them.

"It's because I'm not there." Yveun stopped moving, as if punctuating the words. He spoke mostly to himself. "It is because I have been invisible to my people."

"Yveun—" This was dangerous. This was wild autonomy fueled by frustration and blood lust.

"I will go fight."

"My Dono, I implore you to rethink." Coletta felt as though she was scolding a child and not a man nearing ninety.

"You have done enough holding me back."

The words stung. No, not the words—the shock of them, the outright audacity. Anger flashed hot in her blood, a response very few could draw from her, but it was there. Coletta cooled it. If one let it linger, anger was a poison for which there was no antidote.

"I have done everything for the good of our house, for the good of your rule." All reminders were proving futile. Her Dono, her life mate, the man she had worked to see to power and then worked alongside to keep it, suddenly saw her as having no more utility than a set of Fenthri tools.

"I will go to Ruana." Yveun started for the door.

"With more time and just some Xin captives, we will have an army of Perfect Dragons. They will not see it coming. We will blindside them."

"Or we will lose our chance entirely." Yveun's head whipped back to her. "Waiting has given us nothing and the tides are ever shifting against us."

Coletta had one more request of him. One final attempt to save her Dono's life and salvage all they had worked for.

"At least become Perfect first," she implored, knowing the matter futile. "Give yourself the strongest chance."

He stared at her with abject horror, a look that was the final breaking of any love or kindness or even rapport between them. "How dare you suggest your Dono is anything less than perfection. I will not accept Xin organs—not now, or ever. I will not have them in me unless I am sinking my fangs into the hearts of the fallen. And as long as I breathe, I will not stand to see our house sullied by them either."

He strode past her, starting for the door. Coletta merely stood, looking at the lone throne. A seat she knew would never have a master again.

"Yveun—"

"No half measures, Coletta." He paused, briefly, but she refused to look at him. She gave him all the disrespect of her back. "When I return, I will deal with you in the same manner."

Coletta did not cry. She did not scream or shout or rake her claws over the room. She breathed in through her nose, and out through her mouth, three times to regain her composure.

Then, Coletta'Ryu started back for her garden, to prepare for the end of the world.

ARIANNA

It was night when they finally had a reprieve.

The reprieve was short-lived, as a frustrated Cain stomped in and disrupted their peace with an endless string of scolding for their recklessness. Cvareh impressed and pleased her in equal measure when he finally stood up for himself, telling off the man.

The break was short-lived, however, as with the dawn came a new swarm of Riders, and a new host of bloodshed.

More fell on both sides, and at long last Arianna was forced to recover her magic. It was like a seemingly never-ending source now. *Seemingly.* For when she hit her limit, it came fast and hard.

"How do you feel?" Cvareh was the only Dragon who would go out of his way to talk to her. No matter how much the Fenthri bled for their cause, the Dragons regarded them with wary eyes. The inverse was also true. Perfect Chimera huddled in groups, avoiding all contact with the Dragons.

"I'm fine." Arianna continued her inspection of the gun in her hands. "This, however . . ."

"Is it broken?" Cvareh sat next to her heavily.

"No, but it's reaching its limit. I thought Flor and I had reached a solution, but it seems not." There were hairline fractures along the barrel that promised years more of testing and dozens of iterations down the line.

"Florence . . ." Cvareh repeated thoughtfully. "How is she?"

"She's found her place." *Not unlike you*, Arianna added for herself alone.

"I suppose we all have."

"Get out of my mind, Dragon."

Cvareh laughed, and Arianna let the sound smooth away her mock ire. She would miss the man, when it was all over. The place he had ultimately found had no room for her. His world, Florence's—neither was Arianna's. As Florence had seen it, so would he, when the time came.

They sat on his balcony at the manor. The glider barely fit and his boco swooped back every now and again, cawing in angry protest at having to share its post. They were away from prying eyes and combat.

Arianna listed to one side, her temple meeting his shoulder. She closed her eyes the moment his cheek pressed against her head. How she, of all people, had come to enjoy the company of this Dragon, Arianna would never know. But with Florence starting her new life, and Eva and Oliver dead, he was the only one who knew her. He was the only one who'd seen her in her entirety.

"Cvareh," she began, softly. "When you're King—"

"*If*," Cvareh emphasized.

"*When*," she shot right back. Arianna would not tolerate dismissive language now. They'd come too far for it. "Do not forget the promises you made to Loom."

"I would never."

"Because I will hunt you and kill you if you do."

"I wouldn't have it any other way."

She wondered if it was true—if he was sincere in appreciating that some part of their relationship—whatever it was—was strung together with vengeance and inter-world power struggles. It was certainly odd, but she'd lived an odd life. It was only fitting that the only companion she'd found at the end of the road would be the most inconceivable of them all.

"Cvareh—"

Arianna never finished her thought, which was likely a good thing, as she'd suddenly begun to feel dangerously sentimental. Cain bounded onto the balcony, and the expression on his face told them everything. Even still, nothing could've prepared her for his words.

"Yveun approaches."

"What?" they said in unison.

"Are you sure?" Arianna had fully expected the battle against the Dragon King to be drawn out until its bitter end. She never expected the man to make the same mistake she had—to deliver himself neatly to her.

"I don't think I would mistake the Dragon King," Cain replied testily.

Arianna was too distracted by their luck to even think on it. They ascended through the manor to an upper level. Sure enough, a whole flock of boco cluttered the sky, approaching fast. Flanking one man were two Riders with large pennons strapped to their backs bearing the sigil of House Rok.

Arianna adjusted her grip on her weapon. One shot—all she needed was one good shot. The gun had that much left in it, at least. Arianna slowed her breathing as they neared. Just when she was about to take a sharp inhale and lift the barrel—

Cvareh stopped her. "Don't."

"We can kill him right now. We can *end* this."

"You know I must. For Nova to see me as Dono, it must be a proper duel."

Arianna glared at him, the gun, at the approaching king, but more at her circumstances in general. She knew it to be true, though every instinct screamed for her to just end it. Grand acts only created great openings for error.

"A duel?" Cain's hand went slack as he became distracted by Cvareh's words. "You're going to duel him *now*? Why not before?"

"Because now, we can thrive. Tam will undoubtedly side with the victor. With more weapons like the one Arianna is holding, with Perfect Chimera, none will attempt to subvert our victory." Cvareh's eyes drifted back to her. "Because now, time is on my side."

Did she hear him right? Arianna studied his face, searching. She wanted more—needed confirmation of what he was planning. Had his plan all along been to use her lungs against Yveun?

"Cvareh'Ryu," Yveun called out, finally within earshot and hovering just above the platform. "I seek to challenge you. Are you finally done shaming your house with your subversions?"

"I seek to challenge you as well." Cvareh ignored the bait and Arianna silently commended him.

She watched as Yveun landed. Her hands itched—to pull the trigger, to summon claws, to attack. She stood silently, however, forcing herself to stay in place, play her part.

Yveun's eyes found her and then the handful of Perfect Chimera in their midst. "I wouldn't have believed it if I'd not seen it with my own eyes. Xin has stooped so low as to work with Fen. How do you follow such a weak ruler that he must turn to the gray scourge of the earth for power?" Yveun asked the Xin assembled.

"How does Rok follow a man who drives his House to failure because he is too afraid of progress?"

"'Progress,' as you call it, is a threat to all of Nova, as it undermines the foundation of our traditions."

There it was. There was the crux of it. Arianna watched as the other Dragons, both red and blue, considered what side of this line they fell on. Did they stand with an evolving world? Or did they cling to the order that had seemingly served them so well for centuries?

"Progress cannot be stopped once started, not even by a King." Arianna made her voice heard. She made Oliver's voice heard. She made Eva's, and Florence's, and every other Fenthri who had ever worked and died for the idea of a free Loom, heard and accounted for.

"And who would believe a Fen?" he sneered at her.

"Because I am evidence of it." Arianna gave him space to challenge her on the claim, but Yveun's silence was the loudest reply—so loud that the other Rok Dragons exchanged glances. "Because Perfect Chimera are here and will come to Nova in droves. The God's Line will protect none of you. Work with us, or find out what it is like to live beneath a greater race."

Enough Dragons actually seemed to think on her words that Arianna considered the whole claim worth it. Frankly, Loom had no interest in ruling over Nova—at least, she sincerely hoped that sentiment remained unchanged. But the Dragons didn't need to know that. Let it cloud their minds and cast the shadows of doubt on their every movement.

"You lie." Someone from Yveun's entourage.

"Do you really want to take that chance?"

"Enough!" Yveun regained his control the only way he knew how, by shouting it back into place. It was the move of a desperate man. One that had Arianna wondering how she had ever allowed herself to be bested by him. "Will you duel me or not?"

"As the Xin'Oji," Cvareh proclaimed proudly. "I will—for honor of Xin, for my sister, and for the title of Dono of all of Loom."

There was no waiting in Dragon duels.

Arianna watched as both men exploded into motion. Yveun was a stronger, faster, and better fighter than Cvareh. But Cvareh had a weapon that he now deployed.

She felt the strange ache that followed a time stop, and looked on with everyone else as Cvareh moved from where he'd been about to be attacked, to the space just behind the Dragon King.

Yveun looked on in confusion; by the time he realized where his adversary had gone, Cvareh had plunged his teeth into the man's back, drawing blood with fervor.

"Time?" Yveun roared. He bucked backward and Cvareh rolled off. Yveun twisted, lunging for him.

Another snap of magic. Another ache between her temples. Cvareh was holding the Dono's arm, bleeding him from the wrist.

Yveun reached for the man, his hand stopping just before Cvareh's neck. As soon as Cvareh released the Dono's flesh, he took another sharp inhale of air. Arianna's ears barely had time to hear the start of Cvareh's lungs filling before time stopped again.

It was like watching two fighters moving through completely different sequences of events. When Cvareh was in one place, he suddenly appeared in another. It was jarring and sustained purely on Yveun's own magic.

Arianna shifted her gun in her hands, ready to kill. Even by imbibing off the Dragon King, she could see the toll stopping time took on Cvareh's body. He wouldn't last much longer as he was.

Exhaustion lead to mistakes, and Cvareh let go of time a second too early. His jaw snapped shut on air; Yveun pulled his hand back, plunging his claws forward to Cvareh's chest. Cvareh tumbled backward at the last moment.

Yveun was on the offensive, like a sea monster that had spotted a lone ship. Cvareh dodged and sidestepped, but he did not stop time again. He was conserving his energy.

Arianna caught Cvareh's eye. The distraction was just enough for Yveun to land a clean hit, sending Cvareh reeling, blood pouring from his shoulder. He stumbled backward, and half-fell into her.

By the time she realized what he'd done, time was stopped. Arianna gripped onto him, holding him, so she would not be pulled from the pocket of time he'd created for her. Her eyes met his, and Cvareh looked at her with a mouth pressed shut into a firm line. Cvareh rose his free hand, blood still pouring from his shoulder where his magic was failing to heal him, and pointed at Yveun.

Finally, it clicked.

"Y-You want me to kill him?"

Cvareh nodded.

It was a kindness, a gift unlike any he had ever given her. Together, they walked. Arianna clutched him tightly with one hand and drew her dagger from the other. She'd dreamed about savoring this moment—of what Yveun's face would look like when she killed him slowly, purposefully.

But as she had told Florence, she was not the one destined to kill the Dragon King, at least not in the eyes of the world. So, unceremoniously, just outside time, with Dragons looking on, seeing with unseeing eyes, Arianna carved out the heart of Yveun Rok'Oji Dono.

Cvareh shuddered and quickly yanked her away, half dragging her back to where she'd stood before. Arianna watched as he released her and then—

Time snapped back into place.

There was Cvareh, standing over the fallen corpse of Yveun Dono, heart in hand. He collapsed to his knees over the dead Dragon, coughing blood. Arianna wanted to run to him. She wanted to chew the King's heart herself and spit it into Cvareh's mouth if she must.

But he had given Arianna her moment. Now, she gave him his.

With almost frail weariness, Cvareh raised the heart to his mouth and plunged his teeth into it. He tore off pieces ravenously, snarling at the Rok Riders.

They all watched as their new king bathed in the blood of his predecessor.

COLETTA

This was the day the world stood still.

Coletta was among her flowers when the Riders returned. She stood, feeling frozen in time herself, as they recounted the magic Cvareh had been hiding in him all along. The men and women regarded her as the Rok'Oji now, but they looked on with skeptical eyes even as they said it.

How could one so frail be the Oji? she could almost hear them say. She had served a purpose between her and Yveun. He was the visible strength, and she the invisible.

She had never been made for the grand stage.

Coletta went to her laboratory and sat on a bench. She tilted her head back, staring at the blue sky that peeked at her from between the rooftops of the estate and the foliage. It was as if the opulence of the manor threatened to suffocate her. It was as if the vines of her plants wanted to strangle her, for all that she had loved and nurtured them. It was as if the sky itself mocked her, reminding her of the new world order that had been thrust upon them, the future stolen from her claws.

There was no word from Fae, and even if the woman was still alive and somehow proved to be successful, too much momentum was stacked against Rok to have the assassination of one rebel leader deal a crushing blow to Loom. Xin would prevail, which mean Loom would as well, no matter what happened now. A new world was being designed, one that she no longer had a part in crafting.

Coletta sighed softly, and closed her eyes. It had been a good run, while it lasted.

With her by Yveun's side, they had been unstoppable for more than half a century. They were the last in a long line of noble and fearsome Rok leaders. Just over a thousand years of dominance was now coming to an end. But none of Rok's former glory mattered any longer. History was written by those still alive to hold pens. Her magnificent house would be cast as a cruel, tyrannous rule overthrown by a noble insurgence. They would be painted as the last holdover of an era steeped in respect for tradition that was long gone, an era overthrown by engineered perfection.

It was a dishonor too unbearable to conceive.

Coletta moved to the back corner where certain concoctions were locked away. She had one more obligation to her home and house. They would never sing her songs, would never abide by her as Oji. Her life was forfeit. So, before any upstart could challenge and kill her, Coletta would play one final, masterful stroke.

She had been preparing for this inevitability since her final confrontation with Yveun in the Red Room.

She pressed the gold panel, summoning both Topann and Ulia. By the time the two women reported, Coletta had their tools assembled. One look at them told her all she needed to know. They had heard the news of their new "Dono."

"Lord Xin now rules." She did not mince words in life, nor would she in her death. "The great end comes for Rok as we know it."

Both women kept their eyes downcast. Ulia gave a soft sniffle.

"But we will not go quietly. We will not let all we love be consumed by those we hate." Coletta smiled at what had been assembled on the table before her. "We will take that from them. We will make sure that for generations to come, the name Rok is whispered, for fear that we will spring up from underneath our falsely appointed rulers and seek our vengeance."

"What must we do?" Topann's bravery assured Coletta that she was ready for this mission. So, the harder task would go to her.

"You will take this." Coletta motioned to the portion of the table covered with poisoned daggers and vials, enough to take down an entire estate. "And kill all those here."

"My . . . lady?"

Coletta had expected the order to kill her own to be particularly difficult for Topann to stomach. She'd been the most loyal of them all. But it was for that reason that Coletta had chosen her.

"Topann, you will be the only one among us to survive." Coletta took her flower's hands in hers, in a reverse of their usual interactions. "You will plant the seeds of Rok's return. Kill those here, and be the only one to tell the tale. Speak of Loom's savagery and Xin's disregard for our ways. Kill them all in the estate and force Rok to rebuild from the ground up in vengeance, in hate."

There was a brief moment when Coletta thought Topann would refuse, thought she might have to kill the woman and do this most important work herself. But Topann was a warrior, and loyal to her above all else. "I will, my queen. I will unleash every savagery I expect of Loom and Xin on our estate. I will go to the southern cities and tell them of your sacrifices, of the betrayals our house has endured."

"Good." Coletta turned, scooping up a separate dagger from the table. "Ulia, sweet Ulia," she cooed, summoning the girl's attention. Ulia steeled her watering eyes and pressed her mouth into a line. There was anger there, and anger made for sloppy actions. "You will take this, and give the Tam'Oji our regards."

Ulia took the dagger, inspecting what little she could see of the blade at the top of the sheath, by the hilt. "Gold?"

"Because he so loves it. Because his loyalty only extended as far as the gold we provided him."

Ulia's brow furrowed briefly. *Yes, child*, Coletta told her silently, *I have been planning for this for some time*. Granted, in Coletta's plan, Finnyr would have been the Xin'Oji, and once Xin was stabilized under him then they would turn their efforts onto House Tam, replacing *that* Oji with someone far more loyal. But plans adapted and changed. The dagger would gain new purpose.

"I will do this." Ulia took one deep breath that shuddered into stability, and then nodded. She accepted the dagger like it was a boon from a god.

"I bid you both farewell. Topann, any yet living flowers may grow to you." Coletta dismissed them for one final time.

Topann left promptly with a handful of supplies, as though she could not spare one final look for her soon-to-be-dead queen's face. But Ulia lingered. She searched Coletta's posture for answers the Dragon Queen would not allow herself to reveal.

"What will you do?" she whispered.

It was the one time Coletta allowed herself to be questioned, allowed her designs to be known. "If it is chaos the world seeks, then I will see it done." She took up one final dagger and a handful of vials for herself.

Ulia's eyes spoke volumes, but only two words fell from her lips. "Thank you."

Coletta nodded and watched the girl leave. She had done all she could, but it had not been enough. Coletta slung a large pouch over her shoulder and took the last of her supplies.

Perhaps it was not all she could've done. Coletta began to wonder as she started from her garden for the last time. Perhaps she should have been the bold and strong Ryu the house had wanted. If she had been, they would have seen her as the Oji now. She could've continued to lead the charge with Perfect Dragons. But without Yveun at her side, no one would heed her long enough to see the salvation she could offer them.

As she had been in life, in death, she'd be relegated to the shadows.

Coletta walked through the Rok Estate and down to the Gray Room for the final time. She set free the Perfect Dragons. They would live to be fearsome creatures. Rumors of their feats would bubble to the surface of Nova's consciousness until they could no longer be ignored.

Then, amid the growing chaos of the Rok Estate, Coletta'Oji took to the skies one final time, charting her course for Ruana.

CVAREH

He could have eaten three more of Yveun's hearts, and it still wouldn't have been enough. Cvareh chewed and tore his way through every last bite. He didn't care much for the taste of Rok blood—even though victory was its own spice—but the magic it brought back to him was essential to merely breathing. His lungs felt in no better state than they had following the Alchemist's removal of them for Arianna. If anything, they could be worse.

His joints ached, and his body was ravaged. But he was Dono. So Cvareh consumed every last bite of Yveun's heart, both for sustenance and for ceremony.

All eyes were on him, and not one Dragon or Fenthri moved. Cvareh wiped his mouth with the back of his hand. He needed to stand, needed to step into his role as Dono.

But the moment he tried, his legs buckled and he struggled to right himself. A strong arm appeared around his waist, connected to a sturdy and familiar form. Arianna had tugged his arm over her shoulder, supporting him before Dragon and Fenthri alike.

Yes. The word coursed through his mind at the woman's presence. He wanted her to be seen at his side. He wanted the world to know that she was his and now that he was Dono, there would be no questioning the fact. Cvareh saw the wary eyes from those assembled, but not one Dragon stepped out of place.

"We need to get to Lysip," he wheezed. Cain appeared before him, offering to help support him as well. Cvareh waved away the offer, trying to stand on his own. "We must get a boco—a glider, it will be faster—to Lysip."

"The battle is won, Dono." Hearing the title from Cain's mouth made it all the more real.

"Not yet." Cvareh pulled his arm from Arianna. The moment he tried to step away, however, the world tilted and he lost balance yet again. Cain moved for him, but Arianna was faster.

"Coletta," Arianna finished the thought he couldn't quite seem to get out before.

"Yes."

"What about the Rok'Oji?" Cain hadn't quite kept up. Cain was close, but the Fenthri woman at Cvareh's side was the other half of his mind.

"Do you think she'll accept Cvareh as Dono gracefully?" Arianna spoke loud enough that everyone could hear.

"She doesn't have a choice," Cain insisted.

"Like she didn't have a choice at the Crimson Court?" Arianna fired right back.

Cain floundered.

"Cain Xin'Ryu To," Cvareh announced, elevating Cain to the societal rank of To with a breath. "I request for you to defend my honor on Lysip. See that Coletta assumes her responsibility as the Rok'Oji, under me as Dono, or that she perishes."

Whispers and a few gasps arose from those observing. But there was nothing else he could do. Even if he was the Dragon

King, a title alone would not replenish his magic enough to give him the confidence to fly to Lysip. He knew he was sending his friend into the asp's nest. But what else could he do?

"And," Cvareh continued, "you will take Ari Xin'Kin To with you. She will assist however you deem necessary." Whispers and gasps grew louder as Arianna was quickly elevated in both society and House as well.

He locked eyes with the woman at his side. Arianna almost wore a frown. Was she not happy? He'd won, and he could see her forever have a place on Nova.

"We should go." She looked to Cain with renewed purpose. "I'll pilot the glider."

"Lead on," Cain agreed with a nod. To the others assembled, he said, "See your Dono is well cared for and recovers to full strength. We will need him in the months ahead."

Cain's order spurred the scene to life. Arianna disappeared from his side, replaced with a woman that he'd never seen before. Cvareh remained focused on his childhood friend, but mostly his eyes were on his lover.

"Go safe."

He wanted to say so much more. But the woman was strong. Cain was strong. There would be many more opportunities, he assured himself, to say all that needed to be said.

ARIANNA

Wind whipped her hair into the face of the man riding the glider behind her.

"It's there, ahead." Cain pointed over her shoulder and Arianna thought, not for the first time, of dislodging him from his spot with a particularly sudden roll.

"Yes, I can see that. Just focus on staying on." Did he think that she honestly couldn't tell where the isle of Lysip was? There were only three main islands in Nova and, given that they floated nowhere remotely close to each other, she could only assume that they had successfully made it to Lysip when another gigantic land mass came into view.

"I am on." He said it as though the fact should be obvious.

"Stay that way." Arianna ground the words between her teeth. He was very good at acting like he hadn't nearly fallen off twice already. Though Arianna was equally skilled at acting like one of those hadn't been her own attempt to shake him.

"The estate is there." Cain pointed at a massive complex that was unmistakable even to someone who'd never seen it before.

"My eyes still work fine under my goggles." She sighed loudly, wanting to make sure he heard it over the wind. Arianna pulled on the handles and pitched the glider toward the estate.

As they approached, a sharp tang hit her nose and went straight to her head. Her lungs burned, her magic fighting whatever the wind carried. Arianna slowed, making a wide arc and banking away.

"Why aren't you—"

"Can't you smell it?" She pulled on the levers, bringing the glider into a hover.

Cain seemed as though he was going to protest, on principle more than anything else, but when he stopped and took a proper breath his expression changed.

"Coletta." She said the name they were both thinking.

Arianna lowered the glider, moving slowly over the estate. A glimpse of one of the outdoor arcades, corpses lying prone, confirmed her suspicion.

"Twenty above... what did she do?" Cain whispered in horror.

"She refused to let us win." Arianna scowled and tried not to be angry or frustrated at the fact that she would not be the one to kill Yveun's mate. Was one kill really so much to ask for? Her neck ached, reminding her of Coletta's handiwork all too well.

"She killed her own? No that's impossible, even for her . . ."

Arianna finally brought the glider down, bringing a hand over her nose to combat the smell of death, blood, and poison. No one rushed to meet them, no one swarmed in greeting or combat. Their only company was wind. The whole manor was unnervingly still.

"I think you need to come to terms with the impossible," Arianna suggested as she rolled over a corpse with her foot. In the center of the dead woman's chest was a slit, right between her breasts, that had gone a dark gold from the festering poison that oozed from it.

"Why?" Cain muttered, looking at a loss. "Why would she kill her own?"

"She'd lost." Arianna looked in the room attached to the landing area they'd chosen at random. Sure enough, no signs of life. "And she couldn't handle the idea of us besting her house."

"But—"

"It's not a Dragon-like thought, I know. But take it from me, this woman knows no limits."

Cain was silent, respecting the darkness that hovered over her words at the mere mention of Coletta. Arianna knew well enough how low the woman would stoop.

They wandered the estate, looking for signs of life, for any signs of the woman who had reaped such destruction. But none were to be found.

"It's as if she's disappeared into thin air." Cain slammed his fist against a doorframe, splintering the wood and bloodying his hand in anger. "How many bodies have we looked through?"

"Not enough." Arianna crossed her arms over her chest and thought. If she had been in Coletta's position, what would she do?

The realization dawned on her as a Rok man stepped through the doorway.

"I found them!" he shouted, presumably to others. "I found the Xin murderers! They have a Fen!"

"Wait, what?" Cain stalled in his hesitation.

Arianna sprang into motion. She lunged for the man, claws drawn and honed on his chest. Before he even had a chance to react, he was dead.

"We have to get back to Ruana."

"What?" Cain stared at the Dragon she'd just killed, as if debating if he should feel remorse over the death of a Rok.

"We need to go." Arianna grabbed his forearm and tugged him forward. He began running on his own as they sprinted through the manor, toward the glider, and away from the sound of rising voices.

"I don't understand." He skidded to a stop as she jumped on the glider, grabbing both handles firmly.

"Coletta means to pin these murders on Xin. The longer we stay, the more we play into her plans."

"But she—"

"She's not here!" Why couldn't he see that? It had become so painfully obvious to Arianna. It was so objectively clear how stupid they had been.

"Where is she?" The horror in Cain's voice betrayed the fact that he had finally been brought to understanding.

"Get on," Arianna demanded, disturbingly calm. She was going to take off with or without him.

Cain made the smart choice and quickly jumped on behind her.

She yanked the handles and her magic shot into the wings, pulling them upward. Arianna leaned into the movement, as if with force of will alone she could see the glider all but teleport back to Ruana. She ran through everything again in her head, but there was no other option.

"You don't really think she . . ." Cain trailed off, no doubt running through the same probabilities and series of ideas as Arianna.

Coletta was a woman who'd lost everything to one man, who was now not only the Dragon King, but the head of the House she so despised. If she was willing to kill her own for the sake of vengeance against them, what would she do to him?

Arianna swallowed hard and struggled to keep her grip on the handles as her palms grew abnormally slick.

She had to get to Cvareh.

CVAREH

His bed didn't feel different.

One would think that, lying beneath the weight of kingship, one would sink further into the mattress. But he didn't feel any differently. In fact, he felt so very much the same that Cvareh was worried he had somehow missed an important step in becoming the Dono.

It did not feel real yet. He, Cvareh Xin, was the Dono for all of Nova.

Every member of House Xin had begun to fawn over him with renewed intent. Every man and woman seemed to want to get him something. He wished he hadn't sent Arianna and Cain away. House Rok could wait; he needed his two greatest allies to fend off those who would seek to pour praise on him to the point of nausea.

Exhausted and overwhelmed, Cvareh had ultimately sent them all away.

His lungs still ached from the quick successions of stopping time. They'd felt raw from the harvesting; now they felt utterly foreign. They'd been taken out, grown again, ripped apart, and put back together so many times that it was still laborious to breathe.

Yveun's heart had helped exponentially, but even that surge of power wore off. Every inch of his frame had sustained enough wounds and expended enough energy that all he wanted was quiet. All he wanted was sleep.

So, he allowed the attendants to look after him long enough to make minimal treatments to his wounds and then dress him for bed. But it was the silence after they left that he'd truly relished. Silence that now was his only companion in the wake of his ascension to Dono.

Cvareh closed his eyes. His thoughts did not drift to leadership. Nor was he visited by some prophetic vision of Lord Xin blessing him with divine right to rule. Behind his eyelids, he found the face of one woman—Arianna. And with no one to know, or judge him for his daydreams, he indulged the thought.

He saw them sitting together, thrones to match. They would be a beacon for Loom and Nova, a symbol of what their worlds could be, of the partnership that was required for all of them to seek the freedom they had long desired. And, as Dono, he would see that she never wanted for anything.

Dreaming numbed the pain, and soothed him enough that sleep could take its hold.

Movement stirred him. His mind was sluggish, but his body was already feeling much stronger from however much rest he'd gotten. Cvareh groaned softly, trying to dismiss whatever unnecessary helper had disturbed his sleep.

His eyelids fluttered, and he caught a glimpse of red.

Red.

Cvareh's eyes shot wide open as he felt a blade plunging between his ribs, straight into his heart. They took in the face of a woman he'd only seen in passing before. Her eyes were dead and emotionless. She could have been sipping tea, rather than killing the Dono in cold blood.

The blade burned as she removed it. The hole closed, magic knitting over the small incision quickly, but the fire remained.

"Coletta," he snarled.

"A gift, for the new Dono." She smiled, exposing teeth that looked more like worn-down knives. Her gums were gnarled and recessed. "I used the same poison on your sister." Coletta's hand cupped his cheek, almost lovingly. "I thought you would want to die as she did."

With a primal scream, Cvareh summoned energy he did not think he possessed, bolting upright. One hand gripped the woman's frail shoulder, feeling bone snap under the force of his fingers as the other hand plunged into her chest. Coletta coughed blood onto his chest, leaning against his cheek. She reeked of death and strawberries.

"Rok will forever seek to regain the throne that is rightfully theirs," she swore darkly.

Cvareh ripped out her heart with ease and pushed her away. Coletta posed no struggle; her triumphant eyes remained wide open even in death. She collapsed onto the floor, and Cvareh discarded her heart across the room, not daring to sink his teeth into the flesh of the poison mistress. Just her blood on his shoulder seemed to burn his skin.

The excitement and exertion quickened his heart. Cvareh collapsed back onto the bed, trying to slow the flow of poison throughout his body. It seared his muscles and sapped his strength.

He stared up at the ceiling above his bed, and wondered what Petra had seen as she lay in an agony that mirrored his.

The door opened and three Xin rushed in, responding to the commotion. Cvareh didn't know their names, but these would likely be the last faces he saw before he died, so he took them in as though he'd known them all his life.

"I have been poisoned," he whispered, as if speaking too loudly would cause his blood to pump and his body to give out faster. He wanted to slow the take of poison for as long as he could. He wanted to stall the inevitable. He would say only what needed to be said and preserve all remaining words for the one woman he wanted to lay eyes on before the God of Death cast his shroud over Cvareh's form at last.

"Who?" They looked at Coletta's corpse. No doubt, they had never seen the woman before. Coletta avoided public appearances at all costs, since they only sparked rumors of her frailty.

"Coletta Rok'Ryu," he answered. "When—" the word got caught. He thought of Petra again. His sister had endured the same pain as he, likely worse. He would not break down, would not let the pain get the better of him. "When I am gone, Cain is the Xin'Oji, and the Dono."

Cvareh closed his eyes, taking a deep breath. Stasis. Stillness. He had to persevere, had to hang on.

"When Cain'Ryu and Ari'Kin return, send them to me..."

"Dono, what can we do?" one of the men asked hopelessly.

Had he not heard a word Cvareh had said? Death was inevitable.

"Imbibing will sustain me... but not save me." It was the only thing he knew to say.

He shouldn't have been surprised when they returned with a heart in hand a short time later. Cvareh wanted to refuse. It had no doubt been cut from some under-island dweller, someone under the shade of House Xin that he was supposed to protect. But his mind was delirious and focused on only one thing—seeing Arianna again. *He had to see her again.* It was a drive beyond anything else. A drive that could push a man to madness.

He brought the heart to his lips and ate, and when he could no longer eat it himself, it was fed to him. Every bite was smaller than the last, his chewing slower.

But still, he held on.

He held on until he saw white against a colorful world, a peaceful break for eyes overwhelmed by the all-too-bright kaleidoscope he found himself in. He held on until Cain's booming voice summoned his consciousness back toward the surface of the inky darkness he was drowning in. He held on until he felt her hands on him again.

"Ari—"

"Cvareh, I need you to listen to me." Her voice was hurried, thin, frantic.

He smiled tiredly. She had to be forceful up to their very last moment together. Well, call him a romantic, or just insane, but he wouldn't have it any other way.

"Cvareh, listen, stay with me. It won't work if you won't listen." She was talking too quickly for him to really listen, and her voice had an odd pitch he didn't quite recognize. "Cain, help me sit him up. We need him awake—we only have one chance."

Cvareh groaned in protest as they hoisted him upright. The groan turned into a hiss of pain. It was as if jostling his blood reinvigorated the poison, spreading it further through his veins. Their efforts were long past the point of fruitlessness. Three hearts, now cold and void of magic, littered the bed around him.

But still, Arianna clung to him. He felt her arms around him. He felt her strength. His body ached to return the same to her in kind.

"I know what I want my boon to be." She was whispering now. It was soft and low, like a lover, like how he'd always wanted to hear her speak to him. Warmth enveloped him, warmth in the shape of a woman. "Listen closely, Cvareh, because all the magic in the world will be yours to see my boon fulfilled. You will have no choice. You must do this for me."

He leaned against her, let her voice flow through him. This was what he had wanted. This was what he had waited for. This was what kept him clinging to life. To fulfill the contract he had made with a Wraith.

"For my boon, I want . . . I wish . . . I wish for you to heal, stronger than you were before, completely and utterly. Cvareh, for my boon, I wish for you to live."

The words echoed within him, and with them, magic exploded anew.

ARIANNA

S he felt him return to her.

Magic that normally smelled of woodsmoke took on a new depth. The rich aroma cleared, like a window being opened to some greater beyond, and a crisp smell like rain flooded the room. Arianna continued to cling to him, tighter than she'd ever admit in the future to any who dared recount this moment.

She doubted doing so helped the magic. If anything, it likely hindered him, as she was giving Cvareh new bruises for his magic to heal. But she wasn't exactly thinking logically. All she wanted was for him to return to her. Until that moment her every want and wish had been death—the death of Finnyr, of Yveun, peaceful deaths for her old friends and lover when there were no other options. But now she wished for life. A long and fruitful life, for him.

It was a twitch at first. A movement in his biceps that could have been nothing more than instinct or involuntary reaction. But then it happened again.

His arms found movement, coming back to life. Rain turned back to smoke, and Cvareh breathed normally once more. The sound of his life filled her ears—the shifting of his movement, of his exhales against her cheek. He wrapped her in his embrace, responding with as much fervor as she held him.

Arianna didn't want to open her eyes. What if she was wrong? What if somehow this was all some illusion of a desperate mind too broken to handle the loss of another love?

"Arianna . . ." he breathed, soft enough that she could lie to herself and say she hadn't heard it.

But she did, and the sound had her choking in a sigh of relief. Emotion was raw in her neck and she wanted to scream or cry or laugh, but did none of it. She merely held on to the man she loved, and gulped down her relief. Cain was watching, after all, and there was only so much she'd allow the man to witness.

Cvareh's muscles gained strength, his back straightened, his breathing leveled. He continued to hold her as his heartbeat steadied once more, regular and strong. It was a sound Arianna could listen to for days—years, even.

Finally, he straightened away and merely stared at her with a wonder she'd never seen on anyone before.

"You saved my life."

"Well, it'd be really inconvenient for Loom if the man who has all the deals for our freedom just up and died." She couldn't say what she really felt—not even if she wanted to, which she didn't. It was far too terrifying and grossly romantic to utter aloud. "Plus, I really, really hate that woman." She nodded toward Coletta's corpse, more than a little upset that was yet another death Cvareh had over her. "And I loved the idea of thwarting—"

"I love you too, Arianna," he interrupted boldly.

Bloody cogs, he had to up and be the brave one, once again. Here he was professing his love for her in front of his right hand, as the King of the Dragons, and all Arianna could do was muster sarcasm. "That's one way to say thank you, I suppose."

She forced her arms to go slack.

King of the Dragons, the words repeated in her head, imprinting as fact. It had all happened so fast, and there was always one more enemy. But now that there were no more standing against them, the future was upon her.

This man was the King of the Dragons, Dono, leader of Nova. He was not just Cvareh anymore; he had a far greater role to play. One dark corner of her heart uttered in reproach for its self-preservation: *you should have let him die in Dortam.*

She'd been the one to save him, to deliver him to the Alchemists, to see his house succeed, to see him become King . . . only to have to let him go.

Arianna stood quickly, before she could allow herself to be trapped by him. He would draw her in and then there would be no escape. She'd damn them both with her sentimentality.

There was practice in her movements. Life had prepared her with an unofficial training to do what needed to be done, even when doing so was impossibly hard. She had dedicated her life to fulfilling her duty, and the dreams of others. It should be instinct, putting her wants second and doing what must be done. But all her preparation wasn't enough now that the moment was upon her. Walking away, what should have been the easiest task of all, had never demanded more strength. For, if she stayed, he would focus on her. He would defer to her. He would hesitate, and pause, and steal moments with her. While his time was what she wanted to steal more than any other thing, it was a heist she wouldn't allow herself to make.

"Where are you going?" His confused, questioning gaze made it all the harder.

"Back to Loom. My job here is done." Arianna attempted to make her escape.

"You can stay."

"I don't belong here." She didn't know why she was indulging argument, but her feet had gone into mutiny against her brain. They were in cahoots with her ears to hear what he'd say next.

"You have a place here," he insisted.

"Cvareh, she's—"

"She's the one we owe the world to," Cvareh snapped at Cain's protest. "I am the Dono and I can decree it."

"You don't get it." She looked back at him and, for the first time ever, was thankful for every hardship she had endured. For it had all hardened her enough to survive this parting. It had given her enough training to turn her face, and her heart, to stone. "Cvareh, this is not something you as a Dragon can decree. I am made of steam. I am hot-blooded, strong and free. I was cast in steel, on Loom, and that maker's mark is not something you can expunge from my soul.

"I don't belong here," she finished. It was said with almost enough conviction to fool herself.

"You belong at my side." Arianna watched him deflate with every word, and had to tell herself that what she was doing was for the best.

"I do not belong here, and you know it."

"What will you do instead?"

"There's always something to steal." Arianna smiled nonchalantly, as if one option was as good as the next. If he dug in his heels now, that carefully crafted façade would crack. She would find some excuse to stay, she knew.

But her bluff was good enough that Cvareh didn't call it. He stared right back at her until she could take it no longer.

Arianna turned and walked out of his room, past all the Xin gathered in the hall, as though nothing in the world were bothering her. Every bit of ease on her exterior hid the heartache inside, as she left behind the Dragon King she loved.

FLORENCE

There was no weapon like hope, and no ammunition for
it like good news.

Word of the victory up on Nova spread faster and
thicker than the clouds overhead. Helen, who had
been up with Arianna, had whispered back to Will—their
decision to get Dragon ears and set up a whisperlink hadn't
been the least bit surprising to Florence. Will informed the
rest of the Queen's minions, who ultimately dispersed the
news to Shannra.

Florence knew the moment Shannra had appeared in
her office that there had been victory, just by her expression
alone. And because she had already had the information
from someone else.

"You already know."

"Emma was here not minutes before you left. Word
funneled through the Revolvers who were up with House
Xin when it happened." Florence looked back at the list of
tasks she'd begun drafting, already several items deep.

"We have claimed victory, and you are still busy at
work." Shannra looped around the desk, draping her arms
over Florence's shoulders.

"It is only the beginning—freedom is only the beginning for us. Now, we must rebuild Loom, not as it was but as it could be." Florence was having a hard time deciding what to prioritize. Everything seemed like it needed to happen at once. And when everything was a priority, nothing was a priority.

"There is to be another Tribunal?" Shannra had no doubt focused on the first item on Florence's list.

"At Garre. Emma is spreading the word now."

Shannra sighed, though the noise was without any sort of real weight. "What is it with you and Tribunals?"

"I am a vicar, after all." Florence ran a hand up Shannra's arm, starting at where her hand met the desk, helping prop her up, all the way to her shoulder and back.

"You are the Vicar *Revolver*." Shannra turned her head back to Florence. "Your place is in Dortam, not Garre."

"And so it shall be," Florence affirmed. "Once we are all in agreement, every vicar will return to their rightful home to begin rebuilding."

"Will you return home alone?" Shannra asked, staring out the window behind Florence's desk in what had become her makeshift office.

"I think you know the answer to that."

"I want to hear you say it."

Florence didn't bother concealing a smile. "You will accompany me, if you so choose, as a Master Revolver."

"Don't think you can win me over with titles." Shannra tilted her head coyly.

"What can I win you over with then?"

"I asked you once if we could share a flat in Dortam when all this was over. You never answered." Shannra stared her down, as if trying to pin Florence with her eyes. "It's all over now. I need an answer."

Florence stood slowly. She pushed in her chair, and leaned against the desk with Shannra, facing the window, at just one small scrap of the world that was now theirs.

"Let's see . . . A flat in Dortam, right by the Guild hall, I think it was." Shannra hung on her every word. "I'm not sure if, as the Vicar Revolver, I can live outside the hall proper."

"I could be coerced into being flexible on the location."

"Could you?" Florence rounded the woman—her lover, in all her scarred and battle-weary glory. She reached a hand, cupping Shannra's cheek, weaving her fingers in the tangled mess of hair. "What must I do to coerce you?"

"I think you will come up with something creative." Shannra's voice had fallen to a hush, her lids heavy. She leaned forward, ever so slightly, and Florence felt herself moving to meet her.

"I will certainly try, Moonbeam."

Shannra halted, brows furrowed, lips pursed, eyes alert. "Moonbeam?"

"You asked me to be creative." Florence smirked. "I can be dangerous when I'm creative."

"Spoken like a true Vicar Revolver." Shannra was back to whispering. "I like you dangerous, Gunpowder."

Florence smirked at the equally heinous petname. She needed a partner who could roll with the punches and dish it out as well as she took it.

Before either of them could conceive something worse, Florence claimed the woman's mouth with her own. Shannra's tongue was sweeter than any cookie Florence had ever eaten.

"What about all your work?" Shannra asked after several long minutes, gasping for air.

"It will keep."

Florence pushed aside her papers, scattering them to the floor. Yes, there was work to be done, decisions to be made, and things to be settled. But first, she had a woman to hoist onto the desk and more hard-earned flavors of freedom to relish.

CVAREH

She never told him outright that she loved him.

She had fought at his side. They had made love countless times. He had invited her to stay on Nova and be his queen, his paragon for the new bond between Loom and Nova.

In reply? She couldn't even say that she loved him, even though he knew it was more than true with every beat of his heart.

He wanted to point it out to her. He wanted to demand it from her. But it would mean nothing if he did . . . So, the words were left unsaid in her wake, where he lapped along the shores of all they could've been.

Cvareh stared at where Arianna had just stood. He had done everything Petra had ever dreamed. He had accomplished the dream of hers he had adopted—a Xin'Oji now wore the title of Dono. He, Cvareh, of all Dragons, was now the Dono.

It should have been a cause for celebration. His chest should have swelled with pride so great that his ribs would shatter and be rebuilt with magic now bolstered with the knowledge that he held all of Nova in his palms. But it wasn't.

There was no pride and no fullness. He had achieved everything, but he didn't have the one thing he'd come to want more than anything else. He'd lost the one woman who made everything in his world worthwhile.

"Well, I suppose that makes sense." Cain reminded him of his presence.

Startled, Cvareh half-jumped, as if pulling his feet from the tar of his own thoughts. "What does?"

"You had a boon with her this whole time." Disapproval ran rampant between Cain's words, though his friend didn't pursue it. There wasn't much to be done now about it and the fact that Cvareh had forged such had just saved his life. "Explains your obsession with the woman."

"It's more than that," Cvareh mumbled.

"Is it?" Cain asked, though Cvareh knew he was already aware of the answer so he didn't dignify the question with a response. "Call her back, then. Make her stay."

"I can't."

"Why not? You're the Dono."

"You heard her." Cvareh motioned to where the woman had been standing. "She can't be contained here and I couldn't make her."

"You're the Dono," Cain repeated, as though those three words should explain away everything.

"It means nothing if she doesn't stay of her own will. I can't order her presence just as I can't order her love."

Cain was given pause at the word "love." Surely, his friend must have seen it already. The man's brow knitted, furrowed lines digging over his eyebrows. "And that means something to you?"

It meant more than Cvareh could ever put into words. But all he said was, "It does."

"Then, if you will not command her to stay or order her affections, you must stop giving her your own."

As if it were that simple. As if it had ever been that simple.

He hadn't chosen to love her. He simply did. It had become as undeniable to him as winter's chill and as warming to his soul as summer's sun. Trying to do anything but love her would be like trying to halt the seasons: pointless and impossible.

"I can't do that either," he confessed in a whisper. Cvareh continued to stare after Arianna, the vacant spot where she'd once stood now filling with a new regret that he had not properly imprinted her image on his memory. With her as the Wraith on Loom, and he as the Dono in Nova, their paths were likely to never cross again.

"Then learn how." Cain moved into his field of vision. "Xin needs, *deserves*, an Oji who will celebrate this time and lead with all his heart." Cain shook his head, his tone becoming even more serious. "All of Nova, Cvareh. Not just Xin, but all of Nova needs you now. We are fractured and bleeding, and we need a Dono who will unite us."

"You're right," Cvareh admitted.

"We need someone who knows the Fenthri and is willing to work with them but still defend Nova's interests," Cain continued as if Cvareh hadn't just agreed with everything he'd said. "Someone who can carry on Petra's vision. Someone who has the esteem of our House. We—"

"I know, Cain." Nothing the man had said was untrue. But the whole of it had made Cvareh realize that he was not the only one who fit such a description.

"I will be here for you. It will be my supreme honor to serve as Ryu to the Dono." His friend squeezed his shoulder in a sympathetic display.

"Don't be so sure."

"What?" Cain's brow was back to furrowing. Cvareh could almost feel the panic rising from him.

Cvareh merely smiled at his friend's confusion. "This is a tumultuous time, Cain. Kings are dying left and right…"

FLORENCE

Dear W.W.,

Shannra tells me that I'm writing to a ghost. Fear not, I corrected her that the proper term is "Wraith."

You've been very good at not being found, this past year. I can only presume it was intentional when all of my efforts to leave no stone unturned left me empty-handed.

At first, I thought perhaps you were worried about my focus not being properly on my duties as Vicar Revolver. I could only imagine though, given the speed at which I've seen the hall and refinery rebuilt, that such was impossible. A distracted vicar does not make for an effective one. And, if I may be so bold, I've been fairly effective.

So, I'm only left to think that you do not want to be found. I attempted to corner Helen on the matter, but she was only slightly less slippery to get a hold of than you. It seems she's settling into her assumed role of rebuilding Mercury Town as well. Perhaps a little too well. (Do not make me send Revolvers down there to clean up any messes.)

In any case, now that I've come to terms with such a realization, I'm left with only one final course of action—this letter.

We are women of action, you and I, not words. Thus, I've toiled over what to put here for weeks now. You are aware, I am sure, of the overall state of affairs in Loom. And judging from the recent report of the "Queen of Wraith's Grand Return to Dortam," I think you're keenly aware of the status in our city. (It's a bit of a flashy title to re-assume, don't you think? For a woman who supposedly died in the battles on Nova.)

I digress, yet again... I want you to know, if nothing else, that I have looked for you. That I will continue to keep my eyes out for a woman in white at every corner I pass, every junction I cross. You, my teacher, my mentor, one of the most talented women I have ever known, will always have a place with me.

And should you never walk through the open door I'm leaving for you, then so be it; know you have my thanks. This runaway Raven will forever be in your debt as the woman who pulled her shaking and scared from the Underground, and once more, showed her the light.

Sincerely,

F.

P.S. I am truly sorry about what happened to Cvareh. However, if you said or did anything to ensure Cain would be so open to keeping positive relationships with Loom, I thank you.

ARIANNA

The moon peered down through the clouds onto the streets of Dortam.

The light was bright enough to cut one's shadow into the cobblestone of the streets, wet and glistening with the night's chill. It was the same moon that had borne witness to the rise of the White Wraith years ago, and was now the sole member of the audience witnessing the rebirth following the metamorphosis of that lone creature.

Arianna darted between back alleys, the hem of her freshly-tailored coat flapping against her legs.

Two Revo grunts were on her tail. They had all the persistence of fresh journeymen let out for the first time to "keep the peace." Yes, they were determined, but Arianna wasn't dissuaded.

Even as rubble and ruin, she knew the pathways and side-streets better than anyone. The farther she got from the center of Dortam, the rougher and more broken things became. It was an area that was still mostly untouched by time—a holdover from the days of Dragons.

She pushed deeper and deeper, knowing she'd lose them eventually. They were already tired of wasting ammunition by taking cheap shots at nothing.

This part of the city had been far enough away from the epicenter of the Revolvers' self-destruction that it had been spared from total ruin. Dortam was a target now; the bullseye was the new metropolis, springing from the ashes of the old. Out from that center was ruin, still in the process of being rebuilt. Further still, a peace of Arianna's heart would always live—Old Dortam. Buildings here jutted at odd angles and collapsed rooftops sagged holes between persistent walls. It was the city of Dortam's criminals and less-than-desirables. It was home for her.

She waited out of sight, tucked in a shaded alcove, listening carefully to the footsteps of the Revos slow. They cursed aloud, debated further pursuit, and eventually decided to let her go. *Smart men*, Arianna applauded. After all, she so hated killing talent. The Revolvers had little and less of it, in their present circumstances.

Arianna reemerged into the moonlight, looking around at the street she'd tracked to for the first time. It was instantly familiar. She remembered the sounds of industry—welding, hammering, the buzz of saws—that filled the air by day, and yielded to the revels of gambling parlors at night. Now, there was only silence, and her footsteps breaking the stillness.

Two streets down, one over, along a back alley, was a stairwell. Some stairs were missing—the iron rusted out and peeling away from itself like rotten flower petals. But the main joints to the building were still strong enough to hold her weight.

She didn't have anywhere else to be tonight. Her patron could wait until morning to get the trinket Arianna carried. For now, she'd rest in what was an all-too-familiar flat.

The door was ajar, but the room showed almost no signs of life.

Almost no signs.

Arianna waded through the familiar smells and nostalgic sights over to the kitchen table, where a letter sat among cookie crumbs that had somehow evaded rats for years. It was pristine, fresh, and on it were the letters "W.W." in a familiar hand. Arianna turned it over, and paused.

The floorboards behind her creaked under the weight of another presence. Another ghost reemerging from the memories of past lives she'd given up when Arianna had died.

"It's a bit much don't you think, to have the Dragon King himself hunt me down?"

Arianna turned, setting the letter back down on the table to have her hands free. She didn't know what she should anticipate… a fight? A flight? Or something more?

A Dragon emerged from the bedroom. His hair had grown out in the months since she'd last seen him. It almost brushed his shoulders in its burnt orange disarray. Cvareh wore dark pants and a long-sleeved, high collared shirt in the current fashion—if any of Loom's tailoring could really be called that compared to the pomp of Dragons. It was plain, functional, and everything she'd never associated with him.

"Very much Dragon, not quite King."

Arianna tilted her head curiously.

"You have not heard?" He seemed genuinely surprised.

"When you're a ghost, you don't hear much." Arianna leaned against the wall, folding her arms over her chest. Seeing him was like running her fingers over the dried ink of long-forgotten schematics. She'd not realized just how much she'd missed the familiar designs.

In truth, Arianna had only been truly oblivious until she'd return to Dortam no more than a week ago. Her attempts to fade away had been sincere. She'd secured a cottage in the mountains to the north, far outside the city, that had everything she'd needed.

Or *thought* she'd needed.

For she still found herself drawn back to the city that had been her home following the last rebellion. She'd made the excuse that it was for fresh supplies alone. Then, somehow, a new coat had found its way onto her shoulders, and her feet had found themselves standing before Helen, asking if there were any odd jobs that needed doing.

"Apparently not." He chuckled deeply, a sound that could turn moonlight to sunlight. "Though, I'm coming to realize such myself. We are both ghosts."

"Oh?" She could do little more than make noncommittal noises that encouraged him to continue until he gave her enough information to work with.

"I fear it falls to me to regretfully inform you that the Dragon King you worked so hard to save perished due to poison from Coletta'Ryu."

The words sank into her flesh slowly, seeping through her. They eventually reached her brain and elicited the most ineloquent response of, "What?"

"I hear, however, that his replacement is every inch the man both worlds hoped for in a Dragon King."

"Cvareh, what are you saying?" Arianna truly had been gone too long. No one on Loom had ever said the Dragon King's name; it was always just "Dragon King" or "the king." Surely, Helen had known. Arianna was already fantasizing about how she'd wring the girl's neck for neglecting to mention the "death" of Cvareh.

"Cvareh is dead." He phrased it in a different way, as if she hadn't already figured it out on her own.

"A pity I couldn't kill him. I'd so wanted to kill the Dragon King in the last rebellion." There it was again, the sarcasm that arose in defense of the fragile hope her heart had begun to bleed.

"I have it on good faith that you accomplished that task."

"You should check your sources, as Yveun'Dono was killed by Cvareh'Oji."

They both shared a smile that was quickly stolen by silence. She'd fantasized about seeing him again, but Arianna had never let the thoughts take hold. He was the Dragon King, needed in the sky world, and she had no place there. Now that he was in front of her, she was at an utter loss of what to do.

"You should go back to Nova," she whispered. Arianna knew it was pointless.

"I don't belong there, not any more."

"You're a Dragon. Isn't the only thing that matters to you your place? In society, in the hierarchy?"

"You're right," he affirmed. The man hadn't moved a muscle and she wanted to tackle him for it. Though she had no idea what would happen once she had him on the ground.

"Then why are you here?" And why was she whispering?

"Because this is my place."

Arianna wanted to scream at him for the answer that wasn't an answer. She swallowed hard, but couldn't dislodge the lump in her throat that was blocking all sound. He took a step, and then another. Arianna burned the sight of him into her eyes. The idea that the end of this rebellion, the true end, might not require her to sacrifice everything she loved, rooted itself unbidden in her mind. It was a notion she'd not considered with even the smallest corner of her heart, and now it burrowed so deep, she feared the hole it would leave would have no bottom.

"Is it my place?" he asked, standing toe-to-toe with her.

"I can't choose that for you." It was the only response she could muster. He hadn't forced her to choose, in the end, and so neither could she.

"I long ago made that choice." Cvareh leaned forward with all the slowness of a man who had her daggers shoved at his throat the last time they had occupied this space. His forehead met hers, their noses almost touching. And for a moment, for a brief and blissful moment, they merely breathed. "Do you want me?"

"Yes," she confessed to herself, to him, to his twenty gods, to every maggot and rat and cut-purse that might be listening.

"Do you love me?"

Arianna opened her mouth to respond and closed it. She swallowed once more. She couldn't make this easy for him, not now, not ever.

"Follow me, and find out." Arianna stepped away and locked eyes with him for one deliciously long moment, before she strode out the door, his footsteps close behind.

With the moon watching, the Wraith and the Dragon stepped into the night together.

The WORLD Of L⊗OM

Pronunciation Guide

People

Arianna	Are-E-ah-nah
Cvareh	Suh-var-ay
Florence	Floor-in-ss
Leona	Lee-oh-nah
Yveun	Yeh-vu-n
Louie	Loo-EE
Petra	Peh-trah
Sophie	So-fee
Agendi	Again-Dee
Finnyr	Fihn-er
Dawyn	Dawn
Coletta	Koh-let-tah
Soph	Sah-f
Luc	Luke
Theodosia	Thee-Oh-doh-sha
Faroe	Fuh-row
Topann	Toe-PAh-n

Places

Ter	(Short for Territory)
Lysip	Lisp
Holx	Hole-ks
Keel	Key-uhl

Ruana	Roo-AH-na
Easwin	Ees-win
Abilla	Uh-bih-luh
Venys	Veh-nis
Napole	Nah-pole-Ee

Things

Peca	Peh-kah
Royuk	Ree-yook
Fennish	Fehn-ish
Dunca	Duhn-kah
Boco	Boh-koh
Endwig	Ehnd-wihg
Glovis	Glow-vihs
Raku	Rah-koo

Dragon Houses/Titles

Xin	Shin
Rok	Rock
Tam	T-am (same as 'am' in 'I am')
Oji	Oh-jee
Ryu	Re-you
Dono	Dough-no
To	Tow
Bek	Beck
Da	Dah
Vicar	Vih-kur

The Five Guilds of Loom

Harvesters   Alchemists   Rivets

Ravens   Revolvers

Guild Brands

Found on the right cheek, tattooed guild brands were imposed by Dragon Law to designate a Fenthri's rank and guild membership. The tattoo is elaborated upon as new merits are achieved.

 Initiate

 Journeyman

 Master

Dragon Houses

All members of Dragon society belong to one of three Dragon houses. Ties into the House can be by blood, adoption, mating, or merit.

Rok

Tam

Xin

Dragon Names

All Dragon names follow the structure:

[Given Name] [House Name]'[House Rank] [Societal Rank]

Shortened names are said as one of the following:

[Given Name]'[House Rank]
or
[Given Name] [Societal Rank]

House Ranks	Society Ranks
Oji – House Head	Dono – King/Queen
Ryu – Second in Command	To – Dono's Advisors/High Nobility
Kin – Immediate Family to the Oji/Ryu	Veh – Nobility Chosen by the Dono
Da – Extended Family	Soh – Upper Common
Anh – Vassals/Lower Members of the Estate	Bek – Lower Common
	(nothing) – Pauper, Slave, Disgraced

Acknowledgements

NICK—I wouldn't have made it through this manuscript without you. I push, and you push me harder. Your thoughts, suggestions, insights, were all imperative for me to make it through this story that demanded so much of me. Thank you for having both the strength to demand the world of me and hug me hard enough so I keep it together when I may crack under the pressure.

ROBERT—thank you for all the inspiration you gave to me, however inadvertent. You're an exceptional friend and a role-model for me on how to be a decent human being (even if I'm pretty sure I regularly come up short). Thank you for being a parallel river of temperate waters.

MY EDITOR, REBECCA FAITH HEYMAN—there should be a saying that behind every marginally decent author is an editor who's ten times more amazing. Thank you for working with me on this manuscript and helping me from throwing ideas around to cleaning up my structure when it needed it most. I am so, so glad we met and are getting to have this experience together.

KATIE—as always, thank you for keeping me sane. You give me something no one else does in your unique blend of encouragement and love. I would've long gone crazy if I didn't have you to get turkey clubs and fancy tea with.

JEFF—Thank you for all the love and support you gave me over the years and throughout the writing of this novel. You were there when I needed you and supported me through this crazy dream.

SABRINA—You were so very helpful in organizing the Loom read-along and more when I needed it most. Thank you for your continued support!

ROB and the KEYMASTER PRESS TEAM—thank you for your continued belief in me and, you know, not deciding I'm not worth your time. It's been a delight to work with you and I can only hope we continue to bring worlds into readers' hands together.

THE TOWER GUARD—my dear street team, thank you for everything you do! You're always there when I need you and such a great group. I'm so honored to be surrounded with people who really take care of their own.

About the Author

ELISE KOVA has always had a profound love of fantastical worlds. Somehow, she managed to focus on the real world long enough to graduate with a Master's in Business Administration before crawling back under her favorite writing blanket to conceptualize her next magic system. She currently lives in St. Petersburg, Florida, and when she is not writing can be found playing video games, watching anime, or talking with readers on social media.

Subscribe to Elise's mailing list for the latest news and updates:
http://EliseKova.com/Subscribe/

CONNECT WITH ELISE KOVA
http://www.EliseKova.com/
https://twitter.com/EliseKova
https://www.facebook.com/AuthorEliseKova